THE FIFTH BANDIT

JASON KASPER

THE FIFTH BANDIT

Severn River Publishing
SevernRiverBooks.com

This is a work of fiction. Names, characters, businesses, places, events and incidents are either the products of the author's imagination or used in a fictitious manner. Any resemblance to actual persons, living or dead, or actual events is purely coincidental.

ISBN: 978-1-64875-493-7 (Paperback)

ALSO BY JASON KASPER

Spider Heist Thrillers
The Spider Heist
The Sky Thieves
The Manhattan Job
The Fifth Bandit

American Mercenary Series
Greatest Enemy
Offer of Revenge
Dark Redemption
Vengeance Calling
The Suicide Cartel
Terminal Objective

Shadow Strike Series
The Enemies of My Country
Last Target Standing
Covert Kill
Narco Assassins
Beast Three Six

Standalone Thriller
Her Dark Silence

To find out more about Jason Kasper and his books, visit
severnriverbooks.com/authors/jason-kasper

To my father, Ray

1

BLAIR

Blair tightened her grip on her backpack straps and picked up her pace to keep the businessman in sight amidst the midday crowds on 58th Street.

The weather in New York City was unseasonably cool on this early April day, allowing Blair to dress in layers of clothing that she'd desperately need if the proceedings ahead went wrong in the slightest. She proceeded with the flow of foot traffic, unnoticed by the many pedestrians traversing the sidewalks amid the blaring car horns. There was something decidedly unnerving about being in public during the day, sauntering about with the citizens of Lower Manhattan, but this was perhaps the safest place for her.

At least for the time being.

Less than a month removed from their last operation here, no one expected her LA-based heist crew to be *back* in the Big Apple—least of all the NYPD, a fact that the team made no small effort to confirm in the weeks of meticulous planning leading up to this moment. Combined with Blair's carefully selected ballcap, sunglasses, and red wig, the civilian masses around her provided a cloak of anonymity through which she could pass unnoticed on her way to the final destination. The exposure still involved risk, however, and that risk was going to swell exponentially in the coming minutes.

She heard Marco's Russian-accented voice in her earpiece, his announcement tense.

"Target is in position. Blair, send it."

Blair withdrew the cell phone from her pocket, unlocking the screen to reveal a preloaded text message. She tapped the send icon with her thumb and looked up to see the man to her front react almost immediately.

He palmed his phone and began texting back, his keystrokes registering as an ellipsis on her screen as she waited, her throat constricting with anticipation. If this exchange didn't work as planned, then her crew was running perilously low on options.

She quickly scanned the text she'd just sent.

Germinaro gave away my table. Meet me at Paolo's on 58th.

Finally the man's return message flashed on her phone.

On my way.

He diverted course, stopping at the crosswalk to turn left as Blair hurried across the street while transmitting a casually whispered message to her crew.

"The hijack worked, I'm moving into position as planned."

"Copy," Marco replied. *"We've got about two minutes before he's running late, so make your sweep fast."*

Blair needed no encouragement in that regard. Her exposure on the street was second in danger only to Sterling, who would now be approaching from the opposite direction. Both of them were known fugitives, and the sooner they concluded the operational phase of their plan and proceeded to the getaway portion, the better.

She felt momentarily relieved as the entrance to Le Diamant came into view, stopping with her cell phone in hand and glancing from the screen to the street as if her ride would arrive at any moment.

"In position. Marco, pipe me in."

She heard a garbled sequence of coded messages as the police transponder feed came over her earpieces, and Blair scanned the cars parked along the curb, her focus narrowing in on an NYPD cruiser at the front of the row.

The Ford Police Interceptor Sedan was emblazoned with two blue running stripes, its rear door boasting the motto *COURTESY PROFESSION-ALISM RESPECT*. Rather than being dismayed by the sight, Blair felt a surge of hope: if there was a sting in progress, the police would employ a far more subtle degree of presence.

She searched for indicators of that now, her gaze sweeping first across the car tops and trunk lids in search of UHF, VHF, and hockey puck antennas, along with unusually dark tint and the presence of light bars at the top of inside rear windows. There were other tells—dual exhaust pipes on a car that didn't come with them stock, and unusually clean, late-model Dodges and Chevrolets with black steel rims and chrome hub caps—but she saw none of these now. Instead, she homed in on the next most likely subject: a yellow taxi cab.

The NYPD operated seven such taxis spanning Ford, Nissan, and Toyota models, each virtually indistinguishable from regular cabs at this distance save for one key detail: the NYPD taxis had license plates beginning with 2W or 6Y. But the cab in question began with the number seven, and while Blair was confident no unmarked police vehicles were in the lineup, that didn't mean undercover cars weren't present. Those would have none of the usual indicators, and unless a cop jumped out of one, there was simply no way to tell.

But for now Blair felt satisfied in her assessment, giving a discreet glance to a decidedly non-police vehicle parked beside the entrance.

The Rolls Royce Cullinan was six thousand pounds and a half-million dollars of aluminum space frame chassis, plush leather interior, and lambswool floor mats. It looked the part, its hulking jet-black mass rising imposingly above every other car on the street. A pair of gargantuan men were

standing beside it, sunglasses glinting as they watched every person
diverting from the sidewalk toward the Le Diamant entrance.

The chatter from the police transponder muted as Blair transmitted.

"We've got a marked cruiser, no other visible police. Two bodyguards at
the Cullinan. They're staring down anyone going inside, so keep your head
down."

Then, swallowing uneasily, she concluded, "Sterling, you're clear to
proceed."

2

STERLING

Sterling entered the foyer of Le Diamant, doing his best not to look bewildered as he approached the hostess stand.

But his restraint didn't come easy.

The opulent entryway opened to a thirty-foot-high wall adorned with inlaid sections of colored glass, the mosaic a dazzling array of light and color. Sterling walked with all the grace he could muster under the circumstances, his runner's frame adorned in a cotton and polyester bodysuit to which his business attire had been tailored. Added to that indignity was the irritation of the silicone facial prosthetics that altered the curvature of his cheekbones and nose, the disguise completed with the application of a movie-grade fake beard made out of hand-tied hair.

The combined effect seemed to work thus far—the bodyguards hadn't paid him more than a passing glance when he strolled past.

That wasn't to say his entrance went completely uncontested. Sterling hadn't made it halfway to the hostess stand before a man with gray hair and black-rimmed glasses stepped into his path and asked, "How can I help you, sir?"

Sterling sized the man up with a glance—both the elegant cut of his suit and the obvious manicure indicated he wasn't a member of anything security-related. Nonetheless, the problem with walking into a place like Le

Diamant was that the clientele was simply too exclusive for any entrant to fly under the radar. In this ultimate bastion of the New York City power lunch, regulars included celebrities, real estate moguls, Wall Street tycoons, and visiting politicians. To Sterling's knowledge, he was the only fugitive to ever set foot here, and very likely the only one who ever would.

Smiling, he replied with a well-practiced Texan lilt, "Yes, I'm meeting Mr. Dembinski. I believe he's seated at his usual table."

"Of course." The man nodded but made no move to clear a path. "Am I correct in assuming this is your first time dining with us?"

Just his luck, Sterling thought—room for 120 people in the main dining room and this man knew at first glance that he'd never seen Sterling before.

"Yes, it is."

The man extended his hand. "Then allow me to welcome you to Le Diamant. I'm the manager, Fran Germinaro."

Sterling accepted the handshake. "Doug Carriker. Pleased to meet you."

Only then did the manager lead the way into the dining room, gesturing for Sterling to follow as he spoke over his shoulder.

"I hope you'll allow me to send over a complimentary dessert for your meal today."

"That would be great," Sterling replied, knowing full well that the coming engagement would be cut short long before that point. "Thank you so much."

They proceeded into a red-carpeted space filled to half capacity with tables where the New York elite chatted over appetizers and sparkling water. A central column formed an enormous wine rack, the corked ends facing outward like an artillery section ready to fire an opening barrage in all directions.

Sterling caught sight of Eric Dembinski toward the rear of the dining room, where the Wall Street financier preferred to sit in seclusion. Not too surprising, he thought, given the dexterity with which Dembinski negotiated campaign finance laws on behalf of his industry. That kind of legal tightrope walking—and the number of years Dembinski had been doing it successfully—probably required no small amount of meetings that were better conducted away from prying ears.

The man was texting furiously, probably trying to reach his associate, who was currently headed to a different restaurant altogether. Sterling was grateful to approach unnoticed, and saw that his current impressions of Dembinski had changed little from the last time they'd met.

His half-closed, lifeless eyes remained fixed on his phone, hair gelled into spiky peaks. Dembinski's rotund belly was concealed by the table at present, but his shoulders were broad enough that Sterling hoped to avoid a hand-to-hand engagement.

The manager stopped politely a few feet away and announced, "Mr. Dembinski, your guest has arrived."

To Sterling's surprise, Dembinski didn't even look up; he merely gave an impartial nod as he ended his text and opened an email app. The manager departed as Sterling took a seat, and only then did Dembinski finally set his phone on the table and make eye contact, his expression quickly shifting from composure, to surprise, to confusion.

"I'm sorry," he stammered. "Do I know you?"

Sterling felt a wry grin playing at his lips. The bodyguards hadn't recognized him through his disguise, but they hadn't met Sterling face-to-face just six weeks ago. Dembinski had, though that had occurred in Washington, D.C. under vastly different circumstances.

"You know who I am." Sterling now made no attempt to disguise his normal voice. "And if you don't tell me what I want to know, the next time you see me I'll be in your Park Avenue apartment. Trust me, you'd rather get this over with now."

Dembinski's hand flew to the cell phone, but Sterling intercepted it in a lightning-quick snatch, relocating the phone to his side of the table as he continued.

"In Albany, you lured me into a trap. Since that betrayal was a marked departure from our previous agreement, you were either bribed or intimidated."

Dembinski nodded quickly. "Intimidated. Otherwise, I never would have...I mean, no one in their right mind would—"

Dembinski was cut off again, this time by a waiter who appeared beside them.

"Good afternoon, can I get you something to drink?"

"We need a minute," Sterling said forcefully, causing the waiter to give a deferential nod before leaving. Redirecting his gaze to Dembinski, Sterling continued, "Let me guess—they were going to expose you if you didn't play ball."

"That's right."

"Who contacted you?"

"I have no idea. The call was anonymous, even the voice was scrambled. If I knew, I'd tell you. Believe me, I've got no reason to protect whoever he was."

Sterling couldn't gauge the man's response—his dull shark's eyes were flat as ever, not betraying the slightest indication of either honesty or deception. Responding with a sympathetic grin, Sterling gave one more attempt at the soft approach.

"You've got every reason in the world to protect him."

"What? Why?"

"Because you don't want to piss off someone more powerful, and I get that. But you're the man responsible for funneling dark money from the banking industry into political campaigns, and you're smart enough to do your homework on everyone you're in bed with."

Dembinski's mouth fell open.

"You're going after the mentor, aren't you?"

At the sight of Sterling's fixed glare, Dembinski continued, "Why? What could you stand to gain?"

"It's what I stand to lose. He's coming after my crew, and my mother. I'm going to get to him first."

"To kill him?"

Sterling shook his head. "Nothing we steal is worth a human life. What I need is leverage, and to get that I need a name. Now, who threatened you?"

Dembinski turned up his hands. "I really have no idea. You've got to believe me."

This time, Sterling knew with the gut-level certainty of all his considerable intuition that Dembinski was lying. He was overplaying his hand, his dull monotone quavering in an uncharacteristic tic, betraying a nervousness that seemed excessive in the current setting—after all, Sterling couldn't hurt him now.

At least, not here.

He pressed, "I know you did your own investigation."

"Of course I did my own investigation," Dembinski admitted. "But my people couldn't trace the caller."

Before Sterling could respond, he was distracted by the transmission over his earpiece.

It was the last duty position he wanted to hear from at that moment, or at any moment during an operation—his lookout, who wouldn't speak without some imminent crisis.

And sure enough, Blair hadn't interrupted without good reason.

"*Run*," she said urgently. "*Someone called the cops, and his bodyguards are inbound.*"

3

BLAIR

Blair ended her transmission in time to see the two massive bodyguards darting into Le Diamant.

She was too late to stop the men even if she'd had the physical ability to do so. But that didn't stop her from following them up to the restaurant's front door and scanning wildly up and down the street as she considered how this could have gone bad so quickly. Sterling wouldn't have let Dembinski use his phone; he must have had some concealed transmitter to alert his bodyguards, who would respond by notifying the police and racing to his side.

And that was exactly what was happening now.

The police transponder crackled over her earpiece with a response to the dispatcher's initial call of a 10-10 Hotel, or possible crime with a request for help.

"*149 in vicinity. Say again location.*"

She glanced at the squad car parked up the street, assuming but not certain they were the responding officers.

The response to this query wasn't the dispatcher at all, but rather Marco's voice as he hijacked the police transponder.

To his credit, he concealed his Russian accent well, sounding almost neutrally American as he transmitted, "*Be advised, suspect is a white female, slight build. Red hair, ballcap, blue jacket. Wearing a backpack and possibly armed. Last seen exiting Le Diamant."*

That description narrowed down the police's focus from every pedestrian on the sidewalk to the garishly attired Blair, now standing at the exact location they were being directed to approach. And right on cue, the squad car doors flew open and a male and female officer exited the vehicle. Blair noted with resignation that their level of physical fitness appeared to be just fine, thank you, as she felt her hopes of overweight pursuers dashed.

They rushed onto the sidewalk as Blair performed her final action before being spotted—tightening the straps of her backpack, an act she'd scarcely finished before both cops locked eyes with her and shouted in unison, "Police, don't move!"

But movement was the only thing on Blair's mind at present. Her job as lookout had faded, in one fell swoop, to a secondary role that was much less enviable and performed only when utterly necessary to protect the operation.

Turning away from the officers, Blair began a desperate sprint down the sidewalk.

4

STERLING

Sterling leaned forward and spoke quickly to Dembinski, who had assumed a more confident stance—he knew help was on the way.

"You know who I am and what I can do," Sterling began. "Now you can remain a rich free man, or become a dirt-poor inmate in about six months. Because Jacobson's fate is going to look like a vacation compared to how hard I bring you down, and if I find out you gave me a false name, that's exactly what will happen."

This had the effect of softening Dembinski's composure, but no sooner had the words sunk in than both men heard an outcry at the entrance to the dining room and Dembinski's gaze flew to the two bodyguards racing between the tables. He only had to stall for a few more seconds before they reached him.

Blair transmitted, *"Rabbit heading south,"* as Dembinski sputtered, "I can't give you *any* name. How can I tell you what I don't know?"

Rising from his seat, Sterling flipped the table sideways. It landed with a crash of scattered silverware and broken glass, eliciting shocked cries from nearby diners. He advanced one step toward a terrified Dembinski, grabbing his shirtfront with both hands and shaking him hard.

"I will take everything from you. I will leave you penniless—"

"Geoffrey Lambert," Dembinski gasped.

Sterling released him and said, "Blastoff."

Dembinski's face contorted with confusion. "What?"

A moment later it became clear that Sterling wasn't speaking to him, but to some outside party listening in on the proceedings.

The shrill cry of a fire alarm sounded inside the building, and the overhead sprinklers emitted a gushing torrent of water on the diners. That was all it took for the restaurant to erupt in pandemonium—the crowd leapt to their feet, scrambling to safeguard their phones and purses as they rushed toward the exit.

Sterling took off as well, not with the crowd but against it, fighting his way through the flow of people on his way to the kitchen.

5

BLAIR

Blair sprinted past a parking garage on her right, ordinarily a great place to lose police pursuit but far from it in New York City, where the subterranean structures were manned by parking attendants. She could still hear the cops behind her, along with shouts for her to stop. Mercifully, however, the surrounding crowd only responded by attempting to film the pursuit with their phones.

Skidding to a halt at the corner of 58th Street and 3rd Avenue, Blair took a hard right turn and regained her momentum, footfalls hammering at the pavement as she negotiated the scattered pedestrians moving in both directions. She heard the traffic over the police transponder but paid it no mind; her focus was on the path ahead, perhaps slightly diluted by the consideration of alternate routes. The sunglasses were the first item of her disguise to go, easily removed and tossed aside while on the run.

Sterling transmitted, *"Headed for the service exit."*

At least he'd made it out before the bodyguards could grab him, she thought.

Her new trajectory put her in line with a new NYPD officer, this one having emerged from traffic duty at an intersection as evidenced by the fluorescent green-yellow vest and gloves. Marco could block the police dispatcher's transmissions and replace them with his own, but he couldn't stop the responding officers from reaching their local counterparts on a UHF band—and these two cops had apparently succeeded in redirecting backup.

Blair came to a stop between the two sets of opposition, one with his arms spread like a defensive lineman to her front, the other two closing to her rear. Turning left, she launched herself into the stop-and-go traffic of 3rd Avenue.

She pirouetted sideways to duck a taxi, then leapt ahead of a delivery truck whose driver slammed his horn in protest. Once Blair reached the far side of the street, she continued her southward sprint to the next street corner before evaluating the location of the three pursuing officers.

All had made the crossing intact, and Blair knew they'd see her next move—sprinting past the civilians on 57th Street during their lunch break. She stopped at the far corner, allowing the officers to commit to the cross-walk before violently lurching into the four-way intersection, this time headed diagonally toward the far corner in a zigzagging course to bypass cars screeching to a halt at the sudden intrusion.

"Headed to Saks," she transmitted breathlessly upon reaching the side-walk, a momentary safe haven from traffic collision as she cut left, moving west along 57th Street toward the intersection with Lexington Avenue. The storefronts to her right were a blur until she stopped at the corner, performing a quick backward glance to confirm that all three cops were thundering down the sidewalk toward her.

She cut right onto Lexington Avenue, her move occurring in full view of the officers before she disappeared around the corner. Only when she confirmed no police were in her immediate view did she perform the next phase of costume ditching, stripping her oversized ballcap and red wig attachment to expose a honey-blonde hairpiece firmly affixed to her scalp. The hat and wig combo got tossed into a trashcan before she ran halfway up the block, then slipped through street traffic stopped for a red light.

Her path took her to a Starbucks, where she slipped inside and maneu-vered through the line of customers toward the far door. A look out the window revealed the officers heading north on Lexington Avenue, pursuing her last known direction of movement as she reached the side door leading back onto 57th Street.

She exited onto the sidewalk at a walk, emerging beneath a construction scaffold and gliding past a real estate office and bank before yanking open the department store's glass door.

Once inside, Blair made a beeline to the clothing racks, pretending to appraise the merchandise before ducking down out of the employee—and surveillance camera—lines of sight.

Her blue jacket was retrofitted tearaway, allowing Blair to split its buttoned seams and discard it without so much as removing her backpack.

But that wasn't sufficient to alter her appearance completely, and Blair knelt to rifle through the backpack's contents. In addition to a Gucci purse with an emergency evasion kit that she slung over her shoulder now, it contained folded bags from commercial establishments along every possible route away from Le Diamant: Victoria's Secret, Bloomingdale's, T. Anthony, Oak & Barrel, and most pertinent to her at present, Saks OFF 5th.

She whipped the shopping bag open and deposited the backpack inside before rising and making her way to the exit. Her transition now complete, it was just a matter of making the facade of a New York trophy wife convincing for bystanders. Blair procured her cell phone as if it had just buzzed in her pocket.

"Tanya, hi!" she exclaimed. "How was Grand Cayman?"

She closed the distance with the front door, approaching to within ten feet before emitting a burst of explosive laughter.

"Dinner next week would be great," she said, sweeping through the front doors.

A moment after setting foot on the sidewalk, a passing man stopped to grab her arm.

Blair winced before seeing that it was Alec smirking self-righteously, one eyebrow raised as he lifted a bouquet of flowers for her to see. She accepted them with an astonished grin before giving him a kiss on the cheek.

But then Alec looked down, shaking his head at the sight of her shopping bag. "How much did you spend? I leave you alone for five minutes and you've depleted the kids' college fund on what, more shoes?"

"Just two pairs," she replied. "And I need a minute, dear—Tanya is back from the beach."

"Tell her I said hi."

"The ball and chain says hello," Blair gushed into the silent phone as they strolled down the sidewalk, hearing Sterling's next transmission.

"I'm away clean, clear of pursuit and moving to linkup with Marco."

Alec asked, "How'd you pull that off so fast?"

"That's the problem with hiring muscleheads for your security detail," Sterling replied calmly. *"Those two lumberjacks were winded in thirty seconds."*

"You're not looking so light on your feet either lately, pal."

"It's called a fat suit, Alec."

"I'm not talking about the fat suit," Alec objected. "Feels like you've put on your freshman fifteen since shacking up with Blair. But I'm pleased to report she's seen the light and gone for the better man...since leaving Saks we've already gotten married and had kids."

His voice was drowned out by the shrieking wail of a fire truck fighting its way through 58th Street traffic toward Le Diamant.

So Alec went silent, using the opportunity to slide his arm around Blair's waist. She didn't object to the overture—at least not until they were away clean—and the ostensibly happy couple threaded their way westward toward a waiting getaway car.

6

STERLING

Sterling slipped silently through the warehouse, peering around corners with the benefit of late-afternoon sunlight filtering through wax paper plastered over the windows.

They were less than two hours removed from the city, and despite driving an elaborate surveillance detection route prior to returning to this dusty staging area, Sterling didn't feel any safer now than when he'd exposed himself to Dembinski at the restaurant.

He angled his view through the final doorway on the northeast corner of the building, first scanning the empty ground level for anything suspicious before his eyes ticked upward, meeting the lens of a wireless camera positioned in the corner.

Then he transmitted in a whisper, "East side is clear."

Marco's voice came over his earpiece a moment later.

"*So is the west.*"

Sterling spun back to the hallway, flipping on the light switch before striding to the office and transmitting to the other half of his team.

"Blair, Alec, the warehouse is clear. Wave off pickup duty and head on back."

It would take them a few minutes to return; they were staged on an adjacent road, ready to intercept Sterling and Marco if they had to flee the warehouse on foot and execute a pre-planned evasion route through the strip of woods behind the facility.

And before they arrived, Sterling wanted to find out everything he could about Geoffrey Lambert.

He made his way toward the hall that stretched the length of the warehouse, and in the process passed another two cameras.

They had outfitted the temporary staging area with a full network of the devices, whose feed Marco had surveilled ahead of their return from the city in addition to checking the door, window, and motion sensors for any sign of disruption. When you spent your entire adult life bypassing security, you became fairly paranoid about your own, Sterling thought, and given their opponent's resources, his crew needed to cover every angle.

He emerged into the hallway, seeing Marco at the far end as both men converged on the door to his ad hoc office.

Before Sterling could speak, Marco called out to him with a preemptive admonition.

"Don't get crazy. I need to check the status of my data scrub—"

"Later," Sterling cut him off without breaking stride. "Geoffrey comes first."

Even at this distance he could see the disappointment in Marco's eyes. As a world-class hacker, the man was loath to delay any opportunity to check his digital penetration-in-progress. But if his data scrub hadn't worked in the last few weeks, Sterling reasoned as he walked, there would unlikely be a breakthrough today.

The short-term warehouse lease was located in Poughkeepsie, an otherwise unremarkable town equidistant from New York City and Albany. Apart from convenience, they'd chosen it for the presence of multiple airports ranging from international and regional to small private airstrips. If the cops managed to track them back to this area, they'd have their hands full trying to cordon every avenue of air escape.

But flying didn't come easy when you were a fugitive, and the airport ruse remained just that—a ruse.

Sterling passed the real method of transport seconds later, striding past the warehouse bay where the team's twin Sprinter vans were parked facing the rollup door, each bearing the logo of his crew's security consulting LLC.

The company was legit on paper but not much else, providing them a pertinent cover to haul a few hundred thousand dollars' worth of sophisticated equipment cross-country from their LA hideout. Each van was equipped with a false bottom to conceal the most incriminating cargo of all: Sterling and Blair themselves, both known fugitives of national notoriety and, after the previous few months, a gradually spreading international one as well.

Sterling entered the office shortly after Marco, who took a seat and powered on his computers. The bootup passed with interminable slowness for Sterling, and he paced impatiently behind the hacker, mind racing through the implications of what was about to happen. Right now they needed a lead, and they needed it desperately.

As the first screen glowed to life, Marco began his search and ruled out possibilities with the same name. Soon he landed on a promising employment history.

"Geoffrey Lambert is a consultant at KBS, Killeen Business Solutions. Website is out of Switzerland."

Sterling leaned in as Marco opened the official webpage, then read, "Mission statement: 'We further our clients' strategic objectives in challenging regulatory climates while assessing, developing, and capturing emerging market opportunities.'"

Marco continued, "Looks like a go-between, a proxy for investors to remain legally safe while someone else does the dirty work. That means Geoffrey isn't the mentor we're looking for; he's a middleman."

"No," Sterling shot back. "He's a middleman who knows the mentor's identity. There's a big difference."

An outer door to the building banged shut, and Sterling heard footsteps approaching before Alec's voice echoed down the hallway.

"So Geoffrey is the mentor?"

Marco called out, "Not the mentor. A middleman."

Alec appeared in the office a moment later, throwing up his arms in exasperation.

"Great. So this entire op was a waste of time."

Blair strode in behind him, still wearing the blonde wig. "Sounds like it."

"No," Sterling corrected them as Marco continued his research, fingertips clattering across the keyboard, "all it means is we found a stepping stone instead of the goal. Geoffrey knows the mentor's identity, so he's our next target."

But Blair was already shaking her head. "If Geoffrey was chosen to call Dembinski, that means the mentor trusts him."

"So?"

"So," Alec intervened, "even if you put on your fat suit and traipse into another face-to-face meeting, Geoffrey's got to be a hardliner. He won't reveal the mentor's identity unless he's threatened with death. And we can't exactly kill him, can we?"

"No," Marco replied, his keyboard suddenly falling silent. "We can't. He's already dead."

Sterling whirled around, leaning over Marco's shoulder and exploding, "What do you mean, he's dead? He would've had to call Dembinski last month—what could have possibly happened between now and then?"

Marco said dryly, "A single-vehicle crash just outside Boulder two weeks ago. And alcohol was a factor."

Blair asked, "You think the mentor took him out?"

"I'm not convinced Dembinski was telling the truth in the first place. Maybe Geoffrey was his fall guy because he knew we couldn't confirm it either way."

"Or maybe," Alec pointed out, "we'll never know. "

Sterling felt the onset of nausea in the pit of his stomach.

Marco's gaze was fixed resolutely on the screen as he spoke with measured cynicism. "May I check the status of my data scrub now?"

Sterling gave a sullen nod. "Yeah, why not."

No sooner had he spoken than Marco opened a new set of browser windows filled with tiny text spelling out indecipherable lines of code—it wasn't just another language but an alien one, utterly meaningless to three of the four people standing in the room.

Except, Sterling noted, the final line of code that was now highlighted in green.

"Ha," Marco said. "It is done, exactly as I predicted."

Alec was less enthused. He muttered, "What are you so excited about? It didn't even involve a heist."

Marco's body went rigid, and then he turned slowly to fix Alec with a smoldering glare.

"Neither did the meeting with Dembinski, or anything we did in D.C. or New York over the past month. Yet we all very nearly got arrested, spent a tremendous amount of money from our dwindling cash reserves, and certainly pissed off someone far more powerful than our original opponent. Besides," he concluded, "why steal a burner phone from an evidence room when the FBI has already backed up all its data to the cloud?"

"He's not wrong," Blair pointed out.

No, Sterling thought as the hacker returned to his screen, Marco was many things, but most definitely not wrong when it came to such matters.

Technically, digital evidence was more secure on the cloud, not less. Computers and their servers crashed, after all, while the cloud was both evergreen and continually updated with the latest cyber security patches. That was to say nothing of storing multiple copies of the evidence for access by other law enforcement analysts or, in this case, a weeks-long penetration effort by the one man in the room with the skills to do so.

"FBI has already done network analysis," Marco announced, "so that makes our job even easier."

Sterling watched him download a file, then open it to reveal a constellation of blank face images—identity unknown—connected by a spiderweb of lines indicating phone calls placed.

Alec pointed out, "But their analysis was of a network of burner phones, which were probably replaced monthly—"

"Weekly," Blair said, "at least."

"Okay, replaced weekly. That's even worse. And I don't see any positive IDs among those blank faces, so this hasn't exactly been helpful."

Sterling was undaunted.

"The FBI doesn't have the connections we do. Marco, run those numbers through our database of thieves, fences, anyone and everyone on the criminal side."

"Relax," Marco said. "I'm getting the .csv file now."

Sterling turned to appraise his other two teammates. Alec looked bored, staring dejectedly at the computer screen as if he already assumed this was a lost cause. But Blair met Sterling's gaze with a neutral expression that betrayed no emotion—at least until Marco spoke once more.

"No hits."

Blair's face fell, and Sterling said, "Run it again."

"Sterling," Marco began, "the computer isn't like Alec. It doesn't make mistakes."

"Run it again," Sterling repeated, more forcefully this time.

The hacker did—and after a momentary pause, he said, to Sterling's dismay, "Still no hits."

Silence fell over the crew, broken only when Alec chimed in, "So we've got the name of a dead guy, and a network of phone numbers that are utterly meaningless to us. Bang-up job, guys. That road trip was a great use of our time and resources. Dembinski could have been lying about Geoffrey, and after today, he'll be surrounded by bodyguards 24/7 for at least the next ten years."

Sterling folded his arms. "We can get to anybody."

Marco turned to face him and countered, "But that doesn't mean we should. Dembinski isn't the one coming after us; the mentor is. And until we find out the mentor's identity, we're powerless to stop him."

Blair said, "There's still one person we can ask."

Sterling shook his head adamantly. "He's not going to talk to us."

"No, he's not going to talk to *you*. But I've got history with him. It's worth a shot. We staged here for a reason, we've prepped for this contingency, and we all know getting in would be child's play. We could get it done tomorrow, maybe the next day at the latest."

"It has to be tonight," Marco said grimly, "because tomorrow is his sentencing. We all know how that's going to turn out."

7

BLAIR

Blair leveled her taser, taking slow, cautious steps as she approached the open doorway.

Slipping through a dimly lit house late at night was no easy task—while she'd studied the floor plan, a single errant step risked colliding with some obstacle the homeowner had carelessly left on the floor, and the slightest noise could trigger any number of reactions from calling the cops to a room-by-room search with a personal firearm. Blair's covert entries for the FBI had universally occurred in empty facilities, while her forays into professional thievery were usually undertaken long after employees had left work for the day.

Now, she was not only inside a building with two unsuspecting people —paranoid ones at that, judging by the corporate-grade security system they'd had to disarm before she made entry—but advancing despite the knowledge that one of those people was fully awake.

Blair sidestepped around the doorway, visually clearing the room before entering.

The kitchen was palatial, a pair of vaulted ovens flanked by what appeared to be custom maple cabinetry. She made her way around the granite-topped island, passing a row of barstools and stopping at the edge of the dining room as Alec transmitted.

"No movement upstairs. He's still in the living room."

She could see it ahead, the short corridor opening into a large room glowing with lamplight. Blair advanced quickly now, each step bringing her closer to a compromise that she could only forestall by maintaining the element of surprise. The living room spread before her, the far wall marked by a cut fieldstone fireplace filling the gap between wide built-in bookcases.

But her attention was focused on the leather sofa, and more particularly the person seated there, facing away.

She held the taser in a two-handed firing position as she advanced, training her aim on the silver-haired man who hadn't yet detected her presence.

Blair silently rounded the couch until she was almost within his peripheral vision, then whispered, "Don't make me use this on you again."

She fearfully anticipated what would happen next—he would shout a warning to his wife upstairs, or make an immediate move to call the cops if not pull a gun on her. God forbid he have an emergency notification device like Dembinski had, she thought, or this entire exposure would be over before it began.

But to her surprise, Jim Jacobson seemed not to have heard her at all; he simply lifted the glass in his hand and took a sip.

Only when he'd set his glass back down did he reply, his voice hoarse.

"Why'd you come here, Blair—to rub salt in my eyes?"

Certain that this was some kind of deception ploy, she rounded the couch while keeping her taser aligned on his body. A bottle of Macallan sat on the table beside his glass and nothing else. Not even a phone in sight, much less a gun.

But the most shocking thing about the entire situation was the sight of Jim himself.

He was unshaven, disheveled, almost unrecognizable. His eyes were rimmed with red, set above dark circles, and for a moment, against all odds, Blair felt a profound sense of pity for him.

"No," she said, "I didn't come here to—"

"Well for once, I don't care about turning you in. Say what you came to say, and leave me alone."

It wasn't until then that Blair took in a previously unnoticed detail. The

couch Jim was sitting on had its cushions covered by a blanket and a single
pillow mashed against an armrest.

She'd been primed for a confrontation, ready to do whatever it took to
get the information she came for; and now, it was all she could do to
remember fragments of her rehearsed speech.

"You're paying for your own defense attorney. That means your mentor
has written you off."

A pause. "So?"

"So tell me who he is."

Jim's voice was flat now. "Now why would I go and do a thing like that?"

Adjusting her grip on the taser, Blair said, "I went to prison for you."

"And tomorrow, it will be me going to prison—*because* of you. When I'm
convicted, the FBI will revoke my Medal of Valor, and Sandra"—he
gestured to the blanket and pillow—"will be all too happy to send it back.
She's barely speaking to me."

"Well," Blair pointed out, "you got that award on a lie. This is what
coming to terms with the truth looks like."

Jim snickered then, as if an impudent child had just raised a pointless
and incoherent counterargument. Then he lifted the bottle and poured
himself another drink—three fingers by the look of it.

Taking his glass in hand, he said, "You've already gotten what you want.
Your crew is famous, and the cops have been reduced to auctioning off your
physical evidence as memorabilia. Congratulations, Blair. You've earned it."

He took a sip as she shifted uneasily, unsure how to feel much less react.
The back of her neck was burning now, whether out of guilt or fear, she
couldn't tell.

"I never wanted to be famous," she said, composing herself with a shaky
breath. "I wanted to be good at my job, and that didn't stop when I got
kicked out of the FBI. But your mentor is going to come after us, and there's
no reason for you to protect him."

Jim cut his eyes to her sharply, his gaze searing into her.

"No reason? You know what my life expectancy would be if I told you?
I'd have a shank in my ribs by this time tomorrow night. And frankly I'm
surprised you haven't already stolen the burner phone they confiscated
during my arrest."

"We didn't need to," Blair said with a self-satisfied grin. "We hacked the FBI's network analysis. Is there a clue in it?"

When Jim said nothing, she continued, "It doesn't matter. I'm going to find his identity, one way or the other."

"No, you won't." Then he shrugged, leaning back on the couch and crossing one leg over the other. "Or maybe you will. But it won't be from me."

Blair gave a frustrated sigh. "What difference does it make? He'll never know you told us. You don't have to protect him anymore."

Jim's eyebrows flew upward, and he barked a shrill laugh. "Protect? Did you honestly just say that? My mentor doesn't need any protection. The crimes of Sterling's father are well within the statute of limitations, which means Sterling's mom is screwed. That means you and your crew are, too, and...and I'm screwed right alongside all of you." Taking another swig from his glass, he raised it in a mock toast. "I've reached acceptance, and so should you. This is how it ends."

"That's where you're wrong, Jim. Because my crew is just getting started. This isn't how it ends; it's how it begins."

Jim swiveled, eyeing her black-clad figure from top to bottom, then shook his head slightly. Then he leaned forward and, without taking his eyes from hers, set his glass on the table.

"I can't tell if you're delusional or naively optimistic, Blair. So let me explain something to you: you've made a lot of money stealing, sure. But there's one currency more powerful than cash in this world: *power*. And that's what my mentor deals in. The fact that you even came here to ask tells me everything I need to know. Whatever happens during my sentencing tomorrow—and I've got a pretty good idea of what that will be —your crew is going to have it ten times worse. If you survive at all, which, let's be honest, isn't going to happen."

Blair felt her forehead wrinkling. "If we survive? What's that supposed to mean?"

"It means," he said forcefully, "that once you're in this individual's crosshairs, you don't come out of them. Not alive, at least. So go ahead: go after my mentor. Or run now, because I'm sure you've got a good retirement plan in place. But it won't make a difference either way."

"I don't believe you."

"Why would you? You've got no reason to trust me."

"Understatement of the century."

Jim sighed. "We weren't always enemies, Blair, so I'll say it anyway. The best thing you can do is have your whole crew turn themselves in."

Blair scoffed. "Not going to happen."

"I wasn't finished," Jim continued. "You won't be safe from my mentor in prison, not by a long shot. But you'll be far safer there than you will be on the run. At least if you're all in solitary confinement, it will take my mentor longer to get to you. So take my advice, or don't—"

"We won't."

"—but with every possible emphasis a condemned man can muster, believe me when I say that you're all condemned too. You're not even going up against Goliath, you're going up against an army of Goliaths. And there's not going to be a happy ending, Blair. Not for any of us. My mentor is going to burn you and Sterling, and his mom and your whole crew."

"I think we'll be just fine without your sage advice, Jim. Some of us have had to work to get where we are, and you don't stay free as long as my crew has without learning a few survival skills along the way."

"There are no skills that will help you with this one. There is no amount of money that will get you out of this. If I thought there was, maybe…" He gave an ambivalent shrug. "Maybe I'd help you."

"Then help me. Help me bring down your mentor."

"My mentor doesn't get brought down, Blair." He gave a pitiful laugh. "May God help you now, because no one else will."

8

STERLING

Sterling's cell phone buzzed in his pocket.

Leaning against the seatbelt, he shifted his night vision to glance at the screen. The phone was merely an alternate communications method with his team, but their radios had functioned seamlessly all night, and thus Sterling was somewhat unsurprised to see the display flashing *UW*.

The shorthand was for Uncle Wolf, not a blood relative but rather a friend of his late father. Not only was Steve Wolf a lifelong role model for Sterling, he was also a recently retired master thief who'd helped the crew immeasurably on their last trip to New York.

Sterling silenced the call and deposited the phone in a cupholder, resuming his two-handed grip on the steering wheel as he focused his night vision on the glowing green landscape beyond his windshield.

He'd already completed his driving prep in the rented Ford Mustang GT, warming up the engine and performing a few high-speed runs, weaves, and sharp braking maneuvers to transfer heat from the brake discs and pads into the tires before staging for Blair's pickup. The vehicle's interior and exterior lights were off, the result of replacing the relevant contents of the fuse box with custom fuses linked to a kill switch. With the press of a wired button assembly now strapped to the bottom of his steering wheel,

Sterling could restore the car to fully legal illumination—and he would, once he traversed the short stretch of road between his current location and Interstate 90 to the south. That alone would provide the anonymity of high traffic, and once the road merged with I-87 and routed east of Albany, he'd be as good as invisible amid the flow of civilian cars.

At least, if everything went according to plan.

The odds of that were up for debate, and Sterling felt his apprehension rising with each minute that ticked by without a transmission from Blair. Seeking a personal audience with Jim was an act of desperation, plain and simple, but what other option did they have? Dembinski's information had been a dead end, as had their digital pilfering of Jim's burner phone activity. If Blair didn't get any help from Jim—and Sterling couldn't see how she would, as the disgraced congressional candidate was many things but not dumb—then his crew was at a complete loss on how to proceed. They'd staked everything on this trip, and were now minutes away from confirming it had been for absolutely nothing.

His phone buzzed in the cupholder, the screen once again glowing with Wolf's name. As Sterling silenced the call, he heard Blair transmit over his earpiece, "*Moving to exfil.*"

"How'd it go?" he replied.

"*It didn't. He wouldn't tell me anything, except to say—*"

"We're screwed?"

"*Yeah. His words exactly.*"

"We'll just see about that—" Sterling's transmission was interrupted by Marco's voice over the net.

"*Police are responding now to a home invasion by a known fugitive. First units are eight minutes from Jim's house and they're going to set up a cordon.*"

At least Jim had given Blair a thirty-second head start, Sterling thought, putting the transmission into drive as he awaited her arrival.

His phone flashed a text from Wolf.

Pick up your phone, cracker.

Sterling ignored it. He didn't need any distractions, and there would be ample time to return the call on their drive back to Poughkeepsie. The cops would be swarming his current location soon, and Sterling needed at least three minutes to reach the interstate.

Another text flashed.

NOW.

Sterling briefly weighed the prudence of taking a call at this critical juncture in the op. Then, after a moment's hesitation, he decided that Wolf had never sent him an SOS before and was not particularly subject to theatrics.

He tapped his phone to dial Wolf, hearing the call connect over the vehicle's Bluetooth speakers.

"Mexican Clint Eastwood, what's shaking?"

Wolf's already menacing, gravelly voice sounded especially threatening as he responded, "I've been trying to call you."

"I'm a little busy right now."

"Yeah, I heard the transponder. Cops are on their way."

"We're on it."

"No," Wolf hissed, "you're not. The problem isn't the police, it's that everyone knows you're in Albany."

"So? We're not exactly strangers to avoiding capture—hang on."

The passenger door flew open and Blair climbed into the seat. Sterling accelerated before she'd had a chance to close the door, carving a right turn by the time Blair put her seatbelt on.

Albany Shaker Road extended before him in mottled green hues, completely barren at this hour as he floored the gas and felt the five-liter V8 spool to full power as they rocketed past trees and the occasional residence. The automatic transmission seamlessly shifted through gears as he reached 82 mph before applying the brakes for a stoplight ahead.

The three-way intersection was free of headlights, and Sterling slowed until the car was entering it before cutting the steering left and yanking up on the handbrake. He felt the rear wheels lock as the Mustang spun sideways, then dropped the handbrake and applied countersteer until the front bumper was pointed toward a gloriously straight half-mile stretch of Everett Road.

Then, with his bootlegger's turn completed, Sterling floored the gas.

As his Mustang sprinted to sixty in just over four seconds, he continued, "Go ahead."

Wolf replied, "There's a message circulating in the underworld."

By now the car was blasting through the quarter-mile mark at 115 mph, and Sterling held the speed steady in anticipation of braking for the first gentle curve in the road.

"What do you mean, 'the underworld?'"

"I mean everyone," Wolf said angrily. "Current and former thieves, our fences, our equipment suppliers, and everyone who supports them through black market channels."

Sterling slowed to 90, guiding the Mustang in a gradual left-hand turn as a car approached in the opposite lane, momentarily blinding his night vision before vanishing in a blur of motion.

"So what's the message?" he asked, impatient. Surely Wolf could hear the V8 growl, and if he was already tracking the police scanner, then he should've known Sterling had better things to do at present than talk.

Wolf continued, "One million dollars bounty for actionable information on the location of the Sky Thieves."

Sterling smirked as the Mustang barreled past an urgent care clinic and then a pub, both closed for business and gone as quickly as they appeared. Undaunted, he replied, "Anyone who could find us isn't going to cooperate with the police."

"The police aren't offering the bounty. It's from a private party. And whoever it is doesn't want you arrested—they want you killed. There's an additional one million bonus for every dead member of your crew."

Sterling felt the first pang of fear tugging at his stomach as Wolf went on, "And that kind of money is going to draw every bounty hunter, mercenary, private investigator, and crooked cop in the US. Plus any thieves who think they could locate you. So trust no one; don't even contact me, because anyone who knows about my connection with your father will be watching. Get out of New York, reach someplace safe, and then go into hiding. Your heist career is over."

9

KRISTEN

Kristen Shedo strode before the full-length mirror in the foyer of her private collection, noting with pleasure that she looked resplendent as always.

She wore a casual Christian Dior long dress, the striped silk fabric a shade of candy red that accented the warm skin tones of her long-distant Egyptian heritage. With matching lipstick and makeup done to perfection, to say nothing of her yoga practice, regular BOTOX, body contouring, and microdermabrasion treatments, and a personal chef and nutritionist on her household staff, Kristen looked and felt better at age 52 than many of her counterparts in their thirties. The cutthroat world of business investment had a tendency to age people quickly, but she'd played the long game, and as she appraised herself now, she was pleased to see that the continued efforts had paid off in full.

She adjusted the yellow gold BVLGARI bracelet on her right wrist, then used manicured fingertips to brush a tendril of chestnut hair behind an ear adorned with a pear-shaped ruby earring surrounded by a halo of diamonds. Everything about her appearance was perfect, and had to be—she wouldn't just be representing herself in the minutes ahead, but also the team of thieves whose efforts had occupied much of her waking thoughts as of late.

A muffled man's voice announced, "Ms. Shedo, Paul Schmidt from Darien Insurance to see you."

Kristen glanced once more at the room behind her, gaze sweeping across the breathtaking collection, every item in its place and illuminated to perfection—her pride and joy ready to inspire awe in the heart of her visitor.

"I'm ready," she called back in a singsong voice.

The door swung open in a near-silent arc that belied its seven-inch thickness, held ajar by a member of her security staff as the insurance appraiser nervously entered.

She suppressed a frown at the sight of him: a slender man with birdlike features, he bore an unsightly pencil mustache beneath his rimless glasses. In what universe he thought that appearance would be acceptable, she had no idea.

But she glided toward him and extended her hand, announcing, "Mr. Schmidt, thank you so much for taking the time to come."

He nervously shifted a ledger to his left hand, returning her handshake with a weak and clammy grip.

"Ms. Shedo, I appreciate you having me. I've completed my inspection of the exterior, and just need to confirm the interior contents and placement before submitting my report."

She flashed him a polite smile, then stepped aside and extended her arm into the room behind her.

"Mr. Schmidt, welcome to my personal exhibition to honor the legacy of the most elite heist team to ever spark the public imagination—the Sky Thieves."

"I, um, see. And you constructed this room to hold your collection?"

"It was formerly my personal library," she replied, "reappropriated into a collection space when law enforcement began auctioning evidence no longer needed for forensic analysis. Note the track lighting on the ceiling, Mr. Schmidt—the credit belongs to a senior member of the Illuminating Engineering Society who also serves as the lighting designer at the Smithsonian Art Museum. Every piece has its own point of illumination, or multiple points, according to its texture and positioning. The end result, as you can see, is a variety of lighting intensity that establishes a rhythm and momentum as you pass through the exhibits."

She led him to the first pieces, each occupying a considerable portion of wall space.

The twin panels were twelve feet long and eight feet high, the inner edges of the elaborate frames lined with narrow red-and-blue ropes that had been shaped into elegant cursive Latin script across the surfaces.

With a respectful nod to the wall, she began, "These are the two rappel ropes used in the Century City heist. Both are Black Diamond 9.4 with a 2X2 woven sheath and a factory middle mark, 80 meters in length. The one on the left was used by the unidentified crew member, while the piece on the right was constructed from the rope utilized by Sterling and Blair."

Paul glanced from one frame to the other. "And the Latin script?"

"Of course." Kristen extended an upturned palm to the left frame. "*Audentis Fortuna iuvat.* 'Fortune favors the bold,' Spoken by Turnus in the *Aeneid*. And this one"—she gestured to the second rope script—"is from the same epic poem. *Flectere si nequeo superos, Acheronta movebo.* 'If I cannot bend the will of Heaven, I shall move Hell.'"

"I'm sorry, did the ropes...did they come like this?"

Kristen, taken aback, stared at Paul in an attempt to discern whether he was serious or making some ill-informed attempt at humor. After a moment of analyzing his clueless expression, she concluded the former.

"Of course not. No, Mr. Schmidt, this is the work of Debra Lego."

"Lego?"

"The artist, of course. She traveled here to Seattle from Venice, and I hosted her for two weeks to complete the work on these premises for a considerably greater sum than I paid for the ropes themselves. And these," she continued, proceeding to the next exhibit, "are the panels used by the Sky Thieves to block the underground tunnel access point they used to escape."

He followed her and examined the twin metal squares, each bearing a yellow triangle with a lightning bolt symbol over text reading, *DANGER: High Voltage. Back of this panel is live.* Leaning in, he squinted at the smaller print that said *Follow ALL requirements in NFPA 70E for electrical safe work practices, including all protective equipment.*

She folded her arms triumphantly. "A brilliant means of covering their tracks, wouldn't you say?"

"Yes," he agreed with hesitation, standing upright and jotting notes into his ledger. "It's...very clever. And this is from the getaway car? Same heist?"

He pointed to a BMW badge mounted to the wall on a small frame. She strode beside it and explained, "That's correct, this is the actual hood roundel from the modified BMW M3 used in the high-speed chase that ended in El Segundo. I tried to obtain the entire vehicle, of course, but the LAPD insisted the remains were required for forensic evidence. Though I can't possibly see why, as any DNA was thoroughly denatured by the aqueous foam of sulfuric acid. No one as brilliant as Sterling Defranc would risk leaving clues behind."

"Wasn't he arrested?"

Kristen bristled at the comment, then composed herself and took a graceful step toward the next exhibit.

"Following his successful robbery of the Sky Safe, the subject of my next display—" She swept a hand toward a shelf with a firefighter mask propped upright on an ebony stand. "This is the mask he abandoned on the construction crane. The visor fogged, you see, and yet he risked every-thing to continue his entry while tethered by the item displayed here."

Beside the mask was a large frame adorned in cursive script of a similar style to the climbing ropes—but rather than being formed by rope, the quote was composed of a meticulously shaped cable.

"And the Latin?"

"Ovid, the *Metamorphoses*. *Fas est ab hoste doceri*. 'One should learn even from one's enemies.' Quite a useful reminder, in my line of work. The cable is constructed from high-strength twisted steel filaments covered in a slick phosphorus-based fire-retardant coating. It was also"—she paused, forcing a measure of humility into her voice—"crafted into this work of art by Debra Lego, on her second visit to my home."

Paul nodded, then cocked his head to the side and asked, "Was the diamond ever found?"

"What diamond?"

He blinked, tapping the point of his pen against the ledger. "The one stolen from the Sky Safe."

She swatted at the air with a dismissive gesture. "I'm quite certain the Sky Thieves fenced it at the earliest opportunity. Anyone can dig up a rock, Mr. Schmidt. There's no brilliance involved in that, only luck and the distasteful exploitation of the poverty-stricken masses used to mine the earth. But only this crew was capable of engineering the breathtaking feats, and it is highly unlikely we'll be witness to any equivalent criminal genius in our lifetimes."

Wrinkling his nose in confusion, he replied, "And the...the doll, Ms. Shedo?"

She followed his gaze further down the wall, then proceeded like a curator leading a guided VIP tour.

"That 'doll' is the Tasha Edenholm, a poseable, weighted infant replica with hand-rooted hair built by Ashton-Drake. It was carried by Blair Morgan herself, along with the open-weave cotton muslin nursing cover. She used both, you see, to hide in plain sight at the Albany Institute of History & Art."

"I see. And these—are these grenades?"

She took a step forward, stopping next to the three expended canisters as she narrated, "Purchased as a single lot, these are three of the nine tear gas grenades they used to flee the museum in Albany. The others are being held as evidence, though I assure you, I plan on one day possessing all of them."

He raised an eyebrow.

"Legally," she hastily clarified. "The remaining six will one day be up for auction, I'm quite certain of it. But as of yet it appears that the Albany PD doesn't want any more of my money."

"I'm afraid the Albany reference is lost on me. What did they steal from the museum, art?"

"The Sky Thieves do not steal *art*, Mr. Schmidt. Their presence at the Albany Institute was an attempt to recover the tapes that incriminated Jim Jacobson."

His mustache twitched as he pursed his lips. "I see. So that's where they got the tapes."

"What?" she huffed, exasperated. "My God, man, no. They recovered the tapes four days later outside the fundraising dinner in Manhattan—

you know what? Never mind. What is important right now is that these items of impeccable provenance are housed securely within a safe room that provides near-absolute protection per all FEMA guidelines. A tornado could wipe away this house, Mr. Schmidt, and still this room would stand intact."

Lowering the ledger to his side, he said, "I must warn you that my company will only underwrite these items for their assessed value, which may fall short of what you paid the auction house."

"Their value? They're priceless. Your report had better indicate that, and I want as much coverage as I can get, Mr. Schmidt."

"Your passion is inspiring, Ms. Shedo. But I'm afraid my company may have to insist on some ballistic glass to protect the items from theft and fire—"

"Glass? Mr. Schmidt, if I wanted to see these items behind glass, I could have donated them to a museum. Instead I collect them, because I can do this."

She strode to the center exhibit, pausing before the firefighter mask and taking a resolute breath. Reaching for the mask, she let her fingertips graze the polyarylate face shield—the same lens that Sterling Defranc had gazed through on his way to what was arguably the single most audacious heist ever carried out. Kristen felt the electric energy flowing into her hand, as if it was transmitting its power through her, and shuddered slightly as a chill ran up her spine. Closing her eyes, she emitted a soft gasp.

"Do you see? It's the touch—the touch is the thing. That is why I collect, Mr. Schmidt. When I have an important business decision, a merger or acquisition that must be decided upon, I don't sit in front of a computer and examine spreadsheets. I come here, to this very room, and draw my inspiration from these items. My muse isn't in the data, it's in this room."

Releasing her hand from the mask, she opened her eyes and spun toward him, speaking accusingly. "What would you have me do, barge in here with a jailor's keyring to unlock my cases first?"

He shrank back from the verbal assault, then offered a nervous smile.

"We're being generous in offering to underwrite these items outside of a safe, Ms. Shedo, and—"

"My *house* is a safe." She raised her arms halfway, spinning in a circle before facing him with hands on hips. "You've seen my security. And this entire room has the highest possible protective rating."

Paul wrinkled his nose. "Yes, ma'am, that's technically true—the room is UL Class 350 certified. But while your vault door has a six-hour rating, the walls, ceiling, and floor have a *one*-hour rating, and the UL system only accounts for temperatures of 1700 degrees for a given time period—"

"Seventeen hundred degrees? The nearest fire station is less than five minutes away and Lake Washington is in my backyard, not Mount Vesuvius. Short of a volcanic eruption, Mr. Schmidt, I don't see how my collection is in any danger of being eradicated by fire."

"It's not eradication I'm worried about, Ms. Shedo. My greatest concern is, I suspect, the same one causing you to seek insurance in the first place: the possibility of theft."

"The only thieves," she said, "who would stand a shot at making it into, much less out of, my residence are the Sky Thieves. And I don't think they'd go to all the trouble of stealing their own equipment back, do you? I seek insurance because I'm a cautious woman, Mr. Schmidt, and it always pays to hedge one's bets. This is about peace of mind, not fear."

Paul shifted his weight from one foot to the other, then back again.

"Well, I think I have everything needed to submit my report—"

"Then my security team will escort you out."

He hesitated, clearly considering whether or not to offer a handshake.

"Thank you for your time, Ms. Shedo. We'll be in touch."

She replied with a disaffected murmur, turning her back on the man without bothering to watch him leave.

Instead she surveyed the collection before her. It wasn't complete yet, of course, and wouldn't be until she obtained the unauctioned pieces of evidence as they became available.

Her gaze settled on the single open space remaining among the shelves, a prominent gap between the Sky Safe memorabilia and the items from New York. The clueless insurance appraiser hadn't seemed to notice the disparity, nor would she bother informing him until it had been filled. Kristen Shedo was not a suspicious woman, but she knew by now not to declare victory until it was well in hand.

She strode up to the empty shelf and set her palm flat atop it—the slab of wood was hollow, meaningless, but it wouldn't be for long.

No, she thought, because there was one item left to acquire. It was to be the first and, most likely, the only piece of evidence to be sold from the Sky Thieves' greatest heist—a daring operation that wasn't really a heist at all. Or maybe it was, she mused with a droll smile, depending on how you looked at it.

Removing her hand from the shelf, she stared at the empty space with the languid assurance that within 48 hours, it would be filled with her most treasured possession yet.

10

BLAIR

Blair found Sterling leaning against the second-story rail, gazing out across the main warehouse bay below. She knew what he was thinking even as she approached, and could read the look on his face as he stared at the rehearsal area.

To her, the warehouse hideout in the industrial district of Moreno Valley east of downtown LA was just that: a warehouse hideout. Sure, it had some sentimental significance; after all, they'd planned and rehearsed every heist here from the time she joined the crew up until the present day. This was the site of those nervous hours leading up to the departure for an op, and the place where they returned afterward, jubilant at their success and continued freedom. And for her and Sterling, both known fugitives, it was out of necessity a home as well.

But Sterling viewed the warehouse as much more than that. This was his legacy, the command post for a criminal empire that he'd built from the ground up along with Alec and Marco.

She stopped alongside him, taking up a position at the rail as she asked, "You okay?"

"Yeah, of course. You?"

Blair nodded. "It's just a warehouse, Sterling. Four walls and a lot of equipment."

"We're not leaving," he shot back, cutting his eyes to hers.

"I didn't say we had to leave. But if we have to relocate to stay safe, it'll be okay."

He swept an arm over the rail. "This warehouse isn't just the safest place for us to be, it's the *only* place for us to be. It's withstood every attempt by law enforcement to locate us, up to and including a dedicated federal task force."

"That doesn't mean it'll be safe forever."

"Why not?" He turned to face her. "We've bought up every peripheral property overlooking the compound, no outside thieves know about it, and we only come here through a series of drop cars and routes that bypass traffic cameras. It held up after my arrest, and that wasn't because the government wasn't using every means at their disposal to locate it."

He wasn't wrong, Blair thought, though she could see this was not the time to make any headway with Sterling's expectation management. It wasn't that he didn't know how bad their situation was—at this point, that much was hard to miss—but he was too emotionally attached to this site to be reasoned with.

At least, for now.

"Come on," she said, taking his hand. "Let's go to the conference room."

They walked there in silence, a rare interlude of awkwardness between two thieves who'd shared everything together: victory, defeat, and for the past month, a bedroom in the warehouse.

But that silence ended the moment they entered the conference room.

Alec, filling mugs from a coffeepot in the corner, called over his shoulder as they entered, "Well if it isn't the narcoleptic lovebirds. While you two have been sleeping in along with the staggeringly worthless Marco, I've been keeping up with current events."

"What's the verdict?" Sterling asked.

Alec turned to face them, a coffee mug in each hand.

"Jim just got sentenced to six years without possibility of parole. That comes with being barred from government service, so his political career is over. And the FBI has revoked his Eagle Scout Award—"

"The Medal of Valor," Blair said, accepting the mugs and handing one to Sterling.

"Right, that. After all this time fighting back and forth, you can stick a fork in Jim because he is D-U-N *done*."

Blair and Sterling took their seats at the conference table, its surface covered in the items of their collective brainstorming efforts: notepads, pens, random toys that they tinkered with as they debated ideas.

Sterling said, "Jim got what he deserved. But his sentence doesn't help us with his mentor."

"I wasn't finished." Alec pulled a chair back and slipped into it. "We are now in the midst of yet another law enforcement auction of our evidence."

Blair frowned. "I thought they were done with the auctions. Haven't they sold all our stuff already?"

"Nay, my good woman. One more is being bid upon as we speak, and since it's the first and only item to be released from the Supermax breakout, they expect it to break all the previous records."

"Well," Sterling asked impatiently, "what is it?"

"You ready for this? You'll think I'm joking, but I'm not: the prison loafer you lost in the concertina wire during your escape."

"Isn't it covered in blood?"

"It is."

"Who would want that?"

"Apparently someone who's willing to pay"—he consulted his phone—"465,000 dollars, according to the last bid."

Sterling shook his head in disbelief and leaned forward, folding his hands on the table. "Whatever. Let's get back to work."

Marco entered the conference room while groggily rubbing one eye. "Get back to work on what, exactly? Wolf is the only thief outside this group that we trust, and if he's telling us to disband it's not because he's uninformed."

"We're not disbanding," Sterling shot back, glaring at Marco as he indifferently crossed the room to the coffee pot and poured himself a mug while replying.

"Every attempt to uncover the mentor's identity has been unsuccessful, and between our last trip to New York and the previous expedition to take down Jim, we're running perilously low on funds. And while I applaud the virtue of our philanthropy, you must admit that giving half our earnings to charity hasn't helped."

"The fifty-percent cut is nonnegotiable," Sterling replied. "That's how my father operated, and that's how we operate, period."

Marco wore a half-smirk as he carried his mug to the table, then lowered himself into a chair. "I'm not debating you on nobility, Sterling, just timing. Maybe we should have held onto some of it until we were out of the woods here."

Blair interceded before the argument could escalate.

"We need to look at what's best for our crew as a whole. Sterling, you and I would need to flee the country. But Alec and Marco have never been implicated as Sky Thieves—that means they could still find legal employment in America."

Sterling repeated, "We're not disbanding."

"I'm just saying, if we did...life would go on. We've had a good run; maybe it's time to hang up our spurs. It's not like we couldn't get your mom out of the country before she's prosecuted. And didn't you once tell me there was more to life than heists?"

Alec grunted. "He was trying to get into your pants when he said that."

"I was," Sterling conceded, "but that's not the point. We can't run away from this."

Alec responded without hesitation.

"As much as I hate to agree, you're right. We don't have a choice. If Jim's mentor is half as dangerous as everyone would have us believe, there's no place we'll be safe. Just because he doesn't know who Marco and I are at this moment doesn't mean he won't find out. And I've got a medical condition called 'wanting to stay alive and out of prison for as long as possible.'"

Sterling nodded enthusiastically. "So let's go back to how this started: anyone as financially and politically connected as the mentor will have skeletons in his closet. It's our job to find them, and bring him down the same way we did with Jim. Just because we haven't found a way yet doesn't mean it's impossible. Our problem right now is money—we need a heist."

Blair took a sip of coffee and set her mug down as she offered, "Or we could tap our go-bag fund."

"Absolutely not." Marco's eyes went wide at the suggestion. "That fund is enough for new IDs, a trip out of the country, and a fresh start. That's the final safety net, and if we use it now, there is nothing beneath us but the fall. We don't access it unless we're leaving for good. I agree with Sterling: if we're not going to run, we need a heist."

"But for once in our career," Blair pointed out, "we don't have the time to plan one. Money aside, what can we do with what we've already got?"

"At present, we don't have anything."

Blair mused, "What about the audio from Jim's tapes, the content we've withheld for future ammunition? Since releasing the footage from the Sky Safe robbery while Sterling was in court, we've got like a million YouTube followers."

"2.7 million," Alec clarified, "as of this morning."

"We could release that audio today. It would cost us nothing, and maybe someone else could use the clues about political connections to piece together the mentor's identity while we work on a plan."

Marco shook his head adamantly. "That audio is only useful once we know who the mentor is. Paired with a name and some further proof of their misdeeds, it becomes evidence. Without it, the audio is useless to us."

She asked, "Then who can we ask for help?"

"No one," Sterling said, "according to Wolf. He said not to even contact him, because he'll be under surveillance due to the connection with my father."

"What about Wraith?"

The room fell completely silent, and to Blair's surprise, the first person to speak wasn't Marco in his usual capacity as team naysayer but Sterling.

"Are you serious? The woman who stole the tapes from us in the first place?"

"She helped me escape," Blair countered.

"Only because you saved her life."

"True, but I briefly spoke with her after the fact. I think she's trustworthy, and we all know by now that she's got the tradecraft to help us."

Judging by his expression, Alec seemed at least semi-receptive to the proposal, but Marco crossed his arms and spoke in a grave tone. "Wraith is anything but trustworthy. She'd sell us out for the bounty in no time flat."

"I agree," Sterling said. "She robbed us once and she'll do it again, this time with our lives. And even if we did want to commit suicide by asking, we have no way to contact her."

Blair eyed him with a rising sense of irritation. "You're wrong. I told her the email address we used to communicate with Dembinski. Theskythieves@gmail.com, remember? She's surely hacked that account by now to see what we're up to. We could send a self-addressed email there, and I guarantee she'd read it almost immediately."

Softening at Blair's withering glare, Sterling said, "The only person outside this room who knows the stakes as well as we do is Wolf. He said to trust no one. We're being hunted and we're running low on funds. This isn't just a regular war; it's a financial one as well. We need a heist."

Alec seemed to have lost interest, and was now playing with his phone as Marco responded.

"Aside from the money required to plan and execute it, a heist would strain our two key resources: time and effort. And it would place us at an even greater risk on a good day, much less while everyone in the world is looking for us to get the bounty."

Finally Alec looked up from his phone and interjected, "The hammer just dropped on Sterling's stinky shoe."

"And?" Blair asked.

"1.2 million."

There was an audible groan from the group, and Marco was the first to recover his wits enough to speak.

"Who pays this kind of money for our old crap? It's undignified."

Alec shrugged. "Crazy people, I suppose. But as usual, you've all left it up to me to save us, so I'll point out the obvious."

"Which is?"

He grinned. "We don't need a heist, necessarily. What we need is *money*. Now Blair could resort to stripping, or we could do something less enticing but far more lucrative."

"Like what?"

He held up his phone. "Some wacko is buying up anything we've ever laid our hands on for astronomical sums of cash. What if we figure out who that is, and sell him something ourselves?"

Sterling leaned forward, apparently intrigued but shaking his head nonetheless.

"Whoever the buyer is, he's not going to pay top dollar for average stuff. We'd need something that is irrefutably used or obtained in a famous heist, something that would complement his collection. And we don't have anything like that on hand."

"Sure we do," Alec casually replied.

"Like what?"

"Only way we got into the Sky Safe was by stealing one of the Kryelast jigsaw planks prior to construction and replacing it with one of our own. We've still got the original plank—it's sitting in my workshop right now, laid across two safes. I've been using it to hold my coffee."

Marco asked, "Didn't we set that on fire with thermal lances during our testing phase?"

"Of course we did. Only way to know our plan would work was to try it on actual Kryelast. It's partially burned up, sure. But it's the stolen plank all the same. Think about it: proprietary lightweight material, unique jigsaw pattern...the authenticity is beyond all doubt to a prospective buyer."

Blair asked tentatively, "If this person paid a million for a bloody prison loafer, how much would they pay for the plank directly from us?"

"Three million," Marco said. "Maybe four."

Sterling was nodding now. "Given their demonstrated wealth, they're a legal citizen. That means they don't know about the bounty, and even if they did, a million bucks in exchange for ratting us out is nothing to them. And they're clearly a fan, so there's zero risk of them turning us in."

Marco cautioned, "There's low risk. The risk is never zero."

"Sure, agreed. We'd have to approach it like we were walking into a trap, just like we do with everything else. But think about it: we'd replenish our funds without tapping our emergency accounts, and that amount of cash buys us a lot of financial leeway to keep pursuing the mentor."

Blair thought about that for a moment, then asked, "What if this collector doesn't want to buy the plank?"

"We go down the list of bidders for each item, one at a time. Someone's going to bite."

Alec set his phone on the table. "We're forgetting about one thing—

crazy rich people like to remain anonymous. The auctions all occur through representatives making the bids. Before we can pitch any buyer on our plank, we have to figure out who bid on our team memorabilia in the first place."

"I've got a guy for that," Sterling replied. "Marco, can you hack the auction house?"

Marco leaned back in his seat, putting his hands behind his head before answering with unshakable confidence, "Anything can be hacked."

11

STERLING

"It can't be hacked," Marco said, his eyes fixed on the computer screen.

Sterling rubbed his temples. This was the most disappointment he'd ever felt in Marco's lair.

The only light in the room was provided by Marco's computer screens —which was more than sufficient, Sterling thought, because there were ten of them.

Four elevated monitors were tilted downward, hovering over an additional six screens perched atop the semicircular desk that held so many keyboards and computer mice that Sterling wouldn't know where to begin drafting an email, much less monitor a hacking effort. Which was just fine by him—he'd never had to, relying instead on the man at the epicenter of all this ridiculous technology.

Marco was so good at what he did that Sterling actually wondered whether the hacker was joking with this latest declaration, and it wasn't any easier to tell when the central chair swiveled toward him, casting Marco's face in the shadows as he turned away from the computers and spoke.

"Go ahead, ask me if I'm serious."

"Are you?"

"Always."

Sterling's hands balled into fists in an involuntary spasm. "You hacked the FBI's cloud storage. How can you not penetrate the records of an auction house?"

"With the FBI," Marco began, "we had the benefit of law enforcement's obsession with evidential integrity and chain of custody. Storing evidence on a cloud is subject to local, state, and federal regulations that specify the encryption requirements, audit trails, and authentication protocols, so I could analyze the regulations to reverse-engineer a digital penetration."

"Right. Using the law to break the law, a Marco specialty. So?"

Marco spun his chair to the side, lifting his legs to cross both ankles atop the desk.

"So auction houses are subject to no such regulatory guidelines. High net worth individuals usually buy anonymously as a contractual require-ment from their insurance company, or security service, or both. Keep in mind that a single compromise of buyer identity could cost an auction house hundreds of millions in sales over the course of a year, and you'll understand why they don't exactly keep these records in the public space."

"Then where do they keep them?"

Marco gave a helpless shrug. "Presumably, only on a limited internal network with no online connectivity. During each of our memorabilia sales, the winning bids were submitted by auction house staffers working the phone banks. It's safe to say that the caller was a proxy representing a legally anonymous entity, and very few people inside the actual auction house will know who that is. If I had to guess, they're using a courier to personally relay shipping information to an armored car company that transports the items to their final destination."

"All right," Sterling conceded, "what do we know about the auction house?"

Marco lowered his legs from the desk and spun his chair to stop at a peripheral computer monitor, accessing the commercial website as he continued.

"JB West. They're a major international auction house, and the second largest in California after Bonhams. Main office is on Melrose Avenue, and they employ 47 specialists to represent 25 categories of collectibles with over 300 auctions each year."

"And they've sold all of our team gear so far?"

"All of it."

Sterling lowered him into the chair beside him. "What's so special about JB West? Why not Sotheby's, Christie's, or Phillips? I thought they handled all the high-dollar stuff."

"They do," Marco said. "Most of the important art goes through them—impressionist and modern, contemporary, old masters, most of them selling for orders of magnitude more than our crew paraphernalia could fetch at auction. But JB West has made a name for itself with the lowest commission rate, which appeals to law enforcement who are selling evidence to raise funds, and by being the first to accept cryptocurrency, which attracts buyers who want an extra layer of anonymity."

Then he interlaced his fingers, locking out his elbows to stretch and adding, "The bottom line is, I can obtain the records of each proxy bidder and use them to trace the actual buyer. But that will require a physical penetration—we will have to go to JB West headquarters. Be grateful they're in LA."

"I'd be grateful," Sterling retorted, "if we didn't have to risk a break-in to get buyer info so we can pitch them on a direct sale that might not work in the first place."

Marco frowned in the glow of the computer screens.

"As would I. But you said we needed a heist, Sterling. And I'm telling you, we just found it."

12

BLAIR

"Here we are, my pet," Alec said, stopping on the sidewalk beside an ornate wooden door and resting his palm on the handle. "Shall we?"

Blair paused to examine the exterior of the JB West headquarters building, which was, she thought, deceptively elegant.

The two-story structure had an ornate art deco facade that wasn't out of place amid the shopping and entertainment venues on LA's fabled Melrose Avenue. From the outside, there were no more visible security measures than after-hours door gates and the ubiquitous black dome cameras.

But inside was where they kept the items for upcoming auctions, some of them valued in the millions, and that was where things got interesting.

"Yes," she said, "let's get this over with."

Alec held open the door and Blair stepped through, entering the lobby to find a lavish space, with crystal chandeliers hovering over waxed marble floors and oriental rugs spaced at regular intervals. There were four separate viewing tables, only one occupied at present by a portly middle-aged man being catered to by a sales rep.

Blair stopped in place, allowing Alec to sweep to her front and approach a gray-haired gentleman manning a reception desk beside them.

"Welcome to JB West," the man said. "How may I help you?"

Alec sauntered up to the desk and exchanged pleasantries as Blair checked the path to her line of egress, a fire exit leading to the rear parking lot where Sterling waited with a getaway car. If she was somehow recognized and the cops were summoned, Marco would transmit a single codeword—*avalanche*—and cause the ostensibly married couple to flee.

But if that hadn't come to pass within the first few minutes, it was unlikely to; after all, Blair bore about as much physical resemblance to her normal appearance as she did to any number of unrelated women.

Facial prosthetics had transformed her smooth features into high cheekbones and a slim nose, complete with an abnormally perfect chin that conveyed the appearance of both plastic surgery and filler injections. Neither was out of place in Los Angeles, and she'd completed the look with ghostly blue colored contacts and a flowing wig of perfectly styled light brown hair with warm blonde highlights. The goal was to fit in without standing out, to belong without being too memorable in the aftermath.

Her exposure here was certainly a risk, but a calculated one.

Alec went on, "I'm interested in Lot #389 for Monday's auction. It's an Official Major League Baseball, signed in blue pen by 26 members of the historic 2004 Red Sox lineup that won our first World Series since 1918. The lot includes a letter of authenticity by PSA/DNA Authentication Services, and I'd like to see that as well."

The receptionist replied, "I'm sorry, you said a...a baseball?"

"Yes, sir. Lot #389."

Typing on his keyboard, the man appeared vaguely troubled as he responded, "I can't seem to find your appointment in our system."

"Appointment?" Alec sounded offended. "My accent is my appointment, sir, and any Boston native should be allowed—nay, required—to pay homage to the team that broke an 86-year stagnation and, I might add, set the stage for an additional three World Series titles."

Frowning, the gray-haired man responded, "I'm afraid we don't typically host viewings for items with a starting bid below 25,000 dollars. And it appears that Lot #389 doesn't qualify."

"Well," Blair said, "you heard the gentleman, honey. Time to go."

But Alec was undeterred, setting his left hand atop the desk in a final impassioned plea.

"Sir, the item was just posted on your website last night and I didn't see it until this morning. Now tomorrow is our wedding anniversary and we're headed out of town for a romantic week in Napa Valley, and I'm afraid this is my one and only chance to evaluate the auction lot in person."

The receptionist didn't seem to be listening; as Blair had expected, his eyes dropped to Alec's wrist on the table before him.

Wealth was a hard thing to gauge in LA, a city where the ultra-rich were as likely to be in shorts and a T-shirt as a suit. The only surefire indicator most salespeople had was on the wrist, as even the most shabbily attired millionaires tended to wear some heinously expensive watch.

And Alec didn't disappoint: he wore a platinum Vacheron Constantin, a timepiece purchased at great cost as part of a plan for him to impersonate a Wall Street executive with whom he bore an uncanny physical resemblance. That plan had fallen apart but the watch remained, much to Sterling's irritation, and today was the first time it would pay off for the crew.

The receptionist didn't care about the sale of a baseball; he cared about the potentially far more expensive items that such an eccentric client could bid on in the future.

Smiling politely, he replied, "Congratulations on your wedding anniversary."

"Thank you," Blair said.

"I'd be happy to make an exception." He looked behind them and raised his arm, summoning an attractive woman in her mid-twenties to approach and greet them warmly.

"Hi, I'm Kagan and I'd be happy to help you today. Please follow me."

She led them to a viewing table, asking over her shoulder, "And what lot number are you interested in seeing?"

"389," Alec said, "and I'd like to review both the sacred baseball and its certificate of authenticity, if you wouldn't mind."

"Of course," Kagan replied. "Please have a seat here. Can I get you something to drink—coffee, tea, champagne?"

Blair shook her head as Alec pulled out a chair for her and said, "No champagne could be as sweet as the 2004 World Series ball. We're fine, thank you."

Taking a seat, Blair watched Kagan's departure.

She walked to the right side of the lobby, pulling open an unlocked door and vanishing inside. Blair knew from blueprints that it represented the stairwell entrance—no lock, no RFID card reader required to enter—although that was a far cry from what would be encountered at the doors leading to each sublevel, where the real valuables were stored.

Alec assumed his place in the chair beside her, pulling back his shirt cuff to check the time before saying, "Sorry for the inconvenience, darling. This won't take long."

"I trust it won't," Blair replied, scanning the room with the appearance of a casual first-time visitor.

As a former member of the FBI's Tactical Operations Section, Blair was the undisputed crew expert in the use of hidden surveillance devices. Her previous job experience had endowed her with a keen eye in spotting the often barely discernible signs of security measures not intended to be seen. Scanning for those would take up the majority of her effort once she completed her primary task of confirming or denying the type and place-ment of overt devices. If there was a significant deviation from the layout detailed on JB West's insurance policy, long since hacked by Marco, then the crew had a very real problem on their hands: an overhaul of lobby secu-rity would almost certainly indicate the same in the considerably more secure basement sublevels.

Alec asked, "Everything okay, sweetheart? I feel like you've been giving me the cold shoulder all day."

"Everything's fine," she said icily, "as long as we don't miss our dinner reservation. Keep that in mind when you're authenticating your toy."

"*Baseball*. A very rare and historic commemorative *baseball*, my love. Not a toy."

Blair didn't reply, noting with pleasure that so far everything appeared to be as expected. She'd observed the ADT door contact sensors on her way in, followed in short order by the six cameras providing every possible angle of coverage over the visitors and staff.

Those were the least of their concerns. Marco could hack the cameras with relative ease, conducting a routine digital takeover that would allow him to freeze the images at will without upsetting the onscreen clock. Like-wise, the door contact sensors and their corresponding audit trail documenting which were opened and when was an entirely digital process that he could simply suspend at will.

She let her gaze drift up to the corner of the ceiling where a small white box was mounted. It contained a square lens mounted at a downward angle, the shape of the casing confirming to her that this was, as they'd expected, a Kronos Max 619.

And that was where the real problem lay.

The stairwell door opened, followed by Kagan reappearing with two items encased in rigid plastic.

She set them down on the table's velvet-lined tray, first the certificate and then the baseball itself, the rounded surface covered in the scrawling signatures of the 2004 Red Sox. Blair appraised each with disdain, quickly looking away to play the part of the inconvenienced wife down to the last ragged detail.

As Kagan seated herself across from them, Alec seized the baseball and turned it over in his hands to view the signatures through the glare of light reflecting off the transparent cube encasing it.

"I take it you're a Red Sox fan?" Kagan asked.

"Born and bred," Alec replied without breaking his gaze from the ball. He began flipping the cube at regular intervals, muttering to himself, "Johnny Damon, Doug Mientkiewicz, Bill Mueller...my God, this is a thing of beauty."

Blair gave an indifferent sigh as she glanced around the room, concluding her search for overt devices and segueing into a hunt for those meant to go unseen. While the classified devices she'd emplaced on behalf of the FBI were virtually undetectable, visually or otherwise, only a finite number of reliable options were available for purchase on the retail market.

But so far the Kronos 619 appeared to be their single greatest obstacle.

It wasn't that the motion detector used a combination of microwave and passive infrared sensors, or even that it was among the most effective and highly sensitive models currently in production. The crew had extensive experience in neutralizing similar devices on any number of heists.

Instead, the problem was that this particular motion sensor, as well as others in the levels below the lobby, were hardwired into the building's central alarm and thus completely impervious to any digital disruption. Since the wiring ran inside the building, they'd have to excavate a section of exterior wall to interrupt the circuit, a lengthy and noisy process that would eliminate any possibility of their incursion going unnoticed.

Likewise, if they simply cut power to the building the system would trigger automatically, meaning an auxiliary power unit in the lowest sub-basement would simultaneously activate every interior and exterior emergency light, send wireless and cellular distress signals to the police, and—Blair's least favorite of the available outcomes—sound an audible alarm. At 130 decibels, the sound would be equivalent to a fighter jet taking off with full afterburners, the noise level a half-step removed from eardrum rupture and sufficient to be heard for close to a mile in any given direction.

Alec gave a breathless moan and said, "There you are."

He looked up at Kagan, beaming with joy. "Hall of Famer Pedro Martinez, right there. Beautiful, simply stunning."

Tapping Blair on the shoulder, he said, "See, honey? Pedro, right here next to the MLB logo."

Blair looked at the ball and then away.

Alec's shoulders sagged. "You broke my heart when you left us for the Mets, Pedro. You broke my heart."

Then he set down the ball and lifted the certificate of authenticity, reading aloud.

"'The signatures are consistent considering slant, flow, pen pressure, letter size, and other characteristics that are typical of the other exemplars that we have examined in our professional career.'" He huffed a laugh. "You're darn right they are, PSA/DNA Authentication Services."

Then he set down the certificate and asked Blair, "What do you think, dear?"

She shrugged, then pointed to the floor.

"I think we need a rug like this in our dining room."

The reference to acquiring any item of decor in the lobby was her indication that she'd completed her sweep, and Alec responded in kind to Kagan.

"Well," he began, "I think we've crossed the threshold of my wife's attention span. However, I find this commemorative baseball to be in impeccable condition and will be bidding on it come Monday up to ten—"

Blair cut her eyes to him, and he quickly corrected himself. "—eight thousand dollars. Thank you for your time, Kagan. This has truly been a day to remember."

Kagan collected the items and bid them farewell before retreating to the stairwell. Blair remained seated until Alec rounded her chair and pulled it out for her, then led the way to the front door as he scrambled to hold it open for her.

Blair smiled as she exited into the warm air and vehicle exhaust of Melrose Avenue.

The next time they set foot in this building, she thought, would be to rob it.

13

BLAIR

Blair walked in step with Alec, each of them holding a long metal pole with a tripod base as they crossed the empty rear parking lot behind the JB West building. At two o'clock in the morning, the facility was abandoned, but there were a sufficient number of neighboring structures to warrant an extra layer of concealment for their entry.

Upon reaching the back door, Alec and Blair spread their poles apart and set the tripods down, fully extending the eight-by-eight vinyl backdrop displaying a photographic copy of the rear entrance they were about to breach. It wouldn't hold up to close scrutiny, of course, but from the perspective of a passing driver, the facade did a surprisingly good job of presenting a routine appearance—and besides, Blair thought, hopefully they wouldn't be relying on it for long.

She and Alec slipped around the sides, tucking themselves in the space between the canvas and the building's outer wall. Alec immediately set to work on the after-hours gate, using a covert entry tool to pick the lock in a matter of seconds. The inner door was another matter altogether, though Blair had plenty to do in the time it would take her teammate to bypass the deadbolt and keypad. Kneeling, she removed her backpack.

The first item Blair removed was a mobile handset. She unfolded two antennas before directing her attention to the display, an attached iPhone programmed with the relevant software. Unlocking it to illuminate the screen, she saw a set of crosshairs hand-drawn with an extra fine permanent marker as she considered the delicate matter ahead.

Manually defeating the Kronos Max 619 required an intimate knowledge of its motion threshold, the smallest movement required to detect an intruder. Anything at or past that threshold would trigger the alarm, while anything below it would be undetectable. While these thresholds could be adjusted via sensitivity settings designed to eliminate false positives, the crew had to plan for the worse end of that spectrum.

The sensor mounted in the lobby had a minimum possible motion threshold that would allow it to detect a person moving at a rate of four inches per minute anywhere within twenty feet. It would take an extremely small, precision robot to move with the painstakingly calibrated sluggishness required to evade the sensor's attempts to detect it, and that was exactly what the crew had decided to use.

"Almost there," Alec whispered. "You ready, Maverick?"

Blair didn't respond immediately, her focus directed on the delicate process of removing the next item from her backpack.

The drone's body was small enough to fit in the palm of her hand, weighing in at just over half a pound. An X-shaped brace separated four tiny propellers, their blades safeguarded by a flexible plastic prop guard that would allow the drone to remain in flight if it bumped into a wall. Blair doubted that would occur tonight—the drones were purpose-built for precision flight, and as the crew's designated pilot for the evening, she'd spent the better part of the past week flying this device with incredible accuracy.

And tonight, that accuracy would be required.

She carefully set the drone on the ground, comforted by the fact that it was small enough to evade motion sensor detection even with the team's two modifications: a small LED light that Blair activated now, and a six-by-six-inch screen of wax paper held aloft by lightweight poles superglued to the roof of the drone's body casing.

"I'm set," she whispered to Alec, who completed his final step on the door breach before replying.

"*Sésame, ouvre-toi.*"

He turned the handle and pulled the door outward with astonishing slowness. By their analysis of the blueprints and security plans, there should have been two feet of blind spot before the motion sensor could detect movement, but they didn't intend on testing that. Blair took hold of the handset and waited for the door to open sufficiently wide for her drone.

They'd tested the aircraft extensively at the warehouse, putting it up against a newly acquired set of Kronos Max 619 units set to the highest sensitivity. After Blair inadvertently tripped the test sensors with manual control, Marco adjusted the software to restrict the drone's speed to a level sufficient for remaining beneath the motion threshold. Since then, the drone had functioned almost flawlessly, though it required Blair to carry a mobile GPS transmitter to maintain a continuous signal—a lesson they'd learned only after the drone lost signal indoors and crashed to the ground.

Finally Alec had the door halfway open, holding it in place as Blair prepared for liftoff.

Gingerly placing her thumbs onto the twin joysticks of her handset, she pivoted them to the bottom corner of their movement range until the drone's propellers whirred to life; then she thumbed the left stick up until the tiny aircraft glided upward.

Her next actions were pure muscle memory. Using her left thumb to adjust altitude and orientation and her right to move the drone forward and sideways, she watched the iPhone display as the drone buzzed inside the doorway, its progress heralded by the LED light that illuminated a swath of the lobby. Then she guided the drone to the far right corner, gradually increasing its altitude until she could make out the motion detector mounted near the ceiling.

This was the trickiest part of the entire affair—even with its size and speed remaining beneath the motion threshold, a sudden movement close to the sensor could nonetheless trigger the alarm. Blair slowed her progress the closer she got until the aircraft was barely moving at all, easing forward and up until the crosshair marking on her screen was flush with the bottom edge of the Kronos Max 619 sensor casing. The wax paper screen atop her drone now blocked the unit's microwave and passive infrared sensors, allowing them to enter the building at will.

Releasing her control inputs to hold the drone in a hover, she transmitted, "Lobby sensor is blocked—clear to move."

14

STERLING

Sterling slowed his jog to cut around the canvas facade.

Blair didn't look up from her handset, her lack of attention to his approach serving as a welcome confirmation that the drone remained in place. Alec held the door ajar and Sterling slipped inside, activating his headlamp while cringing at the thought of the earsplitting alarm sounding through some unanticipated facet of the building's security plan.

But the well-furnished lobby was silent aside from the angry buzz of Blair's drone holding its position in front of the motion sensor. Sterling ran past opulent administrative offices to the stairwell door, jerking it open by the time he heard Marco's footsteps behind him.

Sterling recovered a keyring as he descended the steps two at a time past the first two basement sublevels, where any concessions to occupant comfort ended abruptly. The climate-controlled and dehumidified rooms housed a stockpile of art, jewelry, and wine among countless other collectibles set to be auctioned at events around the world, to say nothing of Alec's stupid baseball. While a few of those items would be prime targets for a heist, Sterling's crew preferred to rob the deserving, and in any case, valuables weren't their real targets tonight—information was. The sooner they recovered that and exited, the better.

He was pleased to see Doorking telephone entry systems beside the first two doorways, the metal boxes instantly recognizable from the trio of round, vertical buttons beside the keypad. As he negotiated the stairs leading to the third and final sublevel, Sterling flipped through his keyring accordingly. It held a variety of options, all easily procurable through installer catalogues or eBay; each would open a huge number of similarly keyed units.

The CH751 key was a staple for accessing a majority of lockboxes, file cabinets, and wafer tumbler locks. There was also the FEO-K1, which could be used to activate the fire service override in a majority of US elevators, along with the 1284X Ford Motor Company fleet key. That particular gem could open and start the ignitions of a staggering number of Ford vehicles across police departments and, courtesy of the reappropriated Crown Victoria auction process, taxis as well. He flipped past the A126, which would universally open control units produced by the Lanier Electronics Group. The only one he cared about at present was the 16120 key, pinned in his fingertips by the time he set foot on the concrete floor at the bottom of the stairs.

There he rushed to the single doorway ahead of Marco, who stopped with his fingers on the handle. Sterling squared off with the stainless steel Doorking telephone entry system on the wall—the unit allowed authorized users to unlock the door via a keycode, and unauthorized employees to request entry via the intercom. Sterling was neither, and he instead pushed the 16120 key into the lock, where it turned cleanly as it would in any Doorking telephone entry system produced since the early nineties. Lowering the outer metal panel, he exposed the inner workings of inter-connected wires, circuit boards, and, most pertinent to him at present, the terminal block of dry contacts through which he could manipulate the solenoid door lock.

Adjusting a U-shaped piece of wire on his keyring, Sterling simultaneously touched the tops to bridge contacts four and six on the terminal block, grounding the circuit as the lock emitted a satisfying *clack* of deactivation.

The noise was followed by Marco twisting the handle but not opening the door—yet.

Alec thundered down the stairs, which served as Sterling's first indication that the back door vinyl backdrop facade had been relocated inside the building. Blair followed a moment later, holding the drone in one hand. With the other, she produced a spare battery unit from her pocket, replacing it with the partially expended one as she moved.

Sterling closed the Doorking unit casing and stepped out of the way, allowing Blair to set the drone on the floor and resume her control of the handset.

"Go ahead." Her eyes were fixed on the iPhone display, and Marco pulled the door open with impossible slowness. Blair waited until it was half cracked and then sent the angrily buzzing drone aloft, where it hovered three feet off the ground before drifting through the doorway toward the motion sensor in the corridor beyond.

As he waited for the drone to reach its destination, Sterling prepared the next tool in his arsenal: a Phillips head screwdriver.

After a minute of tense silence, Blair announced, "Hallway sensor is blocked. Clear to move."

Sterling was the first to enter, jogging toward the second door on his right. He tested the handle out of instinct, felt it hold firm, and then turned his attention to the RFID card reader mounted beside the door frame.

The deadbolt controller on this unit was installed on the secure side of the door, removing any possibility of bridging wires to effect an entry. This presented a delay, but certainly wasn't a showstopper; instead, Sterling would have to exploit the unencrypted communications between the card reader and the controller that deactivated the deadbolt.

This process began with using his screwdriver to remove the single screw at the base of the unit, then pulling the R90's front cover away to expose the two screws affixing it to the wall. Sterling set to work on these, depositing the screws into a drop pouch on his belt before moving the unit away from the wall to pull a two-foot section of cord through. He held the cord steady as Marco clamped a wire stripper to cut through the rubber insulation, then twisted the tool and carefully peeled back a five-inch strip.

The process exposed a cluster of five color-coded wires within, and Sterling placed a postage-stamp-sized chip known as an ESPKey beneath the bundle. He ignored the blue wire, instead clipping the rest into the chip's connection ports. Used for its intended purpose, the ESPKey would serve as a "sniffer" to collect the credentials of authorized users, transmitting the data wirelessly for the user to clone as many access cards as they wished for hasty repeated entry.

But this particular chip had been modified to transmit as well, and Marco used his phone to initiate a logic-analysis software program that cycled through multiple numerical combinations per second, interrogating the controller and using the time delay in unit response to determine correct digits one at a time. The end result was a six-digit code determined and transmitted back to the controller on the far side of the wall within half a minute—and once that occurred, the deadbolt thunked into its retracted position and Alec cranked the handle open for the crew to enter.

15

BLAIR

Blair was the last one inside the office, which, she could tell at first glance, had a better than passing chance of containing the information they'd come here to find.

In stark contrast to the auction house's ground-level commercial area, this room was strictly utilitarian. No art on the walls, no oriental rugs lining the floor. Instead there were two desks with computers, both in the process of having their hard drives imaged by the crew's plug-in devices. Alec was seated at the nearest one, while Marco manned the station at the far wall, using a separate plug-in to open the user account at the same time.

He'd already determined passwords for the auction house's online computers using a procedure that tested just under three billion passwords per second, enabling him to crack the sophisticated alphanumeric codes within days. Now Marco was running a more refined version of that process, operating under the assumption that the unit's intended operator used the same password or a slight variation of it for their offline work.

And that computer would hold the key, Blair knew. They'd selected this office as their destination for a simple reason: it contained the only ethernet hookup that didn't correspond to an online access point in Marco's initial hacking efforts, which was, according to him, indicative of a computer impervious to remote access. Now he was sitting before it, having already accessed the administrative mode and initiated his software plugin to cycle passwords as Sterling rifled through a bookcase with binders of sales records.

Blair's only task at present was to keep her drone hovering in front of the hallway motion sensor, recalling it to switch the battery if the effort exceeded the twenty-minute mark.

But no sooner had she glanced at her handset display to confirm the drone remained in position than Marco called out, "I'm in."

She looked up to see him accessing the computer's search directory, entering the lot numbers of the crew memorabilia by memory to confirm the hard drive imaging would bring with it the bidder and buyer information. Within seconds he had six different windows open on the screen, and she felt goosebumps across her forearms as he spoke again.

"I've got what we need."

Blair actually chirped in surprise. Nothing could be this easy. "You know the buyers?"

"No," Marco replied. "But I have a list of middlemen. From there we should be able to trace the source."

"How many middlemen?"

"At a glance? Hundreds. So hopefully one will stick out. Let's go."

16

STERLING

Alone in the warehouse conference room, Sterling paced before the long table that had been cleared to make way for a new item—the Kryelast plank.

Sterling had mixed feelings about being in such close proximity to it.

On one hand, of course, the plank was a marvel of modern engineering. The proprietary material was created solely for use in a freestanding safe hanging off the side of a building, a theoretically impenetrable concept made more so by its unique jigsaw edges, which eliminated any possibility of exploiting a linear seam with a ballistic or mechanical breach.

Blair had come up with the only feasible way to get in: by altering the Sky Safe's construction before it was built. Thus the crew had stolen this plank from its manufacturer, replacing it with one of their own design. And while they'd gone to great pains to match the exact weight and make their replica visually indistinguishable at anything less than a microscopic analysis, its construction differed considerably: it held a core of thermal lances, pressurized oxygen, torch, and, of course, the transmitter to allow the crew to ignite it. They'd essentially built one giant burning bar and allowed the builders to unwittingly install it in the safe's roof. When the time came to rob it, they'd been able to enter at will—or Sterling had.

And the memories of that night were the source of his emotional tumult upon seeing the plank now.

Sure, he'd managed to overcome inconceivable odds to steal the Sierra Diamond, an eight hundred and seventy-two carat, uncut white whale of a prize, and hand it off to Blair. But in the process, Sterling had walked into a trap of Jim's design, been arrested, and faced lengthy court proceedings before being sentenced to incarceration at the same Supermax prison normally reserved for terrorists. There he'd spent 23 hours a day in solitary confinement in an eighty-five-square-foot concrete cell, the bare minimum allowed by federal statute.

His time at the Supermax had been one long, continuous nightmare spanning various degrees of horror that had tested his spirit and found him wanting. By the time Blair and his crew rescued him from the abyss, he'd been questioning his very humanity.

The Kryelast plank was partially scorched from Alec's thermal lance testing, which had rendered one side into a molten fray that had since congealed into an onyx-like strip that was incredibly hard to the touch. But the opposite side of the plank bore the undisturbed jigsaw pattern, and there would be no doubt as to the item's authenticity for their buyer—if they could find one.

Sterling continued pacing then, though not for long.

Alec's voice boomed down the hallway. "Sky, Sky, Sky Thieves—ho!"

Blair, the first to enter, took in Sterling's appearance. "You okay? You look like you just saw a ghost."

"I'm fine. Did we determine the buyer or what?"

"I assume so. Marco's been in his lair all day, and Alec's been with him for the past hour."

Alec burst through the door a moment later, continuing his rendition of the *ThunderCats* theme song.

"The Sky Thieves are on the move...the Sky Thieves are loose....feel the magic—"

"You find the buyer?" Sterling asked.

Marco entered next, holding a file folder. "We did."

"And?"

Before the hacker could respond, Alec said, "The Forbes 400 is an annual list of the richest Americans ranked by net worth. How many can you name?"

Sterling crossed his arms. "Can you just get to the point?"

"Nope," Alec said firmly. "Start rattling them off."

"I don't know—Jeff Bezos, Bill Gates, Elon Musk."

Blair added, "Mark Zuckerberg. Larry and Sergey from Google."

"Warren Buffet."

Alec grinned. "Yes to all. Nice work, but you're not there yet."

"Maybe a Kardashian?"

"No. Anyone else?"

When neither Sterling nor Blair replied, Alec continued, "Well here's one that neither of you guessed, who, incidentally, is the same individual who has purchased literally *all* of our crew gear at auction: Kristen Shedo."

A dumbstruck moment of silence followed, broken when Blair and Sterling asked in unison, "Who is Kristen Shedo?"

Marco set the file folder atop the table and slid it to the far end.

Sterling intercepted the folder, flipping it open and rifling through pages still warm from the printer as Alec narrated, "She's 52 years old, lives in Washington State. She's a serial entrepreneur and venture capitalist."

"I thought all those lived in Silicon Valley," Sterling replied, turning over another page.

"Well at least one lives in Medina, just across the lake from Seattle. Her house is on Evergreen Point Road—same street as her fellow Forbes 400 members Bill Gates and Jeff Bezos."

He felt his eyebrows shoot up at that, then stopped flipping through the pages when he located a professional photograph of Kristen Shedo. She was beautiful, with dark hair and piercing hazel eyes, her very image conveying a surefooted sense of authority.

Then he shrugged. "We knew our fan would be rich."

Marco replied, "'Rich' doesn't begin to describe her. Net worth is somewhere around 33.7 billion."

Then Alec added helpfully, "And she's insane."

Sterling looked up from the picture. "Insane?"

"Okay, so insane is too strong a word."

"You mean eccentric."

Alec shook his head quickly. "That's not strong enough."

"Then what are we talking about here?"

"Start with eccentric, then stop three-quarters of the way to all-out, full-fledged, card-carrying, straight-jacket-level insanity. That's Kristen Shedo."

Marco tried to clarify.

"She owns twelve properties outside of Medina, including a castle in Germany and an island in the British Virgin Islands—"

"So?" Sterling cut him off. "I'd own some real estate if I had her kind of money."

"She's spent over eight million dollars on grand champion koi fish for her garden pond."

"Who doesn't like pets?"

"And," Alec added, "a rumored 200,000 dollars on plastic surgery."

Sterling tossed the professional photograph on the desk. "Well apparently it worked. She looks great."

Seeing Blair's eyes narrow, he hastily followed up with, "You know, for an old lady."

Alec took a step forward, placing the fingertips of one hand on the desk as he said, "I'll take it from here, Marco. Sterling, she paid a hundred fifty grand for John Lennon's toilet."

Sterling hesitated. "So she's got some quirks."

"And allegedly owns a sex tape of Marilyn Monroe."

"You wouldn't be curious?"

Blair's gaze was heating up now, and Sterling was grateful for the interruption when Alec spoke again.

"Okay." He nodded. "I see we're playing hardball. How about the fact that she routinely participates in seances to communicate with the ghost of W.B. Yeats?"

"He was a great poet."

"Or has a collection of shrunken pygmy heads?"

Sterling threw up his hands. "What do you want me to say? If she buys the plank, does it matter how weird she is? Alec, I've caught you literally breakdancing to Miley Cyrus songs on no less than three occasions, and you're certainly not in any danger of paying us millions."

"It was a joke," he snapped, face reddening. "I knew you were watching."

Marco sighed wearily. "All right, so we now know who bought our heist gear. That was no small feat. Are we going to contact her or not?"

"Depends," Sterling replied. "Can you get a direct phone number?"

Marco nodded. "I've already initiated the data scrape. I expect to have a personal contact number within 24 hours."

17

KRISTEN

Kristen Shedo followed her lead bodyguard down the corridor, pausing only to allow him to push open the heavy steel door. The hammering chop of a helicopter filled the void, and she slipped through the doorway to feel the air disturbance of idling rotor blades whipping wind across the open rooftop.

The first thing she saw upon exiting was the sleek body of her Eurocopter EC135, painted in a dazzling shade of candy-apple red, as were the rest of her aircraft and, indeed, many of her cars as well. Consisting of pure red mixed with 3.14% green and no blue whatsoever, the resulting color achieved a wavelength of 610.91 nanometers on the visible light spectrum. Aside from the fact that this particular hue of red complemented her skin tone like no other she'd seen, her predominant obsession with this color stemmed from the mix of green.

Green, of course, was representative of both rebirth and immortality, the very skin color of the Egyptian god Osiris, king of the underworld. Equally if not more compelling was the 3.14 numeral, and while most people only valued that as the mathematical constant of Pi in Euclidean geometry, to Shedo it combined the three most important energy attributes she'd used to expand her consciousness.

That significance began with the number 3, which, as anyone knew, symbolized expansion, growth, and freedom. It was the frequency of the spiritually advanced beings who had undergone many lifetimes as ordinary humans in their past incarnations before ascending to the state of Ascended Master.

Then there was the number 1, the treasured representative of initiative, inner guidance, and manifesting desire into reality. Paired as it was with number 4—stability, the earth, mankind—it was little wonder she had an affinity for hex color code #ff0800, resulting from a numerical pairing of green with red, whose symbolic meaning was courage and life itself.

Her attention shifted to the skyscape around her and she halted abruptly, noting with pleasure that her lead bodyguard, even a relatively short term into his employment, had accustomed himself to these pauses on the roof. He had stopped a respectful distance away and was holding up an index finger toward the pilots, allowing her to direct her focus to the 360-degree panorama around her.

And what a panorama it was.

The perpetual blanket of clouds over Seattle had lifted, giving way to a glorious sunset where apricot hues transitioned to a cornflower-blue sky. It was breathtaking, really; she felt the vibrant radiance of her life energy rising in equal proportion to the view.

She gazed southward toward the Cascade Range, the mountains standing out in stark relief to the urban landscape. The horizon was graced by the outline of Mount Rainier, its unmistakable profile carving a swath across the sky.

Westward was the glassy surface of the Puget Sound followed by the Olympic Mountains, the glacier-capped summit of Mount Olympus visible amidst the old-growth forests along the coastline. Kristen gasped in appreciation, swinging toward the north where Seattle's iconic Space Needle rose from the sprawl. Then she cast her gaze eastward across Lake Washington to the distant shoreline that she called home.

And then, as her bliss reached a dizzying crescendo, she felt her personal phone buzz in her pocket.

Kristen released an anguished shriek of protest that was lost amid the noise of the idling helicopter, then ripped out her phone before confusion set in at the sight of *No Caller ID*.

That was, simply put, not possible—very few people possessed this number, and she'd saved every last one of them as a known contact.

She answered the call on speaker and shouted, "How did you get this number?"

But the helicopter racket erased any reply if there was one at all, and Kristen took the call off speaker before bringing the phone to her ear.

A man answered, "Good evening, Ms. Shedo."

Feeling a surge of anger, she cried, "I said, how did you get this number?"

"Most people," the man said calmly, "would want to know who's calling first."

"I'm not most people," she hissed.

"So I've heard. But when I tell you who I am, you'll understand how I reached you—my name is Sterling Defranc."

"Very funny."

"I'm not joking."

"Who is this, really—Kamal? Elon?"

"It's really Sterling."

"Well I don't believe you."

A pause before the man continued, "Ms. Shedo, it's my understanding that you are well versed in my crew's history. Ask me any relevant trivia question and I can guarantee I'll ace it."

Kristen pursed her lips, then said, "Two rappel ropes were used during the Century City heist. Law enforcement never released the model details, but upon acquiring them I commissioned an independent assessment—"

"Black Diamond 9.4 climbing ropes, 2X2 woven sheath. Both 80 meters in length, which gave us 60 meters of usable length from the tie-down point — sufficient for reaching the 23rd floor of Geering Plaza, where we re-entered the building and moved to an elevator shaft whose cables were rigged with hydraulic descenders."

Her rage turning to elation, she frantically waved an arm over her head and shouted to her bodyguard.

"Shut it off! I can't hear—shut it off!"

He patiently waved a flat hand back and forth across his throat, after which the rotor blades powered down.

Kristen swallowed, then said, "The tether cable used for the Sky Safe—"

"Within the phosphorus-based fire-retardant coating, a core made of high-strength twisted steel filaments. Fifty meter total length."

"My God," she gasped, "it really is you."

"Yes, Ms. Shedo, it is."

"Call me Kristen," she blurted, cursing herself for sounding desperate and hastily adding in a businesslike tone, "and to what do I owe the honor?"

"It seems you've acquired every item belonging to my crew that's ever come up for auction."

She put a hand over her throat. "You want them back?"

"No. I want to add to your collection."

Kristen felt an almost delirious sense of lightheadedness. She gasped, "I'm listening."

"There's an item that you won't be able to get at auction, now or ever. The Kryelast plank—"

"That you stole from the Wellington Safe Corporation," she finished for him. "The one you replaced with a replica concealing your entry mechanism, before the Sky Safe was constructed."

"That's right. I must warn you, it was partially burned during our testing procedures."

"Even better."

"But it's intact, and about 60 percent of the jigsaw pattern remains."

Her heart was fluttering now. "Name your price."

"4.5 million," came the immediate response.

She gave a short, rasping laugh. "If you have what you say you have, I'll pay you an even five—with one caveat."

"What's that?"

"You deliver it in person. I want to meet the man behind the legend."

"Done," he agreed. "And is this the best number to reach you at?"

"It is."

"Good. Transfer will require you to clear your schedule for a day and wait for my call. Will that be a problem?"

"Absolutely not."

"Am I correct in assuming the background noise at the start of our call was your helicopter?"

"Yes," she said, watching the now-drooping rotor blades on the aircraft she used to ferry herself to work five to six days each week.

"Perfect. On the day of the exchange, please have it standing by, fully fueled. For security reasons, I'll need to provide your pilot instructions on a private frequency."

"Is that it?"

"Payment must be instant crypto transfer at the exchange point."

"Easy day, Sterling."

"I'll be in touch," he said. Then he added an additional three words that sent her spirits soaring.

"Thank you, Kristen."

"No," she said, a dreamy grin forming on her lips, "thank you, Sterling."

He ended the call, though it took her a few repeated efforts of, "Hello? Hello?" before she allowed herself to confront this reality.

Once she did, Kristen Shedo cast a shocked glance to her lead bodyguard and managed, "Tell them to...tell them to spin it up." Forcing herself to draw a breath into lungs that were now constricted, she spoke the last words she would manage for the next five hours.

"I'd like to go home now."

18

BLAIR

Blair gazed out across the windswept landscape visible between the trees of her perch near Red Top Lookout. She'd had to avoid the summit, of course, where a tourist-infested panoramic lookout tower maintained a commanding view. By contrast, Blair's position was less advantageous in terms of visual majesty, but almost equally suited for long-range communications with a distant aircraft—and besides, she thought, the refreshing Pacific Northwest air with its hints of moss, pine, and musk held equal sway at both vantage points.

She took a deep breath, trying at least for the moment to focus on the staggering beauty around her.

That should have been easy, even from Blair's comparatively low elevation. To her north, the snow-capped Cascade Range spanned peaks that were easily recognizable from her mission preparation: first Ingalls Peak and Mount Stuart, the slope descending into Sherpa and Dragontail Peaks. And while her view to the south was blocked by the hillside, the west nonetheless revealed traces of the distant Seattle skyline through the trees.

The alternative view was much less compelling: Marco, presently focused on monitoring multiple police transponders, screening through the overlapping chatter for any mention of fugitives or air support. His eyes were fixed on a tablet display depicting an overhead view of their surroundings dotted with multicolored plane icons—the locations of active flight transponders operating at any altitude, which Marco had to surveil to ensure there were no flight hazards to the soon-to-be inbound helicopter.

Blair's job, by contrast, was relatively easy.

She checked her watch, seeing the time tick over to four p.m., a full five hours after Shedo and her aircrew had been told to stand by. The ensuing gap was contrived to detect any effort to notify authorities.

Whether or not that would occur remained to be seen; for the moment, Blair satisfied herself with transmitting, "All elements, check in."

Alec answered, "*Your most beautiful Bostonian is hot to trot at the pickup.*"

His voice was followed by one far more serious.

"*Sterling, in position. Let's get this over with.*"

Marco continued his silent vigil, attending to his devices with a half-hearted thumbs up in recognition of her operational control request. She transmitted over the crew net.

"All stations are ready. Stand by."

Blair palmed her alternate radio hand mic, preparing to initiate the entire operation.

She occupied a key role in the proceedings ahead, one that involved far less risk of arrest than either Alec or Sterling.

And yet, Blair's predominant emotion at the moment was unbridled fear.

She forced a breath, steeling herself for what was to come. At the auction house break-in, she'd been the pilot; now, she'd be the air traffic controller. Keying the mic in her hand, she transmitted, "Eurocopter, this is Sky Thief, please send your status."

The response was almost immediate, spoken in crisp pilot lingo.

"*Sky Thief, this is Eurocopter six-mike-whiskey. Currently stationary at Ms. Shedo's residence, fully fueled, range approximately 360 miles. We can be airborne within ten minutes of your call and will comply with all instructions—*"

The transmission was cut off by a new voice.

"*I want to speak to Sterling.*"

Blair recognized the voice from watching Kristen Shedo's interviews; here was the basket case herself. She felt frustrated by the interruption; nonetheless, there were precious few advantages to being a known fugitive, and one of them was the fact that you could use your real name and achieve instant recognition.

"This is Blair Morgan," she said, "and I am transmitting to relay instructions to *your pilots*. Not to you, Ms. Shedo."

Then Blair did something incredibly stupid, her mind flashing through the memories of uncovering Kristen Shedo's identity, a jubilant moment soon crushed under the heel of two subsequent facts: one, Sterling thought she was attractive, and two, he was apparently undisturbed that this woman supposedly owned a sex tape of Marilyn Monroe.

Keying the mic, she said, "If you want to receive this plank, which I'll remind you is the only item to ever be sold by us directly, then I suggest you let me communicate with the people flying your aircraft so they can transport you safely to the exchange point. Are we clear?"

Those final three words came across with far more hostility than Blair had intended.

But the apologetic response was swift. "*I understand*."

Blair, to her immediate shame, offered a consolation prize. "Sterling will be present at your exchange point. It's my job to get you there."

Quickly composing herself, she transmitted, "Now, for the pilots—and only the pilots—be advised, all bearing guidance on your route will be approximate and backstopped by major landmarks. Precise headings and altitude are at your discretion for the safety of your aircraft and passenger, over."

"*Good copy, Sky Thief*."

"You are cleared for takeoff. Please report back once you're in the air."

The pilot paused briefly before confirming, "*Cleared for takeoff, Eurocopter six-mike-whiskey*."

Blair appraised the afternoon sky, considering their timing for this mission.

While the Seattle PD didn't have their own helicopter, the King County Sheriff had three that operated on a full-time basis. The fact that all three possessed FLIR, forward looking infrared cameras, was the chief reason this exchange was occurring now; it was comparatively easy to hide from overhead observation when the sun was out. At night, the FLIR would highlight the team's heat signature in no time flat, queuing the pilots to activate their "Night Sun" searchlight to illuminate the crew at 30-million candlepower.

And since their Air Support Unit routinely assisted neighboring counties, the fact that this exchange was taking place close to 20 miles outside the King County line provided precious little consolation.

Marco suddenly said, "Their transponder has shifted. Looks like they're on the move."

A half-minute later, Blair heard the pilot's voice through her earpiece.

"Eurocopter six-mike-whiskey is airborne and loitering, please advise."

She keyed the mic and said, "Turn heading one-eight-zero and check in for further guidance once you have visual on Interstate 90."

"Turn heading one-eight-zero en route to Interstate 90, Eurocopter six-mike-whiskey."

This was the tricky part, she thought. Her goal at this point was to reveal just enough information to keep them moving in the right direction without providing the ability to summon effective police reinforcement.

The pilot came back on the net. *"Sky Thief, Eurocopter six-mike-whiskey has visual on Interstate 90 on Mercer Island, please advise."*

She consulted her notes. "Turn left heading zero-nine-zero; your instruction is to handrail Interstate 90 east past Tiger Mountain State Forest. Report back once you have visual of Washington 18 and 202 intersecting with I-90, approximately twenty miles from your current location."

"Eurocopter six-mike-whiskey, turning left zero-nine-zero until intersection with Washington 18 and 202."

Blair should have felt better at this point, but she didn't.

The reason behind her fear was hard to explain—this exchange was far lower risk than any heist she'd done with the crew, and barring some unlikely betrayal by Kristen Shedo, it would probably go off without a hitch. But a betrayal wasn't outside the realm of possibility; Sterling's meeting with Eric Dembinski at Washington Park in Albany came to mind, along with his narrow escape.

In the end she decided that her fear wasn't out of concern for being compromised; they'd planned for that, and she trusted her crew's responses in the event of a crisis. Instead, the looming sense of terror came from the fact that *Sterling was alone out there.* The last time he'd set off on his own, he'd been arrested and imprisoned. Blair couldn't stand to lose him again, and the last place she wanted to be was out here, completely helpless, as he remained exposed to whatever occurred at the exchange point.

Before she could consider the thought any further, the pilot transmitted, *"Eurocopter six-mike-whiskey confirms approaching eastern limit of Tiger Mountain State Forest, have visual on Washington State Routes 18 and 202. Maintaining one-five-hundred feet until advised otherwise."*

"Copy," Blair replied. "Proceed along I-90 eastbound, check back in when you are between Kachess Lake and Cle Elum Lake, both north-to-south-running terrain features approximately fifty miles to your southeast."

Another brief pause—the gap, Blair presumed, was for the pilot and co-pilot to reference their flight charts and confirm the instruction.

"Got it," the pilot transmitted back. *"Eurocopter six-mike-whiskey is en route and will advise when we are between the lakes."*

Blair exhaled wearily as she dropped her hand mic and rubbed her temples.

Then she lay back on a bed of leaf litter and pine needles, staring up at the treetops with a sense of dread that the real wait was about to begin.

19

KRISTEN

Kristen Shedo kept her eyes fixed on the outline of the lakes out the helicopter's port window, each carving a near-parallel semicircle amid the trees and forests below.

She spoke without keying her mic, ensuring her voice reached the pilots, and only the pilots, over the aircraft's internal communications system.

"I see the lakes—check in with Blair."

The lead pilot sounded annoyed as he replied, *"We see them too, Ms. Shedo, but her instructions were to check in once we were between them, not before. And since she's monitoring our transponder location, we—"*

"Well *my* instructions," she cut him off, "are to check in now. Blair Morgan doesn't sign your paychecks; I do."

A brief hesitation before she heard him speak again, this time in a more muted tone that indicated he was transmitting over the designated frequency to reach Blair.

"Eurocopter six-mike-whiskey is approaching the lakes at this time. Request further guidance on flight path."

Blair replied with measured forcefulness, *"I'll provide further guidance once you are between the lakes, not before."*

Kristen felt her shoulders tense with apprehension. As awestruck as she was with the Sky Thieves' accomplishments, Blair was revealing herself to be a grouchy little she-devil. If this were a boardroom setting, Kristen would shred her to pieces; but for now, she had to play by the rules of this game she'd found herself in, suppressing any aggressive instincts with the knowledge that, if all went according to plan, she'd soon be meeting Sterling Defranc face-to-face.

And that, she thought, would justify any indignities required to make it happen.

The helicopter glided past Kachess Lake, scarcely crossing the eastern shore before her lead pilot contacted Blair again.

"*We're between the lakes,*" he transmitted, "*handrailing I-90 and maintaining one-five hundred feet. Standing by for further guidance.*"

Blair answered, "*Shift heading to zero-nine-zero toward Lauderdale Junction. Report in once you have reached US 97, running north to south, in approximately 11 miles.*"

The pilot echoed, "*Heading zero-nine-zero, Eurocopter six-mike-whiskey.*"

Kristen turned away from the window, looking to the lead bodyguard positioned in the leather seat across from her.

He was the only other passenger, currently scanning the digital map on his phone as she covered her headset mouthpiece and called out across the vibrating cabin, "Where is she taking us?"

He glanced up, leaning forward and replying in his Southern accent, "Ma'am, next turn is gonna be north or south to parallel US 97. South takes us to the Yakama Indian Reservation, which is mostly open ground. North would lead toward the Pasayten Wilderness. My money is on her taking us north, followed by specific instructions to land in a clearing. There are hundreds that would fit their purposes, a few dozen of which are close enough to roads and trails that would provide them egress to the hardball. Bottom line, the risk assessment remains that—"

"I don't care about risk to me," she shouted back, alarmed. "I care about getting the plank, about...about meeting Sterling."

His eyes went dull at this comment, and while he wisely refrained from providing any response, she could tell he was perturbed by her overenthusiasm.

The sound of her pilot's voice caused her to press her fingertips against the window beside her, searching the landscape below.

"*We're crossing over US 97 roughly 1.5 miles north of Lauderdale Junction, please advise.*"

Kristen could tell from the urgency in Blair's response that they were getting close to the exchange point, could feel it in her bones.

"*Turn left, heading zero-one-zero to follow US 97 north.*" The helicopter banked as the pilot obeyed, completing its turn as Blair continued, "*In approximately five miles, the road will break east. When it does, I want you to continue following it and check in for your next instructions.*"

The pilot repeated, "*Turn left heading zero-one-zero, continuing to follow US-97, Eurocopter six-mike-whiskey.*"

Flinging her gaze toward the bodyguard, Kristen asked, "What will happen after the road breaks east?"

Her bodyguard took a moment to pan across the map on his phone, then gave a resolute shake of his head.

"We're not gonna make it that far. After that point, the terrain gets too mountainous for there to be many good landing zones, and this crew isn't gonna give us much lead time to anticipate their location. Before the road turns, she'll give us new guidance."

Kristen frowned. "Are you willing to stake your career on that?"

He stared at her. "Yes, Ms. Shedo. I am. And I must remind you that if this turns into a hostage situation—"

"They wouldn't do that to me."

"Just the same, ma'am, I'll need you to do exactly as I instructed in our rehearsals."

Kristen rolled her eyes. "Yes, yes, I know. Hit the deck and let you deal with the so-called 'threat.'"

He nodded. "And if they manage to take me out, you comply with whatever they say and wait for the cavalry to arrive. Don't try and resist them; just know that my people will be combing the area looking for you, along with every local and federal police asset in Washington and beyond."

She was opening her mouth to respond when Blair spoke again.

"*Eurocopter, turn left heading two-seven-zero effective immediately. Descend to approximately seven hundred feet, and comply with all instructions as you receive them."*

The aircraft banked sharply and began to dive, assuming its new westward heading as the pilot responded.

Kristen didn't hear what he said—she was scanning out the window at a mountain ridge below, watching an elevated fire lookout station sweep by off the port side, its wood construction rising from an exposed summit of rock.

"Red Top Lookout," her bodyguard informed her in his slow drawl, "and we're headed back toward the lakes. There's a valley about two miles ahead, paralleling the North Fork Teanaway River. Our LZ will be in that valley, mark my words."

"LZ?"

"Landing zone, ma'am. Plenty of fields for them to choose from."

Blair spoke over her headset. *"Adjust your heading ten degrees left."*

The ground below was a wrinkled landscape of trees descending toward a river valley as Blair announced, *"Five degrees right."*

Kristen felt the helicopter skew in compliance as they soared over the valley, the trees becoming sparse before her aircraft overflew the river. For one fleeting moment of terror, she thought they'd somehow missed their linkup.

But Blair coolly transmitted, *"Reduce airspeed to 110 knots and descend to three hundred feet."*

No sooner had the pilots complied than Blair ordered, *"Left turn heading two-six-zero. Reduce airspeed to 100 knots and descend to two hundred feet."*

Kristen's heart was hammering now, her pulse racing by the time Blair gave a final command.

"LZ is half a mile to your 12 o'clock, marked by VS-17 panel and red smoke. Ground winds are light and variable. Recommend an approach heading of three-five-zero degrees; once your skids touch down, cut all power. Then Ms. Shedo can exit, and take all instructions from Sterling."

Kristen felt her heart leap into her throat at the mention of Sterling's name and quickly pressed her fingertips against the window to look outside.

Her Eurocopter soared seventy feet over the treetops. The first thing she noticed was a tall windsock beside the landing marker; this was no random cash grab, she knew. Sterling really, *really* cared for her safety.

As the aircraft angled into its final landing approach, she caught sight of a blaze-orange cloth panel held down at the corners by rocks. Beside it was a canister spewing plumes of crimson smoke that whipped into a low blanket against the aircraft's rotor wash, and no sooner had she registered the significance of the smoke matching her signature color than she lost all power of speech.

Sterling Defranc stood at the edge of the clearing, wearing khaki pants and a green plaid shirt, the Kryelast plank held over one shoulder with a single hand.

He looked casual, relaxed even, watching the helicopter through eyes shielded by aviator sunglasses. Kristen felt suddenly self-conscious, removing her headset and tossing it on the seat beside her before smoothing out her hair.

Her reverie was shattered by the imbecile bodyguard, who leaned forward and announced, "Ma'am, I must insist that—"

"You stay right here!" she screamed back, preemptively ending his overture as he held up both palms in a gesture of compliance.

Kristen used the final seconds before touchdown to reach into the Hermès Birkin bag on the seat beside her and withdraw her phone. Noting with dismay that it had no cellular signal, she opened the camera app on selfie mode to check her hair and makeup. She realized her expression was one of a starstruck schoolgirl and forced herself to assume a confident, power-dripping eye contact with the device, pouting her lips for an added degree of sex appeal.

That did the trick; she was once again radiant, awe-inspiring especially at her age, defying all notions of having dipped a toe into the pool of a fifty-something existence. Sterling was two decades her junior, and yet she managed to reassure herself with the fact that she'd been able to sexually subdue even younger men to her will.

But with the soft lurch of her aircraft touching down in the field, Kristen Shedo felt insecure once more. She forced herself to take a resolute breath before jerking a thumb impatiently toward the helicopter door, her bodyguard's cue to slide it open.

She started to rise, felt her movement arrested by the seatbelt.

Kristen emitted a high-pitched giggle at the realization, wrenching the clasp to free herself from the seat before climbing down onto the skid as the aircraft powered down.

20

STERLING

Sterling strode toward the gleaming red helicopter, whose engine cut out to the whine of the internal power systems, its rotors continuing to spin out of sheer momentum.

Instinctively scanning the edges of the field, he rotated the Kryelast plank off his shoulder as Marco transmitted, *"Scanners and aviation frequencies are clean. Blair and I are relocating for exfil."*

"Got it," Sterling replied, watching Kristen Shedo exit the helicopter.

She turned to face him, pushing a wave of dark hair over her shoulder and puffing out her chest, which was practically shrink-wrapped in a thin top beneath her open jacket. Adjusting the handbag in her grasp, she tottered forward on high heels that were remarkably unsuited for negotiating the uneven field.

But she did a decent job of it nonetheless, her sculpted legs emerging from an absurdly short red skirt. Somehow, though, Kristen Shedo pulled off the look with grace and, indeed, beauty.

Sterling set down the Kryelast plank and extended his hand.

"It's nice to meet you—"

Kristen barreled past his handshake and hugged him, causing Sterling to tense before he relaxed and patted her on the back. The air was cut with her perfume, a subtle floral scent with overtones of vanilla and citrus.

She pulled away and clasped her hands over his shoulders. "It's really you."

"Really me." Sterling tried to smile as he took a step back to break the physical contact. Kristen was staring at him with wide eyes, the lack of sunglasses making her piercing gaze all the more apparent. He couldn't tell if she wanted to fight him or take him on a date, and forced himself to continue in a professional tone, "Here's the plank, as advertised. If you'll kindly exchange the funds—"

"No," she said breathlessly. "Not yet."

Kristen reached into her handbag as suddenly as if she was going for a gun, but her manicured fingertips emerged with a paint marker. She extended it toward him, hand trembling slightly. "If you would be so kind as to sign it for me, Sterling."

He hesitated, then accepted the marker from her with a shrug. Five million dollars was five million dollars, after all, and if she wanted his John Hancock in the process, then so be it.

Kneeling, he scrawled his signature on the Kryelast surface, then capped the marker and handed it back.

"I must warn you, Ms. Shedo—"

"Kristen," she blurted. "Always Kristen, to you."

"Well, Kristen, strictly speaking, this exchange is illegal in every conceivable way. I have to advise you not to tell anyone about it."

"Relax," she replied easily. "From this moment on, my collection is for my eyes alone. Though I must ask, what do you have planned for your next heist? The Louvre?"

"You know enough about us to know that we never steal art."

"Of course—then the Kremlin, perhaps? Something more exotic?"

Sterling wasn't sure what bothered him more about the inquiry—the fact that she had an eerie sense of entitlement, as if these purchases made her a de facto member of the crew, or the growing apprehension that by inviting her to effectively sponsor them, he'd courted a new kind of trouble.

"I can't discuss what we're working on now. But when we succeed, you'll hear about it. I can promise you that."

"I have no doubt," she said in a near-gasp, gaze dropping to his wrists.

"Your watches—are those... are those the ones you wear when conducting heists?"

Sterling held up his right wrist with his father's vintage Seamaster. "This Omega has been on every job—Blair even wore it on the Supermax rescue."

Her nose wrinkled.

"Are you and Blair an...an item?"

"We are. And this"—he pointed to the digital watch on his left wrist— "is a replacement after my early release from prison."

"I'll buy the Omega," she said, eyeing it greedily. "Five hundred thousand."

Sterling shifted uneasily. "It's not for sale."

"Of course. One million."

"I'm afraid it has sentimental value—"

"One point five."

Smiling awkwardly, Sterling said, "Kristen, this watch belonged to my late father. I'm afraid I won't let it go at any price."

Then he nodded toward her timepiece. "Besides, it looks like you have a nice enough watch already. Vacheron?"

She quickly unbuckled the watch and handed it to him with the word, "Patek."

He took it from her, eyeing the brushed silver surface with the words PATEK PHILIPPE, GENEVE above a second hand subdial, dauphine hands and solid gold hour markers surrounded by a gleaming hobnail bezel. Turning it over, he admired the elaborately finished movement through the sapphire caseback, then mournfully handed it back to her.

"It's beautiful."

But Kristen refused to take it, instead throwing up a hand.

"It's yours. Keep it."

Sterling recoiled. "I can't accept this, it's...magnificent."

"Oh, please," she groaned. "My bag cost more than the watch. You've given me an incredible memento, Sterling. This is the least I can do. I can't accept you not accepting it—take it, or the deal's off. Besides"—she shrugged—"I'll buy a new one tomorrow."

Sterling felt an odd sense of guilt-laced shame at the thought of taking the watch, but his mind soon returned to priority number one: getting the money exchanged and leaving as soon as possible.

"Thank you," he said, carefully tucking the watch into his shirt pocket.

Reaching into her handbag again, Kristen procured a device that looked like an old Blackberry phone on steroids. Sterling handed her a slip of paper with the account and routing information and cleared his throat loudly, which was Marco's cue to kill the directional cellular and wireless jammers they'd positioned in advance around the field. Only a narrow band correlating with their team frequency was allowed to proceed unhindered.

Marco transmitted, "*Jammers off.*"

Kristen completed her funds transfer with a final keystroke before tucking the handheld device back into her bag and returning his account information. "Honestly, Sterling, it is I who should thank you. You know what happens when you have more money than you can spend? The world is devoid of a sense of imagination. There is nowhere you haven't traveled, no toy you don't own. Nothing you can't replace. Except one thing that your crew has provided, to me and to the public."

"What's that?"

Her eyes tilted dreamily to the treetops at the edge of the clearing. "A sense of wonder. Of adventure. Every heist ignited my imagination, caused me to resume my daily pursuits with a vigor that had long since disappeared. Your crew's items remain, in a way, my most prized possessions, more meaningful than art. What you've done with your crew...it's an art form of its own, would you agree?"

Marco transmitted over his earpiece then, his voice partially obscured by an engine revving in the background.

"*Payment received in full, jammers are back on. Get out of there.*"

Sterling gave her a demure grin. "It seems the payment went through. The plank is all yours."

By then she seemed to have forgotten about her new purchase altogether, seeming confused as to how Sterling could know about the payment status.

"Of course." She nodded. "You must have the rest of your crew nearby. Blair and...only two others? Or are there more? I've always wondered."

"I'm sorry, Kristen, I can't discuss that. And I have to ask that you remain here for one hour before departing, as an additional security measure."

Taking a step forward, she extended her hand. As he shook it, she said, "You don't have to explain yourself, Sterling. I'll gladly wait. And if you ever have any more memorabilia you'd like to sell, you know where to find me. I'll gladly pay top dollar."

"We just may, Kristen," he said, releasing her hand after she made no move to do so. "We just may...thank you, and take care."

She advanced toward him with surprising quickness, planting a kiss on his cheek before he had time to react. His nostrils were once again filled with the rich floral scent of her perfume, and as he considered how to best end the engagement without offending her, she did it for him.

The kiss was over as quickly as it began, and Kristen dipped out of sight, easily hoisting the Kryelast plank to one side in a surprising display of strength. Then she turned and marched back to her helicopter, her hips rocking the miniskirt a few additional degrees to each side than the walk required.

Sterling found himself waiting for some rearward glance to acknowledge with a farewell wave, but Kristen Shedo didn't look back—and, turning to face the treeline behind him, Sterling broke into a jog.

21

BLAIR

Twisting the steering wheel, Blair guided the Polaris Razor around a sharply declining turn in the trail before reaching a short straightaway and accelerating.

The forest on either side of the vehicle was a blur as she throttled the 110 horsepower side-by-side vehicle toward the linkup site. While the Razor had room for four, only Marco accompanied her, his head bouncing with each bump in the trail as he studied the tablet in his hands.

The Razor was fully licensed, displaying the required metal tag with dual tabs authorizing it for on-road and off-road use. Although the vehicle had seatbelts and a roll bar making helmets optional according to Washington State law, both of them had full-face helmets and goggles, along with clothes in full camouflage print. The side-by-side was strapped with a hard case containing a pair of unloaded Browning 12-gauge shotguns, making this the first operation in crew history involving fully functional firearms.

In this case, the weapons were necessary.

Washington's wild turkey season was in full swing, and Kittitas County had a bag limit of one for anyone with a small game license and a valid turkey tag—which they could produce if asked. Before completing their road trip, Marco actually had to decrease the resolution in his digitally fabricated documents before printing so they could be held beside actual copies without appearing "too real."

Working to their current advantage was the fact that the trails leading away from their command and control site were wide enough to accommodate a side-by-side, allowing Marco to ride in the passenger seat while monitoring law enforcement and aviation frequencies and simultaneously watching the streaming footage from the remotely transmitting cameras positioned around the exchange point.

That latter point interested Blair the most—she hadn't gotten to see the exchange, too preoccupied with piloting the Razor down the perilous slopes surrounding Red Top Lookout. But she wanted to see what Kristen Shedo would do now that the exchange was over. If she took to the air against Sterling's guidance, they could reasonably assume it was an attempt to flee the range of the crew's jamming systems to summon law enforcement.

She braked sharply before the next turn, whipping the steering wheel clockwise as the Polaris's all-wheel-drive system held traction and sent them rocketing toward a long and relatively flat straightaway.

Blair used the opportunity to glance at the tablet screen in Marco's hands.

Kristen Shedo had emerged from the helicopter, this time without her jacket, revealing a scandalously tight tube top, cleavage on full display as she kicked off her high heels and began—dancing.

Blair forced her eyes back to the trail, then looked at the screen again to see Kristen performing an odd, erotic dance for no one in particular, caressing her body as she moved.

The Razor hit a tree root at the side of the trail, jarring them. "Eyes on the road!" Marco shouted through his helmet.

Then he tilted the screen away from her, further chastising her with the words, "Try to get us to the linkup alive. You can be jealous later."

She felt her hands tighten on the steering wheel. "Jealous? Of that hag?"

"Yes," Marco muttered, holding the screen closer to his face in the bouncing seat. "She's some hag."

Blair felt her blood pressure rising, and she accelerated to a breakneck speed before slamming on the brakes and whipping the Razor around the next turn.

22

STERLING

Sterling accelerated the quad-cab pickup down the dirt road, hearing the low-hanging tree branches scraping off the roof.

This phase of the getaway was relatively simple: drive the pickup as fast as possible to its stopping point. And Sterling, ever a fan of speed, pushed the truck as quickly as it would go without catapulting into the trees. It was a fine vehicle, a low-mileage Toyota Tacoma that negotiated the trail without issue. They'd acquired it for cash two days earlier, had it serviced and inspected, and test driven it extensively—and in a matter of minutes, Sterling would abandon it in the woods.

This was the cost of doing business. Between the road trip, vehicle acquisition, reconnaissance, and equipment setup, his brief exchange of the plank had cost the crew just under two hundred thousand dollars. But with nearly five million in profit, selling that scrap plank had proven to be a stroke of genius on Alec's part...provided, of course, that they weren't walking into a trap.

Sterling doubted that would be the case.

His mind still reeled with the memory of the plank exchange. The rest of his crew maintained that Kristen Shedo was crazy, but he was the only one who'd met her in person...and that fleeting encounter provided all the proof he needed to know they were right. A sudden embrace was one thing, but what was the deal with that kiss? It wasn't romantic per se, but that didn't make it any less disturbing. To the contrary, Sterling found it a troubling indication of the woman's obsession with his crew. But these were desperate times.

As he carved a left turn to follow one branch of the dirt path, he heard Marco transmit over the crew frequency.

"*Blair and I are ten minutes out from linkup. Chopper is still at the LZ, radio frequencies are clean.*"

Alec replied, "*Still waiting for Sterling to figure out that the gas pedal is the one on the right.*"

"I'm two minutes out," Sterling replied testily, scanning the trees for the piece of orange ribbon he'd tied around a trunk to denote he was a half-mile from his stopping point. When it flew by his window, he revised his time estimate. "Make that one minute."

The dirt road was the obvious path of egress for anyone looking to track him from the exchange point, and its various outlets were accessible from the nearest paved road leading north to a major campground. In the event of police response, that road would be the first thing locked down in a search for the newly surfaced fugitive. Various trails and dirt roads would soon follow, but enough of those existed for the crew to outpace the cops—at least, after he completed his upcoming maneuver.

Braking the truck to a near-halt between a rock formation on one side of the road and a massive oak tree on the other, Sterling swung wide before cutting his steering in the opposite direction.

The pickup's front bumper crunched into the rocks, jolting him in his seat. Ensuring the vehicle was sufficiently angled to block all road passage, Sterling yanked the parking brake and killed the engine. Then he grabbed the two-pound metal bar assembly from the passenger seat, a steering wheel lock that he hastily applied before inserting a generous dollop of super glue directly into the keyhole.

Sterling exited and locked the vehicle, pocketing the keys before darting southward into the woods. Now the pickup would serve its final purpose as a roadblock.

The first police cruiser to arrive would find the road impassable, the stationary pickup presenting both a time delay and necessitating a 360-

degree search by ATVs, which would take far longer to coordinate. Actually blocking off every trail outlet where they connected to small towns lining State Routes 903 and 970, to say nothing of U.S. Route 97 and I-90, would require more patrol cars than the Kittitas County Sheriff's Office had to offer, and by the time they summoned support from the adjacent police jurisdictions, the crew would have already outpaced the cordon.

He charged up a steep incline, pulling himself upward with handholds on the surrounding trees before emerging onto a narrow trail where a squat black ATV sat on massive all-terrain tires. A full face helmet dangled from one of the handlebar grips, and Alec, wearing an identical helmet, approached with a detection wand.

Sterling stopped with his feet shoulder-width apart, holding his arms straight out to his sides as Alec guided the wand from head to toe on his front, scanning for any location transmitting devices.

His Boston accent was muffled through the helmet as he rotated to Sterling's backside and asked, "Any physical contact?"

"To say the least."

"Lucky guy," Alec muttered, then completed his sweep. "You're clean."

Only then did Sterling produce the Patek Philippe wristwatch. "And she gave me this."

Alec shoved the wand in his cargo pocket, replacing it with a zippered pouch with the explanation, "Marco's rules."

Sterling accepted the bag and deposited the watch inside before zipping it shut, folding the water-resistant ballistic nylon material, and tucking it away as he made for the ATV. The pouch's interior was lined with two layers of Faraday fabric to provide RF signal blocking up to 5GHz. If Kristen Shedo had attempted to hand off a tracking device—and given her obsession with the crew, that wasn't outside the realm of possibility—the pouch would block its signal.

Alec grabbed the spare helmet and tossed it to Sterling, who hastily pulled it over his head and tightened the strap, dreading their next steps.

His teammate had already straddled the ATV, and now fired the engine with a high-pitched whine that quickly receded to a low, throaty rumble as the 90-horsepower engine idled. In contrast to the trails that Blair and Marco had to drive, Alec's route was far too narrow for a side-by-side;

which, Sterling thought mournfully, left him in the unenviable position of having to ride piggyback.

Sterling mounted the seat and routed his arms around Alec's waist. He was in the process of announcing that he was set when the ATV lurched forward in a neck-jolting burst of acceleration, and Sterling tightened his grip as Alec steered up a rocky path on their way to the linkup point.

23

BLAIR

Blair's next turn revealed a steep decline, and she eased off the accelerator to let gravity and momentum take her side-by-side down the hill and into the clearing beyond.

Marco braced himself for the streambed at the bottom of the hill, which the vehicle thundered into before vaulting up the far bank and emerging into a worn clearing bisected by a sandy dirt road. Steering left, Blair directed her side-by-side toward a gray Jeep Wrangler parked beside a stand of trees.

She braked to a stop next to the four-door Jeep, cutting the ATV engine before she and Marco leapt out to begin their transition procedures.

Depositing their helmets upside down into the seats, they stripped off their camouflage outer garments and stuffed them in the back of the Jeep as soon as Marco had unlocked it and opened the rear swing gate. He transferred his digital equipment to the Jeep as Blair stripped the case containing the shotguns, sliding them diagonally into the Jeep's cargo area. As much as they didn't want to have firearms in the vehicle during an escape, they couldn't leave them behind—but the side-by-side itself was a different story.

She recovered a spray bottle and sanitized the vehicle, generously hosing down the seats, steering wheel, and helmet interiors with foul-smelling sulfuric acid. It didn't much matter if anyone figured out she'd been involved, but Marco was a perfectly legal citizen in the eyes of the law. And while ammonia or bleach might do an adequate job of eliminating DNA, sulfuric acid would also destroy the friction ridge skin left behind by fingerprints.

Taking the bottle with her, she abandoned the side-by-side along with its key. The only preferable option to destroying evidence was to ensure it got stolen, and Blair guessed that an outdoor enthusiast was going to make the vehicle vanish in short order. Besides, she thought, any self-respecting redneck would be able to kick start, hot wire, or jump the starter relay even if she took the key with her, so she may as well help them out.

Marco took the driver slot as Blair slid into a rear seat; now that they were minutes from crossing onto public roads, known fugitives would have to remain in the back for the rest of the escape.

This transfer point was at the juncture of multiple dirt roads that could be traversed to reach either of the nearest towns, Roslyn and Ronald, each located just under a mile away. The crew had staged follow-on vehicles at both so they could flex around police response as needed. Blair loathed buying and staging so much equipment only to abandon it, but it was a necessary evil in the event anyone tried to capture them—which, as Marco's next transmission indicated, didn't appear to be happening.

"Frequencies are clean, Blair and I are staged for primary exfil to Roslyn."

Blair felt her breath hitch as she awaited a response. After miles of mountainous trails in the side-by-side, she felt like her bones were still vibrating as she finally sat stationary on the canvas seat.

"*Got it,*" Sterling finally replied over her earpiece. "*You should see us any minute now.*"

The confirmation that he was okay sent an immense wave of relief over Blair, who still harbored the irrational fear of losing Sterling. He was everything to her now, their unlikely romance now more important to Blair than the job itself, formerly a life's purpose that drove her every waking thought.

And however ecstatic she was at his check-in over the radio, the emotion doubled in intensity when she actually saw Alec steer his ATV into the clearing and race toward their parked side-by-side. Sterling was holding onto him like a damsel, his helmet jerking sharply as Alec carved a final turn and came to a stop.

Blair wanted to run to Sterling's side, to hug him as if in need of physical touch to assure herself he was okay, but she forced herself to remain in the Jeep. Feigning a professional composure that betrayed her every instinct, she watched both men ditch their helmets before sanitizing them and the ATV with sulfuric acid.

Alec reached the passenger door a moment before Sterling slid into the backseat beside her, and Marco accelerated the Jeep forward, careening down the dirt road toward Roslyn.

Blair grasped Sterling's hand and squeezed it. He looked at her with all the suave confidence that he seemed to emanate at times like these, then cracked a reassuring grin that told her he was fighting the same emotions she was, restraining himself from an impulse to kiss her.

No words were spoken, and none needed to be. As Blair smiled back, their eyes communicated everything they wanted to say, until her smile abruptly faded.

"Is that lipstick?"

She ripped her hand from his and launched it toward his cheek, pinching it and examining a greasy red smear on her fingertips before repeating, "Is that *lipstick*?"

Sterling's expression faded to shock, then embarrassment—the master criminal had failed to hide the most incriminating evidence of all.

"Not my call," he hastily replied. "She just did it."

Blair felt heat rushing to her face, breaths becoming erratic as he tried to assure her, "Relax, it was like being kissed by your grandma."

Alec turned around from the passenger seat. "Yeah, like being kissed by your hot, D-cup, bubbling sexpot of a grandmother. We've all been there, am I right?" He pantomimed tapping an imaginary microphone. "Come on, people, is this thing on?"

Blair turned away, looking out her window at the forest rumbling past before saying in a low tone, "Shut up, Alec."

Undeterred, the safecracker continued, "Marco, you know what I'm talking about, right?"

Marco's voice was grim. "Shut up, Alec."

"Sterling, what about—"

In unison, the three teammates shouted, "Shut up, Alec!"

Silence fell over them, unbroken save the rumbling tires negotiating the bumpy dirt road as they made their way south toward Roslyn.

24

STERLING

Huntington Beach was Sterling's favorite place to clear his head.

He gazed out across the Pacific waves, now shimmering with the golden-orange sunset, the ocean stretching endlessly before him. A cool breeze washed over him as he sat in the sand, sighing in a state of long-overdue relaxation. Sterling looked left to the pier, perhaps a quarter mile away and strangely deserted at present. Usually it was packed at sunset, and for good reason—the view was without equal, and tourists and locals alike flocked here for the same reasons that Sterling did.

Or at least, for the same reasons he *used* to.

Gone were the days when he could saunter to the beach, strolling the shores or sitting in the sand with a cooler containing a six-pack, absently watching the surfers. His last visit to Huntington occurred on July 3rd the previous year, one day before his crew robbed the Sky Safe. After that...well, one of the more irritating aspects of being a wanted fugitive was that venturing into public necessitated a serious disguise, and Sterling had chafed at the notion of returning to this most sacred of locations with something as crude as a fake beard.

He brought a hand to his face, automatically probing for hair or facial prosthetics and finding none—he was completely undisguised, though why he'd assumed this monumental risk, Sterling had no idea.

At any rate, it didn't appear that anyone would see him out here now. The crashing waves were free of surfers, and as he glanced around in search of witnesses, he found no beachgoers, no volleyball games in progress, no human beings whatsoever with the exception of a figure approaching to his right, carrying an object in each hand.

No sooner had Sterling spotted him than the man called out in a hoarse voice, "Think fast," before tossing one of the objects in an underhand arc.

Sterling caught the pass, finding it to be a cold can of Pabst Blue Ribbon.

Laughing, he said, "Still drinking this swill?"

By now the man had taken up a seat in the sand beside Sterling and opened his own can. "It's a classic."

Though Sterling would never admit it to anyone else, there was something infinitely intimidating about Steve Wolf.

He had a way of squinting with his eyebrows solemnly furrowed, a gaze of intense focus that remained whether he was offering praise or criticism —the only distinction between the two was to be gleaned by the words spoken in his gravelly whisper of a voice, because Wolf always meant what he said. There was no subtext with him, no mincing words, and there hadn't been since a teenaged Sterling had looked up to him as a second father figure.

Nodding to the unopened can, Wolf said, "Drink up, whiteboy. You're going to need it."

"Why do you say that?" Sterling asked, cracking the tab and watching the foam gush into the sand.

Wolf replied with a question of his own, spoken with a low, methodical intensity.

"What part of 'your heist career is over' didn't you understand?"

"We didn't do a heist," Sterling said, "not exactly. Washington was more of a...private sale."

"Wrong. When you're in this game, every exposure is a heist whether you're stealing or selling. I told you the last time we saw each other—you've changed things, forever. Too much media spotlight, too much public intrigue. You didn't have an exit plan then, and you still don't."

Sterling was suddenly grateful for the beverage. He took a long pull from the can, thinking to himself that if he was going to get a lecture from Wolf, at least it came with a free beer.

Then he replied, "The last time we saw each other, I told you we were about to deal with a puppet master. Well, I'm dealing with it. You told me to protect my family; that if I did right by that, I'd do right by everything in the world."

Wolf turned his gaze to the horizon.

"I meant what I said, and it still applies. But with an enemy of this magnitude, protecting your family means pulling them out of the flames. Instead, you put them closer to the fire."

"We made it out of the sale, didn't we?" Then, feeling inexplicably foggy about what had occurred after their getaway from Roslyn, Sterling dropped the rhetorical tone of his question and asked again, "Didn't we?"

Wolf nodded. "You did. Eighteen-hour car ride back here and that brunette didn't speak to you during much of it."

"My crew is safe?"

"That depends on your definition of 'safe.'"

Sterling took another drink of beer, squinting at Wolf before asking the obvious.

"What are you doing in LA?"

Wolf shrugged, then pointed his can to Sterling's opposite side and said, "The same thing he is."

Sterling looked left to see a second man standing beside him, then dropped his beer and scrambled to his feet.

It was his father.

That was the first moment Sterling knew he was dreaming. The recognition brought with it a vague sense of fear, as if acknowledging that fact would fracture his current reality.

And right now, he didn't want it to end.

Suddenly he was no longer on the beach at all; instead, he was sitting in the living room of his childhood home in New York. The huge stone fireplace blazed beside him, and across a low table, seated on the opposite couch, was his father.

Walter Defranc appeared as he had in the peak of good health, long before the pancreatic cancer had ravaged his body. His eyes were sharp and focused, a thief's eyes, analytical and noting every detail of his surroundings. There was a degree of vigilance in his presence that no law-abiding civilian would ever experience, and Sterling resisted the urge to embrace this phantom in his mind, wary that any sudden action would cause him to wake up.

Instead, he whispered, "It's good to see you, Dad. I could really use your advice right now."

His father didn't move, didn't react at all; he was stone-faced, sitting completely still as if frozen in place.

Then he said, "You know what my advice is going to be, son. Three words."

"Yeah." Sterling nodded. "I do: figure it out."

"That's right. It doesn't matter whose fault it was, how much luck, good or bad, has hit your plan. In our game, it's usually bad. All that matters is what's happening right now, son, and what you do about it. That's why 'figure it out' is the operative term here, like it always is. You remember the other lesson I taught you?"

Sterling quickly supplied, "RTB: Remember the Baron."

"Tell me why."

He leaned forward. "Because in the '20s, Herman Lamm was the king of bank robbery. He pioneered everything we do today—casing the target, rehearsals, planning getaway routes."

His father finally moved, giving a curt nod as a log popped in the fireplace. "So good they called him the Baron. You remember what happened to him?"

"Yeah—on a bank getaway his driver jumped a curb, popped a tire, and caused their spare gas can to fall out. His crew got far enough away to change the tire, and their spare went flat. Rolling gunfight with police and vigilantes. First car they stole had a speed governor set at 35. The next one was a truck without enough water in the radiator. Then they stole another vehicle, and it was almost out of gas. Ended up at a farmhouse where someone had taken the family car on an errand, and that's where the Baron got cornered and killed."

"Exactly," Walter agreed. "So why did I teach you RTB?"

"To remember how much can go wrong even when you do everything right. That doing a heist in the first place is pushing your luck, so not to make things worse with stupid decisions. And as a reminder that the universe will fight you every step of the way."

Walter turned his head to look at the fire, his face lit by the orange glow. "The more you disrupt the universal order, the more repercussions there are. And you, my boy, have disrupted it about as much as any thief could. Fundamental difference between you and me is that after four generations of Defranc men going to prison, I figured out how to stay the gray man. You've become a celebrity."

"Thank you."

"You're still unbelievably good at twisting anything I say into a compliment. And you're still wearing my watch, I see."

Sterling eagerly lifted his wrist. "Of course I am."

"You wore it when you stole the Sierra Diamond?"

"I've worn it on every heist, and I always will."

Walter rose with athletic grace before standing with his hands at his sides.

"You're getting reckless, son. Remember what that diamond was going to be used for, before you stole it?"

"What does that matter?" Sterling replied defensively, rising to meet his father's eyes. "I'm taking risks, yes. But my crew just made millions without stealing anything, and that opens up a whole world of options we didn't have before. Mom is going to be safe. I'm going to find out the mentor's identity."

"I'm afraid you already have."

Sterling burst awake, his heart speeding along at a dizzying clip.

He sat up, finding Blair asleep beside him.

Spinning his gaze in the other direction, he saw the Faraday bag on his nightstand containing the Patek Philippe watch. He hadn't so much as unzipped the bag since leaving Washington, but suddenly the timepiece had gone from a trophy to a troubling indication of something he was just now starting to piece together.

Sterling swung his legs off the bed, snatching his phone from the wireless charger before flinging open the bedroom door.

He ran down the warehouse corridor barefoot, fumbling with his phone to activate the flashlight. Once he succeeded in illuminating a swath of hallway, he picked up his pace until skidding to a halt before another door that he jerked open.

"Marco," he called out, "get up. We're going to your lair."

To his credit, Marco awoke with surprising coherence, brushing past Sterling in T-shirt and boxers. He looked eerie with his long hair down, far more savage than he appeared with his usual low bun.

"Start talking," Marco said, and Sterling rushed to follow him.

"I need to make sure I'm right about something, because there's no going back if I am."

"Specifically?"

"Kristen Shedo. She tried to buy my Omega, and she gave me a Patek."

Marco opened his office door and slid into the chair to power up his computers. "So? Rich people all like nice watches."

"That's what I'm afraid of. Is it possible that Patek has a transmitting device?"

The hacker cast a wild-eyed look at Sterling and said accusingly, "Have you taken it out of the bag?"

"Of course not."

Calming somewhat and returning his focus to the computer screens, he said, "Then it doesn't matter if it's transmitting or not—the Faraday fabric will block it. Now, what am I looking up?"

Sterling began, "JB West is the new hotness in accepting crypto as payment—did they sell the Sierra Diamond?"

Marco's fingertips danced across the keyboard before he confirmed, "Yes, it was sold through JB West."

Sterling felt a rush of validation that was quickly snuffed out under a growing sense of terror. This was a rare situation where he desperately hoped he was wrong, where every step closer to confirmation brought him head-to-head with an unavoidable reality that he didn't want to face.

"Search the databases we copied from the auction house. Find out who bought it."

Marco was clicking through folders with alarming speed, delving into the depths of their recovered data as he spoke in a cautionary tone.

"The winning bid would have been placed by a middleman, and I'll have to trace the cutouts to find the actual buyer. Last time it took me three to four hours per sale."

"The middleman might be all we need. If it's one of the same guys who bought our heist gear, then we know the real buyer was Kristen Shedo."

"Meaning?"

Sterling's face felt flushed now, the heat descending through his neck at the very real possibility that his inattention to detail prior to this point could have doomed his entire crew. He had to force the words out now, his voice frail.

"The Sierra Diamond was too appetizing to pass up—it was a white whale item placed right in our backyard. Now the buyer was never announced, but we found out it was a billionaire who intended to have it cut into 24 baguettes to line the hour markers of two custom wristwatches. Remember?"

"I do."

"Well do you remember how quickly the Sky Safe got built? Someone used money or connections to cut through all the bureaucratic red tape, then laid a trap knowing we'd try to hit it. If Kristen Shedo bought that diamond, it also means she used it as a sacrificial lamb to get us caught."

"Which would make her—"

"Jim's mentor," Sterling cut him off. "If I'm right."

By now Marco had opened a spreadsheet, leaning in to examine the rows.

"Here's the winning bid for the Sierra Diamond."

Sterling leaned over his shoulder, trying to see the name but unable to read the tiny strings of text spanning the screen.

"Does the name match any of Shedo's middlemen?"

"No, but I recognize it."

He spun his chair to face Sterling and said, "Geoffrey Lambert."

Reaching for the wall beside him, Sterling flipped up a protective cover to expose a flat red button. He placed his palm against it, hesitated for a split second, and then pressed as hard as he could.

25

BLAIR

Blair awoke to a fire alarm.

The low, blaring tone rose to a high-pitched wail over the course of three seconds; after one second of silence elapsed, it began again and brought with it the auto-activation of every light inside the warehouse, her room included.

She was out of bed as the second tone sounded, quickly pulling on clothes staged at her bedside and donning her running shoes by the time she looked back to see that Sterling was gone.

The fire alarm system was networked across 32 devices throughout the warehouse installed on one signaling line circuit, the speakers positioned to cover every room with their volume adjusted to be audible only within the building. Since they'd disabled the digital alarm communication transmitter, this alert was for the crew alone—and its use meant that their nightmare scenario had finally occurred.

As the alarm continued to blare, she burst into the hallway to see Alec emerging from his room, fully dressed.

"Go!" she shouted. "I've got your room!"

He was gone without so much as a word of acknowledgement, racing to the stairs before descending them three at a time on the way to his workshop. Blair entered his room and moved to his dresser, pulling out the top drawer and upending it to deposit the clothes and contents onto the floor before tossing the drawer aside and repeating the process.

She turned to the bed, stripping the comforter and leaving its underside facing the ceiling on her way to the far nightstand. Those drawers were ripped out exactly as she had with the dresser, and then she darted into Marco's room.

It was empty when she entered, though she noted with dismay that his pre-staged clothes and shoes were still on the floor beside the bed. She tossed these into the hallway on the off chance that he'd actually have time to don them, then proceeded to scatter the contents of every drawer and strip the bed the same way she had in Alec's room.

Once that was complete, she made the run to Marco's lair.

The first black duffel bag came soaring out of the doorway as she approached, landing a moment before a second one followed. Blair scrambled to hoist one bag at a time over her shoulder, glancing inside the room to see Marco and Sterling feverishly unplugging laptops and hard drives and stuffing them into bags.

Sterling looked at her with a panicked expression. "Did you leave the Faraday bag in our room?"

"Yes," she gasped over the alarm's wailing cry. "Do you want it?"

"No," he yelled back. "Get out of here, we'll get the rest."

Blair made for the stairs, descending toward the ground floor to see Alec running across their main rehearsal area wearing an enormous hiking pack with whatever safecracking equipment he'd chosen to salvage in the time it took for Sterling and Marco to join them. Most of the crew's critical equipment was kept loaded in the twin Sprinter vans as a matter of standard procedure, along with their personal wallets and identification, for precisely this contingency—one that Blair never thought she'd see executed outside of their monthly practice drills.

She turned toward the main rolling door and, beside it, a massive gun safe. Alec came to a stop, hoisting open the safe's unlocked door.

Inside was 25 cubic feet packed with the crew's non-digital evidence: old technical manuals, physical documents they'd recovered on heists, stacks of paper used to sketch out operational plans and kept for reference. A network of hand-built shelves constructed of thin plastic supported these products, far too great in number and volume for the team to quickly shred or take with them—which was, of course, the reason they were kept in the safe, along with the single item centered on a top shelf.

Blair passed Alec as he reached for the green canister of a thermite incendiary grenade, clasping it in one hand to compress the safety lever as he pulled the pin with a soft *click*. Carefully setting the grenade back on the top shelf, he released his grasp and allowed the safety lever to release from the canister, then slammed the door shut and spun the wheel to lock it.

Blair heard a dull hissing sound as the grenade's thermite converted to molten iron, a process that caused it to burn at over 4,000 degrees, leaving the contents an incinerated pile of ashes.

She stopped at the rear bumper of one of the team's two Sprinter vans, both parked in parallel facing the rolling door. By the time she'd deposited her bags into the cargo area, she heard the rolling door rattling upward on its track, sent into motion by Alec, who was now moving for the opposite van.

Blair left the cargo doors ajar and slid into the driver's seat, keying the ignition and pulling the van forward into the night, stopping once it was just outside the warehouse. Alec mirrored the process, and then they both dismounted while leaving the engines running.

They met at the edge of the main warehouse entrance, their conversation restricted to a brief exchange as Blair asked, "What happened?"

"Don't know."

Marco ran down the stairs with Sterling on his heels, both men still barefoot and carrying two slung duffel bags with the final digital contents to be evacuated. This was Alec's cue to take off for his personal drop car, one of several rotated through a series of parking locations every time he drove to or from the warehouse. The vehicle contained an orgy of his DNA, and getting it out of here was just as important as driving the Sprinter vans to their fallback location.

Sterling called out, "Speed limit, turn signals, rally at the primary fallback."

Marco dumped his two bags into the back of Blair's van, then took off for his own drop car as she slammed the cargo doors shut. Sterling did the same on the other van, then sprinted back inside the warehouse toward a box on the wall where a transparent plastic cover protected a T-shaped pull handle.

Blair knew she should get into her van and depart; Marco and Alec were already peeling out, driving their cars to the perimeter fence where an outer gate now slid open. But she was riveted in place, unable to move.

Partially because she wouldn't leave without Sterling.

But mingled with concern for his safety was a morbid curiosity regarding what was about to occur, and she watched Sterling flip the protective cover aside and yank a handle within, eliciting a loud, angry buzz from an alarm box before he turned and ran back to his van.

He'd barely cleared the threshold of the building before the ceiling and wall sprinklers hissed to life, ejecting a spray pattern drawn from multiple tanks with a combined total of 2,000 gallons—enough sulfuric acid to keep the sprinklers eradicating fingerprints and DNA for the next 17 minutes before the supply drained in full.

"Go," Sterling commanded, making for the driver's seat of the other Sprinter van as she slid behind the wheel. She pulled forward first, knowing full well that Sterling wouldn't depart before she did. As leader of the crew, he wasn't going down with the ship, but he'd certainly stay with it until everyone else was gone.

She cast a quick glance at her side view mirror, catching her final glimpse of the warehouse interior. Torrents of sulfuric acid rained down on the concrete floor before the rolling door slid shut, erasing the scene from view.

Directing her gaze forward, Blair pulled past the open gate and made a right turn, beginning her circuitous way to the crew's linkup point.

26

STERLING

By the time Sterling caught sight of his crew's primary fallback location through his windshield, he saw that he was only the second to arrive: Alec's drop car was already in its slot.

The building was zoned for commercial use, and as far as the city was concerned, owned by a contracting firm that was completely independent of the crew's security consulting LLC. The site was located just outside the industrial district of Moreno Valley, chosen due to its proximity to the warehouse—if they had to flee on foot, they'd still be able to reach it within twenty minutes.

Tonight's journey to the fallback location had taken Sterling twice that long to drive. Each crew member was assigned a separate surveillance detection route designed to follow an inordinately lengthy path with multiple turns, stops, and directional changes to expose any pursuers before committing to the final destination. How useful that would be under the circumstances, Sterling wasn't certain; if Kristen Shedo had somehow planted a tracker capable of transmitting through every material designed to stop it, there was no telling what else she was capable of.

But the crew made detailed contingency plans so they wouldn't have to waste time debating when a crisis occurred, and Sterling's role at present was to execute, not second-guess.

He cruised past the first parking lot entrance, noting with dismay that the building was completely dark. The first person to arrive was responsible for clearing the structure, then flicking on the exterior light next to the front entrance to indicate it was safe. No light meant Alec was either still clearing the building or had been rolled up already, and Sterling had a sinking suspicion that it was the latter a moment before the lightbulb illuminated.

Releasing a sigh of delirious gratitude, Sterling swung his Sprinter van into the second parking lot entrance and toward Alec's drop car.

He backed into an adjacent space, killed the ignition, and took a moment to draw three measured breaths in an effort to compose himself before exiting the vehicle.

Striding to the front door, Sterling knocked six times, waited a beat, then knocked six more—any other combination would indicate duress, cueing the doorman to flee out the back. Sterling heard the deadbolt unlatch before he pulled the door open and entered.

Alec stepped aside to make way for him, clutching a handheld radio.

"Any comms?" Sterling asked, locking the door behind him.

"Nothing yet."

"All right. I'll take over as doorman."

Alec handed him the radio and said, "You want me to grab you some clothes from the stash?"

"No. Head up to the roof and get eyes-on the warehouse. I want to know if you see any indications of a raid, police or otherwise."

"You got it, boss."

Alec disappeared into the building as Sterling keyed the radio and transmitted, "Primary is secure. Check in if able."

No response.

That much wasn't necessarily concerning—with any luck, Marco and Blair were still conducting their routes, and would only take the time to set up their radios if they had to divert elsewhere.

Sterling felt sick to his stomach as he waited, nauseous at what had just occurred. He'd personally and utterly destroyed his crew's hideout, along with a majority of the equipment that was too bulky to keep packed in the Sprinter vans. They'd just profited almost five million from the sale of the plank, and then immediately lost far more than that in hardware to say nothing of the facility itself.

It was far from being just a financial loss—the warehouse was their safe haven, a sanctuary that had taken close to a decade to outfit properly and only minutes to eradicate completely. The current building could hold them temporarily, and was outfitted to do just that, but it was a far cry from the isolated sanctum of the warehouse and its surrounding properties.

So gut-wrenching was the loss that Sterling thought he was going to throw up, and felt prevented from doing so out of consideration for the two crew members who remained unaccounted for. Successfully bailing from the warehouse before a raid was one thing, but arriving at this fallback location unimpeded was another matter altogether. For one thing, he knew Shedo's people were out here looking for them. For another, so much as an errant traffic stop could be a life-altering event. Marco was currently driving in his boxer shorts and bare feet. And Blair was not only recognizable but driving a Sprinter van loaded with incriminating crew gear.

Sterling heard a car engine grow louder beyond the door, then go silent. Seconds later, there was a knock at the door—six raps, then a pause followed by six more. He unlocked the door and pushed it open, hoping to see Blair.

But Marco entered instead, still barefoot but wearing a backpack.

"That your emergency kit?" Sterling asked.

"Yes."

"Meet Alec on the roof, then monitor the warehouse cams. I want to know what we're up against."

Marco set off without a word, leaving Sterling to bolt the door and wait for Blair to arrive. This particular wait, he knew, would be torturous. If anything had happened to her he would never forgive himself, never be able to look in a mirror without anguish.

Particularly, he thought, if she'd gotten arrested while fleeing a warehouse for no good reason whatsoever.

That lingering thought gnawed at the back of his mind now, presenting the notion that he didn't have any proof of his theory, more of a loose string of connections paired with an intrinsic conviction that had rarely steered him wrong. In the past, that gut instinct had caused him to make intuitive judgment calls from moment to moment, sometimes in contradiction to any semblance of logic; and yet on no less than three occasions, it had kept him and his crew out of prison.

The sound of a car door slamming outside brought a dizzying wave of relief, mitigated by the fact that Sterling couldn't see who it was. But the correct knock sequence rattled the door and he quickly unlocked it.

Blair's expression matched his own emotions, her eyes holding an inexpressible gratitude at being reunited safely. She embraced him before he could close the door, whispering, "Oh, God. I'm glad you're okay." Pulling back from him, she asked, "What happened?"

"I'll explain on the roof—Marco and Alec are already up there."

He locked the door and they ascended the stairs together, emerging into the chilly night air that felt more so given Sterling's lack of shoes or, indeed, suitable clothes.

They found Alec and Marco standing at the roof's eastern edge, their shadowy forms in stark relief against the murky backdrop of city lights. Sterling approached quickly and asked, "Anything on the warehouse cams?"

"They're toast," Marco replied, holding up the tablet for Sterling to see as he swiped through security camera feeds that all showed the same thing: blotched splatters from the sulfuric acid erasing any view beyond the camera lenses.

"Any sign of response?"

Alec nodded toward the distance and said, "You're looking at it. All quiet."

Sterling scanned the rooftops ahead, gradually identifying the warehouse. It was impossible to get a good view into the compound, but he'd hoped to identify some indications of a raid, whether by headlights or helicopter.

Alec asked, "You want to tell us the reason for this little excursion, or are we going to hang out in silence?"

"All right," Sterling began, collecting his thoughts to bring his crew up to speed. "Bottom line, we suspect Dembinski was threatened by Geoffrey Lambert on behalf of the mentor. Turns out Geoffrey facilitated the purchase of the Sierra Diamond, I believe on behalf of Kristen Shedo.

Everything about the Sky Safe—how quickly it was approved and built, its impenetrability, its location in downtown LA—were indicative of the mentor's influence. But we hadn't considered that the Sierra Diamond could have been acquired and willingly sacrificed as part of that trap. The diamond was the bait, and that means Shedo is Jim's mentor."

"Huh," Alec muttered, "I thought she loved us."

Blair said, "She's insane. And here I was, thinking I couldn't like her any less."

"How could she have found us here?"

Swallowing, Sterling managed, "I think she put a tracking device in the watch she gave me."

"Why'd you take it out of the Faraday pouch?"

"I didn't."

Alec shrugged. "Then how could it have transmitted, if there even was a tracker inside?"

"We're talking about a billionaire here, someone who spends a small nation's GDP on auction junk every year. She could have dropped a fortune engineering some exotic transmission device, for all we know."

Marco conceded, "It's possible, in theory. But the layers of fabric would still block the transmission almost entirely. It wouldn't be able to throw a signal very far, if at all."

"It wouldn't have to transmit far," Sterling pointed out. "She knew we'd be returning to LA. All she'd have to do is have some signal intercept teams screening block by block, running patterns until they picked something up."

"So," Alec began, "they might not have even detected it yet."

"Maybe not."

"And another thing—you said the middleman was Geoffrey, right? The guy Dembinski fingered for threatening him?"

"Yes. Geoffrey Lambert, one of the mentor's middlemen. That means Shedo bought the diamond, then used it to try and catch us."

"Hang on—we linked Geoffrey to Jim's mentor, not to Kristen Shedo."

Sterling paused, hearing a distant roar and identifying the sound as a pair of fighters taking off from the nearby March Air Reserve base.

Then he said, "Not technically, no."

"Not at all," Alec quipped, then added, "so why'd you hit the evac alarm without any proof?"

"Because it would have taken Marco hours to follow the trail of brokers all the way to Shedo, and we didn't have that kind of time."

"How do you know?"

"I had a gut feeling," Sterling snapped. "All right, this is going to sound dumb. But I had a dream where Wolf warned me I'd put you guys into the fire with the Washington op. Then I saw my dad, he made some comment about my watch, and asked if I remembered what the Sierra Diamond was going to be used for. And it was going to be hacked up to make the hour markers for two custom watches, right?"

Clearing his throat, Alec said, "Uh-huh. So you might have just trashed our only sanctuary over a bad dream."

"I don't think so," Sterling objected, but Blair cut him off before he could continue.

"Look," she said, pointing to the warehouse.

Sterling squinted at it, finding the distant roof appeared exactly as it did before.

But a moment later he saw what she had—a distinct glow beginning to form at the roof's edges, its orange hue indicating that, to his horror, the building was on fire.

Alec spoke preemptively. "Don't blame me. After I pulled the pin on the thermite grenade, I locked the gun safe."

Sterling spun to face him. "Are you sure?"

Blair replied before Alec could.

"I am," she said, "because I saw him do it. And there's no way the thermite burned through. We engineered this destruction plan specifically so there wouldn't be a fire."

Sterling was breathing quickly now. A portal appeared in the warehouse roof as a swath of flame burned through, spreading to emit an eerie red glow over Moreno Valley.

He asked in a choked voice, "Could something have gone wrong with the sulfuric acid?"

"It's not flammable," Marco said. "It *is* highly reactive, and if it contacts combustible materials or extreme heat, it can result in explosive concentrations of hydrogen. What we're seeing now didn't come from anything we left behind. But it's public knowledge that we use sulfuric acid to destroy evidence, and anyone hunting us could have been prepared for what they found at the warehouse. Whoever is doing this, they may have brought thermite grenades of their own."

Blair objected, "But we weren't there. Why would they set it on fire?"

"To send a message."

Sterling felt a lump forming in his throat, his next breath coming up short as he watched his empire burn. Then his eyes started to sting with tears that spilled over a moment later, running in hot streams down his cheeks.

Blair walked over and embraced him tightly. He clutched her, unable to cope with the sheer anguish of this moment.

Then he laid his head on her shoulder, felt his body briefly convulse, and began to sob.

27

BLAIR

Blair kept her eyes on her digital wristwatch, waiting until the final seconds before calling out, "Five. Four. Three. Two. One—stop! Hands in the air!"

Alec threw his arms up, turning toward her from the countertop where he'd been feverishly working for the past twenty minutes. The workspace and the floor around it were littered with discarded plastic wrappers, and Blair leaned against the counter before folding her arms and saying solemnly, "Alec, it's time for breakfast. Please bring your dish up."

He hastily presented a single paper plate, delicately setting a plastic spoon beside her. She took the plate and eyed its contents warily, then asked, "What was your inspiration?"

Alec took a respectful step backward, deferentially holding his hands behind his back.

"My family is from Boston, so I grew up with clam chowder, lobster rolls, fish and chips, and, of course, Boston cream pie and cannoli. As a Red Sox fan, I'd be remiss if I didn't mention the Fenway Frank, which is far more than just another ballpark hotdog. But I'm also Asian, so I've had my fair share of chicken curry, Pho, fish balls, fried rice, sticky rice, Hainanese chicken rice—lots of rice—and my mother's recipe for Laksa, a spicy noodle soup, was to die for. Now I could either stick with Boston food or Asian food and, given my abilities in the kitchen, be relatively safe. But I wanted to make this dish an expression of my heritage. Alec-on-a-plate, so to speak. And so"—he hesitated, puffing out his chest—"I decided on Boston-Asian fusion."

Blair raised her eyebrows. "That's very...ambitious, Alec."

"Yes, Chef. But since the challenge today was making breakfast for the entire crew with whatever prison-grade military field rations we stocked the fallback site with, and given that our fearless leader Sterling has forbidden even the non-fugitives from leaving to bring back edible takeout, I decided to cast my dreams aside and work with this slop."

With a gracious nod, Blair said, "Okay, Alec. Tell me about your main dish."

Alec summoned a resolute breath. "Today I have prepared for the crew a delicious beef stew entree with a crust of hand-crushed crackers, finished with mini bottles of Tabasco, served on a bed of shelf-stable wheat snack bread and drizzled with melted government cheese."

She tilted her head and asked, "Think you made any mistakes here?"

"If I had to do it over again, I may have used a foil packet of jalapeno cheese for the drizzle instead of regular cheddar."

Blair plucked the plastic spoon from the countertop, then stopped herself just shy of taking a scoop.

"How were you trying to cook the beef—medium, medium rare?"

"Medium, Chef."

Carving a small spoonful of the entree, Blair sniffed it and then put it in her mouth, chewing thoughtfully.

"You nailed the temperature."

Alec blushed, tapping the floor with the toe of his shoe and twisting his heel from side to side. "I was worried that I let the flameless chemical heater run a little too long."

"No." Blair shook her head. "This is a true medium. The beef is very delicate, very moist. Cooked perfectly. What did you use to season?"

"Tiny packets of salt and pepper, Chef."

"You can really taste the Tabasco—a lot of Tabasco, as far as I'm concerned."

Alec flinched, and Blair continued soothingly, "Next time, I'd go lighter on the pepper. You're getting enough of that with the hot sauce. But you left the beef in the foreground, which was a smart call. Overall, I think you honored field rations with a thousand-year shelf life very well here. Tell me about your side."

Alec looked flustered. "It's a medley of nuts and raisins with pan-coated chocolate disks, colloquially known as trail mix with M&Ms, along with a pair of meat snack strips that savvy diners will recognize as Slim Jims."

Blair brought a handful of the trail mix into her mouth, then followed it with a bite of stale beef stick.

Swallowing, she said, "Very rustic, earthy, and the nuttiness is balanced with just the right amount of sweetness from the pan-coated chocolate disks. If I may make a suggestion with the meat snack strips—"

"Yes, Chef?"

"I'd use three instead of two. Odd numbers are always more aesthetically pleasing when you're plating a dish."

"Yes, Chef."

Blair suspiciously appraised the last portion of the plate. "Let's talk about your dessert."

Clearing his throat, Alec said, "For dessert, I have prepared vanilla dairyshake powder fused with non-nutritive lemon-lime drink mix, to which I added fresh tap water and a melted packet of peanut butter to achieve a rich, pudding-like consistency. Then I zested with a dollop of carbohydrate-enhanced applesauce to balance out the tartness of the drink powder, and topped it with a crumble of lemon poppyseed poundcake."

Blair scooped the bright green mixture onto her spoon, then licked it off.

Closing her eyes, she smacked her lips once, then remarked, "Texture and consistency are spot-on. The lemon-lime mix is very punchy, a wise choice. Personally, I wouldn't change a thing about this dessert—it's the star of the plate."

Just as Alec smiled, Blair pointed her spoon at him and said accusingly, "Do you think this performance is going to take you to the top three?"

Alec's mouth fell open before he summoned his courage to say, "I hope so, Chef."

"Well we'll find out when I make lunch. Now present your dishes to the customers in Marco's Lair 2.0."

"Yes, Chef."

Blair turned, carrying her plate into the next room and announcing, "Breakfast is ready. I think Alec did pretty well, considering what he had to work with."

The two seated men may or may not have heard her. Sterling was hunched over a laptop, its display facing away from her. He'd been despondent all morning, spending most of it on the roof staring blankly at the smoldering wreckage of their former hideout. He didn't so much as look up when she spoke.

Marco's back was to her, three laptops arrayed before him.

On the leftmost screen, she saw a streaming news report with a suit-clad man proclaiming, "These people are ruthless. They essentially used battery acid to eradicate any DNA evidence—fine. But setting fire to the building with a chemical reaction of some kind shows a wanton disregard for civilian lives, and were it not for the brave work of the Moreno Valley Fire Department, we could be facing an emergency of catastrophic proportions—"

Blair stepped forward and flipped the offending screen shut before dropping into an open seat. "Do we really need any more bad news right now?"

Marco turned to face her, draping an arm over the back of his chair as he spoke.

"They've discovered safes and vault door components in the wreckage, so law enforcement has already concluded that the Sky Thieves torched a hideout. We're all over the news, yet we're hiding about a mile from a crime scene being combed by every cop in Moreno Valley."

Looking up for the first time, Sterling spoke sharply.

"Everyone thinks we're out of the country by now. And the media attention is all the more reason we should remain here—it's our primary fall-back building for a reason, and we've got enough food to last for a month."

As if on cue, Alec waltzed in with a plate in each hand and a third balanced on his forearm, serving Sterling and Marco like a waiter before carrying his own meal to his seat at the table.

"What is this?" Marco asked.

"Breakfast," Alec replied. "Blair liked it."

Sterling lifted his plate, reluctantly sniffed it, then set it aside.

Alec looked crestfallen with the dismissal. Blair snapped at Marco, "Just try it."

The hacker ate his first spoonful, nodded as if in appreciation, then looked to Sterling and cautioned, "We may have enough food for a month, but we'll need takeout within two days or we'll cannibalize each other."

Now curious, Sterling took a small spoonful from his own plate and took a cautious bite.

Swallowing, he said, "Every time I see a servicemember in uniform, I thank them for their service. Now, I realize I should have been begging their forgiveness for having to eat this stuff on a regular basis. This is the best our tax dollars can provide?"

Blair led by example, putting a heaping spoonful of beef stew into her mouth before replying. "Well you both had better clean your plates, because Alec has been slaving away in there. And now that we know Shedo is the mentor, we need to have a serious conversation."

Alec said thoughtfully, "One thing I still don't get. I mean, Shedo's a business mogul, right? Why would she be involved with an FBI agent like Jim?"

"It wasn't just Jim," Sterling replied. "She's probably got an army of candidates across various sectors. It's a self-fulfilling prophecy—she uses her previous connections to propel people like Jim through the ranks of business or government service, and once they reach the top, they owe her. Political favors, influence over policy, advancing the careers of her next generation of acolytes, you name it. Whatever increases her own power base. And when she needs assistance from anyone else, she's got the money to buy their loyalty."

Marco paused from devouring his Slim Jim to add, "Based on my research this morning, I couldn't agree more. There have been numerous attempts to investigate Shedo, and in each case, the inquiry is suppressed long before it reaches critical mass. Given what we now know, she must have a veritable force field surrounding her, and it's going to remain intact until we can find direct evidence of her breaking the law. If we can, she loses her protection and will be subject to prosecution, a freeze on her finances, forfeiture of assets, and jail time. If we can't, the bounty remains in place and it's a matter of time until someone finds us."

Alec said, "And to complicate matters, we no longer have a hideout or any of our gear except what was either bailed out last night or already packed in the Sprinter vans. Then there's the money situation, which was looking pretty good up until we lost 97 percent of our stuff."

Sterling nodded. "Exactly. The question is, how can we take down Shedo after all that's happened?"

"No." Blair was struggling mightily with what she was about to propose. As much as she didn't want to be the clucking mother hen of the group, the simple fact remained that there were some things only she could bring up; Sterling could be so domineering at times that Alec and Marco, she sensed, would suppress their own opinions in his presence.

She continued, "The first question we have to ask ourselves is, do we try to take down Shedo at all? There is an alternative, and since you three are too macho to bring it up—"

"We're not disbanding." Sterling's voice was flat, adamant, as if one further word on her part would be tantamount to treason.

"Sterling," Blair cautioned, "there are four of us. I don't want to run away in failure any more than you do, but the fact remains everyone needs to get a vote."

"This isn't a democracy."

"It just became one," Blair said commandingly, "and will remain a democracy until everyone has a choice on whether to proceed or not. Marco and Alec haven't been incriminated as thieves. You and I can always flee the country, but they don't have to. It's their choice to make, not yours."

Then she turned her attention to the other two, waiting for their input.

Alec was staring mournfully at his plate, scooping up the lime-green sludge of his dessert before replying with his mouth full. "The plank exchange was my idea. If we hadn't done that, we wouldn't be in this position—and I'm not going to leave this crew hanging in the wind. The warehouse burning was my fault."

"No, it wasn't." Marco cut his eyes to Sterling. "After you scanned him for trackers, anything small enough to fit inside the Faraday pouch should have been safe. I don't know what tech Shedo used to penetrate that, and right now it doesn't matter. The point is, I set the procedures for tracking countermeasures, and Sterling followed them to a T. That means the failure is mine."

Leaning forward, Sterling spoke angrily. "This isn't on either of you. I run this crew, and the compromise was my responsibility. If I'd thought of the Sierra Diamond connection sooner, we wouldn't have lost our home. No one here gets to blame themselves but me—"

"No one," Blair interrupted more loudly than she intended, "should blame themselves, period. It doesn't matter how we got here, or who made which mistakes in the process. What matters is that we *are* here, and now that everyone is fully committed, we can discuss our options."

Alec took another bite of his gruel. "Well that should be a short conversation, because we don't have any."

"We could release the remaining audio from Jim's tapes."

Marco shot that option down in record time.

"We still have no evidence that Shedo was Jim's mentor. Until we do, we should keep the recordings in reserve—"

The sound of a soft, two-tone chime coming from one of the computers silenced Marco abruptly, and seeing his eyes go wide before he directed his focus to an open laptop, the crew remained silent until he spoke again.

"News of our hideout burning travels fast," he said, continuing to stare at the screen. "We have a new message on our account for theskythieves@gmail.com." He looked up. "She wants to meet."

"Who wants to meet?" Alec asked.

"Wraith. She says to be at Rainbow Canyon RV & Boat Storage in Temecula, southwest corner of the property, at two a.m. From there, she will take us to safety—and it's a one-time offer."

Sterling gave a short laugh. "Well that's just peachy."

Blair countered, "I think she's being genuine."

"Oh, I think she is too—as in, she genuinely wants to meet us so she can genuinely turn us in for Shedo's bounty."

"At a minimum, we should hear her out."

"I agree." Alec nodded. "Matter of fact, I think we should meet with her, no questions asked."

"Why?" Blair asked.

"In Manhattan, I asked you if she was hot. You said yes."

"So?"

He shrugged. "So, I want to see for myself."

Sterling intervened, "The last time we met with anyone on their terms, it was with Dembinski in Albany. That was a trap, and so is this. Blair, I appreciate whatever psychic connection you think you have to Wraith. Alec, I respect that you have a healthy testosterone level. But on account of both factors, your judgment on this is flawed. Marco, back me up."

Marco pushed his chair back from the table, smoothing his pants before crossing one leg over the other and directing his gaze to Sterling.

"I'll back you up on the possibility of a trap all day, every day. I'm the crew pessimist, and that's my job."

"Thank you," Sterling said conclusively, as if that ended the discussion.

"However," Marco continued, "I think you're missing the point. Two minutes ago, our options were to disband or proceed. Due to lack of any meaningful variations on the latter possibility, our options are now to disband or meet with Wraith. No other solution is possible. Every day we spend at this fallback site is another day of exposure, and if we're not moving forward, we're moving backward. There is no such thing as marking time in this business. Tell me I'm wrong."

"You're wrong."

"Then please enlighten me: how can we possibly attack Shedo under the circumstances without getting outside help?"

Sterling fell silent at that, his mouth partially open as if trying to summon some coherent response that wouldn't come.

Marco concluded, "Thank you for making my point. The only conversation that matters now isn't whether to meet with Wraith, but how."

"Easy," Alec began. "Same as we did in Albany, with Dembinski. We have a bailout plan, and we don't expose the whole crew. If it's a trap, we need to spring it with one member. And as much as I'd like to represent our crew to this potential hottie, Sterling or Blair will need to take point to provide instant verification."

Marco quickly agreed. "Sending myself or Alec will risk spooking Wraith—"

"Nice pun."

"—and cause her to abandon the linkup or her trap, as the case may be. Either one would leave us sitting where we are now, without options and no more certain of Wraith's intent."

Blair nodded. "It needs to be me. Say what you want about her, but I'm the only one who's met her face-to-face. My presence at the linkup is the most surefire way to assure her that we intend to comply. She'll be just as concerned about a trap as we are, maybe more. Anyone want to debate me on that?"

She expected Sterling to object, but he remained silent; so too did Alec and Marco.

Then she continued, "All right, let's take a look at the imagery of this RV and boat storage facility and see what we're working with. I'll need a minimum of two alternate pickup points if the meeting goes bad, but three would be better if we can swing it."

Marco pulled up a satellite view of the location and spun his laptop to face her.

"No," Sterling said abruptly, as if this had been a heated argument rather than a pragmatic discussion between teammates. "It's not going to be you. My picture has been all over the news, and she'll recognize me just as much as you. I'm going to meet her alone."

"Why?" Blair demanded. "There's no reason it shouldn't be me, and you know it."

"There's a big reason, and here it is: you trust Wraith. I don't. And if this is a trap, I'm not putting you or anyone else in it."

Blair started to object, causing Sterling to slam his fist on the table.

"You said we'd stop being a democracy as soon as everyone cast their vote on whether to proceed against Shedo or not. Well, everyone's had their vote and I'm running this ship again. I'm meeting her alone tonight, and that's final."

28

STERLING

Sterling completed another sweep with his binoculars, scanning the intervals between tree trunks from his vantage point in a cluster of woods.

The distant security lights cast their yellow glow onto the dirt and gravel parking lot where RVs and loaded boat trailers were lined up in neat rows. He caught a flash of movement and focused on it, seeing a mangy coyote trot past with four pups in tow. They passed out of sight as quickly as they'd appeared, leaving him to lower his binoculars amid the rattling of traffic along the highway to his left.

If Wraith actually wanted to help them, she couldn't have chosen a much better spot for the linkup. As a tourist and resort destination, Temecula would have no small amount of traffic at all hours, and that was before he considered the road access.

Thieves tended to look at roadmaps with an eye for major traffic junctures. A single road was easy enough for cops to blockade, but Temecula spanned a large grid of local streets along with a two-mile stretch of I-15 that segued into multiple highways and interstates north and south of the city. If his crew had to make a vehicular escape and didn't get caught in the first half hour following a compromise, chances were they wouldn't get caught at all.

As if that weren't enough, Wraith had selected a linkup less than an hour south of the crew's scorched warehouse hideout, which was a welcome concession to the risks inherent in them moving anywhere at the peak of police interest in finding them. All this was well and good, provided the meeting wasn't a trap, a possibility that Sterling hadn't ruled out by a long shot. If he was about to be compromised, his only consolation would be that his team was safe, albeit down to three members.

And regardless of the outcome, Sterling had already failed in every conceivable metric.

He adjusted his backpack straps and knelt in place, feeling his knees pop before rising and stretching, shaking out his legs one at a time to keep some blood flow after an hour in the woods. In that time, the visual scans with his binoculars were about the only thing Sterling could accomplish—with the roaring interstate traffic, he'd never be able to hear anyone coming, and the alternative to watching the abandoned parking lot was to ruminate on the fact that his entire world was falling down around him.

After years of projecting utter composure and control, he had sobbed like a child in Blair's arms in front of his entire crew. He'd been used to approaching his heist career on his own terms, selectively picking and choosing his targets, and now he was forced into a high-risk meeting solely because he had no choice. As much as he hated to admit it, Marco was right—there were no other options. About the only good news to come since leaving New York was that Sterling had made the split-second decision to evacuate the warehouse, and even that was a hollow consolation prize considering he shouldn't have placed them in that position in the first place.

Now he was minutes away from either a successful linkup with Wraith or running for his life from the jaws of a trap springing shut to imprison him for the last time. Actually, that last part wasn't true, he mused—after all, she'd reap a million-dollar bonus for killing him over turning him in, and if she was half as ruthless as Sterling suspected, she would do exactly that.

His first indication of Wraith's arrival was vehicle headlights reflecting down a row of RVs. Sterling quickly transmitted, "Visual, stand by."

"*Transponder is clean,*" Marco transmitted back. "*Good luck.*"

Sure, Sterling thought bitterly. Luck was about the only thing his crew could offer him right now; depending on which way his pursuers came from, he was looking at a desperate eastward sprint into the hills on Temecula's southern edge or, worse, heading westward to negotiate eight lanes of interstate without getting broadsided by an 18-wheeler doing seventy-plus.

A box truck rolled into view then, angling its broadside to him before stopping at the southwest corner of the lot and cutting its engine. At least Wraith was punctual, if she was driving the truck at all.

The driver's door opened and a woman climbed down–was that Wraith? Sterling already knew she was a chameleon, and Blair's two sightings of the fellow thief had alternately revealed a grunge chick with black nail polish and a fashionista who blended seamlessly with the Upper East Side's financial elite.

This woman appeared to be somewhere between the two extremes, wearing jeans and a tight T-shirt, her dark hair pulled into a loose ponytail as she surveyed the woods and checked her watch.

Then she raised her hands to her mouth and shouted words Sterling could just barely hear over the traffic.

"It's two o'clock; you have one minute."

He considered what the back of the truck held, envisioning a team of armed mercenaries ready to jump out at her signal. The gut instinct that had served him for so long was now silent, giving him no indication of either danger or safety in the proceedings ahead.

"Okay," she shouted after perhaps thirty seconds of her one-minute warning had elapsed, "good luck."

Then she walked back to the driver's door, pulling the handle as Sterling transmitted, "Moving," and without waiting for a response, crashed through the trees toward the box truck.

She'd already mounted the seat by the time Sterling cleared the woods, jogging into the parking lot and cutting his eyes in all directions to search for the first indication of a trap before calling, "Wraith."

The woman climbed down quickly, approaching him as he skidded to a stop in the gravel and extended his hand.

"I'm Sterling Defranc—"

"I know who you are," she replied in an Israeli accent, her expression alarmed. "Where's the rest of your crew? Where is Blair?"

"They're safe," Sterling said, lowering his hand, "but they couldn't take the heat. Blair and the others fled the country this morning."

Wraith had a dark, makeup-free complexion and light green eyes that suddenly looked at him with anguish, his first indication that her demand to meet was no cordial offer. She was considering how much money she'd miss out on by only delivering a single member of the crew to Shedo's people.

But instead she gave a resigned nod and said, "Okay. But we won't be able to get much done with just the two of us."

"What do you mean, 'just the two of us?' What about your crew?"

"I am a solo practitioner. I said as much to Blair when we met in New York."

Sterling almost laughed. "We thought you were lying."

"I wasn't." She folded her arms and gave a rueful shake of her head. "Well, I suppose we can put our heads together and come up with something. Is that all you brought?"

Sterling thumbed a backpack strap and replied, "It's all I could carry when we fled."

Wraith clucked her tongue disapprovingly. "I would have expected the Sky Thieves to have a better plan. Do you need to stash a vehicle here? I've used this site before, and can pay the owners over the phone tomorrow."

"No vehicle," he said. "Just me."

"Okay, then—let's go."

"Why are you helping me?"

Wraith's eyebrows shot up. "Are you serious? Because I accepted payment for tapes I never delivered. Once this person finishes the hunt for your crew, I'm next. There's only one way out of this: to join forces. I can safeguard you until we come up with some way to fight back."

"Safeguard me how, exactly?"

She scoffed.

"You think you're the only thief with a hideout? I have a safe place, and if we don't figure out how to take down this opponent, it's going to suffer the same fate as yours."

"All right." Sterling nodded. "Good. Where's your hideout?"

Her posture stiffened, tone growing more solemn. "I've already come clean about my intentions. But you don't need to know our destination until we arrive. Come on, we're wasting time. Get in the back. You'll have plenty of room—I was expecting a crew of five or six, plus equipment."

This was it, Sterling thought, his final judgment call; and while his gut instinct remained oddly neutral, the balance of logic pointed to the risk of going with Wraith being far less than the dangers of remaining at their fallback site.

He said, "All clear, all clear. Bring it in."

Marco replied a moment later over his earpiece, sounding relieved. *"On the way."*

Drawing a breath, Sterling explained, "All right, here's the truth: my crew is still here. They're on the way. I had to make sure this wasn't a trap."

Wraith let out a high-pitched giggle, though whether out of mockery or because she genuinely found it humorous, he couldn't tell.

"Why would I trap you?"

"There's a bounty—"

"Of a million dollars, maybe two with bonus? I'm not a killer, Sterling, and you should know by now that I can steal more than that."

He didn't reply, and didn't have to—by then, both of them could hear the vehicles approaching through the parking lot, and a moment later the two Sprinter vans pulled into view. They turned away in tandem, then backed up toward the rear of the box truck before the crew dismounted.

"Wraith," Sterling said, "meet the Sky Thieves."

Blair was the first to approach, extending her hand to Wraith with the words, "Nice to see you again. Wish it was under better circumstances."

Wraith accepted the handshake and snickered.

"Last time we both almost died—frankly, I prefer meeting you this way."

Blair turned away to begin the equipment transfer as Marco stepped in, briefly shaking her hand.

"Marco. Hacker."

She nodded in approval. "Good to have a fellow cyber-nerd on board."

Marco barely had time to end the handshake and turn away before Alec was upon her, wordlessly intercepting her hand, but not to shake it; instead, he bent at the waist to give it a kiss, then rose swiftly and advanced a half step.

"It is a pleasure to make your acquaintance, madame. I am Alec, safe-cracker extraordinaire and lord of all locking systems; indeed, living proof that any measures of physical security may as well come with a disclaimer that they are for decorative purposes only. From this moment forward, consider my services at your disposal...all you need to do is say the word."

Wraith didn't answer, instead looking to Sterling and asking, "Is he serious?"

"Don't engage him," Sterling warned, "you'll just make it worse."

But Alec wasn't done, continuing in his Boston accent as if this entire situation were perfectly normal.

"Blair told me—quite crudely, I might add—that you were hot, but she made no mention of the radiant beauty of your stunning countenance. I am humbled and honored to be in your presence, and offer you both my undying admiration and tireless gratitude for your assistance this evening."

Wraith pursed her lips.

"Get in the truck, Alec."

Alec made a half turn to face Sterling and whispered, "She remembered my name," before swiftly departing to the Sprinter vans.

Sterling followed him, and within minutes they'd transferred the sum total of their remaining equipment to Wraith's box truck before backing the vans into open spots for long-term parking. Then they climbed in the back of the box truck per Wraith's instruction, and Sterling felt a crippling sense of vulnerability as she pulled the rolling door down. This was followed by the sound of a padlock being snapped into place from the outside, leaving them in the darkness.

Alec was the first to click on a headlamp, his mischievous eyes glinting in the red light. Sterling had never seen him smiling so broadly—the safe-cracker looked like a virgin on his wedding day, brimming with a sense of overeager anticipation.

"Blair, you said hot. Lots of women are hot." He jabbed an index finger at the forward portion of the cargo area. "But *that*, my friend, was drop-dead gorgeous."

Sterling put a hand on his shoulder and shook it slightly. "This could still be a trap, you know."

"If it is," Alec whispered breathlessly, "it would have been worth it."

Wraith fired the engine as the rest of them activated headlights and steadied themselves against the equipment in preparation for the truck to move—for how long or to where, they had no idea.

And no choice.

Sterling felt the box truck lurch forward as Blair settled beside him, sliding an arm around his waist without a word.

29

BLAIR

As the box truck came to a stop, Blair tried not to get her hopes up.

Over the past four hours and twenty minutes in the shaking cargo area, there had been many such stops, and for the last dozen or so, Blair had expectantly looked to the rear rolling door in the hopes that they'd arrived at their destination. Wraith had made no mention of food, water, or rest breaks, which indicated to Blair a strong likelihood that this would be a one-shot trip, spanning no more than six hours. That amount of time could take them as far as San Francisco, Las Vegas, or Phoenix, and since their compasses and communications equipment were inoperative—presumably due to Wraith's counter-tracking measures—they had no way of knowing which direction they were headed.

She felt the truck reversing and then coming to a final stop before the engine cut off for the first time since departing Temecula.

She stood in eager anticipation, seeing Sterling kick a snoring Marco awake as they heard the padlock unlatch. Blair felt her pulse quicken as she considered that outside was either freedom or an army of cops and mercenaries ready to swallow her crew whole. But she'd remained confident about Wraith's reliability ever since meeting her in Manhattan, and steeled herself with the knowledge that her intuition had been wrong since becoming a thief, but never *that* wrong.

The rolling door slid upward and Blair winced against the sunlight streaming in as Wraith announced, "A new day begins, Sky Thieves. My name is Esther. Welcome to my home."

Blair climbed out the back of the truck, seeing a vast two-story residence finished in the contemporary Mediterranean style—white stucco walls, red clay roof tiles—and was surprised to feel a warm, salty ocean breeze wash over her.

As her teammates joined her in the home's front yard, concealed from outside view by a solid, gated perimeter wall, she asked, "Where are we?"

"Ensenada, Baja California, Mexico. But I prefer to think of it as heaven on earth. We'll get your equipment shortly—first, let me show you the view."

Wraith-slash-Esther began leading them around the house, where a stone walkway paralleled the perimeter fence and led downhill at a sharp angle toward the backyard.

Sterling took it upon himself to look a gift horse in the mouth, asking, "What's the risk level from cartel violence?"

Esther waved a dismissive hand, calling back over her shoulder, "That occurs inland, and in the border towns. Here on the coast, your biggest danger is from pickpocketing. I assure you, the biggest criminals in Ensenada are us."

A moment later they arrived in the backyard and Blair's entire crew was rendered speechless.

The sloping walkway threaded into a manicured yard where elaborate stonework surrounded a swimming pool. But the real view was beyond that, past the outdoor seating areas, firepit, and finally the palm trees that marked the rear corners of the property, bordered by a short fence.

Over it was a row of large boulders serving as the top of a seawall, separating the level ground from a sandy strip of rock-strewn beach that gave way to the Pacific.

The crashing waves extended to a breathtaking blue ocean, two small hilly islands jutting out of the water in the distance and flanked by a spur of mainland. Blair took from the shadows of the early morning sun that the view was oriented roughly southwest, toward Hawaii.

"Why," Marco muttered angrily, "have we been working out of a warehouse?"

Esther looked to Blair with a wry smile. "I was going to ask the same thing."

Before she could answer, Sterling asked, "Esther, why did you choose this place for your hideout?"

"America is far too strict for my taste, the cost of living far too high. Here, people mind their business and I have established an extensive network that will warn me if anyone comes around asking questions about a female thief."

"I get that," Sterling agreed. "I mean, why Ensenada?"

Esther's voice assumed a wistful tone as she gazed out over the Pacific.

"I love the water. The Pacific coast suits my preferences: world-class surfing, open sea diving, strong currents—I like a challenge—incredible visibility, liveaboard charters for next to nothing, and access to Guadalupe Island is as easy as it gets, which is to say 24 hours each way by boat."

Blair asked, "What's at Guadalupe Island?"

"Aside from volcanic hikes, cliff diving, and swimming with seals, it has one of the most prolific great white shark populations on earth. It's the Everest of shark diving."

Marco, taken aback, cautiously inquired, "Are you, like, in a cage?"

"Sometimes," Esther replied casually before she announced, "but enough about that. Now we get your equipment inside my house. I'll show you to the guest rooms, and since we won't get any thinking done on empty stomachs, breakfast will be in one hour. Then, we can get to work."

She started back up the walkway to the front yard, and Blair made to follow her before Alec grabbed her arm and whispered, "Could she be any hotter?"

At that moment, Esther, apparently very keen of hearing, stopped abruptly and called out, "Yes. I'm a black belt in Krav Maga."

30

STERLING

After pausing to take a sip of coffee, Sterling continued, "It wasn't until we'd returned from the plank sale that I realized Shedo could have been the Sierra Diamond's original owner and, therefore, Jim's mentor."

Seated on the couch across from him, Esther gave periodic nods that served as the only confirmation she was listening at all—her gaze was riveted by the sheet of paper in her hand, which she'd been staring at for the majority of his update.

Sterling set his mug down on the coffee table, rubbing his hands together in brooding rumination of events he'd rather forget. "The connection with Geoffrey Lambert served as the only confirmation I needed. We evacuated to our fallback site, and the warehouse was on fire an hour later."

The rest of his crew was seated around them on the various couches and loveseats in Esther's living room, if you could call it that—with a cathedral ceiling, stone fireplace, and high windows presenting a commanding view of the waterfront patio beneath the ocean horizon and clear blue sky, it felt more like a resort. Esther sat with her back to this staggering beauty, clearly accustomed to the sight, and Sterling momentarily wondered how she got anything done in this dream estate.

Esther had already served a Mediterranean breakfast for five—smoked salmon, eggs and tomato sauce, wheat bread, various cheeses, and fresh fruit, all of it good. This woman could cook well, in addition to everything else. The thought made Sterling feel insecure. He had a crew of four, and he couldn't even safeguard them from Shedo's attack; and here was Esther, living a seemingly idyllic existence in paradise while working as a solo thief and, apparently, finding time for martial arts and scuba diving.

When she didn't respond, still focused on the page in her hands, Sterling said, "Now that you're caught up on events to date, what do you think?"

Only then did Esther look up, first at Sterling and then the others, finding all eyes on her. With an embarrassed grin, she flipped the paper over for everyone to see—it was a high-definition printout of Kristen Shedo's professional portrait.

"Sorry," she said, setting the sheet on the coffee table. "I just wanted to get a good look at our target. Before we proceed, I need to level with you guys. I've always been a lone operator, and discretion is my hallmark."

"What are you trying to say?" Sterling asked.

"It's in our mutual interests to bring down Shedo. But if we are to proceed with this, we'll have to do some things my way. I don't intend on ending up in jail or dead, and by taking you in, I've increased my risk exponentially."

"Considering our opponent, I'd say five is better than one."

"That depends," Esther crisply replied, "on how we go about it. Don't get me wrong, I'm a fan of your work. But I fear we have very different parameters for acceptable risk. Your crew has a reputation for being a bit...how should I put this? Showy."

"Showy?"

"Ostentatious. Sensational."

"I know what 'showy' means. But our crew has never done anything the job didn't require."

"I'm not debating that. But I am extremely curious as to your choice of jobs in the first place. You seem to pick the most difficult heists as a matter of principle."

Sterling felt his body going rigid; he didn't know Esther well enough to tell if she was simply being candid or trying to pick him apart in front of his crew, but either way he'd have greatly preferred if she'd chosen to have this particular conversation in private.

He began, "Well I'm not sure how much it matters now, because our current job has chosen us. As for acceptable risk, we operate in very different ways. You're a lone operator, and we work as a team. Everyone contributes to each facet of planning and execution. You're a jack of all trades, but we've got four specialists working in tandem. Going forward, that disparity could be a source of conflict, or it could be an asset in giving us the perspective required to get this thing done. We've all assembled here in good faith, and I intend on finding a solution that sees us parting ways with our freedom intact, without making you regret taking us in."

"Fair enough."

Sterling couldn't help himself. "And in the process, I'll try not to be too *showy*."

Blair quickly added, "Maybe we need to level with you now, Esther. Our crew is running low on cash, which is the only reason we sold the plank in the first place."

Esther frowned.

"How, pray tell, are the Sky Thieves low on cash?"

Sterling felt a touch of defensiveness enter his voice as he replied, "We donate half of every score to charity." Esther's eyes went wide as he continued, "A majority of the rest is re-invested in planning and executing future heists."

After a long pause, Esther said, "So you donate half, spend most of the remainder on upcoming jobs, leaving your take-home as—what, exactly?"

"Five percent. Split equally."

"Wow." She laughed. "Well I am happy to finance a majority of this operation, and since I have not been giving my money away, I have the means to do so. The only question is our angle of attack on Shedo—what was your plan before coming here?"

Sterling explained, "Kristen Shedo is deeply networked in political, business, and federal service circles. She identifies people with strategic potential, helps their career progress in record time, and funnels some into politics with the intent of gaining financial advantages. By the time her successful candidates are in power, they're indebted to her for life. It's basically insider trading at the highest levels."

Without taking his gaze off the laptop before him, Marco added, "And in addition to padding her bank accounts, that network provides protection that she desperately needs. Shedo has made a lot of enemies, many of whom suspect her of illegal business practices. But she's defended on so many levels that every investigation gets shot down almost as soon as it's proposed. We need hard evidence of her network, something so incriminating that her people can't suppress it. Then we announce it to the world along with the remainder of Jim's audio tapes. Once that happens, all the prosecutors who've failed in the past will be lining up to have a shot at her. She'll lose everything, including the ability to finance a manhunt against us."

Sterling watched Esther's expression closely, trying to decide if she was negatively judging their assessment as her gaze floated to the ceiling in silent consideration.

She began, "So the plan is to get her into legal trouble, even though she's got a long list of powerful allies, in order to gum up her financial assets, even though she's proven that for her, a few million dollars is a rounding error. Assuming all of this works, she'll be out of commission for how long? And then what? She'll realize you're not to be trifled with and leave you alone?"

"We're not killers," Sterling asserted.

"I'm not either." After a long sigh, she said, "I'm just wondering if there's a quicker way."

"If you can find one, we're all ears. Our theory, however, is that the only solution is making her the subject of a full investigation that freezes her assets and/or removes her legal and political protection. Based on our experience with Jim, public exposure is the fastest way to do that."

"I don't disagree; I just believe her communications will be sufficiently safeguarded. Have you tried hacking them yet?"

Marco shook his head solemnly. "By the time we figured out that Shedo was Jim's mentor, we had to evacuate."

"So a full-court press with digital penetration is step two. You have your kit with you?"

"All of it. I just need connectivity."

"Good. Step one is to analyze what we've already got. And aside from the identity of Geoffrey Lambert, the only remaining thing you've uncovered was the network analysis of Jim's burner phone, correct?"

"That's right," Marco said, "but the FBI found no connections with the other numbers, nor did we—"

"May I see them?"

Marco hesitated, then pulled up the analysis on his laptop before handing it to her.

She crossed one leg over the other, balancing the computer on her thighs as she panned across the graphic with its blank face images over various burner phone numbers.

Sterling was shocked when, in remarkably quick fashion, Esther rotated the laptop to face him and tapped one of the connections. "You don't recognize this number?"

"No."

She turned the screen back to herself. "The 881 country code is specific to Iridium satellite phones. And the number ending in 6200 belongs to an associate of mine, a French national living in Brussels. He's a very successful art thief—I'm surprised you don't know him."

"Don't be," Sterling said. "Art has never been on our target list."

Esther looked perturbed by the statement, but went on, "Given that an art thief is among the numbers called by this series of burner phones, it is reasonable to infer that Shedo is in possession of stolen art. If we steal that back and document that it was in her possession, not only would she be the subject of a federal investigation, but any companies she's doing business with would have to cut their ties. In addition to a potential freeze on her assets, we'd effectively sever her income. Evidence of her illegal network would just be a bonus at that point."

"That's smart," Sterling conceded.

"And why," she asked, sounding troubled, "wouldn't you steal art?"

He bristled; among his father's ironclad rules, the two that had come up thus far—donate half your earnings to charity, and never steal art—had been ridiculed by the woman sitting before him.

Keeping his voice level, he replied, "Because we prefer to rob the deserving, not take priceless works out of the museums where they belong—"

Alec shushed him, then smiled politely at Esther.

"There's a better reason we don't work with art, and it's because art thieves are friggin' weird. You ever met one?"

"I've met quite a lot," she said.

"Then you know what I'm talking about. Always going on and on about the pieces speaking to them, or changing their plans once they're inside because they can feel the artist's presence emanating from a particular painting. It's creepy, am I right?"

"Actually, I—"

"And another thing," he cut her off, gesturing wildly, "calling these people thieves is a bit of a stretch in the first place. Lots of art museums are about as secure as a doggy day care. Minimal cameras, massive blind spots, and not much in the way of motion detection, which, let us not forget, can all be ascertained when you get to stroll through it as a paying visitor. Where's the challenge?"

Esther watched him calmly.

"And how do you prefer to reconnoiter your targets?"

"Easy," Alec proclaimed. "We tell Marco what we need to know, he does some computer sorcery, and boom, we've got all the security specs."

"Doesn't sound so different from walking through a museum, does it?"

Alec shrugged. "Tell that to Marco. This stuff really stresses him out sometimes. But specializing in art is a race to the bottom. You know what the going rate for fenced artwork is? Seller usually gets about ten percent of the appraised value, if that. Not much of a value proposition."

"And do you know"—she tapped the phone number on the screen—"what that percentage rises to when you accept direct commissions, as my friend does?"

Alec hesitated. "He's your friend? Like, platonic, or are you guys, you know, dating? Does he treat you well? Does he have dimples like mine?"

"Fifty to seventy-five percent, depending on the difficulty involved as well as the client's wealth. That sounds a bit more lucrative, no?"

Sterling finally spoke up, though his voice was beleaguered. "It sounds a lot better than we did on the Sierra Diamond, and that was much harder to get than art would have been."

Esther's tone turned curious. "I was surprised you bothered to steal it at all. I mean, given it was in the Sky Safe."

"That's exactly why we stole it."

Marco explained, "Sterling was obsessed. He would have broken into the Sky Safe if the only thing inside was a bag of Fritos."

"Really?" Esther asked. "I mean...why?"

Sterling replied bluntly, "Because they said it couldn't be done, that's why. Now let's get back to—"

"Your relationship status." Alec fixed Esther with a dreamy gaze. "This art thief is just a professional acquaintance, right? Or maybe just a careless fling, one that you regret? He broke your heart and you're on the rebound, seeking redemption?"

Esther kept her focus on the screen; she was becoming, Sterling thought, very quickly accustomed to ignoring Alec.

"This art thief is a pro. I know we all are, but he's...good. Very good."

Alec sounded combative. "Yeah? What's his name?"

"Scott Smith."

"I mean his real name. All these art thieves have weird French names to go with their weird attitudes."

Her eyes narrowed. "His real name is Scott Smith."

"Esther," Blair asked, "can you call him?"

31

BLAIR

Blair and her crew clustered around Esther, who'd just taken a seat at the desk of her home office. The space was almost as extravagant as her living room, facing a second-floor balcony with an ocean view.

Esther checked her watch. "It's close to six p.m. in Brussels. If I can't reach him now, he's probably traveling."

Blair desperately hoped that wouldn't be the case. They needed a win now more than ever, no matter how small.

"Please, do not speak. He will only confide in me if he believes I am alone."

The four Sky Thieves nodded, and Esther placed the phone on speaker mode before dialing his number.

An automated voice notified them that there would be a short delay while the call was connected, followed by a series of clicking noises. After a half-minute they finally heard the first ring, and the second was cut short as a French-accented voice answered the call.

"Esther, it is a pleasure to hear from you."

"Good to hear your voice, Scott. I hope I am not interrupting anything important."

Blair heard a slight breeze on the other line before the man answered,

"Not at all, I am just having a glass of Merlot on the veranda. Am I drinking alone?"

"Afraid so," Esther replied, "it's still a bit early over here."

"Of course. And to what do I owe the pleasure of your call?"

She paused. "I'm having some trouble with a client of yours."

"Oh?"

"Kristen Shedo."

He gave a sad sigh. "This should not surprise me. Kristen accumulates enemies even faster than friends."

Then, in a more concerned tone, he asked, "I should hope you are not the target of this bounty that has been circulating? The one related to the Sky Thieves?"

"Not yet," she said, "but I'm about to suffer a similar fate."

"This brings me great sadness. Those who cross Kristen do not tend to fare well, as she can inflict great...trauma, as they say."

Blair felt a knot forming in her stomach and shot Sterling a concerned glance.

"I'll get to the point," Esther continued. "I understand she's in possession of stolen art that you provided, and I'd like to steal it back to expose her. Would that be a problem for you?"

Now Blair's discomfort turned to surprise—she couldn't believe how forthright Esther was being off the bat. No preludes, no warming him up to the idea; she just laid all their cards on the table. But Scott's response was one of casual support.

"Not at all. She is a lucrative client, but far from my only one. By all means, return her art to the museums. It would give me great pleasure to steal them again if commissioned to do so."

"May I ask what pieces I'm looking for?"

"Of course." The sound of wind vanished from the call, and Blair took it to mean that Scott had retreated indoors. "The focus of her collection is full or semi-nudes of Venus, the Roman goddess of beauty, sex, and above all, victory. Are you prepared to take notes?"

"I am." Esther glanced at the digital recorder beside the phone to ensure it was still running.

"Two oil paintings by Titian: *Venus Anadyomene* from 1520, and *Venus with a Mirror* from 1555. Acquired from the national galleries in Edinburgh and D.C., respectively. Alexandre Cabanel's *The Birth of Venus*, 1863, from the Musée d'Orsay in Paris. In the Met, I picked up a Lorenzo Lotto piece, *Venus and Cupid*, 1530. But her latest commission is the greatest masterpiece of all: *Tannhäuser in the Venusberg* by John Collier, 1901. By far the most daring and startling of the quintet."

A wave of sheer relief swept through Blair, and Esther looked at her with an "I told you so" expression before turning back to the phone.

"And of the pieces you mentioned, are these all at her personal residence?"

"In Medina, yes. I know this for certain, though where in the house they are, I cannot say. She has assured me they are quite secure there, that not even I would be able to reach them. I have no reason to doubt her."

"What if you had no choice? What if your life was on the line if you couldn't get them back?"

A long silence ensued. "Given her finances, how emotionally invested she is in the art, and what I can reasonably infer about the resulting precautions to safeguard her collection, I am ashamed to say I'd take my chances on the run."

Blair winced. It was maddening to confirm that Shedo harbored stolen art in her home, and she didn't need a thief in Brussels to tell her that the residence was far more impenetrable than any museum in the world.

Esther said, "Running would only delay the inevitable, Scott, and I need to get that art back. Would you go operational on this, work alongside me, provided your involvement was perfectly concealed?"

He gave a good-natured chuckle.

"I would do anything for you, Esther, but this is a bridge too far." A moment later, he continued, "But perhaps I can help you in a different way. There is another piece in her possession, one which she did not commission from me."

"If she didn't commission it from you, how do you know about it?"

"Because I stole it for her nonetheless."

"I don't understand."

His tone became wistful, nostalgic. "On the operation to acquire the Lotto from the Metropolitan, I noticed an upcoming addition to one of the exhibits I passed through. One that was not in place during my reconnais-sance. At the time I didn't know what it was—there was not even a sign installed yet—but I was halted by the piece, a relatively simple bronze dragon with three feet perched on the base, and a fourth extended and clutching an orb. The jaws were open, baring teeth and tongue. Although small, perhaps 23 centimeters in length and 12 to 13 in height, I could tell at once that it had Kristen's energy flowing through it. The power, the sheer audacity of the bronze..."

Alec tapped Esther on the arm and nodded eagerly, as if his theory about the weirdness of art thieves was being validated with each word. She brushed his hand away.

"...there was electricity flowing through my entire body, a surge. I knew then I must present this piece to her. So, I took it. Of course, had I known then what I know now, I would have left it right where it was."

"What do you mean?"

"It was on loan from Stockholm. Part of their Old Summer Palace collection."

Blair had no idea what that meant, but it was quite clear from Esther's haunted expression that the term carried some meaningful—and poten-tially horrifying—implications.

He went on, "Only when I saw the news of my theft did I learn that this simple bronze dragon was a piece-mold casting dating to the Shang Dynasty, making it over 3,200 years old."

"Does she still have the piece in her collection?"

"Have it?" Scott asked incredulously. "Esther, she will not stop talking about it. Kristen was delighted to receive the piece and has said that from the moment she held it, she felt the same energy that I did. She actually travels with it, feels that it gives her power. She is not wrong."

"When you say she travels with it..."

"Everywhere," he confirmed. "All her business trips, it is with her. I have cautioned her as to the lunacy of this undertaking, of course, but she is impervious to reason. It actually causes me a great deal of distress, you see, because if my name is ever connected with its theft—"

"That won't happen," Esther assured him. "I won't let it."

"I should hope not, or I am, as they say, cooked. A cooked goose. But I mention this piece to you as I am certain her home is quite impervious to penetration. When she travels, however...the dragon would not be quite so difficult to grab."

Blair felt Sterling's hand on her shoulder, giving a slight squeeze of validation.

When Esther replied, she made no effort to conceal the gratitude in her voice.

"Scott, I didn't think I could like you any more than I already did. But this is huge. This helps me out a lot, thank you."

"You did not hear it from me, Esther. But I should be very pleased if you make it out of this. Our last trip to Guadalupe Island was...magnificent. We must do it again."

"I'd be devastated if we didn't."

"Not as much as I would, my Israeli sunflower."

That made Blair's eyebrows shoot up, and she glanced cautiously to Alec.

"I'll let you know if I need anything else. Give my best to Anette."

The moment Esther disconnected the call, Alec opened his mouth to speak—and was immediately cut off by Blair.

"What is the Old Summer Palace?"

Rising from her seat, Esther turned to face them before leaning against the desk, arms tight against her sides. "How much business does Shedo have in China?"

"A lot," Marco replied. "Close to half of her annual gross income. Why?"

Esther's expression brightened, and she explained, "The Old Summer Palace was the crown jewel of imperial palaces, located in Beijing. It was home to the last Chinese dynasty, and sacked by French and British soldiers in 1860. Thousands of priceless antiquities were looted. Any of this ringing a bell?"

Blair shook her head. "Why would it?"

"Because many of these artifacts have found their way to museums around the world, and starting in 2010, the Chinese government has been stealing them back."

"What do you mean, 'stealing them back?'"

"The most sophisticated art heists of the last decade or so have occurred in Europe: Sweden, Norway, England, and France, among others. In each case, the heists have targeted Chinese relics at the exclusion of everything else in the museums. Most elapsed in two to seven minutes, with all the calling cards of a pro crew: disabling alarms, police diversions, rappelling through skylights, escaping by motorcycle or speedboat. How do you not know this?"

Sterling lifted his chin and said flatly, "We don't steal art. And how can you be certain that these heists are being sponsored by the Chinese government?"

"It's not much of a secret," she scoffed. "Before the first robbery, a Chinese state-run conglomerate sent teams of researchers, historians, and military intelligence officers on a global tour to inventory museum contents. After the first half-dozen thefts, some international museums started voluntarily sending their items to China on permanent loan just so they're not robbed."

Alec looked enthralled by the implications, his voice jittery. "So if we steal the dragon from Shedo, then very publicly facilitate its delivery to a museum while posting evidence of where and how we got it from her, you think she'd be disowned by all these Chinese corporations she does business with?"

"Not just disowned," Esther replied. "They would crucify her, and actively sabotage her entire business. There would be an immediate end to all of her transactions not just in China but in any Asian country, and that's just the beginning. They would further blacklist any Western companies and investors that didn't cut all ties with Shedo at once, and the woman may be rich but no one is going to choose her over China. Then—and this is the most important part—they'd exert considerable political and economic pressure on the US government until Shedo was prosecuted and imprisoned over owning the piece. Her network isn't strong enough to protect her from that, not in the least."

Blair said, "So we don't need the Venus paintings at all—we just need the dragon."

"Exactly. When Christie's was to auction off two zodiac heads from the Old Summer Palace's fountain, they were threatened with unspecified severe consequences by Chinese government officials. So Christie's turned the zodiac heads over to them instead, and were rewarded with the first-ever license to operate independently in China. Shedo plays dirty, but no one plays as dirty as the Chinese government."

Sterling was nodding now, and he looked at Marco with a wolfish grin.

"I think it's time you get to hacking, my friend. We have a travel schedule to uncover."

32

BLAIR

Blair took a seat on the couch between Alec and Esther before the safecracker could begin edging closer to the object of his adoration. Sterling was sprawled out on a loveseat, taking up all the space with apparent disregard for his girlfriend—and while Blair could have been irritated by that oversight, she knew the truth. He was simply too focused on their upcoming op to have considered the thought.

They sat in silence for a moment, preparing notepads and pens for the brainstorming session that was about to begin.

Esther's living room was bright with the sun's descent over the ocean, white walls glowing auburn. Marco entered the room holding a laptop as carefully as if he were balancing a tray of drinks, gently lowering himself into a chair and facing the others.

"I bring bad news and good news. Which would you like first?"

"Bad," Sterling said. "Always start with the bad."

"We can rule out hitting Shedo's house right now. The city of Medina has so many billionaires that it's got more security cameras than residents. Shedo's insurance requires that a former member of law enforcement live on the property full-time in addition to a substantial security force. Geographic restrictions include a yard that slopes sharply into her dock on Lake Washington, limiting ground movement to a hundred and eighty degrees, all of which is patrolled by guards. The home itself is about as well-defended as a military installation, and even if we managed to get inside, we have no way of knowing where the art is located. Balance of probability is on a hidden door that we'd require impulse radar to locate."

Blair asked, "And the good news?"

"I wasn't finished with the bad." Marco drew a long breath. "Shedo has recently curtailed her business travel, public appearances, and speaking engagements. In fact, she's just cleared over three months of her schedule for an extended vacation, likely to remove herself from possible retaliation until we're captured or killed. So she will be traveling soon, which is the only good news. Then I can get back to the bad—there's a lot more of that."

"Traveling," Sterling said, "by plane?"

"Private yacht."

Alec flung his arms skyward and shouted, "Yes! We're hitting that. Case closed, end of story."

When the safecracker provided no follow-up justification for his outburst, Sterling wrinkled his nose and asked, "Any particular reason?"

"Because I've always wanted to be a pirate," Alec said breathlessly. "When I was a kid, I dressed up as Blackbeard for eight Halloweens in a row. Then twice more as an adult. This is my chance."

Then he began scrawling furiously on his notepad with the kind of intense focus she'd never witnessed outside of him actually breaching a safe.

"Moving on," Marco continued, "her yacht is scheduled to pick her up from her personal dock in Medina in 17 days, then travel through a narrow channel to the Puget Sound west of Seattle, and finally north into the Salish Sea before entering the Pacific Ocean. After that she's headed to a superyacht destination in Phuket until her return trip in August."

Blair nodded. "So she'll definitely have the dragon with her."

"Most definitely. And unless we want to test our luck for another three-plus months, or travel to Thailand, then this op will have to occur during or shortly after her transition to the yacht. Because that opportunity is as good as we're going to get. And there's more—she had a safe installed on the boat, a Shrada Safes Model K." Marco began pawing through his notes when Alec, still scrawling on his notepad, spoke without looking up.

"The big one? 392?"

Marco paused, then confirmed, "Yes, that's it."

"You get a make on whether it's basic K, or a Super, Ultra, or Elite model?"

He glanced back at his notes. "Elite."

"Perfect," Alec said, "because that premium model has a time lock feature whose parameters are set through a wireless interface. We can hack that to determine her parameters, and as long as we rob it while the time lock is active, we're guaranteed to find the bronze lizard along with, possibly, some other art as well."

Sterling gave a low whistle of approval. "That's slick. Very slick."

Marco cautioned, "Before we get too excited about the safe, I still have to discuss the yacht's countermeasures. I'll try to keep this brief, but it's not going to be easy."

Everyone braced themselves for his next words—at least, everyone from the Sky Thieves. Sterling was leaning forward expectantly, and Alec continued jotting notes. Blair felt the constriction in her chest that usually preceded such discussions about the odds against them, at the outset of heist planning when everything seemed impossible.

But Esther, she noted, appeared to show no such anxiety; she tilted her head back on the sofa, a dreamlike expression on her face as if she already knew all the answers.

Marco continued, "Starting with the internal systems, we're looking at armed security personnel, deck-mounted pressure sensors, and onboard CCTV. In the event of a security breach, Shedo is taken to the yacht's 'citadel,' a safe room next to the crew mess. And there's essentially a giant fog machine that fills the yacht with smoke to reduce visibility to about six inches."

Sterling gave a dismissive snort. "The smoke is the least of our concerns —we could memorize the floorplans and rehearse moving in the blind."

"Getting there is going to be problematic, which brings me to the external systems. Her boat has an escalation-of-force procedure that starts with an anti-piracy laser device known as a dazzle gun, which causes temporary blindness."

Blair offered, "We can engineer protective goggles to overcome that."

"Then there's the LRAD, or long-range acoustic device. This is a $20,000 sonic weapon that shoots a beam of high-volume acoustics to deafen anyone aboard an incoming ship."

"We wear earplugs," Sterling said. "Next."

"The pain ray, a five-million-dollar active denial system that fires electromagnetic energy in a narrow beam. Makes it feel like you're on fire."

"Protective suits can block that, I imagine. What else?"

"Line launchers that shoot nets to disable propellers."

Folding her arms, Blair said, "My drone had prop guards that allowed it to bump into walls without losing lift. We could build something similar."

"They'll also shoot flare guns."

"We'll be wearing protective suits anyway. Is that it?"

"Not quite. They've also got a water cannon, which is basically a fire-hose with an unlimited supply. They can use that to fill incoming boats."

"We could," Blair mused, "construct a hull shield that keeps us from taking on water."

"And if that works, they'll blast us back into the ocean when we try to board."

She considered her response, distracted by the sound of Alec ripping the piece of paper free from his notepad. Blair looked over to see him meticulously folding the page into a neat square and passing it to her.

ESTHER was written on it, and she passed it to her left as Sterling said, "So we knock everyone out with sleeping gas."

"It's an open-air deck," Marco pointed out. "Gas isn't going to cut it, and if we make our way through all those security measures, they'll just shoot us with good old-fashioned firearms. Plus the internal and deck doors have a simultaneous auto-locking feature in the event of an unauthorized boarding."

Blair looked left to see Esther unfolding Alec's note, quickly scrawling something, and then passing it back without bothering to re-fold it.

She took a quick glance at the paper, considering that, in all fairness, the cartoon image was well-sketched.

A great white shark took up a majority of the page, its jaws filled with what appeared to be a bloody, mangled pile of unicorn carcasses. Sitting side saddle atop the shark were the caricatures of two people.

One was quite obviously Esther, although her cartoon version was considerably more buxom than the real version, with balloon-like breasts tastefully covered by twin clamshells. Her legs had been replaced by a mermaid tail, and one arm was draped around the figure beside her— clearly Alec, also with a fishtail, his body grotesquely muscled. The merman bodybuilder's anatomy contained not six but eight distinct abdominal muscles, and he hoisted a trident victoriously skyward.

At the bottom of the page, a neatly printed line of text read, *sunset beach walk tonight?* Beneath that were the words yes and no, with a heart-shaped checkbox beside each one.

Esther had checked no.

Blair passed the paper along, then volunteered an unorthodox solution.

"What if we didn't hit the yacht at all," she asked, "and got someone else to do it for us?"

Marco cocked his head.

"Explain."

Leaning forward, she continued, "We know Shedo's destination in Thailand."

"So?"

"So why don't we just contact the Chinese and lay it all out there? Her yacht will be sailing through their backyard with a priceless dragon they really want back, and they've been sponsoring their own heist crews in the first place. We could give them her itinerary, all the countermeasures on her yacht along with the specs for her onboard safe, and maybe a validating picture of the dragon from the man who stole it. They could catch her red-handed and spare us the trouble. That would solve our problem, right?"

"It's an elegant solution," Marco admitted, "*if* it played out exactly according to plan. But predictability is not the current Chinese regime's strong suit, and they like it that way. There's no telling if they would believe us in the first place, and even if they did, they're not going to risk putting together a heist of that caliber on a timeline of two weeks and change. At best they'd plan to raid her yacht on the way back to the States."

"And we're not going to last for the three months that would take," Sterling said. "The Chinese might get the dragon on Shedo's route back, but it won't matter to us because we'll all be taking dirt naps by then."

"Exactly," Marco affirmed.

Blair felt dispirited by the counterpoints, but before she could react, Esther spoke.

"It is fascinating to watch how you people think."

Alec, still holding his personal masterpiece with its checked rejection, asked, "What do you mean, 'you people?' Which people? Asians, Esther?"

"I'm talking about your crew." She raised her hands and shook them mockingly. "*The Sky Thieves*. The truth is that we can't rely on anyone to do this for us any more than we can overcome the yacht's security measures. And when that is the case, the only solution is to render them irrelevant."

"Render them irrelevant," Sterling repeated. "How, exactly?"

"I'm sorry. It's not your fault—you've been on the run, and you're all tired. My eyes are fresh, and it's not fair to judge you for not seeing what I see."

Then she smiled. "But I think I know how we'll be spending the next two weeks."

33

STERLING

Sterling's head pierced the surface, revealing a glittering ocean through the partially-fogged lens of his dive mask.

An anchored boat drifted gently in the current, and Sterling saw that Blair was already ascending the ladder, looking about as graceful as a woman could in fifty pounds of scuba equipment. And while his own gear was theoretically weightless as he floated, that didn't make it any easier for him to maneuver—Sterling had always been a mediocre swimmer at best, and any difficulties he had in the water were currently amplified by a factor of ten.

He started to paddle instinctively with his arms, then reminded himself that those particular limbs were more or less useless and instead worked his legs in slow, powerful kicks, feeling the clown-shoe-like fins scraping against each other as he closed the distance with the boat. With his nostrils enclosed by a silicone nosepiece, any breathing was accomplished orally, as his teeth clenched down on what felt to him like a weighted football mouthguard. But Esther was loath to allow any improper dive nomenclature, and Sterling reminded himself that the contraption was a *regulator*, the only thing standing between him and drowning on each subsurface foray.

Before arriving in Mexico, Sterling had never gone scuba diving in his life—and after the past five days of training, he realized he wasn't missing out.

Everything he'd ever heard about the freedom of wafting about beneath the ocean's surface had proven itself to be one massive fabrication of the uncomfortable reality. Humans were meant to exist on dry land for good reason, he'd learned, and violating that natural order required an obscene amount of equipment and training before one could go about spitting in the face of evolution without consequence.

Grasping the ladder with one hand, he stripped off his fins one at a time, threading the ankle straps around each wrist. Then he ascended, nearly losing his grip as the boat crested sideways with the current. As he cleared the water, he felt the weight of his gear return in full, threatening to drag him back into the ocean that he had been desperate to leave during almost every moment of his training to date.

Sterling clambered atop the deck, advancing a safe distance from the ladder before he dared pull the regulator from his mouth. Letting it hang from its air hose, he took a seat and dropped his fins to the deck, then yanked off his dive mask and snorkel.

Blair, in the process of removing her gear beside him, called out, "This is incredible, isn't it? The sun, the surf—can you imagine living like this, without the fear of being arrested or hunted down by a lunatic like Shedo?"

Sterling panted for breath, mercifully without the interference of the eerie regulator valve creating a Darth Vader-like soundtrack to his trying not to die while supplying his lungs with life-giving air.

"Having been arrested as well as hunted by Shedo," he replied, "I can attest that either or both are preferable to scuba-dying."

"Stop, you're doing fine."

"Easy for you to say—you're actually good at this."

"I've dived before. You haven't." Then, with this consolation complete, her voice lapsed into near-ecstasy. "Did you see those fish? The rays of sun shimmering down? It was, I mean this whole thing is..." She gasped, "Incredible."

Sterling didn't respond, turning his attention to the uncomfortable process of stripping off the mess of gear clinging to his body.

First came the pile of junk that Esther cordially referred to as "hard equipment," scuba-specific gear that started with an impossibly heavy aluminum cylinder filled with high-pressure air. After setting down his cylinder, Sterling arranged the spider-like system of attached hoses, careful not to bang the pressure gauge that showed air remaining—and Sterling consumed this precious gas at approximately twice the speed of anyone else except for perhaps Marco, who was of sound mind and therefore almost as uncomfortable underwater—along with a low-pressure inflator hose linked to the most dreaded item of the entire setup, the BCD.

This acronym stood for buoyancy control device, a polite term for a smothering vest that he stripped off his torso next. It could be inflated or deflated as needed to neutralize the difference between a weight belt dragging you down and wetsuit material filled with tiny air bubbles that tried to lift you to the surface. While that dilemma should be enough to convince any sane person to simply enjoy the view from the beach, the BCD allowed a complete defilement of the natural order in letting the user establish neutral buoyancy, a state purported to be a certain type of weightless freedom that was actually a supremely awkward suspension that brought with it, in Sterling's experience to date, a sensation of desperately wanting to return to the surface.

Then he set to work on his "soft equipment," which could serve double duty for snorkeling. He undid his nylon belt, whose lead weights thudded to the deck as he set it down. Fumbling behind his neck, he found the long lanyard for his zipper and pulled it down his back, breaking the seal of the neoprene wetsuit that felt about as comfortable as being shrink-wrapped by cellophane.

As he struggled to peel the suit from his body, he said, "I'll tell you what. If we retire—"

"When we retire," Blair corrected him, already down to her bathing suit.

"—you can dive all day. I'll be perfectly happy waiting on the boat with a cooler of beer, processing oxygen into carbon dioxide without a thousand dollars' worth of life support equipment that could fail at any moment."

"People do this every day."

Sterling finally freed both arms, then pulled the wetsuit down to his ankles.

"People also smoke crack every day," he noted, "but that's not something I'd want to tangle with. This is a whole lot of trouble for a stupid bronze dragon."

Her eyes lit up.

"We should try skydiving next."

"You're crazy," he said, pulling her in for a salty kiss. "That's what I love about you."

He quickly broke the embrace at the sound of a splash by the ladder, looking over to see Marco climbing up and staggering onto the deck like a waterlogged drunkard.

Spitting out the regulator and peeling the mask from his face, he blinked and managed, "This sucks."

"I know," Sterling replied.

Alec was next up, looking considerably more composed—at least, until the boat rocked in a wave and he almost lost his grip on the ladder.

Esther followed quickly behind him, pulling herself onto the boat with twice the ease of anyone from Sterling's crew. She moved like this was all second nature to her, as if the insane burden of scuba equipment were nothing more than an extension of her body.

As the last three aboard began stripping their equipment, Alec released a whooping victory cry and shouted, "This is awesome! Why haven't we been doing this for years?"

Sterling ignored him, instead kneeling to arrange his dive equipment in the orientation that Esther demanded. When no one else replied either, Alec's shoulders sagged and he admitted, "I almost lost a flipper climbing the ladder, though."

Esther chided, "Flipper is a dolphin—you almost lost a *fin*, and if you'd fallen back in the water, that would mean someone else would have to save you."

He straightened.

"As long as it was you, Esther, I'd cherish the moment."

She replied not to him, but to the group as a whole. "All right, I've seen enough to issue assignments."

She looked directly at Sterling. "Your natural athleticism is incredible.

What you accomplished jumping onto the Sky Safe alone...truly, a historic achievement."

"Thank you—"

"But under the surface, you flail about like a deranged porpoise. It's like you're incapable of moving in a straight line. Your swimming is so...cattywampus."

"What does that mean?"

"Askew," Alec supplied. "In disorder, or disarray. It's one of my favorite pieces of grand nineteenth-century American slang, second only to 'kerfuffle.' Well done, Esther."

She concluded, "Some people are cut out for diving; Sterling, you are not."

He felt crestfallen at the admonition, though not surprised.

Alec said, "I think that's a little harsh, Esther. His ego is fragile—go easy on the poor lad."

"That was me going easy," she responded. "And Alec, it pains me to say this for fear that you will take it as more of a compliment than I intend, but you're something of a natural."

The safecracker fixed her with an erotic stare as he used one hand to provocatively slide his wetsuit's zipper lanyard downward.

Ignoring the overture, Esther looked at Blair. "As for you, your previous diving experience shines."

Blair gave a humble nod.

Then Esther turned and went on, "Marco, you also suck. Bad. There's hacking and there's diving, and you're only suited for one of them."

"Point taken," Marco said, "and I offer no defense."

Running both hands through her sopping hair, Esther announced, "We don't have much time remaining for specialized training, and most of that will be taken up by working with the Pruitts. So here is what's going to happen. Alec, Blair, you're our deep team."

The two exchanged a high five.

"Sterling, you're going to need adult supervision. I'll be with you on the shallow team."

Marco snorted.

"Don't laugh," she said to him, "you're training for the same thing. We'll start rebreathers tomorrow."

Marco objected, "I thought I was driving the chase boat."

"In the best-case scenario," Esther replied, "you will be. But we need flexibility in case there is a dive injury in the next nine days of training— carbon dioxide poisoning, burst eardrum, air embolism, anything that prevents someone from diving. In that event they will operate the boat, and since I can switch between deep and shallow teams if needed, we'll still be able to man both elements."

Then she checked her watch and said, "We've got one hour before we can dive again. Let's eat some lunch."

34

BLAIR

Blair carried the heavy duffel bag into Esther's front yard, squinting against the morning sun on her way to the box truck.

Alec was in the process of depositing two kit bags into the open cargo area and Blair followed suit, hearing the refilled canisters clanking against the truck bed. Marco stood inside, taking hold of her duffel and sliding it next to the rest of the dive equipment with a gloomy expression.

Blair tried to cheer him up, offering, "I'm excited about this, aren't you?"

Turning to face her, Marco put his hands on his hips.

"Adding another ten levels of complexity to an op that already has more potential points of failure than anything we've ever done? No, Blair, I don't think 'excited' is the appropriate term to describe how I feel."

Sterling spoke beside her, straining to lift another gear bag aboard.

"I concur," he said, "one hundred percent. Diving is bad enough, and what we're about to do...well, let's just say I wasn't hungry for breakfast."

Alec was in a much better mood, speaking excitedly as he approached with the final two bags of dive gear.

"She should be back any minute. That means T-minus a couple hours until we get to see Esther in a wetsuit. I don't care how dangerous this stuff is, it's worth the risk."

Blair heard the electric gate buzz open before anyone had a chance to respond, and she turned to see Esther's quad-cab pickup roll past the perimeter fence. It was a hulking Dodge diesel with California plates, a nice touch that eased Esther's frequent trips across the US border—but Blair's attention was drawn not to the vehicle but rather the long trailer it now towed.

Esther stopped the truck as the gate closed to seal the courtyard from outside view and exited a moment later, dressed in jeans and a plain T-shirt. Blair didn't think she'd seen the woman wear a hint of makeup outside of her disguises, though that did little to affect her natural beauty. She threw her arms skyward, belting a victory whoop on her way to the trailer doors.

Blair strode toward her and asked, "I take that to mean there weren't any issues with the sale?"

"The only issue," Esther replied, hastily unlocking the trailer doors, "is that I've always wanted one of these and never had an excuse to buy. Now, I have two."

She swung the doors open triumphantly and stepped aside. "Blair, you're a fellow pilot. Get in there and check them out."

Blair reluctantly climbed inside the trailer, taking in the contents with a conflicted sense of amusement. She wasn't sure what she expected to see— her crew had been too preoccupied with operational planning to do much in the way of research during Esther's round trip to San Diego to recover the latest purchases—but the trailer's interior left her unsure whether to laugh or feel intimidated.

The two gray submersibles looked part aircraft and part shark, with ten-foot-long torpedo-shaped hulls tapering to a trio of tail fins at the rear of the trailer. Blair turned sideways to shuffle between them, noting the transparent canopies covered a pilot seat toward the nose, with an additional passenger chair directly behind in the manner of a two-seater fighter jet. Just forward of the midpoint were a pair of stubby wings ending in propeller assemblies.

She turned to see her crew clustered outside the trailer, peering inside as Esther began her brief.

"Sky Thieves, meet the Pruitt Industries Substar IV with twin-diver capacity. Two-time champion of the biennial International Submarine Races at Bethesda with multiple innovation awards."

Sterling and Marco said nothing; Alec began a slow clap, though his eyes were on Esther rather than the submersibles.

Esther continued, "Maneuverability is accomplished through independently rotating propellers, enabling it to rotate in all three axes like an aircraft—pitch, roll, and yaw—as well as to ascend or descend vertically. Backward movement is possible at a reduced speed."

Sterling pointed to the clear canopies. "I thought we were getting wet subs—what's with the lids?"

Esther climbed into the trailer and reached for a handle beneath one of the windshields, pulling it to lift the clear assembly up six inches before sliding it back toward the tail to expose the two seats.

"The lightweight acrylic canopy is there to reduce drag, not keep the water out. The cabin is meant to flood, so we'll still be relying on our scuba equipment to breathe. Not only are wet subs much lower-profile to acquire on the commercial market, they're lightweight as well. With the full carbon fiber hull, each unit is 152 pounds, making it a two-person lift to slide into or out of the water."

Marco looked unimpressed.

"Is there a power source, or are we pedaling these things like a paddle boat?"

"Electric motors powered by two rechargeable batteries, with a maximum speed of six knots. Endurance is three to four hours of continuous operation depending on speed. And since we can store additional cylinders on board, our air supply won't be limited as severely as a normal dive."

Blair scanned the open cockpit, trying to analyze the dual joysticks and array of controls. "Are they hard to drive?"

"To drive? No. To pilot? Well, achieving proficiency will take all the time we have remaining. In addition to all the requirements of scuba diving, these add the complications of three-dimensional navigation, buoyancy adjustment, and depth control. And dismounting one underwater requires finesse, to say the least—just because you've got the sub neutrally buoyant doesn't mean you will be. Try to set off without adjusting your BCD first, and you could either rocket to the surface or plummet like a brick. That means the risks of every dive injury go up exponentially: air embolism, nitrogen narcosis, oxygen toxicity, ruptured lungs—"

"We get it." Sterling ended the seemingly never-ending list of dive-related medical issues that Esther loved to rattle off at the slightest provocation. "And I'm thrilled about this, just so you know. Since scuba diving isn't hard enough already."

"Relax, you won't even have to dive off it. You've got the easiest role of anyone."

She looked from Blair to Alec and continued, "The deep team, on the other hand, will have to learn these very quickly if we're going to pull this off."

"We'll pull it off," Blair said confidently, rubbing a hand on the carbon fiber nose of the nearest sub. "If it's anything like flying a drone, I'll be piloting it well in no time. And Alec's trying to impress you, so not even he will screw this up."

Alec nodded. "She's not wrong. And you will be impressed, Esther, if it's the last thing I do."

"Let's hope it doesn't come to that," Esther remarked. "Now let's get to the cove to break these in—we've only got a week before we depart for Washington. Then the bronze dragon is as good as ours, Shedo will be on the fast track to a jail cell, and we can end this nightmare for good."

35

STERLING

Lake Washington was a far cry from the crystal waters of the Mexican Pacific; the view through Sterling's dive mask, beyond the sub's transparent canopy, revealed a murky world of green extending to distant sunlight overhead. And right now, he would have given anything for the water to be even murkier.

If regular scuba diving was a train ride of discomfort, then riding a wet sub was a rollercoaster of it.

Granted, the acrylic canopy somewhat blocked the sensation of blasting through the water, which was a good thing, because at their current speed, he was afraid the regulator would be ripped from his mouth. But there was no way to disguise their speed relative to everything they passed, whether the underside of the many boat hulls overhead, the occasional school of fish, or litter; Sterling had been momentarily awestruck by the sight of a majestic jellyfish, only to realize it was a plastic shopping bag a moment before it whipped out of sight, lost from view as Esther sped them forward at full throttle.

She was seated directly to his front, piloting the newly christened *HMS Cattywampus* as Sterling straddled the backside. It was about as awkward as riding on Alec's ATV and twice as demeaning, occurring as it was in the terrifying depths whose only consolation was that his oxygen wasn't in any danger of running out—in fact, he could remain underwater far longer than usual, courtesy of the closed-circuit diving gear he now wore. Its mouthpiece was just as uncomfortable as a normal scuba rig, but that was where the similarities ended.

Instead of a single narrow hose, the mouthpiece had wide dual hoses extending from either side. Right now Sterling and Esther looked like combat divers, in large part because they were using the same style of rebreather systems rather than standard scuba gear. The downside was that they couldn't go as deep—anything more than thirty feet would present an exponential risk of dive injuries—but on the plus side, their exhaled breath passed through a carbon dioxide scrubber to filter the remaining oxygen, eliminating any stream of bubbles and allowing them to close with the yacht undetected.

Esther transmitted, *"You doing okay back there?"*

Her voice was disjointed, a side effect of the science behind underwater communication. With a regulator blocking any ability to speak normally, the crew now relied upon bone-conduction microphones that transmitted via ultrasound, converting the speech into reasonably decipherable audio that played out over the receiver's bone-conducting speaker. The result was a slight buzzing sensation from the pocket-sized device attached to Sterling's mask strap.

"Yeah," he replied, "strapped to a death rocket barreling through a watery grave. What's not to like?"

"We're just cruising. This is *barreling."*

Sterling had just enough time to brace himself against the seat as Esther whipped the sub in a counterclockwise barrel roll that lasted for one rotation, then two, before his composure folded.

"All right, all right, I get it. Please stop."

The sub leveled out, and Sterling adjusted the tremendously bulky satchel slung around his neck and over one shoulder.

"Just trying to be specific," Esther transmitted, her voice rattling against his skull.

The downside to all this cutting-edge communications technology was its range. Sterling and Esther could hear each other just fine—regrettably, perhaps, given that anything he said caused his pilot to complete some gut-churning underwater maneuver—but neither could communicate with Blair and Alec aboard the other sub.

They'd had to rely on a surface station to bridge the gap, a solution made possible by the use of a chase boat providing the only unified communications of this entire op. Marco was the only person aboard, currently under the guise of a recreational boater enjoying the Pacific Northwest scenery. In reality he'd lowered a powerful data signal processing unit below the surface via a length of submerged transducer cable, and currently manned a radio unit with a panel speaker that allowed him to hear and communicate with both the shallow and deep teams.

Marco transmitted the next update, giving Sterling some hope that they could finally get this over with.

"*Shedo's yacht is departing the dock*. HMS Cattywampus, *move to loitering position in Union Bay.*"

Sterling felt the sub pivot into a sharp right turn as Esther replied.

"*Two minutes out. You're sure she's on board?*"

Marco answered, "*Positive. I'm watching the remote feed and she's on the deck right now. The time lock on her safe was activated fifteen minutes ago. We are clear to proceed.*"

He could make out a row of concrete pontoons ahead as Esther carved a right-hand turn to parallel them; they extended to the limits of his forward visibility, blocking out the sunlight in a neat bar that represented Evergreen Point Floating Bridge, the longest such bridge anywhere in the world. At nearly a mile and a half long, the structure carried six lanes of State Route 520 from Shedo's ultrarich town of Medina across Lake Washington and into Seattle. For Esther and Sterling, however, the bridge represented the best navigational aid to enter Union Bay, the first chokepoint in a maritime crossing to the Puget Sound and, ultimately, the Pacific.

They'd barely had time to complete the turn and follow the bridge into Union Bay before Marco sent his next update.

"*Yacht is passing under Evergreen Point Floating Bridge at the east navigation channel.*"

Esther transmitted, "HMS Cattywampus *is in Union Bay, entering loiter pattern north of Marsh Island.*"

The radio call provided an update to him as much as Marco; absent any visual landmarks like the bridge, Sterling had relatively little bearing on his actual location. That information was Esther's purview; she was monitoring navigation with the help of a GPS display mounted between her twin joysticks along with a compass, depth gauge, and buoyancy controls. But he knew that Marsh Island was the final piece of land prior to the inlet of Montlake Cut, and he watched the undersides of boats passing by just under thirty feet overhead, mostly smaller recreational vessels whose occupants were completely unaware of the wet sub drifting through the gloomy water beneath their hulls.

Clutching his satchel, Sterling adjusted the wrist cuffs of his wetsuit to ensure they wouldn't interfere with his upcoming action, the sole contribution he'd be making to this little foray against Kristen Shedo.

As they circled the wet sub, he heard Marco's next update.

"Yacht is passing Webster Point, entering Union Bay. Stand by for visual."

Sterling felt the sub bank into a hard right turn and then level out, presumably headed eastward to locate the target vessel, though he didn't bother to check his compass. Instead he scanned through the acrylic canopy overhead, his gaze darting across the boat hulls until he found what he was looking for.

Shedo's yacht wasn't hard to spot.

He'd studied its profile along with his crew, searing it into his memory until he could distinguish it from dozens of similar yachts, much less other watercraft. But upon seeing it in person, he realized that preparation had been unnecessary.

The 130-foot superyacht was like a long bullet searing across the surface, dwarfing every other boat in its proximity as it headed westward toward the entrance to Montlake Cut, where Esther and Sterling were waiting to intercept it. Because for all the speed the yacht was capable of, it would count for nothing when all boat traffic was restricted to glacially slow movement in the 100-foot-wide center channel stretching to the next bay.

Esther flipped the sub sideways, carving a hard left turn until their heading matched the yacht's before leveling out and transmitting to Marco.

"HMS Cattywampus *has visual and is in pursuit, bearing two-seven-zero into Montlake Cut."*

"Copy two-seven-zero, be advised Queen Blair's Revenge *is awaiting visual in Portage Bay."*

Sterling was amused by the choice of title for the deep team's submersible, an Alec-derived play on the flagship name of his favorite pirate, Blackbeard.

"Understood," Esther confirmed, then said to Sterling, *"I'm going to get us through the wake and climb to depth two-zero. Get ready."*

"I am," he replied, barely finishing his transmission before he felt the sub shudder hard as it passed through the wake created by the massive vessel overhead. Esther powered through the turbulence before ascending, and Sterling could see her leveling out directly beneath the yacht's stern as she transmitted again.

"Depth one-five, will be eyeballing it from here on out."

"Opening canopy," Sterling answered, pulling the handle beside him and then planting his hands on the acrylic ceiling to force the shield up from its locked position. Then he shoved it backward, working hand over hand until it was fully retracted and the current flowed freely over his dive mask. The increased drag negatively impacted their speed—yet another reason they needed to get this done before the channel ended and the yacht accelerated once more—and he felt the vibration of the sub's propellers increase as Esther counteracted the effect with more power.

They'd practiced this maneuver on many unsuspecting vessels in their Mexico training areas, but doing it in Washington was a whole different equation. Looking up, Sterling saw the hull of Shedo's yacht looming so close he could almost reach up and touch it, which was exactly what he was about to do.

"Forward one-zero feet," Sterling said, analyzing the hull overhead. It bore precious few visual references for him to work off of, though the largest—a series of vertical slats extending from either side—were fast approaching as Esther accelerated.

Unzipping his satchel, Sterling dipped his hands inside and grabbed the single item within.

The limpet mine was enormous, containing a significant amount of explosives encased in excess metal to attain negative buoyancy. Because while the "boom" would happen either way, Sterling would be in a world of hurt if he lost his grip on the gigantic mine and it went floating up to the surface rather than down into his hands.

Shedo's superyacht had what was known as a planing hull, which carried a significant benefit in terms of speed. On transoceanic crossings, this type of hull, along with a correspondingly impressive powerplant, allowed the captain to escape bad weather in remarkably quick fashion.

But Sterling's present concern was the shape of the planing hull itself, which crested into an inverted V-shaped pinnacle he now coasted beneath. A full 35 percent of the hull volume adjoined the engine room, and while that served as a testament to the yacht's speed capabilities, it presented the disastrous possibility of a miscalculation on his part.

Esther transmitted, *"We're passing under the bridge—hurry up."*

"Forward five feet," he replied, cursing under his breath. Montlake Bridge was located roughly halfway down the canal, and he was almost in disbelief that they'd reached it already. If he didn't get the mine planted now, they'd lose the yacht for good.

But precise placement was key—while Shedo's safe had a time lock that in theory rendered it unopenable for another six hours, when the superyacht would be well into international waters, they couldn't rule out her use of a master-override code. Their goal now was to flood the room as quickly as possible, rendering it inaccessible for anyone aboard to enter much less manipulate the safe.

There was a second requirement for the precisely calculated point, this one arguably more important: to create a hole for Alec to swim through. While limpet mines were devastatingly effective at creating holes through which seawater would flood and cause a vessel to sink, there was precious little way to predict *which way* the boat would lean once that occurred. By placing the limpet mine on the edge of the V-shaped hull beneath the safe, the ensuing demolition would—at least per the crew's best collective calculations—shear a neat hole that would remain accessible from an approach along the ocean floor no matter which way the superyacht settled.

"Forward three feet," he transmitted, readying the mine in his grasp with the magnetic side facing up. "Hold here."

This was the most delicate part of the entire operation. They'd established in training that Sterling's maximum reach was just inches beyond the top of the sub's tail fin when it was moving levelly forward. If he rose too high, the water flow could yank him out of the sub; if he didn't rise high enough, Esther could clip the tail fin into the hull and send the sub spiraling into the superyacht's wake.

He lifted the mine upward, struggling to brace his back against the seat as he shimmied upward.

"Up six inches...three..."

The mine was so close he could almost feel the magnet pulling it toward the hull.

"Two more inches," he gasped.

"*I can't get any closer*," Esther replied. "*We're going to clip it.*"

With a frustrated grunt, Sterling shoved off his heels to cover the remaining distance, feeling the mine slip from his grasp completely.

For a fleeting second, he thought he was going to catch a glimpse of it spinning like a Frisbee through the water, an explosive charge left to descend toward the bottom of Montlake Cut, never to be seen again.

But his feverish glance upward revealed that it had left his hands on account of the magnetic pull, and was securely clamped against the side of the hull.

"Package away," he transmitted, doing the best he could to pull himself down into his seat before the flow of water forced him out.

"*Diving to depth two-zero*," Esther replied, guiding the sub downward and sideways as Sterling readied himself for the inevitable. She pushed the sub to full throttle, but it did little good—the craft was buffeted by the wake of the yacht's powerful engines spooling to increased power as the yacht soared overhead and out of the canal.

With the canopy open, the sudden influx of water yawed the sub into a violent sideways drift as Esther fought to maintain heading. The sudden lurch was nauseating, and Sterling envisioned his vessel slamming into the bottom until it finally leveled out and resumed forward movement.

Esther transmitted, "*Marco, this is* HMS Cattywampus. *Package is in position, we are clear to proceed, please relay.*"

Marco's reply was smugly confident.

"*Copy package is in position, Shedo's yacht is proceeding into Portage Bay. I have control, estimate three minutes to detonation.*"

36

KRISTEN

Kristen Shedo leaned against the rail at the stern of her yacht, continuing to survey the Lake Washington Ship Canal.

There were two typical options for a yacht owner taking to the waters.

The first, and by far the most common, was to remain inside a personal stateroom until any risk of being photographed by gobsmacked bystanders and paparazzi dissipated, and only then take to the deck. To Kristen, this was sheer cowardice; if they wanted to photograph her, she thought, then let them. It wasn't as if she were strutting about in a bikini, not that the view wouldn't be excellent for anyone who saw her. She was merely standing at the rail in a red strapless jumpsuit, her Saint Laurent Loulou bag faithfully draped across one shoulder.

A second choice would be to stand at the bow, but she considered that an even more distasteful option than taking the reclusive route. The true inspiration of sailing wasn't in the new horizons, it was in viewing the final glimpses of the shores one was leaving behind, a last reminder of the familiar before the view shifted to a foreign landscape.

She enjoyed surveying Seattle from the stern during her departures. For one thing, this city was her home, and for another, her only view for the foreseeable future would be of the open ocean.

University Bridge flew by overhead like a glorious hawk soaring through the sky. There was a sense of acceleration from looking backward and seeing the sudden emergence of overhead structures at the top of her field of view and, considering the rectangular stone support pillars, to the sides as well. It was like slipping through a portal into the unknown, something that the forward-looking yacht owners would never know, and she relished repeating the process as the yacht carefully turned southwest toward Ship Canal Bridge.

Kristen had specifically chosen this yacht for its relatively low profile; while many of her counterparts had to fly to coastal locations to board their tri-deck monstrosities, she was able to summon her boat to the dock at her personal residence, step aboard after the staff had shuttled her bags, and set sail with adequate clearance to pass beneath every bridge between her and the Pacific Ocean.

She felt a thudding reverberation along the railing like a car backfiring —could yacht engines backfire?—but the sensation dissipated as quickly as she'd detected it. As she resumed her view off the stern, the boat's loudspeakers came to life with a man's voice.

"Attention all, attention all—abandon ship. All crew and guests go to muster stations; I repeat, all crew and guests go to muster stations. Abandon ship."

A high-pitched siren blared, increasing in frequency until cutting off. Then the signal repeated, and Kristen, annoyed in the extreme, turned to face the deck where her lead bodyguard was racing toward her with a pair of lifejackets in one hand and what looked like two orange flotation suits in the other.

She called out loud enough to be heard over the siren, "I didn't know we had a drill scheduled."

"We don't," he said, skidding to a stop and holding the items out to her. "This is really happening."

Despite her disbelief, she indeed felt the yacht slowing to a stop as two crew members raced to the rail beside her. They opened a deck compartment to reveal a large white case that they hoisted between them, then hurled off the rail. Two white ropes trailed the case as it hit the water, exploding into two pieces as a life raft unfurled and inflated.

Scoffing, she asked her bodyguard, "What did they do, hit an iceberg? It's May, for God's sake."

"Something hit us, ma'am, possibly a torpedo. I need you to put on your immersion suit and lifejacket."

"I'm not putting those on, and neither are you."

"Ms. Shedo, we've been over this—"

"Don't be ridiculous," she shot back, stabbing an arm off the side of the boat. "We could swim to shore from here. And before we go, I'll need to recover some things from my stateroom."

"Your stateroom is taking on water; we can't even get down the stairwell. The captain says we'll sink in fifteen minutes or less."

Kristen Shedo considered this information, wondering who would dare attack her yacht—she'd accrued many enemies over the years who would love to publicly humiliate her in full view of the city shoreline. Whoever it was, she decided, they would pay dearly for the transgression.

Indeed, she could already feel the yacht slipping downward, the water rising ever so steadily toward the rail. As the siren blasted its repetitive cry, she saw the crew members at their muster stations, hastily donning full-body immersion suits. They were quickly turning into blaze-orange marshmallow monsters, going so far as to pull the neoprene hoods over their heads before slipping into life jackets as they went through the ministrations of their carefully rehearsed emergency procedures. On the open sea, the sight would have been comforting, but with a visible shoreline two hundred feet off either side of the yacht, this was an embarrassment to say the least.

"Very well," she said to her lead bodyguard, adjusting the Saint Laurent bag over her shoulder. She could already feel the tumult of a wounded ego taking over, and it was with a deep and unhindered measure of anger in her voice that she concluded, "The raft it is."

And while she still didn't don the ridiculous immersion suit or life-jacket, she allowed her bodyguard to escort her to the rear ladder, where the crew was pulling at the white ropes tethering the life raft, now a fully inflated hexagon with an orange tent roof. Kristen descended the ladder and easily set foot into the wobbling raft through its tent opening, turning to see her bodyguard board behind her.

Then crew members began piling in, one tumbling mass of immersion suit-clad bodies carrying yellow grab bags of survival gear. She pushed past them to reach the tent flap and bear witness to what was happening outside —her yacht was sinking more quickly now, the stern rapidly dipping toward the surface as any remaining crew members and security staff leapt off the sides and swam toward one of the two life rafts bobbing beside her former boat.

And "former" was the correct term, she decided at once.

The ladder she'd just departed was already dipping out of sight as the emergency siren continued to blare, becoming a distorted warble as the bow tilted upward and water rushed over the rear deck.

37

BLAIR

Blair increased the throttle of her wet sub as Shedo's yacht slipped into the depths.

Alec transmitted from the passenger seat, *"She's listing to port; looks like we'll have to approach from the north."*

He wasn't wrong, she thought—at least, not yet.

The vessel was indeed tilting to its left side as it plunged downward, but that didn't mean it would continue to do so. The internal flooding was continuously shifting the yacht's center of gravity, and while they expected it to descend more or less vertically before settling on one side or the other in the shallow water, the erratic torrents of bubbles streaming from the deck-level doors in wavy patterns indicated an erratic and volatile descent. She concluded they'd underestimated the effect of the planing hull, which favored speed over stability, and decided that there would be no way to determine the yacht's final orientation until it had reached the bottom.

Above it she could make out the silhouettes of bobbing life rafts, counting three before refocusing on the yacht. Its highest point—at the moment, the edge of the starboard deck rail—finally slipped beneath her current depth, forcing her to use the columns of air bubbles to orient her approach.

"Descending to depth two-five," she transmitted for Marco's benefit, seeing

that the gush of bubbles was beginning to trickle off to nothing. On one hand, that was a good thing—the faster this sunk, the faster they could leave—but on the other, it meant that the yacht was about to become indistinguishable amid the water's murky depths.

Blair pressed a button on her right joystick, activating a floodlight that blasted a dazzling blade of light at a 45-degree angle downward from the sub's nose. She pivoted the craft accordingly, sweeping the 6,000 lumen beam left and right in an attempt to locate the downed vessel.

But her first glimpse of the now-grounded ship revealed that it hadn't tilted to one side or the other at all. Instead it had settled more or less upright, albeit with the weight of its engine anchoring the stern as a majority of the remaining hull was suspended in a precarious upward angle.

Sweeping her sub around the starboard side, she angled her spotlight over the hole created by the limpet mine, seeing that it would provide sufficient space to enter. From the looks of it, Sterling's placement had been spot-on, though only Alec's upcoming effort would tell for sure.

He transmitted, "*Guess I was wrong about her listing to port. Drop me off as close as you can.*"

Blair guided the wet sub down and forward as she provided proximity updates for the safecracker behind her, whose view was obscured by her body in the pilot seat.

"Thirty feet...twenty-five...twenty..."

This was where things became dicey—the sub could certainly be piloted with precision, but only within a margin of error that accounted for the current tides at depth. She pulled back on the throttle, entering into an underwater hover that she deemed to be the limit of advance given the required control inputs against the flow of water swirling around the sub and the fact that her stability would decrease once the canopy was open. Blair was about to transmit that she'd reached her stopping point fifteen feet off the hull when Alec spared her the trouble.

"*Hold, hold. Opening canopy,*" he announced, and a moment later Blair saw the acrylic shield lift upward, then slide back and out of view.

At this point her hands were maneuvering the joysticks in small jiggling motions to counteract the flow of water in the open cabin, performing a series of continual micro-adjustments to hold the craft as stationary as she could. She felt Alec pulling himself upward, followed by the scrape of his fins on her back as he floated free.

Blair saw him a moment later cresting overhead in a wetsuit and scuba gear with his satchel of safecracking equipment. Then he kicked his fins and began swimming as she transmitted to Marco, "*Alec away.*"

She glided the sub backward and then ascended, working the controls to keep her spotlight centered as the aquatic safecracker approached the hole. Alec activated his own headlamp and transmitted his first message since departing.

"*Five feet out.*"

His next words came as he reached the blast site, where Blair could see him grasping at the edges of the hole.

"*Going internal—*"

The rest of his message was cut short as he disappeared through the gap in the hull and she lost reception. Not even Marco would be able to hear him now: the yacht would block all further transmissions.

She said, "Alec is inside—start the clock."

"*Copy,*" Marco replied, "*clock is running.*"

The confirmation was necessary for reasons that Blair didn't want to contemplate at present—namely, that the risks inherent in diving inside a wrecked vessel were so multitudinous that the crew had to establish hard timelines in advance based on Alec's available air supply, as well as the sub's remaining battery charge and thus range, to account for the fact that he may not be coming out alive. In the perilous realm of wreck diving, it was entirely possible for an otherwise manageable underwater emergency to turn fatal at the slightest complication, and for the first time in her history with the Sky Thieves, Blair faced the very real possibility of having to leave a dead teammate behind if Marco's timing dictated it necessary.

She banished the thought from her mind, and instead initiated her prearranged course of action.

Steering the sub in a narrow orbit around the yacht, Blair gradually increased the diameter of her circles to orient herself to the bridge pillars along her departure route. Anyone looking for submersibles would expect them to egress to the west and into the vast expanse of the Puget Sound and its labyrinth of attached waterways, and thus her crew would do no such thing. She identified the columns of University Bridge to her east, then narrowed her range until her spotlight once again illuminated the edges of Shedo's yacht. Absent any ability to communicate, she had no idea of knowing where Alec was in the safecracking process—at least, until a sharp blaze of fire flickered through the hole.

That was, she knew, the detonation of Alec's "jam shots," a process of blasting a safe's door off the hinges that he'd modified for underwater use by replacing the standard nitroglycerine with C4. It wasn't the most subtle means of penetrating a safe, but it was the fastest, and right now, speed was all that mattered.

Bubbles surged from the hole, followed by a wispy tendril of black debris that drifted toward the surface. Blair repositioned for Alec's pickup, first circling to his drop-off point and then holding the sub as stationary as possible, with her light angled away from the hole to provide Alec a beacon to follow without blinding him.

She felt her throat constricting with each moment that passed without him emerging, and tried to assure herself that the initial jam shot was just the first step in breaching the safe—depending on its effectiveness, he may well have to conduct another demolition shot with his remaining C4, to say nothing of using a pry bar to wrestle the door away from the main body of the safe.

Blair had an almost dizzying wave of relief when Alec's personal headlamp illuminated the hole from within and he drifted upward while adjusting his buoyancy. Then he began his swim back to the sub.

She transmitted, "Alec is out, Alec is out. He's swimming strong, looks uninjured, stand by for pickup confirmation."

"*Standing by,*" Marco confirmed.

As Alec covered the remaining distance to the open cabin, Blair glanced at her compass to confirm her orientation, preparing to make the quickest possible turn to their departure heading.

The wait for Alec's verbal update was unbearable, but she knew that wouldn't come until he was safely inside the sub. Transmitting through a regulator when you were seated in the wet sub with relatively normal blood pressure was one thing, but Alec had just swum inside the yacht and, she hoped, conducted a successful breach of the safe before initiating his return trip with the bronze dragon. Any of those acts taken by themselves would make breathing difficult, and on top of it all he now faced the exhausting final sprint of swimming back to the sub.

He reached the vessel a moment later, grasping the side of the cabin before awkwardly clambering in behind her, the kick of his fins and force of his body causing the sub to rock slightly as Blair fought to hold it steady. She extinguished her spotlight but made no move to depart, waiting instead to hear Alec manage, in a strained, breathless voice, *"Closing canopy."*

The acrylic hood slid back into view, locking into place and sealing the cabin. Blair immediately moved both joysticks in opposite directions with fluid efficiency, pivoting the sub to its departure azimuth and accelerating the throttle as she transmitted.

"Alec recovered, *Queen Blair's Revenge* is outbound on primary route."

She waited until she'd glided past the squat columns of University Bridge before speaking again. "Climbing to depth two-zero, crossing Portage Bay en route to Montlake Cut."

"Status?" Marco asked.

Alec's response was a gasping effort to speak between breaths. *"No joy."*

Blair felt like she'd been punched in the gut.

She asked, "No joy as in no dragon? What did you get?"

"No joy," he croaked, *"any way you want to take it. The dragon wasn't there, and..."* He panted another breath before continuing, *"Neither was anything else. The safe was empty."*

38

STERLING

Marco's eyes were riveted to the screen as he noted, "It looks like you were diving in a haunted house."

To be fair, Sterling thought, the crew's hacker wasn't exaggerating. He continued watching the footage playing out on the laptop, huddled alongside his crew to view the eerie effect of a single disc of light gliding across glowing particles of silt before illuminating the surfaces of a recently flooded stateroom as they viewed Alec's first-person footage from the dive.

Casting a raised eyebrow over his shoulder, Alec said, "Felt like a haunted house, too. But despite the fact that plunging into Shedo's yacht was a highly dangerous and potentially fatal endeavor, I recalled the memory of Blackbeard, cast aside my fears, and drove onward in spite of the fear settling in my belly like a lead weight, drawing upon the deepest reserves of my courage to continue the mission and—"

"You can stop," Blair said flatly. "Esther isn't here yet."

Alec looked over his shoulder in one direction, then the other, confirming that his love interest was indeed not present among the thieves clustered in the dining room.

Then he gave an ambivalent shrug and mumbled, "Anyway, the safe was empty. You'll see in a second."

Sterling focused on the screen, which now presented a view of Alec's neoprene-clad hands executing a jam shot emplacement with C4 before the view rapidly retreated to a covered position behind a wall in the richly appointed stateroom.

The screen vibrated with a long shudder that barely began receding before Alec swam back to the safe, his floodlight assuming the same eerie glow effect on the yacht interior before settling on the partially ajar safe door. He used a pry bar to wrench it away, shining his light inside the safe for a mere second or two before turning away and departing the vessel.

"Hang on," Sterling said, "go back."

Alec groaned. "Why, Sterling, why?"

"Because I want to see it again."

With an exasperated huff, Alec swatted Marco's hand away from the computer mouse and took control himself, rewinding and slowing the footage to quarter-speed before hitting play.

The safe's interior was empty, confirmed by Alec's spotlight moving to the top left before cutting horizontally to the opposite corner, then performing a downward zigzag pattern until it cleared the entire safe.

It was a barren box just as the safecracker had said, an unsettling fact confirmed only after traveling for 1,300 miles from the Baja Peninsula to Seattle, a journey that turned out to have been for absolutely nothing.

Blair said, "Maybe she didn't bring the dragon with her this time."

"She brought it," Sterling said firmly. "It must have been on her person."

"So." Marco paused the footage. "This leaves us back at square one."

Alec quickly corrected him, "Square zero is more like it. Unless we're allowed to take it all the way down to square negative one, maybe two, because we spent a LOT of time scuba diving to get ready for this—"

Sterling turned and left the table, walking briskly to the rental home's adjacent living room.

The lights were off, a row of military-grade long-range surveillance cameras mounted on tripods peering through select gaps in the vertical blinds. He approached the leftmost camera, using a hand to separate the blades of two textured blinds and peering through the floor-to-ceiling window.

The view overlooked Lake Washington, currently a dark expanse with a single boat drifting slowly across the water, its progress marked by green and red nighttime running lights. His gaze drifted past it to the dark shore-line a mile and a half away, marked by a few glowing homes that were utterly massive at this distance, much less in person.

That far shore was Medina, and one of those homes was Kristen Shedo's. He wondered if she was standing at her own window, staring at the Seattle skyline behind him and guessing what the Sky Thieves' next play would be. Sterling found the thought to be sickeningly ironic: he was wondering the same thing, and didn't have any good answers.

The smart thing to do would be to flee the area, which was exactly what the police were expecting. Naturally the crew had done the opposite, though not out of a disregard for their own freedom; they had two highly incriminating wet subs to conceal, and toting them out of Seattle in a closed trailer presented more risk than any of them wanted to assume at present.

Instead, they'd done the most paradoxically logical thing possible—set up shop at a rented lake house on Seattle's eastern shore.

The home provided everything they needed in the short term: tempo-rary lodging for five, a direct line of sight across Lake Washington to Shedo's property, and most importantly, a large private dock.

That last point was particularly important not just for Marco's rented chase boat moored there at present, but for the pair of wet subs that had to be concealed. The crew had accomplished that feat in remarkably simple fashion by rendering the vessels negatively buoyant beneath the dock, then tethering them in place before bringing the batteries inside to recharge. As long as they came and went from the subs using their scuba gear under cover of night, none of the civilians at the adjacent homes were any the wiser. In terms of location it was a near-ideal arrangement, one that cost them a paltry 3,200 dollars a night to rent, with a one-month minimum duration to remain in the three-bedroom home that had last sold for a hair under ten million.

In fact, the only downside to the current setting was, well, the fact that the entire op had failed to achieve its one and only objective—and the team was supposed to be discussing that predicament at present.

He released the blinds and stepped back into the darkened living room. He wanted to pace but was unable to do so in this unfamiliar territory for fear of running into furniture or worse, clipping a tripod with his shoe and sending one of the thermal or night vision cameras clattering to the floor.

Blair entered the room and stopped beside him, sliding an arm around his waist.

"You should get back in the dining room. Alec gets nervous when you pace."

"I wasn't pacing."

"You would be if you could turn on the lights. Let's get back in there and discuss this— you're not going to get any brilliant epiphanies standing in here by yourself."

"I'm not sure there will be any epiphanies in the dining room, either."

"Well," she sighed, "we don't need a plan anyway. Not yet. Because if we don't have everyone's commitment tonight, then it doesn't matter what we can accomplish tomorrow."

Sterling kissed her on the forehead. "You're right. Let's go."

They'd barely entered the dining room before Alec spun a laptop to face them. "Check it out." He beamed. "We're internet famous."

The headline read, *YOU SUNK MY BATTLESHIP!* Beneath it was a subtitle declaring, *Police confirm foul play in the sinking of Kristen Shedo's yacht.* Sterling scanned the text, where a well-intentioned reporter declared that Shedo was suspected of purchasing Sky Thieves memorabilia at auction and that the thieves were therefore likely responsible for raiding her yacht in an attempt to steal their own goods back.

What followed as Alec clicked through the remaining tabs on his browser wasn't any news updates, per se, but rather a long string of memes that consisted of Sterling's and Blair's mugshots superimposed upon a variety of movie posters from *The Hunt for Red October, Crimson Tide,* and, in one particularly audacious display of history melded with pop culture, *U-571.*

He felt sick to his stomach, the feeling only exacerbated when he saw a further internet portrayal of his own likeness in an adaption of the *Jaws* image, with his face digitally distorted in an open-mouthed gape to swallow not a bikini-clad swimmer but a miniaturized version of a yacht.

"Who makes this stuff?" he cried. "This is insane."

Alec gave a short laugh.

"Um, have you been on the internet in the past ten years? If not, I can assure you, sanity is optional."

Sterling's phone buzzed in his pocket and he checked the display to see the name *UW*.

"Wolf texted," he said, reading aloud from the screen. "'Hope the yacht was worth it. Bounty tripled. $5 million bonus for you or Blair dead, decreasing by $500K every month until you're found. This will bring the best international mercenaries and bounty hunters into play, if they weren't already.'" He left off the final three words—*Run, you idiot*—knowing full well his crew didn't need any more reasons to be apprehensive. Besides, he already knew what had to be done.

The hard part, he suspected, would be convincing everyone else.

Sure enough, Marco was the first to respond.

"Remaining here is a high level of exposure. I say we go back to Mexico, lick our wounds, and let Shedo's bonus dwindle before—"

"Mexico is out." Esther burst into the room with a cell phone in hand. "My early warning network just called to inform me that foreigners have arrived in Ensenada and are making inquiries about a local thief."

Sterling looked up.

"How could Shedo know where you live?"

"Shedo doesn't have to," Blair pointed out. "She's got an army of mercenaries and bounty hunters combing the countryside looking for us, and like it or not, Esther's fate is tied with ours because of the connection with Jim's tapes."

Turning to face her counterpart, Blair asked, "Esther, is there anyone in Ensenada who will rat you out?"

"Not among my early warning network. I've taken care of their children, their families. But this bounty is enough to tempt anyone outside this room. I don't want to push my luck. And the bounty against us has just been tripled to—"

"We heard," Sterling cut her off, not wanting to go over that particular detail a second time. "And we need to discuss our next move. Have a seat."

"I prefer to stand."

Sterling and Blair remained standing as well. A long moment of silence passed before Marco continued, "There's still time for us to go our separate ways."

"I'll say," Esther replied.

Detecting Sterling's glare, Marco added defensively, "I'm just pointing out the obvious. And what other choice do we have?"

Sterling jerked a thumb toward the living room.

"We could hit her house."

Esther objected, "Let's not forget why we went with the boat option in the first place. However extensive the security on her yacht was, it's five times worse at her permanent residence."

"Ten times worse," Marco countered, indicating the remote high-resolution video feeds on the open laptops. "Since sinking her yacht, the frequency of foot patrols along the visible portions of her backyard have roughly doubled. That means she's brought in a lot more armed security, and that's just what we can observe from here. Who knows what other countermeasures she's preparing—and we can't sink a house."

Sterling exchanged a concerned glance with Blair, seeing in her eyes that they were in agreement about what to do; but she remained silent, letting him take the lead.

He began, "The bronze dragon is the only piece of stolen art Shedo takes with her when she travels. Scott Smith already told us all five paintings he stole for her are inside the house, along with God knows what else."

Alec snorted.

"A five-million-dollar Kryelast plank, for one thing. And all our other crap."

Sterling continued, "If we go our separate ways, we'll be on the run forever. All five of us."

"So?" Esther said. "We're on the run now."

"No, we're not. We're across the lake from Shedo's house, and as long as we're here I say we double down. Figure out a way in and take her art—if the bronze dragon is enough to send the government after her, can you imagine what the addition of those Venus paintings will accomplish?"

When no one else spoke, Blair said, "For what it's worth, I agree. Shedo hit us where we live, so we do the same. She won't stop, so we can't either. It's all or nothing."

Marco threw up his hands.

"Whatever harebrained scheme you're going to cook up, you won't be able to do it without me. I'm in."

Sterling cut his gaze to Alec, who jutted his chin and declared, "I don't back down in the face of danger. Unless," he added, looking up wistfully, "it means going on the run with the woman of my dreams, my Israeli sunflower—"

"Scott Smith gets to call me that," Esther cut him off. "You do not, and as much as I've enjoyed this little high-profile jaunt to the Pacific Northwest, if I run it's going to be alone."

Alec gave an ambivalent shrug. "Well, then sign me up for hitting Shedo's house."

Sterling watched Esther expectantly. He could tell from her face that while she'd suspected they were all crazy before, now she'd confirmed it. Her support at this point wasn't just a matter of having a fifth skilled thief in their ranks; they depended on her financially as well, and if she left now it would whittle their already-bad list of options to a few catastrophically dangerous ones at best.

"Esther," he said, "we're already here. Whatever plan we come up with, we'll be able to execute it quickly."

"As if we had the luxury of delaying."

"Fair point. Be that as it may, we've prevailed against bad odds before. Nothing this bad, it's true, but think about what our crew is capable of."

"Your crew."

"No," he shot back, "*our* crew. You trained us, you carried us here, and you did a heist with us today whether we were successful or not. You're a Sky Thief now—the only question is whether you remain one."

Esther didn't reply immediately, instead looking over at the entrance to the living room. Sterling could practically read her mind, the mental image that was forming of Shedo's estate across Lake Washington, now containing the entrenched adversary who'd bested them earlier today. No pep talk he could conceive would possibly match the motivation provided by Shedo herself, a simple fact he could see in the festering resentment lingering in Esther's eyes.

"All right," she said at last, "we hit Shedo at home. But if that doesn't work, I'm gone. No second chances, no more excuses. If we can't succeed now, we never will. Is that understood?"

"Yes," Sterling and Blair blurted in unison. Feeling embarrassed, Sterling collected himself—the best thing to do now would not be to start planning in their fatigued state, but to get some sleep and approach the problem set with fresh eyes in the morning.

Besides, he feared that any other outcome would cause Esther to change her mind.

He said, "Nothing else to do for now. We should rest up for the night."

Alec set his elbows on the table, interlacing his fingers and laying his chin on them like a lovesick schoolboy as he said to Esther, "The sofa is big enough for two."

"No," she replied, "it's not."

"All the better."

"I'd break you into three even pieces."

"I'd hope you would."

39

BLAIR

Blair lined up four clean mugs on the kitchen countertop, aligning their handles next to the coffeemaker as it burbled toward completion of a second pot. The first had already been brewed to half-capacity, the entirety consumed by her and her alone as she pored through every scrap of open-source intelligence regarding their upcoming actions against Kristen Shedo.

She'd set her alarm for a full two hours before Sterling's designated meeting time, not because she didn't trust the crew's planning abilities but because she wanted them to have the best starting point. Sure, they'd all agreed to take the op into divergent territory, but Sterling couldn't hold the crew together on his own. Alec and Marco might follow him without a second thought, but Esther was clearly nearing the end of her patience. And with the current op creeping into increasingly dangerous territory with a yacht raid turned residential penetration, they couldn't afford a single misstep going forward.

Marco entered the kitchen a moment later, bleary-eyed and clearly following the scent of fresh-brewed coffee. Blair hastily filled a mug and handed it to him with the words, "Projector is already set up in the living room. I took the liberty of using your computer, hope you don't mind."

"Mind?" he said, gratefully lifting the mug. "After yesterday, I'll be brain dead until noon."

He stopped abruptly, sniffing the mug's contents before inquiring, "Is this Greaney's?"

"What can I say." Blair shrugged. "Whoever stocked the house had excellent taste in coffee."

By way of livening the early-morning mood, she sang the opening line of the Greaney's coffee jingle, "'At Greaney's, we don't brew coffe-ee...'"

It was no use; Marco had already turned and shuffled off to the living room. Blair's shoulders sagged until she heard the hacker complete the song, although somewhat comedically with his Russian accent.

"We brew happin-e-ess.'"

He was gone a moment later, and no sooner had he departed than Esther strode into the kitchen, alert and poised as if she'd already consumed the same amount of caffeine as Blair had.

"Good morning," Esther said, "did you save a cup for me?"

Blair handed a mug to her. "If there's anyone on this crew who needs to be sufficiently caffeinated, it's you. Presentation is set up in the living room."

"Thanks," the Israeli thief replied dismissively, as if she'd intuited that an original member of the Sky Thieves would have prepared a brief prior to the designated meetup time.

Then she was gone, her quiet conversation with Marco audible for a full two minutes before Sterling entered the kitchen, arriving perilously close to his own designated rendezvous time. She checked her watch and commented, "Thirty-eight seconds to spare. Really enjoy cutting it close to the wire, don't you?"

He accepted the outstretched mug of coffee, sniffing the contents before taking a greedy sip and, she noted with minor irritation, making no comment that it was Greaney's before he replied.

"Take it as a compliment to my assurance in your punctuality."

Sterling left without further comment, walking toward the sound of Esther and Marco's ongoing conversation in the next room. Like Esther, he'd probably assumed someone else had taken charge of the formal meeting portion.

That was part of his leadership style, she knew by now—if no one else had stepped up, he'd set the example by doing so himself. But the bar he'd set by leaping to the Sky Safe, much less spearheading almost every other heist execution save his own prison break, made that outcome impossible.

With a resigned sigh, Blair filled the remaining mug with black coffee and followed Sterling into the living room.

What she saw there made her beam with pride: Sterling, Marco, and Esther were in a tight cluster, exchanging businesslike quips against Kristen Shedo as they debated how to proceed. The wall of windows was shadowed entirely with vertical blinds strategically arranged to conceal the surveillance cameras lining the view of Lake Washington beyond, and a sidewall was lit by a rectangular image of the slide presentation with the words *Operation Shedo Anarchy* along with the current date and time of Sterling's appointed meeting.

But she reminded herself that this effort was in its infancy: there had been no on-the-ground reconnaissance effort, and the very idea of conducting one was dashed mere minutes into her online research— tourists and reporters were routinely accosted by police immediately after entering Medina to snap pictures of the area, which was to say nothing of the city's formal countermeasures that Blair was about to discuss.

Upon seeing her enter, Sterling announced, "All right, looks like everyone's here. Take it away, Blair."

"Still need Alec," she replied, passing her mug to Esther.

With an inconvenienced sigh, Marco turned and kicked the sofa behind him.

"Rise and shine, scumbag."

Alec sat up from beneath a pile of blankets, blinking to find first that the rest of his crew was already awake, and second, that his favorite member of the group was holding an outstretched cup of coffee in his direction.

He was solely focused on Esther as he took the mug in both hands, sniffed the contents, and mumbled, "Is this Greaney's dark roast?"

Esther and Marco responded in unison, "Yes."

"So," Blair began, "now that we've all got coffee, let's get started."

She tapped the laptop keyboard linked to a projector, summoning an aerial satellite view of two swaths of land bisected vertically by Lake Washington. Across from that, Evergreen Point Floating Bridge connected Seattle to the eastern shore, a peninsula that penetrated the water in an approximate rectangle with outstretched fingers of land.

She continued, "The city of Medina takes up five square miles and contains just under 3,000 insanely wealthy people. Police station is in a building that doubles as city hall, and there's not much in the way of local shopping—just a grocery & deli, a plant store, and a post office. Everything else is residential besides an invitation-only country club. But make no mistake, Medina is essentially a surveillance state."

Sterling asked, "What's that supposed to mean?"

"It means that the city limits have signs stating you're entering a 24-hour video surveillance area, and they're not joking. Every major intersection has traffic cameras that record the license plates of every vehicle passing by, and those plates are automatically run through a database of previous criminal offenders. If there's a match, the system notifies police."

Marco hoisted his mug toward the screen. "We can use that to our advantage by hacking the camera feeds and tracking police movement and response."

"Maybe so," Blair replied, "but the police are the least of our worries." She flipped the slide to a close-up of a north-to-south road paralleling the shore, located just west of the city's golf course.

"Shedo lives here, on Evergreen Point Road. On that street she's just another billionaire—Bill Gates and Jeff Bezos have homes there, as do former politicians, professional athletes, high-level Microsoft executives, and various founders and CEOs of companies like Delta Air Lines and Costco. That means every property is equipped with its own security cameras, motion sensors, and armed security staff."

Flipping the slides to an overhead view of Shedo's property, Blair continued, "Her house is 27,000 square feet, and the other building is a 7,000-square-foot guest house."

"Very modest," Alec quipped. "And we're sure the art is in her home and not that outhouse of a guest facility?"

Marco said, "Positive. She's got a former member of law enforcement living in the guesthouse as an insurance requirement, and from what we've been able to pick up through our cameras thus far, it's being used to house her guard force. Unless our camera hack reveals that she's going there on a regular basis, the art will be in her home. Blair, do you have a depth chart of Lake Washington between here and Shedo's property?"

"I do," Blair said, accessing the slide. "From our dock, the lake bottom descends sharply to a depth of 185 to 195 feet, which extends until the far shore. As you can see here, there's an extremely steep ascent on the opposite side until it reaches Lake Washington's 16-foot surface elevation."

Marco didn't hesitate.

"Terrain slope beyond that point?"

Blair suddenly went from feeling overprepared to underprepared, and she hastily flipped to the next slide before continuing, "Elevation profile continues ascending above water to Medina's high point of 141 feet on the western edge of the golf course. Shedo's house sits approximately 62 feet above sea level, so 46 feet above the Lake Washington waterline."

"She has a basement?"

"Yes. There's a walkout deck on the lake-facing side of the ground level, along with a full basement underground."

"Well this is going to suck." Marco set his mug atop a coffee table before leaning back with his arms behind his head. "But we'll have to dig a tunnel."

Esther sighed in relief.

"Brilliant. I agree."

Blair recoiled at the proposition. "How do you figure?"

Without moving from his relaxed slouch, Marco explained, "Three ways into or out of anything—over, under, and through. We can cross off 'over' right now. Anything from the sky will be noticed immediately. Forget about going 'through.' Too many eyeballs at ground level, period. That leaves 'under.'"

Alec groaned. "I don't know that we can tunnel. She has seismic sensors, and we've never hacked those before."

"Well tunneling is the only way, so we better get really comfortable with the concept. Whatever obstacle those sensors present, it's less of a problem than approaching from any other way."

Esther's next statement was spoken with unflinching conviction.

"I bet a hundred dollars," she said, "that you won't have to hack them at all. They're in place to detect aboveground movement. As far as underground disturbances, they won't do Shedo much, if any, good."

Now Marco's curiosity was piqued. He leaned forward and said, "I haven't even told you the model and make of her sensors, nor did you see them when I performed my initial assessment in Mexico. So how could you possibly know that?"

"You know where I'm from originally, right?"

Alec responded, "With that sultry voice, consistently rated as the single sexiest accent by every man alive, how could we not?"

Esther shot him a stern glare and continued, "Hamas has built dozens of tunnels from the Gaza Strip into Israel. Why do you think that is— because Israel has a vast border to cover? It's about thirty miles long. Because they don't want to spend the money? They're in the international top 20 for defense spending. So tell me, why can't that massive and sophisticated military stop the tunnels?"

"I don't know," Blair began, "but I'm guessing you're about to explain it to us."

"At two tunnel diameters or more beneath the surface, the digging process is effectively undetectable to even the most sophisticated radar, acoustic, or seismic devices. It's the same reason the cartels are able to tunnel across the US-Mexico border with ease. When the tunnels are found, it's only because intelligence locates an entry point at ground level. That's it. We stay deep enough until we hit the basement, and we'll be fine."

Sterling, who hadn't sipped his coffee since Marco proposed tunneling, said, "I hate to point out the obvious, but Medina is on a peninsula."

"Yes." Blair gestured to the projected slide brief. "We've covered that."

"A peninsula that is covered with some of the finest residential and police security in the world."

"So?"

"So unless we want to spend months tunneling under miles of countryside, the only option is to begin our tunnel—"

"Underwater?"

"Yes."

Esther quickly replied, "Of course it is. We've got full scuba gear, two wet subs, and a boat sitting less than two miles from Shedo's backyard. Given the slope of her property, we could start tunneling under her dock."

"Underwater," Sterling said uneasily.

"Obviously. Then we can angle the tunnel upward to follow the rising elevation of her estate. That would put us above the waterline within 30 feet or so, by my estimation, and after that it's just regular tunneling. We establish an access point to her basement. Then it's a matter of repeated penetrations to locate her art collection."

"You say that," Sterling noted, "like it'll be a cakewalk to traipse around her house."

Esther laughed. "A cakewalk? No. But Marco is a self-proclaimed camera master, and if her whole property is covered by video feed inside and out, then we can monitor guard locations and reposition ourselves as necessary until we get what we need. Surely you guys have done similar ops before?"

Blair crossed her arms and pointed out, "Admit it, Sterling—she just described our entire incursion into PRY International to steal blueprints for the Sky Safe."

Sterling looked increasingly nervous as the conversation progressed. "But maybe we're getting ahead of ourselves. If I can just circle back to the tunnel—"

Marco sighed impatiently. "What about it? It only has to be wide enough for us to crawl through one at a time. I think we can all agree that comfort of getting in and out comes a distant second to accessing her art collection as quickly as possible. The bounty is simply too great to waste any time."

"I'm with you there," Sterling said cautiously, "I just think tunneling may be a little harder than we're anticipating."

Blair leaned forward. "I think we can do it. There's plenty of historical precedent in LA alone. The Hole in the Ground Gang took two banks using tunnels in the mid-'80s, and dug a third route to a bank they never robbed. Before that, even—London, Lloyds Bank on Baker Street, 1971."

Esther added, "Berlin's been hit by two tunnel jobs, '95 and 2013."

Then Marco chimed in, "Tunnels are practically mandatory in South America. '05, Banco Central in Brazil—71 million. '06, Buenos Aires, 15 million. Plus the attempted robbery in Sao Paulo. They dug over 2,000 feet before they got caught."

"And," Blair continued, "that safe deposit box robbery in Antwerp's diamond district. Those guys built two tunnels: basement to sewer, then sewer to vault. And they still haven't been caught."

Marco chuckled. "Don't forget the clown in Florida whose tunnel got discovered when it created a sinkhole outside the bank. I mean, come on, Sterling. If terrorists and drug runners can do this on a daily basis, then so can we."

Alec wasn't convinced.

"Well I can give you three reasons why we shouldn't tunnel: mole people, Morlocks, and reptilian humanoids. You guys want to throw yourselves at the mercy of shape-shifting bloodsuckers, go right ahead."

Sterling ran his hands through his hair, looking like he was afraid he was losing his mind. "I can give you one more reason, and it's the only one that matters. Take all those jobs you guys just rattled off, plus all the terrorists and drug runners, and let me know how many of them ever started a tunnel *underwater*."

No one spoke until Esther offered, "To my knowledge? None."

"Right," Sterling agreed. "So how do we do it?"

Alec looked to Marco, who cut his eyes to Blair as if she had the answer —which, of course, she didn't. But Blair nonetheless felt confident as she turned her gaze to Esther in anticipation of a brilliant counterpoint.

To her surprise, Esther gave a simple shrug and said, quite unapologetically, "I have no earthly idea."

Alec smiled. "Nice pun."

"It wasn't a pun. I literally do not know."

Blair quickly intervened, "You don't have to. We'll figure out how engineers do it, and formulate a way to apply their methods to this particular problem set. We don't have to dig very wide, or very far; our main considerations are rate of progress and minimizing any visual or audible signature from the work. And since clouds of silt bubbling up from under the dock will be a dead giveaway, we'll need to begin digging after nightfall and stop prior to sunrise."

Esther nodded. "So now we've got a starting point; a working hypothesis, at least. We'll tunnel from beneath the dock into Shedo's property and establish an entry point into her house that we can use for repeated access. We can work in two shifts if necessary, using the same crews as the yacht job: myself and Sterling on *HMS Cattywampus*, Alec and Blair on *Queen Blair's Revenge*."

Sterling groaned. "Great. More diving."

"Marco operates the chase boat as needed, providing command and control while monitoring the camera feeds and guard communications. Once the tunnel is built, we can determine the best organization for our entry teams."

"Which will," Blair said, "probably be dictated in large part by our observations once the camera hack is in place."

"I agree." Marco reached for his mug and took a sip. "So there's just one thing left: figure out how in God's name we can start a tunnel beneath the surface of Lake Washington."

40

STERLING

Sterling looked up from his computer at the sound of the garage door opening, then rose and made his way through the mud room before pausing.

He waited until he heard the garage door rattle shut, all too aware that absent any disguise to speak of, exposing himself to outside view simply wasn't worth the risk. Then he flung the door open, striding into the garage where Alec had backed in the pickup and now stood in the bed, undoing the bungee cords securing a giant packing blanket over a cylindrical-shaped item.

Marco stood on the opposite side of the cargo, helping to uncover the contents.

"All right," Sterling said, "let's see it."

Alec wasted no time, barely waiting for Marco to release the last bungee from its mount before he whipped off the packing blanket with a flourish and cried, "Lord Sterling, I give you—the mole!"

Sterling tried to reconcile the disparity between what he'd been expecting to see and the machine before him. In his mind, there would be a massive conical drill bit on the nose end of a giant, sinister-looking device, the type of thing villains used to penetrate bank vaults in cartoons.

But this machine was, for lack of a better word, small, with a height somewhere around four feet and a length of perhaps twice that. Just looking at it made him feel claustrophobic at the thought of crawling through a tunnel of the maximum diameter it could dig. And it was almost absurdly simple, just a plain cylinder of white plastic shielding with various configurations of carbide disc cutters set at seemingly random angles between holes to allow the displaced earth to pass through.

In technical terms, the object he was looking at now was a TBM—a tunnel boring machine.

"This is it?" he asked. "This is the big bad TBM we've been talking about?"

Alec climbed down from the bed, shaking his head.

"That kind of language might have been okay a few decades ago. But times have changed. It's not okay to refer to this as a TBM."

"Then what is it?"

When Alec didn't immediately answer, and Marco merely clambered off the tailgate without a word, Sterling gave a frustrated sigh and said, "All right, sorry I've been busy with a deep dive of Shedo's basement construction. The good news is we're only looking at concrete, which is nothing we can't get through—"

"Like Andy Dufresne," Alec asked, "in *The Shawshank Redemption*?"

Sterling summoned a breath and said, "Yes, Alec, just like that."

"So we can use a Rita Hayworth poster to cover the hole?"

"We cover the hole," Sterling replied angrily, "using a facade of whatever her interior construction dictates, most likely a mock drywall panel. The bad news is I barely knew the acronym TBM, which is what I thought you guys left to go get. So if this isn't a TBM, then what is it?"

Alec turned to Marco and whispered, "Did we just time travel back to the 1800s?"

The hacker placed a hand on his arm and whispered back, "Don't judge. Just educate—he's old-school. He doesn't know any better."

"Well," Alec said angrily, facing Sterling with a defiant posture, "anything that digs less than a 4,000-millimeter-diameter—13 feet, one inch, to you crusty WASP types—isn't a TBM. It's a micro-TBM, or MTBM. To call it otherwise is, well, appropriation at best. And at worst, you're just being—"

"Let's move on," Sterling said. "Other than the size of the finished tunnel, what's the difference?"

Marco intervened, "Regular TBMs are designed to dig efficiently without the negative impacts of blasting or drilling in urban areas. The tradeoff is a higher initial cost, as they're not cheap and usually require a human operator."

"And this?" he asked.

"Microtunneling is the same concept at a reduced scale, generally used for constructing utility tunnels or sewer pipes between existing subsurface channels. So the normal principles apply, but at reduced cost and, notably, without the requirement for someone to drive them—micro-TBMs are designed to be remotely operated."

Sterling nodded as if that much should have been obvious.

"So you can drive it with a computer."

Alec objected, "That's a gross oversimplification."

"Is it, though?"

"Okay," Alec admitted, "so that's pretty much accurate. The real finesse will be in positioning the entry eye underwater, then pipe jacking this bad boy into position. But after that's complete—"

Marco interrupted, "We can theoretically outdistance the water line after three to four nights of operation. And it's in our best interests to do so as quickly as possible. It'll mean a bit of a climb at the start of every return trip, but provided we can reinforce the tunnel as expected based on our soil composition analysis, we'll be staged to penetrate the foundation six to seven days from now."

Sterling asked, "What about muddying the waters of Lake Washington?"

"Less of a problem than we initially thought, because they make slurry tubes for that sort of thing. So we'll just redirect the dirt into repurposed fuel storage bladders. Our biggest risk is ground subsidence, or causing a sudden sinking of the ground overhead. That risk is fairly well mitigated by balancing machine advance with soil removal to maintain stability even in very soft ground. But we'll still have to reinforce the tunnel to prevent collapse, especially in the subsurface portion."

"Okay." Sterling jammed his hands into his pockets. "So what's next?"

Marco shrugged. "I guess we have to name this thing, or Alec will freak out."

Alec quickly replied, "Your words, not mine. But since I've been thrust into the hot seat, I'll step up and do what needs to be done by assigning a title."

"Hold up," Sterling objected. "Why should you get to name it?"

"Because while robots can be man's best friend in the best of times, so too do they carry the ever-looming risk of turning on their masters. And since I commanded the robot army of drones during the Supermax break-out, I've amassed the most time and experience dealing with these mechanical beasts." He stepped forward and stroked the cylinder gently. "They respect me, and I...well, I respect them."

Marco rolled his eyes. "So what name do you propose?"

Esther entered the garage, looking like she was about to speak before sensing that the three Sky Thieves were in the midst of some heated discussion. Remaining silent, she walked up to the pickup and glanced at the cargo, nodding in approval as if this absurdly small machine was exactly what she'd expected to see.

Watching her closely, Alec drew a breath before proclaiming in a regal voice, "We will call this device—wait for it—The Mole Holer."

Another moment of silence ensued, and when no one spoke, Sterling offered, "That's the dumbest name I've ever heard."

"Dumbest?" Alec raised an eyebrow provocatively. "Or most brilliant?"

"The dumbest," Esther confirmed.

"I feel like you're not getting it. The slang term for a micro-TBM is 'mole.' Both the micro-TBM and actual subterranean mammals dig holes; so, Mole Holer not only rhymes somewhat, it describes the form and function of this machine to a T."

He looked to Marco for reassurance, but after a strained pause the hacker only shook his head and declared, "Alec, it's...bad. Like, really bad."

"Maybe I'm doing a poor job of explaining this."

Esther cut in, "Your explanation is perfectly fine. Your name is terrible, but we're going to accept it and move on because otherwise we'll lose six to seven hours arguing with your incessantly poor logic, outright stubbornness, and corny sense of humor."

Alec stared at her with a profound expression of hope, as if she really understood him.

"See?" Sterling nudged Esther with his elbow. "You really are a Sky Thief."

41

BLAIR

Blair piloted *Queen Blair's Revenge* east across Lake Washington, straining to read her wet sub's GPS display, which, even at its dimmest setting, presented a blinding glare under her night vision.

She'd spent a lot of time wearing such devices, of course; it was almost a staple of her chosen profession as a thief. But operating with night vision underwater was another matter altogether, and she quickly realized that it turned the previously liberating and beautiful act of moving underwater into an awkwardly restrained, almost mechanical procedure.

For one thing, she was used to relatively small, dual tube devices that provided a wide field of vision in dazzling green hues. But fully submersible night vision technology was more like a clunky shoebox in front of her dive mask, the narrower view presented not in crisp green but murky black and white speckled with a starscape of particulate drifting up from below.

She should be used to it by now; in addition to their in-house rehearsals, the crew had spent two nights doing nighttime dive ops in Lake Washington to prepare for this. Much of that time had consisted of Blair and Esther simply piloting the subs through navigational routes across the lake, familiarizing themselves with reaching checkpoints in reduced visibility until they felt prepared for the culmination, so to speak: a series of actual dry runs to Shedo's property, where they'd repeatedly approached and hovered the wet subs beneath her dock while Marco monitored the guard communications for any sign they'd been detected. Once it was clear they could infiltrate successfully, they'd begun staging underwater gear ahead of tonight's effort.

By the time the sun rose tomorrow, they'd know whether their seemingly brilliant plan had any chance of success.

As the navigational beacon approached on her GPS display, she transmitted through her regulator.

"*Queen Blair's Revenge* passing checkpoint two, left turn heading three-four-five, depth two-zero."

"*Copy checkpoint two,*" Marco replied from the chase boat.

Blair manipulated the dual joysticks to send her sub into a lazy, drifting left-hand turn. The craft was slow to react, her steering feel reduced from the usual hairpin response to a sloppy mushiness due to the cargo strapped beneath the carbon fiber hull. While its weight wasn't an issue underwater, it was sufficiently bulky to increase water resistance to the point that she had to maintain near-full throttle just to make forward progress.

Alec transmitted from the backseat, "*Man, the Mole Holer really isn't doing our maneuverability any favors.*"

"Or our speed," Blair responded, then added, "I'm glad we'll only have to make this run once."

"*Don't jinx it. You and I have still got a long night ahead.*"

Blair didn't need any reminding of that fact, she thought as she confirmed their location on GPS.

The wet sub was now headed almost due north, paralleling the Medina coastline rather than making a head-on approach to Shedo's property. Given the sluggish responsiveness of the burdened sub, Blair couldn't risk striking the shore in the event of a GPS failure. Even with her current approach plan, she wasn't certain the wobbling sub wouldn't require two or more repeated approaches before she'd be able to reach her stopping point.

She transmitted, "*Queen Blair's Revenge* passing checkpoint three, on course."

"*Copy,*" Marco replied. "*Stand by for beacon.*"

For a few seconds, the black-and-white hues of her night vision remained unchanged, and then, as if by magic, a piercing glow appeared in the water to her front right, going dark before flashing at three-second intervals.

"I have visual," she confirmed. "Continue pulse."

Blair continued piloting the sub forward, tracking her convergence with the flashing infrared light. She slowed as she came alongside it, then said, "Right turn, heading zero-eight-five, depth two-zero, final approach."

Marco said, "*Confirm final, will relay until you're within audio range.*"

She gradually advanced ten feet forward, confirming that the wet sub remained controllable at the low speed before transmitting, "Steady on."

A moment later the flashing infrared light transitioned to a continuous glow, the effect akin to flipping on a light switch—her visibility went from five feet in front of her face to twenty or more as she peered between vertical wooden beams supporting the dock overhead.

The first thing she saw in their underwater workspace was the *HMS Cattywampus*, the wet sub's canopy open as it rested against the sloping lake bottom, having been rendered negatively buoyant and tethered to a support column.

Beside it were Esther and Sterling floating in their closed-circuit rebreather units as they watched Blair's approach. They were already several hours into their dive, having first shuttled and then prepared the final array of equipment she saw now.

Between what they'd just brought and the gear staged the night before, it was a formidable assembly. Tied off to the dock supports were sections of PVC piping, metal tanks of bentonite slurry, a vacuum pump, and a coiled tubing. One of those tubes descended to what looked like a giant deflated balloon but was, in actuality, an expandable bladder designed for fuel storage. But the most critical at present was embedded into a vertical section of coastline: two horizontal rails leading to an upright metal ring, marked at the twelve, three, six, and nine o'clock by infrared chemlights that formed a loose crosshair at its periphery. In tunnel boring parlance this was the "entry eye," and as soon as she oriented her sub to face it, she heard Marco's next message.

"*Esther says you're centered, looking good, bring it in slow.*"

Blair might have laughed if the situation weren't so nerve-racking.

Slow was about all she was willing or able to manage at this point in the op; she now had to thread the needle between dock support columns with only three feet of clearance on either side of her propeller wings. And while she'd made this type of approach with relative ease a half-dozen times the previous night, she hadn't done so while toting a micro-tunnel boring machine that made any stable movement something of a small miracle.

She felt beads of sweat forming at the edges of her dive mask as she eased the *Queen Blair's Revenge* forward, the nose coming within ten feet of the beams, then five.

"*Centered,*" Alec transmitted, "*keep going.*"

By now she couldn't see the columns at all; her night vision's narrow field of view was solely focused on the entry eye, which began to skew sideways as Alec called, "*Left two, left two!*"

Blair complied immediately, yawing the sub two feet sideways to realign the entry eye in her windshield as Alec said, "*Give it some power, straight ahead.*"

As she increased the throttle, she heard him continue, "*Props are clear and*"—a pause—"*tail clear. Move to offload.*"

She let out a relieved exhale into her regulator, drifting forward as she replied, "*Climbing to depth one-five.*"

The entry eye slipped below her windshield as she heard Alec call, "*Three, two, one. Hold. Hold. Hold.*"

Blair held the sub in as stationary of a hover as she could manage as he said, "*Opening canopy.*" The acrylic hood had barely slid back before she felt Alec wriggling out from behind her, his shadow descending through the glow in her night vision as he dived under the sub to join the crewmates.

This was followed by a euphoric transmission from Esther, whose bone-conducting microphone was finally within range of Blair's speaker.

"*Well done, Blair. Can you hear me okay?*"

"Crystal."

Esther continued in a more formal tone, assuming her preordained command over the subsurface effort at hand. "*Hold fast, we're inflating now.*"

The sub jostled as her three crew members adjusted the buoyancy on twin BCDs they'd mounted to the micro-tunnel boring machine—without them, the Mole Holer would sink like a brick—before undoing the straps that secured the instrument to her sub.

Esther's next order was, "*Stand by, we're pulling it free.*" Suddenly the joysticks came alive in Blair's hands, the sub startlingly more easy to control.

In a voice now strained with physical effort, Esther transmitted, "*Blair, the MTBM is clear. Move to the staging area and shut down.*"

"Moving," Blair confirmed, effortlessly guiding the sub ten feet backward before dipping it nose down to re-attain her black-and-white view of the entry eye, toward which three swimming figures were guiding the Mole Holer's cylinder into position.

She turned left and approached the sloped bank beside the grounded form of her sister sub, the *HMS Cattywampus*. Once she arrived in position, Blair slowly descended until she felt the front of her hull settle into the silty ground, then throttled down until the tail dropped to leave her with a steeply reclined view of the lake bottom rising before her, the mud scarred with hull marks from her and Esther's dry runs the previous night. She adjusted buoyancy until *Queen Blair's Revenge* was stationary, further reducing the throttle and confirming the sub remained still before cutting the power altogether and transmitting, "Ready for tether."

"*Wait one,*" Alec replied. She scanned the ground to her right to see the trio of divers removing the BCDs from the Mole Holer, now securely in place atop the horizontal rails leading to the entry eye. Then they dispersed a moment later, Esther and Sterling moving to arrange the other equipment into position while Alec finned toward her to secure the lanyard to a dock support. While it was unlikely that a sudden current would dislodge the subs from their resting positions, the last thing anyone needed in this already complicated procedure was for one of their escape vessels to drift off into the dark waters of Lake Washington.

Tying down the sub took Alec just over a minute, after which he confirmed, "*Blair, you're tethered. Time to get to work.*"

She braced her hands on the side of the cabin, pushing herself up and out of the seat before making the requisite adjustments to her BCD until she was neutrally buoyant. Alec appeared beside her, and they swam together toward the entry eye to begin the next phase of the op.

She saw the other two crew members in position, having already clipped pre-staged tubing into the Mole Holer's rear face. The tubes ran from the micro-TBM to their routing points between the round sections of PVC piping, then to a variety of attachment points: one to the deflated bladder, another to the vacuum pump, and the remaining one to the first of three tanks of bentonite slurry.

As Blair approached, she heard Esther transmit, *"We'll have to work fast —we're down to about half an hour of station time, at least for Sterling. Who is, as you know, an oxygen hog."*

Sterling added, *"Sorry, I like breathing."*

Blair felt a moment of sympathy for the man—the only one nearly as uncomfortable underwater was Marco, who'd scored the sole position aboard the chase boat. However exerting this subsurface op was for Blair, it was doubly so for Sterling, who'd already been hard at work setting this up alongside Esther.

She arrived at the entry eye, taking up her designated position to the rear of the horizontal rails atop which the Mole Holer rested, braced against the hydraulic jack that would begin its forward drive. Esther and Blair were to either side of the micro-TBM, activating its systems in preparation for Marco to give them the green light while Alec staged himself ten feet below, adjusting his buoyancy in preparation for passing up the first section of PVC piping.

Esther transmitted, *"Mole Holer and hydraulics are live, check in."*

Sterling was the first to speak in this preordained sequence.

"Right side and vacuum pump, good to go."

"Rear is good," Blair added, followed by a final confirmation from Alec.

"Bottom is cocked, locked, and ready to rock."

All they needed now was for Marco to confirm that he had a good signal from the Mole Holer and provide them the final clearance to begin their insertion. But when he spoke over the net, it was clear that wouldn't be happening.

"Cease work, kill the IR lights—guard patrol is coming down the dock with night vision."

Sterling extinguished the infrared lamps, turning Blair's view into a shallow waterscape of vague grayish hues.

Esther asked, "*Do they have dive gear—fins, BCDs?*"

"*Negative*," Marco answered.

That much, at least, was a blessing. As long as the guards weren't going subsurface, the crew wasn't in any danger of immediate discovery, but even so, the appearance of this hopefully random patrol was concerning in the extreme. Shedo's entire property, much less her dock, was covered in remotely controllable optics ranging from daytime surveillance cameras to nighttime and thermal devices. How had the subs suddenly garnered the attention of the security force?

"*Stand by*," Marco said, "*they're on the dock now.*"

Blair looked up, unable to make out much absent the infrared lights but knowing that the guards stood roughly twenty feet overhead.

Marco continued, "*Well, this is an interesting wrinkle. Good news is the guards are departing. Bad news is that their little stroll onto the dock was to verify that the control room could see them on the display—they're already worried about us hijacking the camera feeds. So we can expect interferences like this once we get inside the house as well.*"

Esther quickly corrected him, "If *we get inside the house.*"

"*We're getting in*," Sterling replied, "*if it's the last thing I do.*"

"*Keep going through your air this fast, and it may well be. Marco, are we clear to proceed?*"

"*Guards are almost back at the house, and I have a positive signal with the Mole Holer. You're clear.*"

Sterling activated the IR lamp, blazing the extensive equipment setup into view on Blair's night vision. She adjusted her position to the rear of the rails and took up a two-handed grip on the cluster of tubing emerging from the Mole Holer's rear face, knowing that visibility was about to go to near-zero in the coming minutes.

The micro-TBM was a closed-face model, a requirement for excavating below the water table, much less through a subsurface starting point. Once fully underground, its internal drive motor would ultimately generate sufficient torque to propel it forward, but only once the hydraulic system had succeeded in forcing it all the way through the entry eye. Then there was the small matter of pipe jacking in the soon-to-be muddied waters, but she had another thirty seconds or so before she had to worry about that.

Esther said, "*All stations, stand by for initiation. Three, two, one. Mark.*"

There was an almost imperceptible vibration in the water as the Mole Holer began its incremental charge, assisted by the hydraulic jack forcing it forward. Blair hardly had time to witness the process; as soon as it began, she saw a slow-motion explosion of muddy silt consuming the entry eye, rolling toward her until her night vision washed out in a hazy gray glow.

But she knew well enough what was occurring through the cloud.

The Mole Holer's cutter head was now filled with the pressurized slurry to apply hydrostatic pressure—the effect was, from a physics perspective, much the same as extensive flooding seeping through a home's foundation, except in this case that structural instability was furthered by the 14 single disc cutters rotating to carve up the earth along the machine's vector.

That slurry had the added benefit of mixing with the excavated dirt—known in the industry as the "spoils"—that was being funneled through the cutter head, flushed down a vacuum line, and ultimately deposited into the collapsible fuel bladder installed on the sloping lake bottom.

Esther transmitted, "*It's halfway in—send up the first section.*"

"*On my way,*" Alec replied.

Blair looked down, unable to see even as far as her handholds on the tubing, when she felt the gentle nudge of the PVC pipe against her bottom wrist. She gripped it with one hand, using the other to pull herself up along the tubing until she reached the rails and hydraulic jack. By now her visibility was starting to clear, the hazy forms of Sterling and Esther dimly visible as they made way for her next maneuver.

She positioned the PVC pipe atop the rails before sliding forward until it was flush with the Mole Holer's rear face. From there it was a matter of edging the pipe forward to match the micro-TBM's rate of progress as it disappeared into the underwater hillside.

"*We're in,*" Esther said.

Blair saw the hydraulic jack's teeth retract from the Mole Holer's rear face, automatically sliding to the back of the rails before re-engaging and gliding forward to catch the rear edge of the PVC pipe. Then it pushed that forward as well, driving it slowly into the hill. As with most legitimate TBM and micro-TBM operations, the crew was combining the excavation and tunnel lining into a single process, albeit in such a rudimentary fashion that any self-respecting excavation contractor would shudder at the sight.

Blair transmitted, "Alec, bring up the next section."

"*Moving,*" he confirmed, soon appearing behind her with the next PVC pipe. Blair took up her position beside the rail, monitoring the first section's progress as Alec began positioning the second in a procedure known as pipe jacking.

Once the first section was fully inserted behind the Mole Holer, Alec waited to ensure the second was progressing in the same fashion before diving down for a third.

Blair said, "Marco, first pipe is internal. You have control."

"*I have control,*" he confirmed.

Now he was adjusting the Mole Holer's hydraulic steering jacks to subtly articulate the cutter head, easing it along its first drive with a laser-guided steering system that provided a line and grade accuracy of plus or minus one inch for every 500 feet. Given that the entire tunnel only needed to be 52.6 feet from start to finish as plotted with the help of a high-fidelity engineering simulation platform, they'd be able to reach Shedo's basement along the most efficient line possible. At least, Blair thought, if Marco's calculations were correct. Real-time satellite mapping was of little use underground, so the crew's hacker instead monitored progress through Mole Holer readings projected on a three-dimensional model of the surrounding terrain.

There was some margin for error, but not much. The sections of pipe were half an inch narrower than the cutter head, allowing a bit of leeway as the micro-TBM gradually adjusted course. And while that gap would normally be filled with a stabilizing lubricant, the crew wasn't concerned with the tunnel's long-term stability. They only needed it to hold for a short time following completion, perhaps as few as two or three days.

The second PVC pipe was halfway into the entry eye when Blair transmitted, "Esther, we've got this."

"*All right, Sterling,*" she said in response, "*wave off to HMS Cattywampus. Time to return to base.*"

Sterling replied, but not to her. "*Blair, Alec, good luck—we'll see you back at the house in a few hours.*"

Then he swam past, following Esther back to their sub.

By then Alec was appearing at the rail, hoisting a third section of pipe into position.

"*All right, Blair Bear,*" he said, "*just you and me now. Let's see how far we can dig before sunrise.*"

42

STERLING

Sterling entered the dining room and set a takeout bag on the table, announcing triumphantly, "Breakfast is served."

Marco didn't look up from his computer. "It's six p.m."

"Well, we're working night shifts. Dinner is the new breakfast. Any action on the—"

"No," Marco cut him off, preempting the question that came before every other concern at present. "I just reviewed the footage in super fast-forward, and the underwater cams are clean."

Sterling held up his palms in mock surrender, considering that his repeated inquiries on the subject were for good reason. They'd installed the camera network beneath Shedo's dock because without continuous surveillance of their tunneling operation during daylight hours, the crew would have no way of knowing whether an outside dive team had discovered the mess of equipment installed below. In that event, they could be returning to their dig site only to find a trap.

He dropped into a chair and rifled through the takeout bag to remove a Styrofoam container of orange chicken. Selecting an individually wrapped pair of chopsticks, he pushed the bag over to Marco.

The hacker flipped open the remaining container to confirm it held his pineapple shrimp with sweet and sour sauce and ripped a plastic fork from its cellophane wrapper before returning his gaze to the screen while shoveling portions of food into his mouth.

Sterling noted, "You're supposed to use chopsticks, you know."

Marco answered him without breaking stride, speaking with his mouth half-full. "And you're supposed to be prepping your dive gear for tonight."

Sterling shrugged, taking his first bite. "Checking in with you gives me an excuse to procrastinate. How's the hacking coming along?"

It wasn't an idle inquiry—with the tunnel establishment taking priority since it would require a minimum of six nights to complete, most of Marco's waking hours had been spent operating the Mole Holer from his chase boat while the only other qualified hacker—Esther—was occupied with dive rotations to set the pipe.

The process had been exasperatingly complex: every night required the first dive team on shift to detach tubes from the vacuum pump, slurry tanks, and bladder, reroute them through the newly delivered sections of PVC tunnel, then re-attach the connection points before the Mole Holer could resume operation with crew members pipe jacking at the entry eye. Throw in the emplacement of new bladders for excavated dirt, a limited air supply, and the dive teams needing to rotate shifts before shutting everything down well before sunrise, and the past four nights had yielded only 37 feet of progress, just under three-quarters of the distance required to come within striking distance of Shedo's foundation.

On the plus side, that meant the tunnel could be complete in another 16 hours of boring, which in turn meant they were most likely within three days of actually entering the house.

Marco set his fork down.

"Hacking Medina's citywide surveillance network was child's play. We now have access to all traffic cameras, and can monitor police movements accordingly."

"What about the cameras on Shedo's property?"

Marco looked irritated at Sterling's utter lack of awe, though, to be fair, Marco over-delivered on so many matters of cyber penetration that it was hard to be surprised anymore.

"Her private network was much more difficult to penetrate. But after lengthy efforts, we're in. I've also got her personal itinerary and guard rosters, and am working on accessing the security force radio net."

Sterling leaned forward eagerly, his dinner forgotten. "What have you learned so far?"

"Since we sank her yacht, she's been primarily running her businesses from home using multiple offices and conference rooms. I haven't seen any indications that she's so much as left the property since returning."

"Poor Shedo," Sterling said mockingly. "I wonder if there's such a thing as cabin fever in a 27,000-square-foot house."

Marco shot him a dismayed glance, then resumed his assault on the pineapple shrimp before adding, "Initial review of her itinerary, which I have yet to cross-reference with her security camera footage but suspect is accurate, reveals two camera blind spots of interest for locating the art. One is her home office, which she only seems to enter alone. But it's not big enough to stockpile a collection of our memorabilia, much less while keeping the art out of sight."

"And the other location?"

"Her master suite, just down the hall from her home office. Problem is, it takes up almost 6,000 square feet and she's had it remodeled extensively since the original house blueprints were drafted. We don't know how many rooms are in there, and won't until we achieve entry."

"Remodeled," Sterling muttered, "to accommodate hiding places?"

"According to the pending request I harvested from her appraiser at Darien Insurance, a Mr. Paul Schmidt, it's extremely likely. His report is for our crew gear, stating that it is safeguarded by a hidden entrance disguising a Wellington C610 vault door, beyond which is a room constructed to UL Class 350 one-hour fire standards. The exact location is not noted beyond the fact that it is within her master suite, nor are there any records of the installation that I could locate."

"I bet you anything the art is hidden within that vault door. So we've narrowed it down to a relatively small corner of her house—that's great news."

"To be counterpointed with the bad," Marco said, setting his fork down. "Shedo has also doubled her number of guards, with a corresponding increase in foot patrols. That doesn't include the personal SWAT team of sorts at her guest house."

"What do you mean, 'personal SWAT team?'"

"I mean eight men standing by at all times. Some are former cops, some former military. They don't pull guard, and from what I've seen on the cameras, every time they've left the guest house is for training and rehearsals on her main estate. They're on call 24/7, and fall under the command of her lead bodyguard...and that's who I need to tell you about."

Sterling shrugged, returning to his chopsticks. "So tell me about him."

"She used to have a retired Secret Service agent in the position. But she recently terminated his employment and replaced him with someone from the FBI."

Alec entered the dining room at that moment, a spring roll in each hand. "Jim's out of jail already?"

Marco shook his head. "It's not Jim. It's Clint Vance."

Sterling felt a jolt of energy hit his system, a primal fight-or-flight response upon the very mention of that name. He deposited his chopsticks into the Styrofoam tray and pushed it away without replying.

Alec was far less disturbed, plopping into an open chair and gnawing at one of the spring rolls as he asked nonchalantly, "Yeah? Who's that?"

"Jim's personal hitman," Sterling said. "The FBI SWAT commander who led the assault during the Century City job. And the one who apprehended me after the Sky Safe."

Alec nodded briskly, taking another mouthful of food before muttering, "Oh yeah, the charming fellow who played soccer with your head to make the arrest. Anyway, Esther says you need to prep your dive gear."

"It can wait," Sterling managed, then asked Marco, "You're telling me Vance isn't an agent anymore?"

"Forcibly discharged, following your trial. Use of excessive force."

"Probably why Shedo hired him. She knew we'd be coming for her. It doesn't matter—this won't impact our op."

"Unless," Marco said evenly, "you consider the fact that the one man who hates you more than anyone is heading up her security."

"So?"

"So if we get caught, he's not going to turn us over to the police. He'll kill us, Sterling. The only reason he didn't shoot you outside the Sky Safe was because you were wearing a body cam—"

"Which we'll be doing anyway," Sterling quickly countered, "to document the art in Shedo's possession."

"I don't know that it will make a difference. Not this time."

"Yeah," Alec agreed, brushing the crumbs off his shirtfront. "Me neither. You really pissed that guy off, Sterling."

Leaning forward, Sterling set his hands flat on the table and said, "I don't care if she's got every Green Beret in the world guarding her house, much less a scumbag like Vance."

He felt his blood pressure rising, and fought to keep his voice level as he continued, "*Nothing* stops this operation."

43

BLAIR

"Never thought I'd say this," Sterling transmitted through his regulator, *"but I'm looking forward to getting back in the water."*

Blair tossed a shovelful of dirt into the Mole Holer's tunnel, now at face level, before directing her headlight's beam through the network of support poles to see her literal and metaphorical partner in crime for the evening's festivities.

Sterling was practically covered from head to toe in wet soil, the black cord extending from his mouthpiece to the air cylinder on his back almost impossible to distinguish against his body as he dug. He looked like a muck-covered swamp monster, and she imagined she must have as well.

Driving her spade into the earth, Blair excavated another chunk and tossed it into the tunnel. Then she replied through her own regulator, "All it took was some time with a shovel. Maybe we should have had you digging prep areas back in Mexico—you would've warmed up to diving a lot sooner."

She heard him chuckle, timing her next scoop to alternate with Sterling's as they continued shoveling dirt into the tunnel. This was, in a sense, the easiest part of tonight's op—not in terms of manual labor, to be sure, but there was something comforting in the mindless repetition after so much highly technical work.

Getting here had occurred courtesy of Sterling, who had first shimmied the entire length of newly completed PVC tunnel while trailing a thin climbing rope clipped to his belt. Once he'd reached the top, he used the rope to hoist a nylon climbing ladder that he affixed for the benefit of the remaining crew. The ladder was neither convenient nor comfortable to ascend; it was, however, sufficient to allow repeated access to the highest point of the tunnel.

The Mole Holer had continued its forward march long after Blair climbed up to meet him. Rather than insert any additional piping, Blair and Sterling had braced the earth overhead with a series of lightweight fiber-reinforced plastic panels ferried up the tunnel by Esther and Alec and held aloft by a network of vertical poles. Once a six-foot extension was established beyond the final PVC pipe, the digging had begun in earnest, this time with shovels.

Their goal now was to create a true prep area, a modest space in which they could stage equipment and change from their soaked, muddy wetsuits into clean gear for their forays into the house. With multiple nights of repeated incursions ahead, each of them involving the transition from wet sub and scuba kit to tunnel climb and vice versa, the transition space was not just a matter of convenience but necessity.

The good news, Blair had soon realized, was that the ground consisted of moist organic soil. That made it a far easier composition to dig than what they would have encountered if Shedo lived in an area with less than 40 inches of annual rainfall. And fortunately, the space didn't need to be completed in its entirety tonight; they just needed enough room to allow them to advance laterally to the basement wall. Penetrating that foundation and establishing a facade to cover their entrance for repeated use would be no quick or easy process; and with room for only two crew members to conduct it, the other two could continue expanding the prep area.

The bad news, however, was the sheer volume of dirt they'd had to displace. It was murderously slow, cumbersome work, punctuated by adjusting the supports for their overhead panels with lightweight poles of varying lengths. They'd continued breathing through regulators, but Blair still felt her nostrils clogged with slimy residue from the wet soil. In the process she'd gained a newfound respect for all the thieves who'd dug tunnels by hand to reach their targets—her crew had been able to rely on the micro-TBM for the vast majority of digging, only confronted with manual labor for the final one percent of the job.

The machine had even taken care of their excavated soil disposal, providing them a long channel to deposit the dirt without having to ferry bags back down the tunnel.

Now the tunneling apparatus had gone silent for the last time.

It was far too cumbersome to remove, not that they had any reason to try. The end result was that the Mole Holer had reached its final resting place, burrowed into the earth beside Shedo's basement wall. As long as their plan proceeded in roughly the same manner they predicted, it wouldn't be discovered until long after they'd left Washington, as Shedo's security tried to determine exactly how a collection of stolen art had simply vanished.

Blair saw her shadow appear on the dirt wall, its profile sharpening as a new light source approached.

She paused her digging and turned to face the PVC tunnel outlet, where Alec clambered into view with a stack of fiber-reinforced plastic panels worn in a pouch beside the air cylinder on his back.

He rotated his legs over the edge of the pipe, then scrambled down the dirt slope to the floor of the prep area and deposited his panels with a breathlessly transmitted inquiry.

"*Sure we can't keep working past sunrise? I don't think anyone will check under the dock.*"

Blair glanced at her watch. "Hard time to leave is 47 minutes, and we're not breaking that. Besides, aren't you exhausted by now?"

"*I mean technically, yeah. But me and Esther are really bonding now.*"

Esther transmitted, "*I can hear you, you know.*"

"*I'm counting on it,*" Alec replied, stepping aside in anticipation of her arrival.

The unlikely duo had been making repeated trips to the entry eye, recovering equipment to carry back up the ladder and clip into place in anticipation of the prep area becoming sufficiently expanded. A large part of that gear consisted of gas cylinders, which would be necessary unless the crew installed ventilation shafts—which, of course, they couldn't.

Esther appeared in the void with a quiver of support poles, which she handed down to her counterpart without exiting the PVC pipe.

Then the two were gone, leaving Blair and Sterling to dig in silence. Once a few minutes had elapsed, enough time for them to leave the audio range of the bone-conducting microphones, Blair said, "I think she's warming up to him."

"*I hope so,*" Sterling replied. "*Because if not, Alec's on a fast track to getting punched in the throat. I don't think his month of high school Jujutsu experience will hold up to her Krav Maga. At any rate, I think the prep area has reached its minimum effective size. Let's transition to our lateral drive.*"

With that, they turned their efforts to the wall of dirt beside them, and this was a far more delicate proposition.

Somewhere beyond the veil of soil, a scant three feet or less if Marco's trajectory for the Mole Holer had been accurate, was the concrete wall around Shedo's basement.

They began chiseling into the earth roughly one-third of the way up the dirt wall, gradually increasing the height of their shovel strikes to probe for any instability in the soil. Once the gap had been widened enough, in went a new fiber-reinforced plastic panel to support the newly established ceiling, held in place by one thief until the other emplaced the requisite pole supports.

Then the process began anew, every inch of ground representing the possibility of striking proverbial gold as they advanced on Shedo's foundation. There were three false alarms—stones, as it turned out, which were angrily wrested out of position and handed back—as Blair continued checking her watch, seeing their hard time to begin moving back to the subs fast approaching. If they didn't reach the basement now, they'd enter a new cycle of daylight uncertainty before they could begin digging again, wondering if their calculations had been off. Sterling would be miserable, she thought, as would she. After all, they'd fully committed to this process, having already entombed their micro-TBM after a full seven days of brutal nonstop effort.

But when the tip of her shovel speared the earth to stop abruptly with a flat *clang*, Blair knew they'd arrived.

"We made it," she transmitted. "The foundation is here."

Sterling transmitted, *"Don't get my hopes up,"* before driving his own shovel forward to achieve the same result. They locked eyes for a moment, then turned back to the wall and dropped their shovels, feverishly clawing at the soil with their hands.

The final sheet of earth crumbled as their gloved fingertips scraped against a perfectly flat, man-made surface: a slab of concrete.

Planting a palm flat against the wall, Sterling cut his eyes to her. His stare was smoldering, eyes alight with ruthless determination as he transmitted, *"Tomorrow night, we'll be standing in Shedo's house."*

44

STERLING

Laying the yardstick flat across the drywall, Sterling used a permanent marker to sketch out a three-foot square before removing the regulator from his mouth to transmit via his throat mic.

"Marco, we are at the drywall. Need final clearance before penetrating."

Then he inserted the mouthpiece, grateful to be done with the bone-conducting speakers—at least outside of actual diving. Now they could work off their usual radios, and had even installed a long-range radio relay with a subsurface data signal processing unit beneath the dock and routed to the prep area by way of transducer cable, allowing them continuous communications with the crew's resident hacker—which were, more than at any other point in the op, necessary tonight.

Marco replied over his earpiece, *"Give me a few minutes to do a final review of all camera feeds. Stand by."*

Sterling added a final detail within the square—an arrow pointing up—before trading his marker for a utility knife. Using the yardstick to align his cuts, he sliced through the exterior paper along his markered lines and partially into the drywall itself. The end result was perfectly clean score lines in the material, the surface primed for his final entry.

Sterling passed the yardstick, marker, and utility knife back to Blair, then kept his palm open and spoke like a surgeon at the operating table.

"First pull."

"*First pull*," Blair repeated, setting a lightweight C-shaped handle into his hand. He examined it, noting with approval that the attachment points had been covered in an ultra-strong epoxy that glistened in his headlamp. Sterling pressed the handle into the center line of the square, holding it in place for several seconds to let the epoxy begin to bond before holding his hand out for the next.

"Second pull."

"*Second pull*."

Accepting the next handle, Sterling affixed it beside the first, keeping it stationary until he was certain the industrial-grade adhesive stuck.

Then Sterling removed the air cylinder from his back, setting it aside without removing the regulator from his mouth. Instead he unzipped the hooded disposable coveralls that had absorbed the brunt of dirt and concrete dust, stripping the suit to his ankles until he was down to his preferred uniform for stealthy penetration work: elastic, moisture-wicking black clothes, along with an equipment belt and lightweight tactical vest containing the required tools of his trade, each secured in a non-rattling configuration.

Pulling his feet outside the coverall booties, he was careful to set the soles of his running shoes atop the clean interior sections of the discarded suit.

Glancing behind him, he saw his crew mirroring his actions—Blair was to his immediate rear, with Alec behind her and finally Esther at the end of the row, already pulling on her night vision head mount.

Sterling faced the drywall and did the same, first yanking his headlamp down around his neck. He'd just finished affixing the head mount when Marco's terse reply came over the frequency.

"*Hold fast—I have a guard entering the two-alpha corridor. Let me make sure he makes a clean pass by the basement staircase.*"

"Standing by," Sterling confirmed, pulling a handheld drywall saw from his kit as he waited for Marco's next transmission.

The crew had infiltrated at sundown, which should have given them ample time to complete the night's work. Nonetheless, Sterling was prepared for every conceivable setback tonight from a radio failure to a breakdown with his cutting equipment. Either could easily cause the first penetration to be delayed by another 24 hours, and he'd emotionally braced himself as much as possible not to fly into a rage at the first indication of a problem. He'd gotten his crew into this mess by bringing Shedo's tracker back to their hideout, and it was up to him to get them out of it—no matter how difficult, or how long the process took.

But he hadn't been prepared for the actual outcome of penetrating Shedo's foundation, which had been remarkably smooth and completed well ahead of schedule. That certainly wasn't because the job itself was simple from a technical perspective—simply getting to this point had required three phases of cutting.

Sterling began the process by making a five-foot square cut, operating a wet electric concrete saw that sprayed water both to lubricate and cool the 14-inch diamond blade and to reduce the amount of dust flowing back into the prep area. With a five-inch depth of cut, the blade had only penetrated halfway through the wall; then it was a matter of using a compact hydraulic jackhammer to exploit the newly formed seam and chisel out the surface all the way down to the steel rebar.

Then Sterling had begun his second cut, sawing a smaller four-foot square within the first. This would be their entry port into Shedo's house, and cutting it was a far more delicate proposition—the tip of his blade was reaching the foundation's inner wall, exponentially increasing the sound level within the basement room beyond. But the good thing about infiltrating a 27,000-square-foot house was that noise discipline was relatively easy to achieve; until Marco transmitted that an occupant was approaching a stairwell or the elevator, Sterling was able to operate the circular saw with relative impunity.

Excavating the entry port exposed the polystyrene rigid foam insulation, easily cut by utility knife until Sterling was face to face with layers of fluffy pink fiberglass that he ripped out to get a better view of the wood stud wall frame. The series of vertical two-by-fours was a priority to remove, comprising the last noisy portion of the job—while they'd been able to operate freely thus far, all that could change in a heartbeat. He'd sawed the wood planks as efficiently as he could manage, feeling almost certain that Marco would transmit at any second a report of a suspicious noise over the guard force's radio net. But Sterling proceeded unhindered, until the final thing standing between his crew and Shedo's basement was the half-inch-thick layer of drywall before him.

And now, all he needed was final confirmation before he could set foot into his enemy's lair.

He received his wish a moment later when Marco transmitted, "*Bogey has passed, basement clear, entry room camera is frozen. You are clear to proceed at your discretion.*"

Sterling's response was directed at the trio of thieves behind him.

"Blackout, blackout, blackout."

They extinguished their headlamps in near-unison, and Sterling flipped his night vision downward, activating the infrared floodlight to guide his coming effort.

Aligning the tip of his drywall saw blade with the top left corner of his precut square, he plunged the tool forward and began sawing to the right. Once he reached the far corner he repeated the process twice more, working down both sides until all that remained was the bottom line.

He worked through this final segment with more care, using one hand to grip a newly-emplaced handle as he neared the end of the cut—the last thing they needed was for this square to tumble forward and fracture. But he reached the final corner with no discernable movement in the panel, and after withdrawing the saw and setting it down, Sterling took a final breath and held it. Then he pulled the regulator from his mouth and left it beside his abandoned air cylinder, gripped the remaining handle, and gave a forceful forward shove.

The square of drywall broke free from the wall, a perfectly clean displacement that ended with Sterling inserting his head into the space beyond, assessing his distance from the floor as less than three feet before carefully laying the panel facedown to the side of his entryway, then clambering inside.

He stood on the carpeted floor, awkwardly negotiating the narrow space before a tall stack of boxes to make way for his teammates to enter. Slipping along the wall, he heard Blair and Alec flowing forward behind him, stepping across the inside-out coveralls to avoid tracking soil into the house.

"We're in," Sterling whispered, waving a hand at the camera mounted in the corner of the ceiling.

Marco confirmed, "*I see you.*"

There had been no shortage of choices in selecting their entry room; nearly every non-bathroom space in the house had one or more cameras, which Marco could surveil at will and, when necessary, manipulate the feed in the interests of deceiving the security force.

But when Marco had said it would take him several minutes to make a final review of the cameras before Sterling and his teammates could enter, it was for good reason.

The basement alone had eighteen individually labeled spaces as per the blueprint, ranging from a lower foyer and lobby at the base of two available staircases and one elevator, to a movie theater, wine cellar, wet bar and kitchen, gym, massage parlor, dry sauna, and four recreation rooms. And although the previous days of reviewing security camera footage at extreme fast-forward to generate a log of movements for Shedo, her staff, and her guards had revealed that the basement was infrequently utilized, the op's success hinged on their entry point going undiscovered while they searched for the art. All of those rooms were off-limits for a potential entry.

The basement's mechanical room was similarly removed from the list—if anyone would notice a detail out of place, it was some repairman with an encyclopedic knowledge of building structure—and the crew was left with a particularly appetizing blueprint option labeled *STORAGE*.

While the video feed revealed that this room contained a tremendous number of neatly stacked cardboard boxes and large plastic crates, no one had entered it for the duration of the team's surveillance efforts and they had no clue what those containers might have inside. Any written text was too small for Marco to distinguish even with the camera's streaming 4K resolution, and it wasn't until Sterling stepped close with his night vision that they solved the almost absurdly anticlimactic mystery: they were simply outdoor decorations organized by holiday.

Sterling moved past them and took up his position near the room's single entryway, a closed door that he turned to face, drawing his taser. His only job right now was to cover the doorway leading deeper into Shedo's domain, remaining poised to subdue in the event of an unexpected guard appearance. Marco had hijacked all the camera feeds, but Sterling had endured enough technical issues in the course of his career to never fully trust any precautions whose single point of failure was a computer.

Just because his current role was simple didn't mean his teammates had it easy, however. He glanced sideways to see Alec hunched over the recently removed panel of drywall, applying a layer of transparent tape around the edges while Esther did the same at the square port from which it had emerged. The goal of both endeavors was to eliminate the scattering of drywall dust on their repeated entries—while they'd use a handheld keyboard vacuum to erase any trace of drywall before leaving, they didn't want to repeat the process every night.

Blair was withdrawing a series of thin silicone strips and sparingly using her headlamp to find the best color match to the wall. Once determined, she'd use the material to adhere a silicone lip over the inside edges of the panel face, allowing it to more closely blend with the wall once reinserted. It wouldn't completely hide the entry point, of course, but concealing the actual cut from anything but an up-close examination was better than nothing. Given the porthole was located behind a wall of boxes, Sterling felt confident it would go unseen.

He turned his attention back to the door, gripped by an almost irresistible urge to probe further into the house.

"Time hack," he spoke.

Marco replied, "*One hour, seventeen minutes until you need to withdraw.*"

Sterling smiled to himself, pleased with how far ahead of schedule they were. He'd have been thrilled if they completed the entryway with thirty seconds to spare; as soon as it was complete, they'd have a full four hours of station time each night to conduct their search.

Once again, the desire to push past the door resumed, pulsing through Sterling's veins in a windfall of instinct telling him to slip farther inside, to go deeper while he still had the time.

He didn't know why the impulse was so strong—it wasn't like the art was going to be in the basement, anyway. By this point they'd confirmed as well as they could that their target was located in her sprawling first-floor master suite, a 6,000-square-foot blind spot in their existing blueprints. With the existence of a seven-inch-thick vault door and fire-resistant walls

known to be safeguarding their crew paraphernalia, the art was undoubt-
edly safeguarded there as well. Sure, they could spend a week or more
ruling out vast swaths of the house, but had instead decided to go for
Shedo's inner sanctum on the first full night of search ops. Since the art was
clearly hidden, they'd need all the time in her master suite they could get; it
would probably take the full gamut of their impulse radar equipment just
to locate the sliding bookcase, false wall, or trapdoor leading to the vault
entrance, which Alec had already begun preparations on bypassing.

He heard the quiet whirr of Blair's handheld vacuum as she cleaned up
the fallen drywall dust, looking over to see Esther reaching out of the
tunnel to grasp the panel's twin handles before lifting it into place and
securing it from the inside, leaving Alec to sweep his headlamp over the
seemingly intact wall.

"*Panel looks great,*" he transmitted.

Blair killed her vacuum and added, "*Area is sterilized. Let's head back.*"

Sterling didn't move.

"I want to continue penetration."

"*We don't have time to reach her master suite,*" Blair objected.

"I don't intend to. I just want to move down the one-alpha corridor,
maybe all the way to the lower foyer. Then we'll turn back."

Esther came over the net then, speaking in a cautionary tone.

"*Advise we don't push our luck. We've got the entryway established; let's count
tonight as a victory and come back after sunset.*"

"Your counsel is noted," Sterling said, knowing full well that her
authority ended at the tunnel's edge. "We're going forward anyway—
Marco, freeze the one-alpha hallway camera."

Begrudgingly, Marco responded, "*One-alpha is frozen. You are clear to
proceed at your discretion.*"

Sterling kept his taser in hand and advanced on the door, laying a
gloved palm on the handle. This was where the real penetration began, and
as soon as he heard Blair's transmission that the rest of the crew was
formed up behind him, ready to move, he twisted the handle and pulled
open the heavy reinforced door.

Then a curious thing happened. Before Sterling could so much as take
a step forward, the handle was wrenched from his grasp, the door slam-

ming shut with alarming speed as an electronic deadbolt automatically engaged.

But his wasn't the only entryway to do this: all throughout the basement were sounds of reinforced doors slamming shut and bolting, and the lights in the supply room blazed to life as an emergency siren screeched throughout the house.

By the time Sterling turned to flee, his crew was well ahead of him—Esther was already disappearing through the open porthole, followed in short order by Alec. He'd barely cleared the tunnel entrance when Blair vanished inside, leaving Sterling as the last man.

He climbed through the gap and turned to reach for the handle on the drywall section, lifting it and its newly attached silicone lip back into position with the arrow facing up. A short tug was all it took to slide it back into place, and then he joined his crew in the emergency evacuation back to the subs.

45

BLAIR

Blair carried her bag of dive gear through the rental house's back door, currently held open by Alec.

"You'd better get in there before Esther delivers her deadly roundhouse kick."

"What? To who?" Blair asked, stepping past him to drop her gear bag beside the other sets that had been abandoned inside the house.

"The only other person here: Sterling."

Blair heard Alec locking up behind her as she made her way through the house, trying desperately to remain calm, to force any semblance of logic into her thoughts.

But the overwhelming tumult of emotions made that difficult; aside from the physical fatigue of operating all night and making a speedy subsurface retreat, she was racked with an unprecedented degree of concern over their current predicament. The situation in Shedo's basement had gone from ideal to dire in a matter of seconds—they'd somehow compromised themselves to Shedo's security, had no idea *how* that happened, and fled in a panic only to arrive back at the rental house without further incident. Now their tunnel was burned, rendering over two weeks of time, effort, and financing completely useless.

Most disturbingly, Marco had not only remained silent for the duration of their return trip back to the rental house, but had yet to check in at all. And that, as it turned out, was the current point of contention between her boyfriend and the Israeli thief.

She heard them before she saw them, following the escalating sound of Esther's voice coming from the living room.

"Don't you get it?" she was saying, "Marco could've gotten rolled up by Shedo's people already. For all we know, he might be ratting us out as we speak."

Blair entered the room to find Esther beside the row of telescopic cameras, where Sterling took a step forward to square off against her. He had a radio in his hand, an unsettling reminder that one crew member was unaccounted for.

"We're not going anywhere. There's nothing tying his boat to this location, and Marco would never compromise us."

"How can you be sure?"

"Because," Sterling shot back angrily, "I did time in Supermax, on top of a lengthy trial, with everyone along the way offering me the world if I turned in my people. But I didn't, and neither will Marco. You're not used to working with a crew, but believe me when I say we hired the right people."

Esther scoffed. "Oh really? What about you, Mister 'I'm just going to peek around the corner?' Are you the right person? You had to keep pushing it, didn't you?"

Sterling looked crushed beyond belief by the accusation, his upper body seeming to deflate as Blair quickly interceded.

"Enough," she said sharply. "However that alarm was triggered just now, it would have happened on our next incursion anyway. We don't even know how we got compromised."

Alec entered the room and clarified, "Because Marco isn't here to tell us."

Blair nodded. "It could be a simple radio failure."

Esther yanked out her hair tie, allowing her wet, dark hair to fall to her shoulders. "There's nothing wrong with our comms and you know it."

As if to validate her point, Sterling's radio came alive with a hiss of static followed by Marco's voice.

"*I'm on my way back. Five minutes from the dock.*"

Lifting the radio to his mouth, Sterling asked, "Are you okay?"

"*I'm fine.*"

Sterling's tone transitioned seamlessly from concern to anger. "If you're fine, then why haven't you checked in?"

"*I'll explain everything when I get there. Just sit tight.*"

Esther folded her arms. "What if he got captured, and they're forcing him to lead them to us?"

"I already told you," Sterling fired back, "he wouldn't do that. Or is that too difficult for you to understand?"

"I have a healthy degree of skepticism that's kept me out of jail so far. Which is more than I can say for you."

Blair spoke more angrily than she intended. "Esther, we're all in the same amount of danger here. And if Marco was going to give up our location, he wouldn't need to transmit—Shedo's people would be kicking in the doors as we speak. Please, we all just need to take a breath and collect ourselves."

Vigorously shaking his head, Alec countered, "We don't need to take a breath. Who wants a beer?"

Esther's eyes narrowed. "It's not even four in the morning."

"I didn't ask what time it was, I asked who wanted a beer."

"I do," Sterling replied. Alec held up a finger.

"Me too," Blair admitted. Lifting a second finger, Alec looked pointedly at Esther, who finally sighed and spoke with resignation.

"Why not."

Alec now held three fingers aloft, then added one for himself and said, "And Marco has lost his drinking privileges until he explains why he gave us all heart attacks by not checking in. Agreed? Agreed."

Then he was gone, disappearing into the kitchen as Sterling began pacing the room. Esther stood her ground, watching him with resentment until Alec returned and handed an open bottle to each of them.

Blair took a grateful sip of the cold, fizzy beer. Alcohol was the last thing they should be drinking right now—they were tired and dehydrated after a long night that had ended in nearly catastrophic defeat. But, she had to admit, beer was probably a far lesser evil than yelling at one another until Marco returned.

They moved to the back door to intercept him, quickly learning that his five-minute estimate had been conservative. They'd barely arrived before hearing the boat pull up to the dock, and no one spoke until his footsteps could be heard traversing the wooden planks toward the house.

Just as Blair allowed herself a relieved exhale, she heard Sterling mutter, "He better have a good reason for ghosting us."

"I'm sure he does," Esther said, "but that doesn't change the fact that our op here is tanked."

Sterling didn't answer that, instead unlocking the door and pulling it open.

The hacker strode in with his kit bag of computer equipment held over one shoulder, and before Sterling could deliver the inevitable barrage of questions, he nodded toward the hall and said, "Let's go, I need to show you this."

"Are we safe?" Sterling asked.

Marco kept walking, calling over his shoulder, "That depends on what you mean by 'safe.'"

Locking the door, Sterling hustled to catch up with the others as they entered the dining room. "You know what I mean. How were we compromised?"

"We weren't." Marco set his bag on the table and swiftly unzipped it to remove a laptop before flipping open the screen. "Immediately after I froze the hallway camera, a guard patrol discovered an intruder on the property."

Blair shrugged.

"Then why didn't you just tell us that?"

"Because the guard patrol didn't report it until after they heard the man and went to investigate."

Alec wrinkled his nose. "Wait a minute, did you just say they 'heard' him? What about all of Shedo's thermal imaging, cameras, and seismic sensors? You're telling me we've been risking an eyeball-to-eyeball encounter with a vicious clan of territorial mole people for nothing?"

Blair circled around Marco's backside, clustering with the others to see him pulling up an automatically generated transcript of the guard force communications.

"As best as the guard force has pieced together," Marco began, "the intruder used a heat-shielding blanket covered in fake plants, then low-crawled along the row of shrubs and trees on the southern edge of the property. They're not sure where he initially entered the yard or how long he'd been moving, but it must have been several days at least."

Esther leaned in, her eyes darting across the transcript. "And the seismic sensors didn't pick him up because of...what, exactly?"

"He'd been timing his movements to correlate with the guards' foot patrols."

"Smart," Sterling said. "We should've thought of that. Maybe once he gets out of jail, we could consider hiring him."

Turning to drape an arm across the backside of his chair, Marco replied, "We won't be able to, because the guards shot him dead on sight."

"Shot him?" Blair asked. "Why?"

"Probably because they thought he was one of us, and—"

"Some overeager guard," Sterling finished the sentence for him, "wanted the bounty for himself."

"That would be my guess."

Esther gave an angry shake of her head. "Well they can have fun trying to explain that to the cops. How many squad cars showed up at the house?"

"None," Marco said.

"They're covering it up? How?"

"Their search of the body uncovered a DSLR video camera along with a Washington driver's license identifying the man as"—he returned to the transcript, scrolling down it before continuing—"Robert Lawrence, a conspiracy theorist from Tacoma. They surmised that he was working on some theory about Shedo given the recent press coverage of her yacht sinking, and once they confirmed he didn't have any radio or remotely transmitting body cam to document his whereabouts, Vance told them to get rid of the body."

"My God," Blair gasped.

By now Marco was pulling up a video player on the laptop. "What concerns our current effort is what occurred as soon as the guards reported his discovery. The patrol leader transmitted a single word—'lockdown'—and then this happened."

He flipped through camera feeds showcasing the moment that occurred, but was cut off by Sterling.

"We saw it. Every light in the house comes on, and the doors automatically close and lock."

"And," Marco said, "Shedo was rushed to a safe room on the first floor. But there's something else."

He continued to flip through feeds until he found the clip he was looking for, one that showed a hallway window overlooking the yard.

When he hit play, Blair saw the feed illuminate and the doors slam shut, along with a new detail: metal shutters slid down over the window, preventing any escape.

"It looks like weather plating of some kind. Safe to assume it's impenetrable short of explosives."

"We're screwed," Esther said flatly.

"It gets worse. Keep watching."

Less than thirty seconds later, a door on screen flung open and a fully kitted SWAT team flowed in with assault rifles, splitting up into two-man elements as a full clearance of the ground floor began.

One of the men pulled security at a locked door, and his partner pressed a fingertip to some kind of wall sensor. The door flung open, and they both vanished inside with their rifles at the ready.

"Biometrics," Alec said.

"Definitely," Esther agreed. "Which we can't defeat."

Marco said, "Not in any meaningfully short period of time, no."

Then Blair spoke up.

"Just because we didn't cause the lockdown doesn't mean we're not compromised. What about the lights coming on in the supply room?"

"That's why I was radio-silent on your way back here," Marco confirmed. "I unfroze the camera feed as soon as Sterling had the panel in place, and since there was a three to five second disparity in lights coming on across the various rooms, that may have been good enough. But the other cameras had a blinding glare as they adjusted to the interior lights, so I had to digitally create that effect in the storage room feed, then splice it into the clip on their backup cloud footage, all from the boat. Since it was time sensitive to say the least, and I couldn't afford any distractions, I pulled my earpieces until the work was done."

Sterling threw back a swig of beer, wiped his mouth with the back of his hand, and said, "You could have told us something."

Marco turned in his seat to glare at him, then looked around in what was seemingly his first recognition that everyone was drinking but him.

"Where's my beer?"

Alec shrugged. "We haven't forgiven you yet."

"Well you should, because unless a control room guard was either staring at the supply room monitor when the lights came on or reviewed that footage within 20 minutes of the alarm going off, they don't know about our entry point." He opened a new window on his screen, this one a live video feed of the storage room containing the assembly of stacked boxes—along with their hidden tunnel outlet. "And if they are suspicious, we're going to see the guards performing a comprehensive search any minute."

"If they haven't by now," Blair said, "I think we're good."

Sterling agreed, "So do I."

Alec put a hand on his hip and waved his beer bottle at the screen. "Us being 'good' is pretty relative at present. I mean, despite all our hacking we had no idea this lockdown procedure even existed."

"Or," Esther added, "that metal frame shutters were installed over the windows. Those automatically locking doors are another matter altogether —given their reinforced construction, it would take a demolition charge to blow them open. If we systematically disable the locks on future penetrations, it will be detected during their routine security checks. And considering that we don't yet know where the art is located, we could end up three rooms deep in Shedo's master suite by the time we got locked in."

Blair said, "So we can get into the house, but if someone triggers the alarm, we can't get out."

"Correct." Marco nodded without taking his eyes off the screen. "Unless the art happens to be in the basement—and we all know it's not—we'd be signing our own death warrant by penetrating any further."

Sterling asked, "What if we carried sufficient explosives to blast our way back to the basement in the event of a lock-in?"

Alec frowned.

"We still wouldn't have enough time to reach our tunnel before Shedo's personal SWAT team mobilized to contain us. And they don't need to waste time with explosive charges—all they need is their fingerprint to pass through doors. That means they'd overrun us in a matter of minutes."

Silence fell over their group, leaving Blair overcome with a crushing sense of desperation. She and Sterling had convinced everyone to double down against Shedo at great personal risk. Now it was utterly impossible to proceed, much less succeed.

Blair looked across the crew, waiting for someone to have a brilliant epiphany, some idea that could turn the tides in their favor.

But she could tell from Marco's lack of response that no idea was forth-coming, that there was no recourse to stealing the art back. Even Alec was sulking, silent as he examined the bottle in his hand. And Sterling was virtually catatonic, his hollow gaze fixed on the far wall.

Only Esther spoke, and her words made Blair's heart seize up.

"Whatever you decide to do," Esther began, "I wish you the best of luck. But today, I go on the run."

"Where?" she asked.

"Not home. I have a way out, but it only supports one person. You four were my first crew, and you'll be my last."

Sterling offered, "After all we've gone through, you can't just quit—"

"Quit?" Esther shot back. "*Quit?* I took a tremendous risk to pull your entire crew in from the cold. Then I spent money like a rapper to bankroll this entire operation. When our yacht operation failed, I agreed to one more attempt. Well, now we've used it and the situation isn't getting any safer the longer we wait."

"Esther," Blair pleaded, "don't do this. We'll find a way—"

"A way to what? Sacrifice ourselves to Shedo's people? Because that's what any continuation will lead to. This op is finished, and everyone here knows it."

Setting her unfinished beer on the table, Esther concluded, "I have to pack."

Then she was gone, retreating to her room with quick strides.

Blair's eyes flew to the computer screen, watching the live feed of the storage room in Shedo's basement. It was still empty, every passing second a confirmation it hadn't been searched and wasn't going to be. This was infuriating, she thought—her crew had established an entry point, could monitor nearly every movement inside the house through Shedo's extensive surveillance system and plan their progress accordingly, but without the ability to exit safely in the event of a compromise, the entire op was doomed.

Her thoughts were a maelstrom of seemingly unrelated memories: how she joined this once-unstoppable crew in the first place, and how Shedo had put the proverbial knife to their throat. The tracking device in a wristwatch, and the warehouse burning down. How she escaped from a Century City high-rise, her first op with the crew before they'd even earned the moniker of Sky Thieves, and how, after the high-speed chase had ended in El Segundo, Sterling explained that the job had been a spider heist.

Everyone sees the spider, and nobody notices the web.

And then these thoughts converged into one shimmering realization, the answer to all their problems arriving in one fell swoop.

"I've got it!" she cried out.

Marco turned slowly to face her.

"You've got what?"

"The solution," Blair said, taking a triumphant swig of beer. "We can win this thing, and do it by turning Shedo's own methods against her."

Alec responded with tentative enthusiasm. "Great. How?"

Blair smiled. "By doing a spider heist."

"Okay," Sterling cautiously replied, "how many people will it take?"

Blair thought for a moment. There would have to be a decoy effort, first and foremost. But the decoy participant would, by definition, be prohibited from executing the actual theft; they had no choice but to operate in two separate elements. Or three, she considered, given Marco's required standoff to monitor the overall situation.

"Five people," she said, "at least."

Marco and Sterling watched her as if she was missing something obvious. Blair looked from one imploring face to the other, wondering what they thought she was overlooking before they'd even heard her plan.

But only Alec spoke, setting a hand on her shoulder. "Then you might want to stop Esther."

Blair turned and ran to Esther's room, stopping before the closed door and pounding on it.

"What," Esther said.

"Esther, I know a way."

The Israeli thief flung the door open a moment later, and Blair was shocked to see tears in her eyes.

Her voice was choked with emotion, cracking mid-word as she asked, "How?"

Blair set a hand on the doorframe, pausing to collect her thoughts.

Then she met Esther's eyes, a wry grin creeping across her lips. "That depends. I know you're an expert swimmer and all, but...how fast can you run?"

46

STERLING

Sterling carefully tapped another spoonful of finely ground, rust-colored powder into the measuring cup.

The food scale display ticked to 47 grams, then 48, before freezing.

He frowned—he'd been getting pretty good at this process over the past few hours, and thought for sure he'd be able to hit his mark on the nose this time. Dipping his spoon back into the bag labeled Fe_2O_3, he procured another small ration of powder and tipped it into the cup, stopping when the food scale confirmed 50 grams exactly.

Setting his spoon on the desk, he lifted the measuring cup and tilted it into a one-gallon Ziplock bag already half-full of the red powder.

To this he added the contents of a second bag, this one containing a pre-measured portion of light silver powder finely ground to 300 mesh. Combined, they looked like almost a 50/50 mix, but this, he knew, was only because one powder was heavier than the other. In reality it was a perfect 8:3 ratio, and he sealed the Ziplock before shaking it vigorously to intersperse the contents.

"How's the insurance policy coming along?"

Sterling turned away from his desk to see Blair standing in the doorway of their appointed bedroom in the lakeside rental home, her gaze drifting across the chemical components spread out before him.

"You might want to go," he said, continuing to shake the bag. "Remember, I've never done this before."

"Are you worried about me, or about getting distracted?"

"Maybe a little bit of both," Sterling admitted.

Blair closed the door behind her, then took a seat on the bed.

"I saw how you reacted when Esther accused you of setting off the alarm. And I need you to know that none of this is your fault."

Sterling chuckled. "Is this your idea of a *Good Will Hunting* moment?"

"Something like that."

Setting the bag on the desk, he shifted in his chair and replied, "No one abused me, Blair. I got us into this mess, now I've got to get us out of it."

"Would you stop blaming yourself? We *all* got ourselves into this mess. Esther included, the minute she stole the tapes from us in LA."

Considering the logic, Sterling pointed out, "If we hadn't fought back, then Shedo wouldn't have targeted her."

"Sure," Blair conceded, "and your mom would be getting indicted because Jim would have already made good on his threat."

When Sterling made no immediate reply, Blair sighed. "As for the rest of us? Well, no one forced us to keep pulling heists. Because you're a persuasive leader, yeah. But being a thief is either in your blood or it isn't. If it is—and make no mistake, the rest of your crew has it as bad as you do, myself included—then there's no way you can pull a normal nine-to-five until you scratch that itch. After that? Well, some people retire and some get caught. If anyone should blame themselves, it's me. I brought Jim against our crew, and Jim brought Shedo."

Sterling broke eye contact with Blair to look at the bag. The mix of silver and rust-colored powder had congealed into a tawny brown substance that he stared at absently as he responded.

"My dad always said the more you disrupt the universal order, the more repercussions there are. He was right, you know. We could've stayed with low-key robberies and continued in this line of work forever—instead, we had to push it to the limit, all the time."

"Well," Blair began, "I think we've found the final limit. You and I are both exposed to the public. We've lost our hideout and almost everything we've earned has either gone to charity or been spent trying to get Shedo.

What little we've got left is reserved for starting over. I'd say we're fairly close to the end of the line."

He met her gaze, eyebrows raised. "Close? I thought we'd blown clear past it by now."

She smiled. "Maybe we have. Just remember, our fates are intertwined. All five of us. Whatever happens, we're in it together. That means we all have to get ourselves out of this, not just you. So don't be too hard on yourself, Sterling. Because for every bit of danger you've put us in, you've also given us—me, personally—the most beautiful and fulfilling moments of our lives."

He extended an upturned palm to her, and when she placed her hand in his, he said, "I love you, Blair."

"I was talking about the heists. But I love you too."

She released his hand, rising to kiss him on the forehead before putting her hands on her hips in a defiant posture.

"Now get back to work, Sterling Defranc, and build me some bombs."

Sterling laughed as she departed, smiling ruefully at her intervention. Blair always seemed to know exactly what to say to get him back on track. Which was a good thing, he thought, because right now he couldn't afford an error. Although her reference to bombs wasn't accurate, he thought—at least, not entirely. He turned his attention back to the bag of freshly mixed brown powder before him.

In chemical terms, the 8:3 weight ratio of iron oxide and aluminum powder was thermite, a pyrotechnic composition identical to that of the grenade they'd used to incinerate the contents of their safe as they evacuated the warehouse.

Contrary to Hollywood's widespread perception, however, as much as thermite served well for quickly eradicating material in a confined space, it was an extremely poor candidate for widespread destruction. The reaction producing its wave of molten iron only affected a small, typically directional area, and to make matters worse, the 275 grams contained in a typical thermite grenade would burn out in under thirty seconds.

And for tomorrow's op, that wouldn't do at all.

So while Sterling continued creating thermite in large quantities, it was only the majority ingredient in a mixture that would ultimately integrate the other chemicals at his workstation—namely sulfur, barium nitrate, and the imaginatively titled substance known as polybutadiene acrylonitrile copolymer, more frequently referred to as PBAN. That last component was the binder formulation most commonly used for rocket propellant, and that fact brought a sense of comfort to Sterling, who was the one most likely to be employing this particular insurance policy should it be needed.

The resulting combination wouldn't be thermite at all, but an incendiary pyrotechnic known as ther*mate*. That one-letter variation didn't mean much on paper, but in application, it made all the difference in the world.

Like thermite, thermate had a high heat tolerance and required the use of a magnesium ribbon to ignite. But once that occurred, at least in the modified grenades that Sterling would soon be assembling, you'd better be behind cover.

Instead of a short-lived, directional projection of molten iron, these puppies would explode in a swath of flame that would ignite anything and everything in the immediate vicinity. The reaction was irreversible, and completely immune to water—these would burn even beneath the surface of Lake Washington—fire extinguishers, or indeed anything but liquid nitrogen. If he had to release this particular genie there was no putting it back in the lamp; the finished devices would be almost suicidally lethal, particularly if employed in a residential setting.

But at this point, Sterling thought, suicidal lethality was the only way to succeed. Blair had been right about that much, and as unsettled as he was to break almost every rule he'd lived by over the course of a lengthy and wildly successful heist career, the only alternative was death or, arguably worse, imprisonment not just for himself and his crew, but his mother as well.

Shedo had decided to play dirty, after all, and now the Sky Thieves had no choice but to do the same.

47

BLAIR

Blair took another pull of air through her regulator and then stripped off her wetsuit, overlooking the fact that she was, once again, semi-naked alongside her three teammates in the underground prep area as they transitioned into dry clothes for the next phase of the op.

At the moment, awkwardness was the least of her concerns; the four headlights illuminated a shifting web of shadows on the plastic panels overhead and the dirt walls around them, the spooky kaleidoscope effect so distracting that she feared she'd bump into a support pole and cause an inadvertent cave-in. The prep area had taken on an entirely different aura since her last trip here. Then, it had represented a hard-earned refuge before they took their first tentative steps into Shedo's basement. Now, the space seemed more like a tomb from which they'd launch their final assault and be lucky to return to alive, much less successful.

She finished dressing, a difficult process when conducted between periodic breaths from the air cylinder grounded beside her. After tying her running shoes, she reached into the bag to retrieve her equipment belt and tactical vest as she glanced over at Sterling, looking for reassurance and getting the opposite.

He was in the process of strapping on a bulletproof vest and tactical vest bearing pouches with three of his modified thermate grenades. As Blair continued her transition, she saw him remove his father's Omega from a waterproof pouch and strap it on his wrist. She'd previously questioned the prudence of this, having already suggested that he hand it off to Marco as a means to ensure its safety. That was what the rest of the crew had done with any items of sentimental value, knowing full well that the risks of losing them were higher tonight than ever before. But Sterling had been adamant: the watch had accompanied him on every heist, and tonight would be no exception.

What else this job had in common with anything they'd ever done, Blair had no idea.

For one thing, this was entirely her plan. There were many ways it could fail, but only one way it could succeed. And while most of her heists had involved the possibility of arrest, this op brought with it the very real chance of death for one or all of them. Shedo's security force had committed a murder and covered it up, and Sterling already had two near-misses with Clint Vance, first in Century City and again after the Sky Safe.

Still, the crew had plunged on, all too aware that they had to put Shedo either in prison or on the run herself. To do otherwise risked keeping the bounty open. Only one chance remained to end the manhunt forever, and this was it. While they may be returning to this tunnel with fewer thieves than when they entered, the alternative was for all five to be picked off eventually, while Shedo continued to reign over an empire of corruption spanning illegal influence in law enforcement, business, and politics.

The fear that Blair had felt all day was rising to a crescendo, counter-pointed with an almost nostalgic sadness—this was the Sky Thieves' final heist, whether they wanted it to be or not.

By now she'd donned her night vision, keeping it flipped up on the head mount as she transmitted, "We're almost set here. Need final clearance."

Marco replied, "*Stand by.*"

As the hacker began his systematic review of camera feeds from inside and outside the house, Blair turned to appraise her crew.

Sterling looked like a commando in his body armor and grenades, and didn't seem to notice her as he made the final adjustments to his kit. Instead he was looking down, tightening a Velcro strap, and Blair caught a glimpse of him smiling around the regulator in his mouth in an incomprehensible response to what was about to occur.

Alec was staging the equipment bags they'd be carrying inside as Esther prepared the precautionary items that would remain in the prep area: a set of spray bottles filled with sulfuric acid, their final means of erasing any traces of DNA or fingerprints before they departed for the subs a final time. If they made it that far, Blair reminded herself.

Sensing her uncertainty, Esther transmitted, *"I'm good to go. You've got this, Blair."*

Alec hoisted a gear bag onto his back and added, *"I'm ready. And Blair, I'd follow you into the fires of hell."*

"If this goes wrong," Sterling added unhelpfully, *"you just might have to. I'm set."*

Then he took a step toward her, set a hand on her shoulder, and whispered, "Slow and steady. We've only got one shot to make it in, so trust your instincts. It's a great plan, Blair, and all we have to do is pull it off. No matter what happens, we'll be together. I'm proud of you."

Blair didn't have time to process his comment, much less reply, before Marco's voice came over the frequency.

"Guard patrol just exited the two-alpha corridor, and there is zero presence on the basement level. Entry room camera is frozen. You are clear to proceed at your discretion."

Turning to face the foundation wall, Blair transmitted, "I'm taking us in. Blackout, blackout, blackout."

She extinguished the headlamp now worn around her neck, flipping down her night vision before ditching her regulator and taking a final step forward. Grasping the twin handles on the wall before her, she pushed outward to displace the drywall panel and set it on the carpeted basement floor, sliding it out of the way before climbing through the gap.

"I see you," Marco said.

Blair was only vaguely aware of the confirmation—she was busy clearing the hole to make room for her crew, performing her visual sweep as she slipped past the stacked boxes to her left. Stepping from the subterranean prep area into a climate-controlled interior room was like entering another world, an experience just as disorienting now as it had been the first time.

Drawing her taser, Blair took up a position at the door and stopped, steadying herself with a few long breaths before glancing back to see how the others were doing. As point man, Blair would be moving unencumbered, but the same didn't apply to the other three teammates, now in the process of passing gear bags through the opening in the wall.

Sterling shouldered a single hiking pack that he could easily hand off should he be required to block their retreat, but Esther and Alec would be weighed down by a tremendous amount of equipment, much of which they'd never used on an operation before. In addition to the heavy iron braces padded with spare duffel bags for soundproofing, they carried a set of waterproof tubes for transporting Shedo's canvases, under door cameras, handheld impulse radars, pry bars, and a high-powered laptop whose services would be critical once they located the vault door.

That was to say nothing of the first aid kits and tourniquets each crew member wore, an unfortunate testament to the fact that there was an insanely high possibility of being shot at some point in the proceedings ahead. And Sterling's incendiary grenades were only slightly less concerning than Alec's enormous bag of explosives and demolition equipment. Blair's own taser felt like a tinker toy by comparison, and she found herself unnerved by having to lead this penetration while being trailed by enough destructive power to level a considerable portion of Shedo's home.

Sterling replaced the drywall panel, then approached her as Alec and Esther donned their load.

Blair transmitted, "Freeze one-alpha hallway camera."

Marco answered, *"One-alpha is frozen. You are clear to proceed."*

She waited until Alec and Esther had fallen into position behind Sterling, then replied, "Moving."

Blair turned the handle and pulled the door open, expecting it to be wrenched from her grasp as the alarm sounded, but it swung forward in an anticlimactic motion.

Assuming a two-handed grip on her taser, Blair took her first step into the hallway.

The corridor extended to her left, past two doorways that she knew from blueprints to be a wine cellar and movie theater. She advanced swiftly but quietly, aiming her taser forward in the event a guard made a sudden appearance. Marco's camera surveillance should keep that possibility at bay —at least until they made it onto the first floor, where the first known occupants were—but none of their preparations could completely alleviate the possibility of a trap.

Her footfalls felt like a leap into the unknown, as if each forward step increased their risk by an order of magnitude over the one that preceded it. In a way, that was true; every inch of this advance transported her crew deeper into the lion's den, a realm that unfolded before her in the spectral green hues of her night vision.

She could vaguely hear Sterling trailing her by ten to fifteen feet, close enough for him to quickly reinforce if needed, but far enough to allow her to commit her senses to detecting a threat. Alec and Esther would remain well behind him; by virtue of their tremendous equipment load, they'd need as much of a head start as possible in the event of a hasty retreat. And if that occurred, she knew, there would be no second chances; they'd be lucky to make it to the subs alive, much less flee the area before Shedo's volunteer army hunted them down.

Sterling transmitted on her behalf, "Freeze one-bravo."

"*One-bravo is frozen,*" Marco promptly replied.

Blair slowed at the corner ahead, stepping sideways to visually clear the lower foyer and its closed doors leading to a wet bar and recreation room. The space was free of people and sound, and she angled left to catch sight of her destination: the base of the staircase leading upward to the first floor and, beyond that, Shedo's master suite.

Without taking her eyes off the stairs, Blair nodded to cue Sterling's next whispered transmission.

"*Marco, freeze the one-charlie stairwell camera. Blair's taking us up.*"

48

KRISTEN

Kristen Shedo strolled down her first-floor hallway, eager to exploit the thirty-minute gap in the morning itinerary.

She checked her watch, more to admire the Patek Philippe than to confirm the time. It was the same model she'd gifted to Sterling, purchased a second time the day after her acquisition of the plank, just as she'd promised him.

And while she had an elaborate collection of watches, Kristen had only worn this simple, three-handed Patek ever since buying the Kryelast plank from Sterling. The timepiece now served as a reminder not just of the day she'd met a Sky Thief in person for the first and last time, but how she'd ultimately vanquished the crew with an elaborate seven-figure tracking device integrated into the watch's alligator leather strap.

Kristen continued breezing down the hall, approaching her home office.

Contrary to its title, she never conducted any official business there; instead, she relegated those tasks to her array of conference rooms with ethernet and fiber connectivity. The space she was about to enter was reserved for her illicit dealings, and the network of burner phones was like a garden that required tending between her entrepreneurial commitments. It could be a tedious enterprise at times, but that garden had borne fruit over the past two decades since she'd started it—careers kindled and catapulted into the top echelons of business and federal law enforcement, a mutually supporting arrangement keeping her apprised of efforts to enforce current legislation and how to bypass them, with both tiers of her network providing a useful funnel into the ultimate outlet: politics.

Now, she scarcely had to contribute her own campaign financing anymore to see her candidates succeed. Most of the funds were eagerly provided by any number of business executives who'd risen to power under her watchful eye, knowing that their continued ascent was all but guaranteed so long as they did what she told them to do, when she told them to do it.

Every once in a blue moon someone fell off the ladder of power due to their own indiscretions—James "Jim" Jacobson was regretful proof of that —but nonetheless, she'd accrued no less than eight congressmen and women between the House and Senate, with an additional half-dozen who would likely be joining them after the general election in November. To date she had yet to send one of her mentees into the presidency, although that, by statistical providence alone, would very possibly occur within her lifetime.

Stopping before the threshold, Kristen breathed a sigh and flung the door open, striding inside before closing it behind her and turning to face her domain.

The tall row of windows overlooked her property's sharp descent to the dock, then expanded to a panoramic vista of Lake Washington and, at the far edge of its rippling expanse, the Seattle skyline, now framed by a stunning array of charcoal-gray clouds. How some people found overcast conditions to be gloomy, she'd never know; to her, this vista represented the greatest achievements of her species beneath the power of Mother Nature in all her glory, a sublime merger of water and sky with her favorite city on earth sitting in the balance.

To either side of the windows were walls of bespoke integrated panels crafted in pink ivory, a rare wood species from South Africa that complemented her signature shade of candy apple red. Those walls were heavily decorated with certificates and plaques from her various philanthropic endeavors, along with framed articles from *Forbes*, *Harvard Business Review*, and *Success* magazines, among others.

She turned to approach the desk, a custom Parnian whose pink ivory surface was lined by a three-inch border of red-stained bird's-eye maple and topped with a slab of glass. This was her real command post, more so than even her Seattle office, and she was halted in her tracks at the sight of someone seated behind it.

It took Kristen a moment to recognize the woman glancing up casually from her Xten office chair by Pininfarina. Part of the confusion was that from this angle a Mary Washington ballcap partially concealed her features, though that was the beginning and end of any attempt at disguise. There was no mistaking the dark, almost black hair pulled into a tight bun, nor the facial features of a woman whose mugshot had been broadcast across every major news network more times than Kristen could count.

Perhaps more surprising, the woman seated at her desk wasn't clad in all black or, for that matter, tactical attire at all: she wore a loose-fitting, long-sleeve athletic shirt in a somewhat shocking shade of emerald green.

Blair Morgan smiled pleasantly and said, "Quite a collection of burner phones you've got in here, Ms. Shedo. A few of them have buzzed while you were in the conference room—you may want to check up on your proteges."

Kristen's shock gave way to beguiled amusement.

"Am I hallucinating, or are you a hologram of some kind?"

"You should be so lucky."

Chuckling merrily, Kristen replied, "I'm afraid that in this house, luck is always on my side. I don't know how you got in, but you won't be leaving. You're breaking my heart, Blair—I half-wanted your entire crew to escape my noose."

"Oh?" Blair asked. "Why's that?"

"I meant everything I said to Sterling. Following your crew's career has given me great pleasure and indeed"—she sighed wistfully—"inspiration for my business endeavors. Most of all, you provided something that has become harder for me to find over the years: a worthy adversary. It saddens me that we've been turned against one another, but..."

Her words trailed off, and she clucked her tongue before continuing,

"But business *is* business. You destroyed one of my candidates, so I have no choice but to make an example of you all."

Now it was Blair's turn to chuckle.

"You're going to find out very soon which side of that opposition will be making an example of the other. And I wish I could say the admiration was mutual." She rose from the chair and picked up a backpack from the floor. "Your methods, however...assuming no personal risk while sending in others to do the dirty work? I wish we'd given you better inspiration."

As Blair stepped out from behind the desk, Kristen saw that she wore black athletic shorts over light pink running shoes.

Reaching into her pocket, Kristen took hold of her cell phone and, without removing it, said, "At least you came prepared to run, Blair. But it won't do you much good now."

"Sure it will." Blair shouldered the backpack and cinched down the straps as she approached. "But before I go, there's something I need to tell you."

She placed a hand on Kristen's shoulder, then leaned in and whispered, "We've already stolen your art."

Kristen pulled back from her, releasing a guffaw of laughter.

"What in the world are you talking about?"

"The Shang Dynasty dragon," Blair responded, a grin playing at her lips, "along with a few other pieces. *Venus Anadyomene, Tannhäuser in the Venusberg, Venus with a Mirror*...you know what's in your collection. Or I should say, was."

Kristen felt a wave of chills ripping up her spine as Blair continued, "Don't worry, though, we left all our crew memorabilia. That you can keep —our gift to you. Besides, you paid for all that fair and square. But stolen art? Well that, I'm afraid, we just can't abide."

She blurted, "You'd never be able to find it. It's...it's simply impossible."

"So was getting into your house," Blair said calmly, "but here I am."

"You're lying."

Blair explained, "You planted a tracker in the watch you gave Sterling. Well, we did the same in the plank from the Sky Safe." She shrugged. "What can I say? You should have known better than to put all your illegal eggs in one basket."

"You're not lying," Kristen said numbly, her mind already racing through options to increase the bounty, to comb the countryside if not the world to recover her collection before the Sky Thieves could sell it off for their own gain. Then Blair's face brightened.

"Oh," she said, smiling as she thumbed the straps of her backpack. "I almost forgot the best part—I took all your burner phones, along with a laptop I found that had its internet connectivity permanently disabled. It might take us a while to hack the password, but rest assured, Ms. Shedo, we will."

Kristen lunged forward impulsively, arcing an openhanded slap at this wench's face as hard as she could swing.

Blair parried the blow, sidestepping to intercept Shedo's wrist before torquing her arm in a painful contortion that sent her twisting backward to alleviate the pressure.

Now bent over at the waist, she felt Blair spin her sideways before thrusting her forward and releasing her entirely.

Kristen's view was encompassed by her Parnian desk growing larger as she fell toward it, bracing her impact with both hands before pushing herself upright and whirling around.

Blair was gone, the office door slamming shut in her wake.

"Lockdown!" Kristen shrieked, jerking her cellphone out of her pocket. "Lockdown!"

No immediate response from her guards, which was to be expected, regrettably, given the size of her home.

No matter—there was only a two-second delay in instituting the procedure, the time it took her to open her security app and tap a red circle on the screen. Metal shutters clanged shut over the windows an instant later and her office door deadbolt latched into place as the siren began howling.

She tapped her screen to kill the siren, then rushed to the door and unlocked it with a press of her index finger to the wall panel. Then she burst into the hallway, thumbing the push-to-talk button on her security app as she looked left and right, speaking quickly.

"Blair just left my office—ballcap, green shirt, pink shoes. Start a room-by-room clearance now."

She immediately heard Clint Vance's drawl through the phone speaker. "Deploying SWAT. I'm coming to escort you to the safe room."

"Don't worry about me," she hissed, "just *find her*, and—"

Kristen stopped speaking abruptly as she detected an odd groaning sound from down the hall.

She raced forward, determining the source as coming from behind the locked door of her media room. Disabling the lock with a fingerprint scan, Kristen charged into the space and came up short.

A single window was ajar, propped in place by an enormous metal brace across the top of the frame. The brace was blocking metal shutters that continued grinding against it in a futile attempt to descend. Moving to the window, Kristen saw Blair Morgan sprinting across the lawn, her legs a blur of motion beneath the emerald shirt and bouncing ponytail.

Pressing the push-to-talk icon, Kristen cried, "Blair is outside, running across the south lawn—get her now."

"We're on it, ma'am," Vance replied.

Kristen stepped back into the hallway, turning to race headlong toward her master suite.

The sum total of her security was designed to keep people out of the house or, should they manage to enter, locking them inside. Blair had somehow succeeded in bypassing both factors, and unless the guards managed to catch her—unlikely, given she'd apparently outpaced any foot patrol in the vicinity—she would be gone along with the backpack containing the laptop with every scrap of Kristen's dirty laundry, to say nothing of every last burner phone in her considerable and ever-rotating arsenal.

But this was only her second concern as she rounded the corner and disarmed the lock on her master suite, then plunged inside and made her way to the dressing room. Despite the obvious implications of her network being exposed, she was overcome with a far more irrational concern for her art. If the astronomical sums she'd spent acquiring legitimate items at auction were considered obscene, then the lengths she'd gone to in acquiring her personal selection of masterpieces were nothing short of insane, and for good reason. Any internet celebrity could throw their money around the auction house proceedings; it took a true collector, one whose passion could not and would not be bound by the usual rules, to actually navigate the murky waters of offshore accounts and straw man LLCs to commission the world's top thieves to obtain some of the most significant pieces ever created.

Kristen passed the final hidden barrier, unlocking her vault door and entering the room where, just as Blair had promised, all of the Sky Thieves memorabilia was present and accounted for. The Kryelast plank from the Sky Safe, formerly the most prized item in her memorabilia collection, seemed repulsive to her now that she knew the truth: the thieves had planted a tracker in the item that bypassed her soon-to-be-fired electronic countermeasures team.

She darted past the plank, seeking instead the false wall concealing the collection that the outside world would never see, as a nauseating anticipation set over her. The thought of seeing that space bare, stripped of everything she'd worked so hard for so long to acquire, made her figuratively and literally sick—until she finally slid the false wall aside and saw everything present just as it had been at her last visit.

She swept her gaze across the masterpieces in disbelief. Had they replaced her collection with replicas? No, she thought, that wouldn't make sense at all. If they had, they certainly wouldn't have told her about it. She picked up her bronze dragon, examining it closely. This was the real deal, she was certain; she knew every facet and curve as intimately as she knew her own body.

Suddenly Vance cried out behind her.

"Ma'am, come with me—we've got to get you out of here."

She spun in momentary horror, only then realizing that she'd left the vault door ajar. Her lead bodyguard was standing amid the shrine to the Sky Thieves, averting his gaze from the artwork behind her as sheepishly as if he'd walked in on her undressing. He didn't know, or want to know, what secrets she kept beyond her formal collection—understandable and even admirable, given the circumstances.

Now confused, Kristen replaced the dragon and stumbled toward him, allowing him to take her upper arm and escort her out.

"I—Vance, I don't understand."

He pulled her past the thief memorabilia while explaining, "There may be other members of the crew in the house, and the SWAT team will be reluctant to open fire unless they're certain you're in the safe room. We need to get you there so they can do their jobs."

"Yes," she agreed distantly. "Yes...kill them all. You tell them, Vance."

"I already have."

"Wait," she cried breathlessly, turning to secure the vault door and then conceal it from view with the locking panel. He allowed her to do so, but just barely, and then they were on the move again. As they passed the media room where Blair had blocked the metal shutters in order to exit, then Kristen's own home office, she realized that both rooms were now horrifying reminders that her home had been penetrated. How or why, she didn't know and couldn't comprehend—unless, of course, Blair's entire break-in had been orchestrated solely to steal her laptop and burner phones. It was a worthy goal, she supposed, and more than enough to bring her down; at least, if her legal team couldn't succeed in getting the evidence thrown out.

No, Kristen thought as Vance half-led, half-dragged her toward the safe room, there had to be some other motive. The Sky Thieves were far too calculated to expose themselves over evidence that could possibly be excluded from any conceivable court proceedings—and even if they weren't, why the elaborate lengths to facilitate a face-to-face meeting in her office? To gloat? To force her to lock the house down? Neither option made any sense, because bold as they were, the Sky Thieves didn't stick their necks out without good reason.

Just as she and Vance reached the safe room, Kristen recalled a line Sterling had said during their meeting together.

You know enough about us to know that we never steal art.

That was no surprise to her; she'd said as much to the insurance appraiser when he dared to assume that their incursion into the Albany Institute was for that purpose. Yet she'd just taken Blair at face value that they'd come to steal art now, from her, if for no other reason than to expose her to the world.

But something about Blair's references to the art was oddly specific, spoken in a tone far too confident for a thief who had no ironclad assurance she'd walk out of this with her freedom, much less alive. That contradiction caused Kristen's mind to flash through the fleeting interaction with the thief, searching for a bluff and considering whether there'd been any physical contact before she recalled that Blair's hand had briefly alighted on her shoulder.

Kristen jerked her arm away from Vance's grip at the safe room entrance, where she quickly undid the pearl buttons of her Versace blouse, stripping it and stretching the fabric to examine the spot of Blair's first contact. There, pressed atop the La Greca printed silk, was a tiny, almost undetectable black dot. Using her fingernails to peel it off, Kristen felt the adhesive backing.

Blair hadn't been lying about the tracking device, she realized—only about its location.

Vance yelled, "Ma'am, get into the safe room—"

"*I will!*" Kristen shrieked at the top of her lungs, now down to her bra. "The Sky Thieves are in the house. They are here for my art. Forget about the room-to-room clearance, and bring the SWAT team to safeguard my collection until the police arrive."

Vance smiled then, almost irrationally enthusiastic. "I'll take them there myself," he replied with an almost childlike joy, flinging her into the safe room with far more force than necessary before sealing the door from the outside to leave her fumbling for the light switch.

Kristen felt herself drawing a relieved breath at the former FBI agent's response as she realized her personal SWAT team wouldn't kill the Sky Thieves; not at all.

Instead, in a staggering justification of her decision to hire him in the first place, Vance was going to do it for them.

49

STERLING

Sterling advanced swiftly, eyes on his phone as he watched his icon traverse a dotted blue line that he attempted to follow as precisely as possible—and with tracking software operating at a resolution of six inches across three dimensions, he was able to do so with surprising accuracy.

But his path was blocked abruptly by a wall that the blue line somehow traversed unobstructed. Looking up, Sterling saw a row of hanging clothes, many of them a startlingly bright shade of red.

He ripped the clothes aside, clearing wall beyond that revealed no noticeable seams, fingerprint scanners, or obvious means of passage. Yet all three had to be in the immediate vicinity, and while it could take hours to determine where they were, much less how to bypass them, Sterling had a much simpler solution in mind. Clicking a retractable pen in one hand, he referenced his phone with the other and quickly marked a cross on the wall where the blue line had mysteriously passed through it.

"Got it," he said. "Set your charge here."

Then he stepped aside, making way for his top demolitions man.

Alec rushed in and began emplacing his adhesive explosives on the wall. No one, Sterling thought with grim satisfaction, could employ controlled demolitions with quite such precision or enthusiasm as a professional safecracker. Sterling tempered his racing thoughts with a stoic reminder that once the charge detonated, it wouldn't reveal the hidden artwork, or indeed anything close to it. Somewhere between his current position and the intended target was the C610 vault door as detailed in the insurance specifications, and cracking that would be a whole different ball of wax for the man setting charges at the moment.

Shedo had surely been surprised to see Blair sitting in her home office just minutes earlier, but she'd had no reason to suspect that four out of five Sky Thieves had been hiding in her master suite since shortly after three in the morning. The penetration had been terrifying, a nerve-racking effort using Marco's remote assistance to selectively freeze camera feeds and guide their movements around guard activity.

But entering Shedo's master suite was another matter altogether.

Picking the lock and tiptoeing inside while she slept wasn't the problem —they were experienced and equipped enough to do both, as Blair had many times while emplacing surveillance devices as a member of the FBI's elite Tactical Operations Section.

The real challenge was infiltrating a 6,000-square-foot space for which they didn't possess the remodeled floor plans all while operating under night vision. So they'd used under door cameras to peer inside rooms without entering, locating Shedo's bedroom and staying well clear as they employed handheld impulse radars in the accessible areas of the suite, scanning walls and sequentially ruling them out until they arrived at the unenviable conclusion that wherever the stolen art was, it resided somewhere behind her bedroom door. Since going there as the billionaire slept was out of the question, they'd determined an expansive walk-in linen closet provided the best balance of concealment along with minimal odds of Shedo entering as part of her early-morning routine.

Once they'd sufficiently rearranged the linen closet's contents in order to hide, Sterling had long hours of motionlessness to contemplate how utterly insane this entire plan was.

During that time he'd repeatedly arrived at the same conclusion his entire crew had prior to mounting what would be their final penetration into Shedo's home, one way or another: not only was there no less risky option available, there was no other option, *period*. If they wanted to overcome Shedo's tremendous resources and live to tell about it, then this was the only way.

So far, however, Blair's plan was playing out brilliantly.

Alec was finishing his explosive setup when Sterling heard Marco over his earpiece, announcing the update he'd been eagerly waiting to receive.

"Esther made it to the car and is on her way out. City traffic cameras are still shut down and I'm blocking calls to Medina and Bellevue PDs—quite a lot are coming in at the moment."

Before Sterling could reply, Alec tapped him on the shoulder.

"Unless you want to see how closely your intestines match the color palette of Shedo's wardrobe, I'd get out of the closet. Like, now."

Sterling retreated through the closet and dressing room, leading the way for Alec to unravel his time fuse as he followed. The path led them to Shedo's bedroom, where Sterling caught sight of a familiar black backpack on the floor. Blair stood beside it, hurriedly pulling fire-retardant overalls atop the running attire that was part of a twin set, with Esther wearing the other.

The flight across Shedo's lawn was a ruse, of course, but a necessary one —after leaving the home office, Blair had just enough time to dart down the hall and round the corner into the master suite, where Sterling and Alec had used door braces to safeguard the route back to them.

Esther, by contrast, had simply hidden beside the braced window in the media room, leaping to the manicured lawn before Shedo had even initiated the lockdown; as the rabbit, Esther's only priority was to time her sprint between foot patrols across the grounds as guided by Marco's careful oversight of the security cameras. The noise from the braced window frame, combined with an identical wardrobe, had accomplished the task of channeling Shedo's immediate assumptions where the crew wanted them to go. Part of the trick with hastily emplacing a micro-tracking device was in keeping the quarry's head spinning before they began sifting through facts to determine what had actually occurred—which, given Shedo had amassed billions through intuiting future market valuations and the like, wouldn't take long.

By then Sterling and Alec had removed the door braces from the master suite and resumed their hiding places in the walk-in linen closet alongside

Blair, allowing Shedo to enter and serve her only noble purpose in this entire operation: leading them directly to the art.

She'd done so with admirable speed, her tracker icon threading into the dressing room, past the enormous closet, and seemingly straight through the wall as Sterling monitored from his phone screen, watching her hover at a fixed location before Vance arrived and initiated her withdrawal.

Now the penetration team consisting of Sterling, Alec, and Blair had followed Shedo's route to a seemingly impenetrable closet wall. All they had to do was get past it.

"Set," Alec called out, his hand braced on the fuse igniter.

Before Sterling could provide final confirmation, Marco's voice came over the crew frequency once more.

"SWAT team is entering through the main foyer, moving toward two-alpha. They're not splitting up."

For a fleeting moment, Sterling thought—or at least hoped—he'd misheard Marco. The response was at stark odds with their response during the previous lockdown, and their trajectory put them on a fast track to the master suite.

There was only one explanation for the disparity: Shedo had already figured out the crew's ploy.

Marco continued, "Passing two-bravo now, 30 seconds from two-charlie."

"Moving to block," Sterling transmitted, then said to Alec, "I'll turn them back—you have control."

He handed his phone to Blair, its display still showing Shedo's path to what had to be the final location of the art. "Don't let him get lost."

"I won't—be careful."

Sterling ran through the door to Shedo's bedroom without issue, along with the unlocked threshold to the foyer. Perhaps the only advantage to Shedo's enormous master suite was the fact that its internal entrances weren't subject to the reinforced construction and auto-locking functionality of her lockdown procedure; but that advantage ended upon his arrival to the main door leading into the hallway.

This one most assuredly was locked, no longer bound by the brace that had temporarily held it ajar for Blair's re-entry.

But as with everything else thus far, Sterling's crew had anticipated this

JASON KASPER

outcome as well: the moment Vance had escorted Shedo out of her master suite, Alec simply rigged the door with pre-positioned explosives so his teammates could exit at will. The procedure was remarkably simple, in this case. Yes, Shedo had state-of-the-art automated locking systems and reinforced door construction, but there was a very simple workaround: namely, setting the explosives over the door hinges.

No amount of deadbolts or locks could overcome the door simply being displaced from the frame, and Sterling took hold of the fuse igniter before retreating a safe distance down the wall and transmitting, "Master suite door, fire in the hole."

Alec replied, *"Closet wall, fire in the hole."*

Sterling detonated his comparatively modest demolition charge, the barking explosion dwarfed by a much louder thunderclap emanating from Shedo's closet as Alec blasted through the wall. Turning to rip the door from its severed hinges, Sterling entered the hallway and approached the corner where he'd make his last stand against the incoming shooters.

"Mine was bigger," Alec transmitted. *"Esther, take note. Vault door in sight."*

A shot of adrenaline hit Sterling's bloodstream. No vault door was a match for Alec, particularly not when he'd come prepared to bypass the exact make and model, and locating it was the veritable tipping point of this op—but that wouldn't make a difference if a team of heavily armed security men came storming inside the master suite.

And that was where Sterling came in.

Beneath his kit was a Cordura vest containing front and back soft armor panels capable of stopping handgun bullets, secured over the strike faces of lightweight Level 3A armored plates capable of sustaining a half-dozen hits from the SWAT team's 5.56mm rifles before fracturing. He also wore a taser, though that wouldn't do him much good at present. This situation called for something far more severe, and he pulled the metal cylinder of a thermate grenade from his vest, stopping at the corner before yanking the pin out and holding it aloft.

As it turned out, he arrived not a moment too soon—he'd barely had a chance to flash the grenade down the hall before a single man appeared around the corner 35 feet to his front, the lead element amid a formation of fully equipped SWAT shooters with what appeared to be top-of-the-line assault rifles aimed directly at Sterling.

"This is thermate," he shouted, "and I've pulled the pin. Shoot me and this whole house goes up in flames. Pull your team out—now."

At the head of the pack wasn't a kitted-out storm trooper like the rest, but rather a round-faced man in a suit, armed with nothing more than a handgun. This was Clint Vance, his face as recognizable to Sterling as his own in the mirror.

And Vance clearly recognized him too, his eyes lighting up with barely suppressed fury. Sterling hadn't bothered wearing a mask, and regretted that decision as he saw the man take a final aim that would only end one way.

In the fraction of a second it took him to duck behind the corner, he hurled the grenade as far as he could. It was too late—as the projectile left his hand in a whipping sideways arc, he heard the blast of Vance's gunshots.

Sterling was acutely aware that at 35 feet, it would take a crack shot to hit a man with only a fraction of his upper body visible. But the first bullet slammed into his chest, knocking him off balance. He began to fall, and the bicep of his throwing arm jolted with an odd stinging sensation at the sound of a second shot occurring a split-second after the first.

A third bullet passed directly over his face as he fell. Sterling heard the cracking hiss as the supersonic projectile soared over his head, considering with an odd sense of detachment that Vance's accuracy with a handgun was utterly devastating—he'd achieved two out of three hits with his opening salvo, and the only reason the third had missed was that Sterling was halfway to the floor by the time it was fired.

Sterling crashed to the ground, impacting painfully on his right side as he realized he'd landed in the worst possible orientation. His head was exposed to the hallway, the barrel of every visible gun descending to align with his skull in a nightmarish slow motion. There was nothing he could do but try to crawl behind cover, but it was far too late—if Vance had landed two bullets accurately with a semiautomatic handgun, then there was no way his fellow guards equipped with assault rifles would miss at this range.

But Sterling made the effort nonetheless, trying to push himself backward even as he realized the effort was futile; he was already about to die, but he could still go down fighting.

Blair's face flashed through his mind, summoned by his subconscious as the last thought he'd ever have. He felt a pang of deep, longing regret— that he'd dragged her into this mess, that he'd left her exposed to Shedo's thugs, that he'd rushed past her in the master suite without any meaningful goodbye. Despite his best attempts, he'd failed his entire crew, realizing too late that he was going to die not retired with Blair at his side but in the home of his enemy.

Then he saw the light of death approaching, a radiating white orb that grew in his field of vision with impossible swiftness. How he was able to process this was beyond him; this was no hospital resuscitation, and once the first bullet tore through his head it should have been lights out, consciousness erased, never to return.

But the light continued to expand toward him, its blinding glow shifting from white to red to blaze orange until he could see nothing else. It wasn't until a searing wave of heat whipped over his face that he realized he was facing not the end of his life but the volcanic explosion of his thermate grenade in the hallway.

He slid behind the corner as a wave of flame flickered past and then receded, the groaning howl of the spreading fire interspersed with angry hisses and pops, then gunfire.

The guards were shooting erratically, slinging bullets into the floor and into the corner where they'd last seen him, but they couldn't cross the lake of fire he'd created in the hallway. The gunfire halted as abruptly as it began, and Blair's voice came over his earpiece.

"Sterling, are you okay?"

"I'm fine," he transmitted, knowing that to tell the truth would be to scrap any hope of penetrating Shedo's inner vault. "Thermate ignited. Vance missed and the rest were firing blind."

Bringing his left hand to the spot just below the opposite collarbone, he probed a hole in the fabric to feel the stinging-hot lump of metal now embedded in his body armor.

The good news ended there, however.

His upper right arm was discharging blood at a torrential rate, spewing from both the underside and top of his bicep in a through-and-through just above the bone; the bullet must have passed through his arm, Sterling realized, while it was still extended from his grenade throw. He felt the hot wetness almost more than the injury itself, a thought that occurred with muted surprise before he considered the small matter of treatment: they'd stocked first aid pouches for this possibility and rehearsed dealing with gunshot wounds, but there was zero chance of him effectively dressing his bicep with only one usable hand.

Sterling reached for a tourniquet instead, ripping it free from the rubber bands on his vest and shaking it until the nylon loop with Kevlar stitching was fully open. Then he slid it over his right wrist and up his wounded arm, pulling out the slack and twisting the windlass once the tourniquet was snug in his armpit.

He was only now beginning to feel the pain from his injury, a horrible blistering sensation at the entry and exit wounds that was soon dwarfed by the immense pressure of the tourniquet compressing muscle and squeezing the veins of his arm shut. Sterling faced a split-second decision on whether to request help and cause Blair and Alec to abandon their heist effort, or deal with this himself and make his way back to them before revealing the true extent of his injury.

Seeing the flow of blood taper off as he completed his cinching and secured the aluminum windlass in place, Sterling decided on the latter— the tourniquet wouldn't effectively control the bleeding, just provide a brief stopgap until he could receive proper treatment from a fellow crew member. But at the moment his priority was the success of the overall mission, and he transmitted, "Marco, give us an update."

Marco reported, *"They're pulling Shedo from the safe room. Everyone's evacuating now."*

They better, Sterling thought, because this entire house was going to burn in record time.

Of their research into mansion fires, the most applicable case had occurred in Maryland. A corroded electrical outlet had set fire to a Christmas tree skirt, whose flames spread to an unwatered Fraser fir. That simple fuel source quickly led to a four-alarm fire requiring over 200 firefighters from three departments, fighting the blaze for hours before finally bringing it under control—by which time the 16,000-square foot residence had been reduced to rubble.

Now Shedo's house was subject to a far greater ignition, and one that would end just as horrifically. But the guards had left him no choice, and barring their voluntary departure from the residence, the only way to prevent his crew from being overrun by Shedo's security, much less the cops who would arrive at any minute, was to torch the entire residence.

Sterling pushed his back to the wall and struggled to stand, using his left hand as a brace to leverage himself upward. He briefly considered the prudence of risking his survival by lying to his crew, knowing full well that Blair would be none too thrilled upon finding he'd been shot—if he survived long enough to make it back to her, that was. Nonetheless, he stood by his decision as he began retracing his steps into the master suite. While he'd do everything in his power to complete the op, as long as his crew made it out, he no longer cared if he lived or died.

Shedo had set his home aflame, and now Sterling had returned the favor.

50

BLAIR

Blair watched the vault door penetration as it unfolded, thinking to herself that this was the most elegant form of non-destructive entry she'd ever seen Alec conduct—which was particularly notable since it was also the only time he'd needed Marco's help to breach a lock.

The Wellington C610 vault door was six and a half feet tall, a slab of steel casing containing protective layers totaling seven inches in thickness. It could withstand a 1700-degree fire for six hours before beginning to fail; the sheer amount of explosives required to breach it exceeded even the considerable supply they'd carried along to negotiate biometrically locked doors, to say nothing of Shedo's walls.

Instead, Alec relied upon an unlikely but effective new tool in his safe-cracker's arsenal: a high-powered laptop.

But the real key was in the computer's sophisticated software, a particularly clever and elaborate piece of coding developed by the Mas-Hamilton Group to exploit a design flaw in the C610 and many other seemingly impenetrable vault doors: their wireless programming port. Neither the software nor the laptop capable of running it had come cheap, but they were proving themselves worthy of the cost. On the screen before him, Alec watched the code cycle through numerical combinations at the rate of 354 per second, a rate of progress that would inevitably guess each of the

100,000 permutations in the entry code's five-digit sequence in no more than 4.8 minutes.

She stood behind him in a short gap between the vault door and the former wall of Shedo's closet, now marred by the jagged hole of Alec's wall charge. Blair glanced back through the blast site, seeing that Shedo's closet was now a snowscape of drywall dust and charred clothes, some of which had been lit by flames that had to be stamped before they could proceed.

Now she hoped to see Sterling making his way back to them, turning back only when it became clear he wasn't going to appear in the coming seconds. At the moment, his all-clear over the radio was the only reason she could focus at all. Otherwise, Blair would have assumed the worst at the pair of nearly simultaneous sounds from the direction of the hallway: a single gunshot, and the hissing explosion of what could only be one of Sterling's thermate grenades. Both were followed by what sounded like a short-lived firefight, but Marco's radio call that everyone but the thieves was evacuating the residence served as confirmation that their plan had worked —so far.

Employing a thermate grenade was a last-ditch effort to protect the penetration attempt and committed the crew to one of two possibilities: leaving Shedo's house intact, or burning it to the ground.

Nothing would stop that latter outcome from occurring now. Marco had disabled the house's sprinkler systems, not that they would have done much good—the exothermic oxidation-reduction reaction of thermate produced its own oxygen, to say nothing of a heat so intense that it could weld railroad tracks together. And while the raging fire would stand up against Shedo's fire suppression system, they'd disabled it just the same for fear that its employment would damage or destroy the art they'd come here to recover.

The resulting predicament was almost sickeningly ironic: Sterling had protected their immediate heist, but only at the cost of guaranteeing the art collection would be wiped out in its entirety unless their effort proceeded quickly and completely.

She adjusted the straps of her satchel, which carried five waterproof tubes of varying lengths for the sole purpose of safeguarding the Venus paintings on their route back to the sub.

"*Guards have taken up perimeter positions facing the house,*" Marco transmitted. "*They're waiting for you to come out a door or window so they can take their shots.*"

Sterling responded over her earpiece, "*Any of them on the dock?*"

"*Negative.*"

"*Then they can aim all they want.*"

"*You're missing the point,*" Marco insisted. "*If the fire prevents tunnel access, you can't just flee out a door or window. They're going to kill you and plant a throw-down piece for the cops to find.*"

Whatever Sterling's reply to that unsettling reality, Blair never heard it; instead, her attention was occupied by Alec speaking in French.

"*Sésame, ouvre-toi,*" he said, closing his laptop and rising to crank the vault door's handle. Pulling it open, he continued, "Ladies first."

Blair rushed through the doorway with her phone in hand, prepared to follow Shedo's path as quickly as possible even as she was momentarily stunned to see that there was no art inside—not exactly.

The space was a certifiable shrine not to the masters of oil painting or even Shang Dynasty bronze work, but to the Sky Thieves.

She moved past the rappel ropes from their Century City heist, now propped in a grotesque contortion of Latin script, before spotting the mock-electrical panels used to conceal their escape route along with a BMW badge from their getaway car. Sterling's firefighter mask from the Sky Safe robbery was propped upright on a stand, looking like a detached human head beside his tether cable, which was, in classic Shedo-insane fashion, another Latin quote. Beside it was a shelf with Sterling's bloody prison loafer from the Supermax breakout.

Blair walked with her torso angled toward the wall, shifting for the benefit of her body cam, which, along with those worn by the rest of her crew, was wirelessly streaming every moment of the heist in the interests of constructing a publicly-releasable compilation to expose Shedo for what she was. But so far the only proof of illegal activity they'd recorded was their own, and she continued following the phone tracker past the creepiest item yet: the baby doll she'd carried into the Albany Institute as part of her disguise.

She swept her camera across a trio of expended tear gas grenades, then the Kryelast plank that Sterling had sold her for five million, now with his signature emblazoned on it. The slab was propped upright at a slight angle before the blaze-orange cloth panel, wind sock, and smoke grenade canister used to mark the landing zone for the exchange. All this place was missing, she thought, were altar candles beneath a picture of Sterling.

"Could be worse," Alec remarked behind her. "I was expecting to find our effigies."

"There's still time for that," Blair said as she stopped at the far wall. Lining up her phone with Shedo's path, she marked the wall with a pen. "Right here. Set the absolute minimum charge; the art has to be on the other side—"

She came up short as the cross she'd just scrawled moved to her left. The entire wall panel had been slid out of place by Alec, who'd located a switch on the right-hand side.

"Demolition complete," he quipped, following her lead into the hidden room beyond until she lurched to a stop at the sight.

Blair checked the phone in disbelief, confirming that this was Shedo's final stopping place with an emotion somewhere between relief and outright horror.

The problem wasn't that the art wasn't here; the bronze dragon was within reach on a pedestal to her left, as was Lorenzo Lotto's *Venus and Cupid* on the wall directly behind it. So too were both of Titian's paintings hanging on frames directly ahead, and finally the Cabanel and Collier's *Tannhäuser in the Venusberg* on the right side of the room, the contents of their canvases seared into her memory from all the preparation that had gone into this op. They'd located everything they'd come here to obtain, and that should have been thrilling.

But the sum total of those five paintings represented a minority of the artwork present—the walls were practically covered in frames from floor to ceiling, an array of canvases forming an almost complete wallpapering of every vertical surface. The paintings were not just of Venus, although some were—the rest were partially clothed or fully nude women, and Blair could tell by their sheer beauty that she was looking upon a room full of master-pieces. To make matters worse, a trio of pedestals held sculptures of naked women, each of them close to two feet tall and chiseled out of solid marble.

She turned to film the collection with her body cam as Alec spoke beside her.

"This is too much. We'll have to prioritize."

"We're taking all of it," she replied, stripping her satchel containing the waterproof transport tubes. "Five, six canvases to a tube should do it."

Alec shrugged and pulled the first frame off the wall, the act mirrored by Blair as they began the same process used by art thieves the world over in getting sometimes massive paintings out of museums with minimal damage.

Laying her first painting face-down on the floor, she used a small pry bar to bend a set of aluminum pipe hangers pinning the canvas to the frame. Extracting the canvas, she tossed the frame into the room with their crew memorabilia—they'd need all the floor space they could get.

She set the painting back down, now using the chiseled tip of her pry bar to unseat the nails holding the canvas edges to the wooden stretcher bars holding it taut. Once she'd completed the sequence along the entire perimeter, she delicately lifted the stretcher free, then tossed the wooden framework aside and began rolling the canvas with the paint side facing out.

They'd planned to roll the paintings as loosely as possible in the waterproof tubes, whose interiors were lined with plastic wrap to prevent chafing. The looser the roll, the less chance of wrinkling paint that had in some cases been initially applied over 500 years ago; but then again, they hadn't been expecting to find such a massive depot of stolen masterpieces here. The more canvases they tried to stuff inside each tube, the greater the possibility for damage; but given that a house fire was raging outside, their options were now limited to making their best effort or abandoning some of the work to the flames that would soon be raging within this space.

Once the rolling was complete, she slid the canvas into the tube before letting it unroll as much as possible to make way for additional paintings. Then she repeated the process, and was halfway through feverishly stripping the stretcher frame from a second painting when the sound of footsteps approaching caused her to look up.

Her blood turned to ice at the sight—Sterling was staggering toward her with one hand holding the opposite arm, which was a blood-soaked mess below a tourniquet cinched at the top of his bicep.

"Sterling," she cried, racing to him.

Alec's reply was significantly less concerned as he continued rolling a canvas. "I thought you said Vance missed."

"He did," Sterling said as Blair threaded an arm under his left armpit. "I'm pretty sure he was aiming at my face."

Blair guided him toward the wall and said, "Sit down."

"It's not fatal—not yet, at least. But I've lost a lot of blood and—"

"I've got you," she assured him, helping him take a seat beside the Krye-last plank display. When Sterling caught his first good glimpse inside the art gallery, his eyes widened.

"My God," he said, "will we have room for all this?"

"If we pack the canvases tightly enough."

Alec continued to work as he added, "As for whether we have enough time, that's up for debate."

51

STERLING

Alec called out, "Number four ready to go."

Sterling accepted the outstretched tube with his left arm as the safe-cracker continued, "We've already gotten all the recognizable pieces—want to jump ship?"

It was a valid question, Sterling thought as he glanced inside the hidden art gallery to see Blair working feverishly on the next canvas. She and Alec had stripped the artwork in record time, working with calm efficiency despite the fact that Sterling was unable to aid in the effort with one good arm.

"No," he said firmly, "get the rest, I'm fine. There's no telling what the other paintings are."

What he didn't add were the words *we're taking everything from her*, a consideration that far outweighed any of his personal concerns for historical provenance of the remaining artwork. The effort to pursue Shedo had been one gradually unfolding nightmare from start to finish, and now he'd been shot for his troubles—Sterling wasn't about to let her get a free pass on any stolen masterpieces destroyed in the fire. He wanted her to be held accountable for each and every one, and at present that undercurrent of resolute anger was holding him together more than everything else.

Sterling tried to conceal the shakiness in his steps as he walked the tube to the base of the Kryelast plank. The fully waterproofed cylinders weren't extraordinarily heavy, just bulky; under normal circumstances, even the addition of multiple canvases wouldn't have affected his ability to easily transport them.

But doing so with a gunshot wound was difficult at best, regardless of the fact that Blair had reinforced his initial treatment with a far more lasting solution. She'd first packed the bullet holes on either side of his bicep with tightly packed Kerlix gauze, then mashed the remainder of the gauze roll into place with a pressure dressing before slowly releasing his tourniquet to ensure the hemorrhage was sufficiently controlled before fully loosening it. She left the tourniquet in place so Sterling could tighten it again if bleeding resumed. He frequently inspected his arm, searching for any droplets of blood seeping through, but so far Blair's treatment seemed effective, and the pressure dressing remained clean.

The room he was in was another story: Shedo's personal Sky Thieves exhibit looked like a disaster zone, the floor covered in wood stretcher beams and elaborate frames now discarded in a trash heap of sorts. Sterling negotiated the items carefully before stopping beside the Kryelast plank, setting his waterproof tube beside a trio of fully packed ones lined up for their final extraction from the house. This was his necessary, albeit minimal, contribution to the final stages of this op—Alec had carried the four sculptures here, and Sterling had already placed the small bronze dragon into a padded satchel before assigning an open duffel bag to each of the three marble pieces depicting the female form. He was far too weak to set the heavy sculptures inside, particularly with one arm.

Sterling took a seat and leaned against the wall, glancing left to see Blair and Alec ripping frames and extracting the canvases to be rolled into the sole remaining tube. Once he confirmed that neither were looking his way, he smeared a hand across his face and took a series of shallow breaths that seemed to represent the maximum remaining capability of his lungs. At this point Sterling could no longer divine which of his symptoms were attributable to blood loss and which were due to shock.

While he'd gone to great lengths to sound and act normal in the interests of convincing Blair and Alec to continue the op rather than abandon it, the reality was that he felt himself fading—his thoughts were becoming increasingly fuzzy and confused, his arm a throbbing blend of numbness interspersed with spikes of searing pain that felt like hot electric shocks. The pit of his stomach was a nauseous coil, his pulse racing. While his two counterparts were sweating at the gradual rise of ambient temperature from the fire outside, Sterling's perspiration was underscored by cold and clammy skin that seemed to indicate the onset of some imminent medical crisis.

Nonetheless, he'd managed to strip his armored vest before donning the backpack containing Shedo's laptop and burner phones. That particular item was the lightest of everything they had to carry out, and would therefore represent the only thing he'd be able to transport apart from his own bodyweight. Sterling tried to ignore the increasingly prevalent concern of having to swim with this injury—he'd wear a buoyancy compensator and only have to make it a short distance to the sub—but no sooner had he comforted himself with this notion than he began to consider the risk of infection from exposing his wound to lake water.

Alec approached swiftly, and Sterling looked up with all the composure he could muster, trying to appear calm if not in control of his faculties. But the safecracker seemed to barely notice him; instead, he knelt beside three marble sculptures and hoisted them into their respective duffel bags before shouldering two of the bags with a pained grunt. On top of this he added his demo bag and two waterproof tubes, assuming more weight than any two crew members should have to carry.

"You good?" Sterling asked.

"Yep," Alec muttered, "just gotta carry 900 pounds out. Easy day. See you in the sitting room."

Then he was gone, leaving Sterling to transmit, "Marco, we're finishing up here—how's the house looking?"

Marco replied, *"Two-alpha, bravo, and charlie are out—I've lost camera feed in all of them, and can see the fire spreading fast into delta."*

That was no surprise, Sterling thought. The temperature in Shedo's illicit display gallery continued to steadily increase, leaving no doubt that the hallway they'd used to access her master suite no longer existed. And while that was the only direct way back to the basement, they'd come prepared for this eventuality, using the same method they had to reach the vault door.

Blair appeared then, carrying the final tube of canvases. "This is the last of it."

Sterling tried to push himself upright, and Blair intercepted his unsuccessful attempt by helping him up. She slung the remaining pair of waterproof tubes over her shoulder, then donned the final duffel.

All that remained was the bronze dragon, which she hoisted with relative ease as Alec transmitted.

"*Sitting room, fire in the hole.*"

The last word had barely come over the net when the room shook with a tremendous explosion, the result of Alec detonating his wall charge to clear a path to the western hallway, their sole remaining path to a set of basement stairs. Sterling hoped the blast was sufficient to clear the wall; if not, they had a dwindling amount of explosives to make a second and possibly third attempt, and if that failed, they'd all be entombed in the flaming debris of Shedo's house.

"*Breach complete,*" Alec said. "*We've got west hallway access.*"

"On our way." Sterling nodded to Blair. "Go ahead, I'm okay."

She moved with alarming quickness despite the heavy load, and Sterling had barely begun following her into Shedo's closet when it became clear that his assurance was more of a hollow platitude than any meaningful insight into his physical condition. He was feeling weaker by the second, struggling to walk even under the weight of a single backpack.

They nonetheless made it to the blast site in the master suite sitting room only to find Alec waving them through impatiently on the far side of the hole, shouting, "You two better hurry it up, the fire's already spreading out here."

Blair assisted Sterling through a cloud of smoke and dust, then over the lip of the newly established hole. He looked down the corridor to see that Alec hadn't been exaggerating: flames licked the ceiling overhead, their crackling pops growing in intensity with each passing second.

And despite summoning every ounce of strength and focus he had, Sterling felt his knees buckle. He fell from Blair's grasp and collapsed in the hallway, his head spinning, thoughts growing increasingly delirious.

"Alec," Blair said, stripping the tubes and sculpture, "you're taking all the art."

Alec began donning the parcels but objected, "There were supposed to be three of us carrying it, and that was before we found out she had half the Louvre hidden behind her wardrobe."

Sterling ordered, "Ditch the demo bag. For once we don't have to worry about leaving evidence behind, and you need to get this art to the sub. Otherwise this was all for nothing."

"Forget the art," Alec said incredulously, "we've got to get *you* out."

Blair helped Alec hoist up the duffel bags and remaining waterproof tubes. "I'll help Sterling move. You'll be faster without us."

Alec hesitated even as he took the last of the art, as if the very act of accepting these final items was tantamount to admitting that Blair and Sterling would probably die inside the house. But he added the pieces to his load nonetheless, insisting, "I'm not leaving you two."

"Yes, you are," Sterling said adamantly.

But Blair took a more tactful approach, touching Alec's arm and repeating the same words that Sterling had used to get her to flee with the Sierra Diamond, despite knowing that his capture was imminent.

"Alec," she said, "you've got the ball. *Go.*"

That succeeded in spurring the safecracker into action, and Alec turned to shuffle down the corridor, hindered by the tremendous weight of Shedo's art collection as he kept his head low against the searing heat radiating from the ceiling flames.

Blair helped Sterling upright, ushering him forward past the abandoned demo bag as they hurried to pursue Alec. Only at that moment did Sterling realize the safecracker didn't actually have the ball—at least, not all of it. Perhaps the most incriminating evidence of all was still strapped to Sterling.

He tried to summon his voice to yell, but was too weak, too nauseous and dizzy. Instead he said to Blair, "I've still got the backpack...with the laptop, the phones..."

Blair looked at him in horror.

"Alec, wait!" she shouted. "Take the backpack!"

By then the safecracker had already reached the end of the hall, struggling under the weight of his heavy load as he stopped to look back.

Sterling had just enough time to make eye contact before Alec disappeared from view altogether. The ceiling between them had given out in one crashing swoop, a torrent of flaming debris blocking the hallway and, with it, his and Blair's last chance of survival.

Blair scrambled in front of him, trying to protect him from a gale force of scalding heat that whipped over them both. When the initial wave of air had passed over them, she once again hoisted him upright, half-dragging him along as they retreated the way they'd come.

Sterling managed, "There's no way to the stairs. We try to breach a window, they'll kill us...where are we going?"

"I don't know," she admitted, "but wherever we end up, we'll be there together."

52

KRISTEN

Kristen Shedo glanced absently out her guest house window. The fact that she'd never spent much time here before now seemed strange, as she'd taken to the energy levels rather well since it had become her primary residence a day earlier. The structure formerly bearing that title was visible outside.

Or at least, what was left of it.

Stone chimneys rose three stories from the ground, bookmarking the skeletal remains of a once-massive framework now reduced to scorched ashes. She could only make out the slightest indications of her previous floor plan amidst the partially standing walls. Devoid of its sprinkler system—disarmed in yet-undetermined circumstances—most of the house had simply collapsed into the basement.

The wreckage was currently being combed by a mix of firefighters and police officers, the former extinguishing the remaining hot spots and the latter conducting a systematic search for criminal evidence as well as bodies. All of her people had made it out before the entire house went up in flames, of course, but the Sky Thieves had more or less publicly announced that Blair and Sterling had perished in the fire. She smiled at the sight of an officer leading a German Shepherd through the wreckage, guiding the cadaver dog in the search for the dead robbers.

Then there were agents from the Seattle Field Division of the ATF. Apparently the Homeland Security Act had succeeded in changing the organization's official wording to the Bureau of Alcohol, Tobacco, Firearms, and *Explosives*, that final word being the key component to the investigation of a residential fire where molten iron from a thermate reaction was quickly revealed to be what had reduced her 27,000-square-foot home to ashes and rubble in an alarmingly short period of time.

The fire's progress had sufficiently outpaced the contracted City of Bellevue Fire and Emergency Medical Services' ability to either respond to, or even attempt to suppress, the ensuing blaze just as it had the later arrival of the Seattle Fire Department.

And Kristen, for her part, was unable to provide any explanation for the radical escalation of force from a heist crew whose exploits she knew and understood better than possibly any person on earth outside of an ordained member. Never before had they utilized destruction of property beyond the bare minimum required to access their intended target, much less to inflict mindless suffering on an unwitting victim. Why had it been any different for her?

She wasn't sure and couldn't begin to speculate, though Vance's initial report—which she could hardly trust, given his emotional investment in the matter—had provided some illumination. He'd made no bones about clarifying that Sterling Defranc himself had held a canister aloft in the hallway adjoining her home office to the master suite, declaring that the contents were not thermite but therm*ate*, a distinction she'd later researched. Apparently it involved particular additives that allowed the reaction to proceed into the realm of the truly catastrophic, an act of violence that the Sky Thieves' previous restraint made almost inconceivable.

Kristen had suspended her business affairs and become more or less a recluse in this room, alternating between watching the news and staring out the window, waiting eagerly for the first human remains to be pulled from the debris. As much as she'd held the Sky Thieves in high regard, nothing brought her greater pleasure than the thought of seeing their mangled corpses being uncovered, and Blair's in particular. That little theatrical stunt in her home office was a particularly sadistic touch, Kristen mused, particularly after she learned that it hadn't been Blair fleeing across her lawn in the aftermath, but an unidentified thief. Not that the deception ended up doing Blair—or her boyfriend Sterling—any good.

Which was a very, *very* good thing at the moment.

Despite the loss of her mansion and, with it, a vast sum of personal possessions, jewelry, watches, and collectibles, she'd gone to great lengths to insure every single legally acquired possession. Nor did she mind the fact that Darien Insurance had yet to underwrite the Sky Thief memorabilia—she'd accept those items as a permanent loss, and even if they hadn't been destroyed in the fire, Kristen would probably do so herself out of sheer spite.

Now she faced the new reality unflinchingly: both Sterling and Blair were dead and the world would move on, herself included. She would rebuild, she would make her empire whole. Kristen had been knocked down before in countless business matters, yet had always risen again—and ultimately, prevailed.

Which was exactly what she would do now.

Turning away from the window, Kristen plucked a remote control from the bedspread and turned on the television again.

It flickered to life on Channel 4, and Kristen watched with a bemused grin the endless merry-go-round of the media presenting the same news in lieu of having anything new to report.

A female reporter stood outside an enormous brick and concrete structure, speaking into a microphone.

"Curators at the Seattle Art Museum were met with a shocking sight when they arrived to work this morning—a treasure trove of historical artwork that had been stolen from museums across the US and Europe over the past twelve years."

At this the view transitioned to the same clips she'd been watching intermittently throughout the morning, all the requisite shots of museum officials examining the now-unrolled canvases under police supervision, verifying the authenticity of each work, and documenting its condition in preparation to repatriate the pieces to their original institutions.

The reporter continued in voiceover, "The works included 26 canvases depicting the Roman goddess Venus and assorted nude women, many of them painted by Renaissance masters such as Titian and Botticelli. Museum officials have confirmed the most valuable of the paintings to be a work by Raphael titled *Three Graces*, worth over 50 million dollars.

"But paintings weren't the only works of art that showed up overnight: also included were three marble statues, three of which were Renaissance-era studies for life-size models. The most valuable item found was also the only one not to depict a woman but a dragon: a Bronze Age relic from the Shang Dynasty, stolen from the Met along with one of the recovered Venus paintings. Museum officials said the small bronze dragon, whose original artist is unknown, dates back over 3,000 years and could only be appraised as 'priceless.'"

Kristen steeled herself for the most unenviable part of this media coverage, and she didn't have to wait long for the reporter to continue, "Included with the artwork was a cryptic typed note claiming responsibility for the return—and placing blame for the original thefts."

The screen transitioned to a scanned close-up of the page, which scrolled downward as the reporter narrated the contents.

To whom it may concern:

Kristen Shedo commissioned the theft of these works, so we decided to steal it all back. They are hereby returned in loving memory of Sterling Defranc and Blair Morgan.

The Sky Thieves

Kristen frowned as the footage cut to what had possibly been the most absurd element of all in the wake of these events: spontaneous vigils for Sterling and Blair, complete with camera angles of shrine-like portraits of their mugshots surrounded by mourning fans who lit candles and wept, depositing bouquets of flowers and teddy bears. Such impromptu gatherings had begun in Los Angeles, at the sites of their most well-known heists: Geering Plaza in Century City, and the Exelsor Building downtown, site of the now-defunct Sky Safe.

Support for the two dead criminals had since spread to other major cities, with gatherings in New York, Philadelphia, Chicago, and Houston. The irony was more than she could bear without being sure whether to laugh or cry. It wasn't that she didn't understand the far-reaching admiration of the same thieves she herself held in awe, but she'd been at the site of two attacks, lost her yacht and her home, and there had yet to be the slightest shred of sympathy for her by either the populace or the army of newscasters covering the events. Instead she was almost villainized in media commentary for nothing more than being a billionaire, as if that distinction stripped her of all humanity in the public eye.

Still, she thought, this was hardly breaking news; every local network had been broadcasting an almost verbatim play-by-play for the past several hours, with a few national outlets presenting a more compressed version. To Kristen this was a matter of damage control, and nothing more—there was no proof that the art had been in her possession, after all, and without that the district attorney would be unable to level charges, much less take her to a trial that would surely be dominated by her crack team of lawyers.

Returning to the window, she considered that out of all the recovered art, only her dragon concerned her in the least.

She'd already received four calls from her Chinese business partners, asking her if there was any truth to her ownership of the priceless bronze artifact. Kristen had simply denied it and, as with all good lies, interweaved some threads of truth into the deception. She admitted to them that she'd purchased every significant item of Sky Thieves memorabilia at auction and speculated that the museum note was a malicious piece of propaganda by a heist crew that had, for some reason, felt themselves slighted by her acquisitions.

Instead, Kristen's greatest fear in the wake of the house fire had gone unfulfilled so far and with it, she knew, any reason for her to be concerned at all.

The real prize for the Sky Thieves wasn't art, it was her laptop and collection of burner phones. When Jim Jacobson's phone had been

captured by authorities, it hadn't mattered in the least—the police didn't
get hold of it until well after a routine weekly rotation of new phones and
numbers. Her current fleet of burners, however, were now within the active
rotation; if any serious investigation began in the next three days before a
scheduled date for everyone in the network to change phones, the authorities could conceivably run real-time geolocation. Paired with the laptop,
which contained not only identities but a virtual ledger of services
rendered and owed, she may as well resign herself to defeat.

But Kristen wasn't worried about that anymore.

Why Blair had chosen to remain inside the residence with the most
incriminating evidence of all, Kristen wasn't sure—nor, it seemed, were the
members of her guard force, who had more or less proven themselves to be
thugs in suits. None could adequately explain how the Sky Thieves had
gotten in, nor had the review of her extensive and clearly hacked camera
feeds provided any insight into the matter.

But if that evidence had made it off the property, it would already be in
police custody and Kristen would be an unlisted passenger on a charter jet
to Dubai. Vance stood ready to make that a reality even now, just to be safe,
and if the Sky Thieves had succeeded in extricating hard evidence of Kristen's guilt, she needed only to call him to initiate her evacuation in the
trunk of a car in the guest house's garage.

Since that hadn't yet come to pass, she knew it never would.

Suddenly her focus was riveted on the firefighters clustering together
on one side of the wreckage, extricating a single item from the remains of
her home. And while she at first thought it was a body, disappointment set
in when she got a clear glimpse of the Kryelast plank she'd purchased from
Sterling. It looked remarkably intact given the circumstances, and she idly
considered that its severely high heat tolerance had rendered it the only
part of her Sky Thieves collection to survive the blaze.

No matter, she thought. Even if the investigators pieced together what it
was, she could simply speculate that the thieves had placed it there. They
were already trying to frame her, as her lawyers would make abundantly
clear, so planting a fire-resistant piece of evidence before setting the house
aflame was only a minor leap of logic. Once again, she would come out
on top.

On the television behind her, she listened to the reporter drone on, "Kristen Shedo is a Seattle-based entrepreneur and philanthropist whose net worth is estimated at close to 34 billion dollars. Her office has yet to return our calls for comment, but she was in the headlines last month when her yacht sank in Portage Bay, later revealed to be the result of a limpet mine to crack her onboard safe, which was empty at the time of the attempted theft. And that was just the first loss suffered by Shedo, whose mansion in Medina burned to the ground yesterday. While the investigation into suspected arson continues, her private security team has publicly announced the destruction occurred at the hands of the Sky Thieves, who allegedly deployed modified thermite grenades in an attempt to injure or kill the responding guards—"

A male voice cut her off, speaking excitedly, "Breaking news in the unfolding story surrounding the Sky Thieves—here's what you need to know."

She whirled to face the screen, seeing that the image was now of a stern newscaster gathering his papers in a studio set. He continued, "A chilling video has just been released across major online video-sharing platforms. The footage purportedly shows the LA-based heist crew known as the Sky Thieves invading Ms. Shedo's residence in Medina. Viewer discretion is advised: some of these images are highly disturbing."

Kristen lost all focus on his words as the screen was filled with a montage of video images—a first-person view down her hallway, where at the far end Vance aimed a firearm alongside the members of her SWAT team. There was a blur of motion as the canister of a grenade sailed away from the cameraman, then the flashes of Vance firing before the view crashed downward and the screen was filled with an explosion of flame.

That must have been Sterling getting shot, she thought, but before she could contemplate that, she was watching a new camera angle, this one sweeping through her vault door and into her collection of Sky Thieves memorabilia, pausing to showcase each item before swiftly passing into her art gallery.

She felt her throat constrict at the sight, which cut to up-close views of gloved hands stripping the frames from canvases, canvases from stretchers, then rolling the paintings into transport tubes. This was compelling viewing, to be sure, but hardly conclusive evidence against her. She had lawyers who would have a field day deconstructing its validity on any number of grounds.

Her bronze dragon was plainly visible, and she cringed at its clear documentation in the film. While Kristen doubted she'd go to jail over this footage, her Chinese partners needed no legal verification to condemn her. This would effectively sever a vast majority of her business first in Asia, then the West, which would in turn cost her hundreds of millions in annual revenue. But she'd still be a free woman, she reminded herself.

She focused intently on the next camera angle, a spinning view that stopped to reveal her west hallway, now aflame. Two thieves were visible at the far end, and she saw that Blair was trying to assist a wounded Sterling when the ceiling collapsed, erasing them from view. Kristen chortled merrily, overcome with an almost gleeful excitement; she'd surmised that both thieves had expired on the basis of the museum note and the fact that her laptop and burner phones hadn't been delivered alongside the artwork, but that footage was them as good as dead.

But her heart seized up when the video ended, the television returning to the studio news anchor, who continued, "The footage then segues into additional audio recordings of disgraced former FBI agent and Congressional candidate Jim Jacobson, in what appears to be a continuation of the tapes released in March. These new clips feature a man with a verbal likeness to Jacobson discussing a mysterious mentor figure who actively facilitated corruption not just across federal law enforcement organizations, but major business conglomerates and even the US government."

Kristen withdrew her phone, her hand trembling as the voice went on, "Four individuals are mentioned by name including current and former congressmen, along with details about offshore money laundering and unlawful political influence. And while the audio recordings have yet to be officially validated, investigators say the authenticity of the footage is in little doubt at present, having been posted by the same user account that made public the video of Sterling Defranc's daring robbery of the Sky Safe during his heavily publicized trial..."

She was suddenly equal parts outraged that Jim had specified so much to someone outside the network, and fearful at the repercussions of this degree of media scrutiny. Lifting her phone, she texted Vance.

Time to go. Come get me.

The newscaster droned on, "But the most shocking parts of the video are the audio segments at the end, alleged to be recordings of radio communications between members of Shedo's private guard force. If proven to be accurate, they indicate the discovery of a Tacoma man named Robert Lawrence as he attempted to establish surveillance on Shedo's residence. According to these recordings, Lawrence was shot and killed by guards, who were then ordered to dispose of the body by Shedo's lead bodyguard, a former FBI agent. KOMO 4 TV has confirmed that Lawrence was a conspiracy theorist, and his family states that he had taken a keen interest in Shedo after her possible connection with the Sky Thieves. On Monday, Lawrence's parents filed a missing persons report with police, stating their son was mentally ill and that they were grievously concerned about his whereabouts..."

Kristen felt almost riveted in place, dismayed by the lack of response from Vance. She tried calling him—no answer.

Looking up, she saw the screen display a press conference with a crisply dressed police chief reading a prepared statement.

"Yesterday evening," he began, "an anonymous informant directed officers to a parcel containing a laptop and some two dozen prepaid cell phones. Out of obvious concerns for obstruction of justice, we withheld announcing this evidence in order to begin our investigation—"

Kristen was suddenly in full power of her faculties, no longer frozen before the screen. She grabbed a Bottega Veneta Alligator duffle neatly packed and staged for the purpose on her bedspread, shouldering the strap as she left the room without turning off the television. Someone would take care of that, eventually—but by the time they did, she'd be long gone.

In the meantime she was irritated that Vance hadn't yet arrived, and strode down the hall as she tried calling him again. As it rang, she reminded herself that there would be plenty of time to consider her legal recourse; for now, she just needed to set her escape plan in motion.

Finally, the call connected.

"Forget about coming to get me," she hissed. "I'm carrying my own bag, thanks to you. Wait for me in the garage."

To her surprise, an unknown and yet somehow familiar male voice replied, "Ms. Shedo?"

Kristen stopped in her tracks. "Where is Vance?"

"If you're concerned about his well-being, I assure you he's quite safe."

"Who," she seethed, "are you?"

He chuckled. "Of course, I'm so sorry for the misunderstanding. This is Damian Horne Wycroft, defender of my client's right to effective assistance of counsel as per his Sixth Amendment Rights under the United States Constitution."

Kristen swallowed against a dry throat before stating, "He can't afford you."

"I hardly see how that would be relevant in the somewhat inevitable trial proceedings, but if you must know, I am providing my services pro bono out of a ceaseless desire to drive forward the principles of justice. I was on the redeye to Seattle as soon as Mr. Vance called to explain his unfortunate circumstances."

"He called you *last night?*" This was unbelievable—she'd spoken to Vance in person less than two hours ago, had in fact thought that he was waiting to evacuate her for precisely this scenario. And the entire time, the slimy little weasel had been plotting against her to save his own skin.

"Indeed," Wycroft swiftly replied, "for just as your yacht crew knew when to abandon ship, so too did my client."

Her jaw clenched, and she spoke between gritted teeth. "Surely you know my resources."

"Your resources? Of course I do. But I'm afraid they won't do you much good in the wake of the enormous body of evidence currently in the hands of the Seattle PD, your local art museum, and the world wide web. I should inform you that my representation of Mr. Vance falls well outside of any jurisdictional, willingness, or conflict of interest issues in the coming legal

battle, thus alleviating any possibility of remedy by way of erroneous depri-
vation in my client's first choice of counsel. Send your dogs against me, Ms.
Shedo, and I assure you I will deal with them in the swiftest possible adju-
dication in the eyes of the law."

She considered offering a bribe but held herself back for two reasons.
First, the call was probably occurring over a speaker in front of multiple
witnesses if not being recorded.

But more importantly—because witnesses could always be bought off
—she felt like she knew Wycroft personally, having followed every minute
of his defense of Sterling Defranc in the wake of the Sky Safe robbery. And
Wycroft was nothing if not a glory hound; he valued public spectacle over
money, making him a dangerous adversary indeed.

"And on what grounds," she began, "will his legal defense be based?"

"A plea deal in implicating the true aggressor, the veritable puppet
master holding the strings in a clear-cut case of following orders, indicating
that my client was remorseful yet nonetheless compliant in executing his
sworn directives out of a fear for his own life. I'm afraid I can't offer any
more details as per—hold on a second."

Kristen's pulse was pounding in her ears now, and she strained to hear a
muffled conversation on the other end of the line before a new voice spoke,
this one female.

"Ms. Shedo, this is Jacqueline Ealey, the King County Prosecuting Attorney. Police officers are waiting at the front, side, and back doors of your
guest house. Please make this easy on all of us, and turn yourself in
peacefully—"

Kristen ended the call.

The phone rang again, almost immediately, with an incoming call from
the same line. She put it on silent, the ringtone ending to the sound of firm
door knocks from the first floor.

Kristen turned and walked slowly back to her bedroom, pocketing her
phone before silencing the television and setting down the remote.
Unslinging her Bottega Veneta duffel, she placed it back on the bedspread
and neatly aligned it to its original position. Then she summoned a deep
breath, crossed the room to the window, and directed her gaze outward.

The smoldering wreckage appeared the same as before, yet somehow it presented a different view entirely: that of her empire being vanquished, her considerable and hard-won earnings and power base eradicated from the face of the earth, her best intentions foiled by a small team who had somehow achieved the impossible against their mortal enemy.

Which, in this case, was her, and her alone.

53

BLAIR

From a comfortable reclining chair on the back deck of her bungalow, Blair watched the world with a profound sense of stillness.

A gentle slope of powder-soft white sand descended into clear turquoise water, the placid expanse covering two hundred yards to a mottled stretch of coral reef. Beyond that, the surface took on the deep sapphire hue of the Indian Ocean, a juggernaut of isolation extending as far as the eye could see beneath a cloudless light blue sky. This was Maldives, a chain of islands spanning 26 atolls nearly 500 miles from the nearest shores of India and Sri Lanka.

For Blair, the sovereign Asian country was paradise in its purest form, although she had yet to travel beyond her new home of the North Malé Atoll, comprising a ring of fifty islands widely considered to be one of the most beautiful such formations on earth. Since arriving, she'd been too busy exploring to take a speedboat or seaplane to the farther reaches of Maldives. Her atoll contained over two dozen resorts ranging from comparatively modest to the insanely expensive, some situated on their own private island and each with their own selection of amenities and view of the crystal emerald waters. The views were superseded only by the locals— Maldivian culture spanned influences from Sri Lanka, Africa, Indonesia, and Malaysia—and the music, dance, and cuisine were unlike anything she'd ever experienced.

She heard footsteps approaching and looked over as Sterling walked onto the deck, scanning down the shoreline to their right as he asked, "Anything yet?"

He was barefoot in board shorts and a T-shirt, skin deeply tanned and hair long and tussled over a beard-in-progress. And while his right arm had yet to heal completely—it was still only partially functional, and he suffered from chronic residual pain—the doctors assured them that he'd enjoy a full recovery in time.

Blair laid her head back against her chair and coolly replied, "Other than the fact that you're about to lose our bet? No."

"We'll see about that." Checking his father's Omega, he said, "Shouldn't be much longer."

"Are you nervous?"

"Of course not."

"You sound nervous."

Sterling drew a deep breath and said, "This is the voice of steely resolve. And I'm not going to lose that bet."

She gestured to the empty seat beside her. "Why don't you sit down. Try to relax."

He shook his head. "Let me check out the towel situation first."

"The towels are fine," Blair began, but it was no use—he was gone, back inside the house to continue doing, well, whatever it was he'd been doing for the past few hours.

The former ringleader of the Sky Thieves had been reduced to the status of clucking housewife all morning, cleaning up the bungalow with a far greater attention to detail than he'd dedicated to anything outside a heist in his entire life. Whether that was out of apprehension for what was going to occur any minute now, or due to the festivities planned for later that evening, Blair wasn't sure. She considered once more that Sterling had been acting a bit weird since they arrived—maybe ever since he got shot. Perhaps it was the simple fact that he was no longer a thief, but his transition to retirement seemed far rockier than Blair's.

He'd get over it soon, or at least she hoped he would. After all, her desire to live in a tropical paradise was only the secondary reason for selecting Maldives as their new home. Access to travel opportunities was the main priority, and in that regard, there was no lack of options here.

With the Malé International Airport less than an hour away by speed-boat, they could board direct flights to major hubs in any number of non-extradition treaty countries—Indonesia, United Arab Emirates, Vietnam—from which overland or overwater travel permitted further access to adjoining nations like Cambodia, Laos, Qatar, and Oman, to say nothing of further direct flight access to Russia, China, Mongolia, Montenegro, along with Botswana and Uganda, among others. The world was a pretty big place even for fugitives from the United States, and given that they couldn't hide forever, that was a good thing.

But travel outside the Maldivian Archipelago had been the furthest thing from their minds since they arrived two weeks earlier.

Instead Blair had busied herself with turning their new beach house into a home, exploring the local area with Sterling, and taking the occasional tranquil boat ride to resorts like the Ritz-Carlton, Four Seasons, or Banyan Tree Vabbinfaru to watch the sunset over dinner and drinks.

But for the most part they'd been content with the view from their beach bungalow overlooking the Indian Ocean as they sat together in silence and, more importantly, immeasurable gratitude that they were, against all conceivable odds, still alive.

They could have just as easily died in Shedo's home, and without Blair's quick thinking after the ceiling collapsed, they would have. Once Alec had been erased from view, she and Sterling had been unable to move in any direction but back—and retracing their route provided the key to survival.

By then they were unable to raise anyone else from their crew over the radio, some interference from the fire causing an unanticipated issue with their communications. It couldn't have come at a worse time: Sterling was still able to move, albeit under such physical and mental strain that he wasn't able to contribute much in the way of creative thinking. And that type of thinking was what they needed at that moment more than ever—they could no longer reach the basement, and as Marco had pointed out, even if they managed to flee the fire by overcoming a window barricade and leaping out, they'd be shot and killed by Shedo's security force.

It wasn't until Blair had spotted Alec's abandoned bag of demolitions that she'd come up with a solution. Rigging another wall charge was out, as the two routes leading to basement stairs were already destroyed by the fire that was spreading with exponential speed.

Instead Blair had set up the remaining explosives not on a vertical surface but a horizontal one—the floor of Shedo's bedroom, above her basement gym.

That controlled detonation ultimately saved both their lives, clearing a twelve-foot drop to the floor below. It wasn't a comfortable fall, but nonetheless preferable to being incinerated; she'd helped Sterling lower himself on his good arm as far as he could before letting his hand slip from her grasp, then followed suit in a hasty and ungraceful descent.

Getting Sterling down the tunnel and into his minimum survivable dive gear had been another matter altogether, but she'd had Alec to help with that. Her cry for help had sent the safecracker scrambling up their tunnel's nylon ladder with an expression of shocked disbelief, as if Blair and Sterling were ghosts.

And while getting Sterling into the sub was a misadventure in itself, it was shocking how compelling the risk of imminent death was in motivating him to be at least somewhat enthusiastic about getting in the water. Between that and his normally abhorrent swimming, it was hard to tell much of a difference in his underwater performance after he'd been shot.

Once they'd recovered him to the safehouse, their gunshot contingency came into play: Esther had cleaned his wound, administered antibiotics, and inserted an IV before taking him on a 20-hour drive to a hospital in Tijuana. Blair, Alec, and Marco were conspicuously absent from this marathon road trip—they were busy planting Shedo's stolen masterpieces in the Seattle Art Museum, along with notifying police on where to recover a package containing the evidence of her insidiously corrupt network.

Authorities had long since finished sifting the wreckage of Shedo's house, discovering the tunnel entrance from Lake Washington but no human remains.

This was all their fanbase required to understand that the key line of their museum note—*presented in loving memory of Sterling Defranc and Blair*

Morgan—meant not a literal death for the two thieves but a metaphorical one: the permanent end of their heist career.

News coverage of the various memorial sites around the country revealed that while candles and flowers remained alongside Blair's and Sterling's mugshots, there were a significant number of imaginative new additions to the now-mock shrines. From LA to New York, the show of support included items like Styrofoam gravestones reading *RIP: Retire In Peace*, along with giant photoshopped placards depicting the two thieves beside celebrities rumored to have faked their own death like Elvis and Tupac, to fictional characters who actually had—Sherlock Holmes and Jon Snow. Blair's personal favorite was a grainy image of Sterling overlaid on an infamous black-and-white Sasquatch video, while Sterling was fond of the campaign posters encouraging a Defranc and Morgan run for president and VP.

There was also a cartoon version of their avatars running down the castle steps from the wedding scene in Disney's *Cinderella*, complete with songbirds holding Blair's veil in what was unwittingly the most accurate of their current depictions.

Public opinion of Kristen Shedo hadn't been nearly as enthusiastic.

She was still a free woman, albeit under house arrest in an extensively negotiated compromise after she'd been deemed a flight risk—and now wore, Blair noted with irony, the same type of ankle bracelet she'd had while on supervised release the day she met Sterling. The biggest challenge to authorities at present wasn't a dearth of evidence, but rather preventing anyone remotely connected with her extensive network from influencing the investigation. Over seventeen alleged co-conspirators had already been indicted on charges ranging from bribery and graft to obstructing justice and election fraud. More indictments were sure to follow, Blair knew, though her own concern centered on Shedo alone and she distantly wondered whether the former billionaire would find a way to flee the country just as she and Sterling had.

It didn't matter, she supposed; the hunt against her former crew had ended at once and in full with a near-immediate revocation of the bounty. Not that any formal revocation was necessary at this point: anyone who could have tried to cash in quickly ended the pursuit when Clint Vance volunteered key testimony against his former employer. So far he was escaping Shedo's mess relatively unscathed, and was on a fast track to a minimal prison sentence thanks to the services of his attorney, Damian Horne Wycroft. The fact that Vance would likely emerge with a relative slap on the wrist after shooting Sterling irked her to no end, but she supposed it was somewhat easy to justify self-defense when a home intruder hurled a grenade in your general direction.

But that was all in the past, she told herself, while the present moment offered a far more enticing view. The future, perhaps, even more so, although she'd figure that out when the time came.

The important thing was that her crew—former crew, she reminded herself—was safe. Things would never be the same, and given their history of near-misses with the law, to say nothing of Shedo's hooligans, that wasn't necessarily a bad thing.

For now, her home on Summer Island had been the ideal compromise, close enough for daily conveniences yet far enough from the main vacation destinations to provide a far lower cost of living than on the larger islands. Their money would last here, and most importantly, they had privacy—a combination of friendships and financial support to local water porters had thus far served to keep meddling tourists at bay.

But there were exceptions, one of which stood on the bow of an approaching speedboat.

She could tell even at this distance that it was Alec, his garish Hawaiian shirt unbuttoned and flapping in the breeze.

"Sterling," she called, "get out here."

He rushed out of the house and stopped beside her not a moment too soon. The boat hadn't even slowed to a complete stop before Alec leapt off, splashing into the shallow water and racing up the beach in an exaggerated sprint.

Blair rose and joined Sterling at the top of the steps as Alec darted up to them, pummeling into the couple as he embraced them in one great bear hug, his exposed torso slick with sunscreen.

"I've missed you both so much," he pretended to sob. Sterling patted his back awkwardly until Alec let go, then asked, "How's life in paradise?"

"You're looking at it," Blair replied. "It's...well, paradise. How's business as a legitimate safecracker?"

"Booming. And being back in Boston makes me realize how much I've missed seasons." He cut his eyes to Sterling and asked suspiciously, "Why'd we ever set up shop in LA, anyway?"

Sterling didn't answer, posing his own question instead. "Is Guadalupe Island as nice as Esther made it out to be?"

Alec stammered, "I...I mean, I wouldn't know. How could I?"

"Mmm-hmm," Blair murmured. "So no trips to Mexico, then?"

"I can't...I mean, I'm not supposed to—"

"Yup," Blair said, "thanks for settling that for us."

Sterling lowered his head. "Guess I owe you twenty bucks."

She gave him a consoling rub on the shoulder. "Or 300 Maldivian Rufiyaa. Take your pick—I'll accept either currency."

Looking up, he asked Alec, "You training for the International Safe-cracking Competition or what? Would be nice to put up a win for the old crew."

Alec shrugged. "My whole nine-to-five is training for it, whether I want to or not. As for whether I'll win it, well...let's just say I'll have to sandbag for a few years. Can't exactly score a world championship in my first year of competition without arousing suspicion."

A Russian-accented voice commented from the stairs, "Sounds like an excuse. I got your bags, by the way."

Marco struggled up the stairs with their luggage, setting both on the deck as Blair approached the lanky hacker and hugged him.

Alec said defensively, "After hauling all that art out by myself, I'm still recovering. Quit your whining."

Marco accepted Sterling's outstretched hand and shook it, nodding toward Blair as he said, "I thought you weren't supposed to see the bride before the wedding."

Sterling gave an uneasy laugh. "It's a small ceremony. Those don't count."

"Besides," Alec chimed in, "they're former thieves living in sin. What's breaking one more rule?"

Blair intervened, "Swiftly changing the subject—Marco, how have you been?"

"Working for other people is vastly overrated. I'm going to poach some talent and start my own cybersecurity company next year."

"That's great," she replied. "Congratulations."

Marco clapped Alec on the back. "If this idiot can run his own business, then how could I fail?"

"He's not wrong," Alec agreed.

She asked, "So your hacking days are over?"

"With one exception, yes. It so happens I met a potential client on the boat ride over here."

He turned to face the beach, where Esther was making very gradual progress toward the bungalow, stopping every few steps to turn in a slow circle as she surveyed the waterscape around her.

"My God," she called to them, "it's gorgeous out here."

Alec hustled down the stairs to help with her luggage, escorting her onto the deck with the announcement, "Lady Esther has arrived."

After hugging Blair and Sterling, Esther spoke breathlessly.

"I've always wanted to visit Maldives. Some of the best scuba diving in the world—I am very glad you two decided to settle here."

"After my crash course with you," Sterling said, "I would've been perfectly fine retiring to the desert. But Blair got twice as many votes as I did."

Blair added, "You'll always have a place to stay, Esther. And to be fair, Sterling has taken to reef snorkeling. We saw some manta rays yesterday."

"And it was terrifying," Sterling confirmed.

Esther raised her eyebrows. "Mantas are terrifying? Didn't you know you've got whale sharks here?"

"Well now I'm definitely never scuba diving again."

"Nor am I," Marco said, "though I would like to sleep if that's okay. I'm exhausted."

Nodding empathetically, Sterling asked, "Jet lag hitting you right about now?"

Marco shook his head. "Alec wouldn't shut up the entire flight. Jet lag is a distant second."

Blair swung an arm to the door behind her. "Guest rooms are set up, and you guys can rest as long as you like."

Sterling checked his watch. "As long as you're rested by five o'clock, which is when the pastor arrives. We'll have a quick sunset ceremony and then a couple local chefs are preparing a Maldivian buffet on the beach. Come on inside—we'll give you the grand tour and show you to your rooms."

The tour didn't take long; Blair had selected this bungalow with more consideration for guest rooms than lavish size, or at least that's how she justified her decision to Sterling.

In reality she'd analyzed the spare bedrooms with an eye for how each would look as a nursery. If she was going to raise a family in Maldives—and she intended to, whether Sterling was actively considering it yet or not—then she wanted the best possible house to provide an idyllic childhood. Or three idyllic childhoods, if her master plan played out to its anticipated end.

Once their guests had retired to their rooms, Blair and Sterling returned to the back deck.

This time Sterling took a seat beside her, seeming at relative ease for the first time all day. They'd barely gotten settled when he jabbed a finger toward the water and said, "There they are again."

She looked past the reef to see a dolphin pod arcing in and out of the ocean, and paused to get a brief count.

"Looks like there's five of them," she noted. "Good size for a family, don't you think?"

"That biological clock must really be ticking now. Your cues are getting less and less subtle."

Blair sighed. "I think they're still relatively discreet. And speaking of family, I'm sorry your mom couldn't be here today."

He shook his head resolutely. "Way too risky for her to visit this soon. At least she's safe."

"That she is," she noted. "And besides, things should cool off enough for her to come see us by the time she gets her first grandkid."

"There you go again."

Blair paused before replying, considering whether she should proceed with the grand inquisition now, or wait until after their former crew had departed for their return trip in a week's time. She decided not to delay the matter—it was important for their marriage to start off on the right foot.

"You've seemed a little off lately. What's up?"

Sterling chuckled. "Just wanted to make sure all the guest rooms were set up for them."

"I'm not just talking about today. I mean, since you left Washington."

His voice grew considerably more grim as he replied, "I'm fine."

"Sterling," she began, "you lied to me about getting shot, and that was your one and only opportunity to be anything but completely truthful for the rest of our lives. By sunset today, I'm going to be your wife. That may just be a silly formality to you, but it means something to me. Your days of playing the resolute stoic are over. There's no need to be strong, not anymore. We're not on a crew, and if you can't be vulnerable with me, then this is going to be a very long and awkward retirement."

Now it was his turn to pause, and Blair watched him closely, making it clear that she wouldn't accept a trivial response.

To his credit, Sterling didn't provide one.

"I'm just not sure about...about how things turned out, I suppose."

"What do you mean?" she asked. "We made it to retirement. Not all thieves do. And just—just *look* at this place."

"You're right. I mean, I know. I just wonder sometimes, about how things would have been if I'd played it differently with our crew. Maybe not pushed everything to the limit, all the time. If we could, you know—"

"Still be operational?"

"Yeah." He sighed. "Yeah, something like that. And sometimes I just feel like I shouldn't be here. Like I should still be locked up in Supermax, or have died in Shedo's house. It feels like I don't deserve you, or this, like maybe...I'm cheating fate just to be here right now."

Blair nodded slightly, looking back out over the water before responding.

"You remember in *Heat*, when DeNiro looks out over the city lights of LA and compares the view to the iridescent algae in Fiji?"

"How could I forget? The last time we saw that scene together was outside DC, when we were still trying to take down Jim. And that was also our first...would you call it a date?"

"I would," she said. "And it's no secret that *Heat* is your favorite movie."

"There's not even a close second."

"That's my point, Sterling. You always wanted to be a thief. You're from New York, but you ended up in Los Angeles just like DeNiro's character. Don't tell me you couldn't have made a successful career anywhere else."

He hesitated. "I mean, sure I could have. But LA is the mecca of high-profile heists; it always has been."

"Exactly. And that's where you met me, and now...now you get to see the iridescent algae at night from the back deck of our bungalow."

Sterling fell quiet at that, then admitted, "Guess I never thought about that connection."

"Well I have," she said, turning to face him. "And all those intercon-nected events put us here together for a reason. As for how much is fate and how much is coincidence, who's to say? But everything works out as it should. From our hideout in LA, to the jobs in Florence, DC, New York—"

"Don't forget Seattle."

"Right. The last one we'll ever do, outside Seattle. It took that entire journey to bring us to this island. Where we'll go from here, who knows? But for now, there's no place else I'd rather be than here, with you. As for the fact that our heist careers are over, well, I have to admit I'm more than a little relieved. Aren't you?"

Sterling didn't respond, but there was a shift in his eyes, a subtle relaxing of his posture that told her he was finally letting go of life as a thief. He looked out over the water. Blair followed his gaze to the emerald surface of the Indian Ocean, a colossal gem shimmering in the sun.

Finally Sterling took her hand and said, "It was a good ride while it lasted."

"Yes," she agreed, squeezing his hand. "Yes, it was."

THE ENEMIES OF MY COUNTRY:
SHADOW STRIKE #1

On a mission to assassinate a Syrian operative, a young CIA contractor uncovers a shocking terrorist plot that threatens his wife and daughter.

David Rivers is very good at killing people.

He's an expert in the art of violence—first as a Ranger, then as a mercenary, and now as a CIA contractor conducting covert action around the world.

But he's never had a family to protect...until now.

Newly married, and with a five-year old adopted daughter, David thinks his family is safe in Charlottesville, Virginia as he risks his life abroad. But when his mission to assassinate a Syrian operative reveals an imminent terrorist attack on US soil, nothing can prepare him for what he discovers.

The attack will occur in one week. The target is in his hometown.

And his wife and daughter are mentioned by name.

ABOUT THE AUTHOR

Jason Kasper is the USA Today bestselling author of the Spider Heist, American Mercenary, and Shadow Strike thriller series. Before his writing career he served in the US Army, beginning as a Ranger private and ending as a Green Beret captain. Jason is a West Point graduate and a veteran of the Afghanistan and Iraq wars, and was an avid ultramarathon runner, skydiver, and BASE jumper, all of which inspire his fiction.

Sign up for Jason Kasper's reader list at
severnriverbooks.com/authors/jason-kasper

jasonkasper@severnriverbooks.com

Printed in the United States
by Baker & Taylor Publisher Services